Confessions
of
Madame Psyche

Dorothy Bryant

by Dorothy Bryant

NOVELS
Ella Price's Journal
The Kin of Ata Are Waiting For You
Miss Giardino
The Garden of Eros
Prisoners
Killing Wonder
A Day in San Francisco
Confessions of Madame Psyche

NON-FICTION
Writing a Novel

ESSAYS AND STORIES
Myths to Lie By

*For complete information on ordering any of these books,
send your name and address to*

ATA BOOKS
1928 Stuart Street
Berkeley, CA 94703

Confessions
of
Madame Psyche

MEMOIRS AND LETTERS OF MEI-LI MURROW

DOROTHY BRYANT

Ata Books

Ata Books
1928 Stuart Street
Berkeley, California 94703

This is a work of fiction

Printed in the United States of America
Library of Congress Number: 86–71677
Cloth ISBN: 931688-13-2
Paper ISBN: 931688-14-0
First Edition

Typesetting: Ann Flanagan Typography
Design: Robert Bryant
Production assistance: Anne Fox, Lorri Ungaretti

In 1985 I received forty pages of typescript excerpted from "a much longer work," along with a letter from Joy Goldman Meyerlin asking for my opinion on whether this material, written by her mother, was publishable. Intrigued by what I read, I visited Mrs. Meyerlin in Santa Cruz where, retired from a long career as a music teacher in New York, she lives with her husband.

Joy Meyerlin had never known either of her parents, who, she was told, died in Europe during the 1919 influenza epidemic, when Mrs. Meyerlin was less than a year old. She had been reared in New York City by her father's sister, who could tell her only that she had been "handed to me in a hotel room in Turin by Erika Newland, your mother's sister." During the 1940s she had written to her Aunt Erika in hopes of learning more about her mother, but received no answer.

In 1970 Mrs. Meyerlin was notified that she was heir to the estate of Erika Newland, who had died in a rest home in San Francisco at age ninety-three. Coming to San Francisco to settle her aunt's affairs, Joy Meyerlin found among her papers indisputable proof that her mother had not died in Italy in 1919, but at Napa State Hospital in 1959. She went to Napa, where her mother's commitment in 1941 was confirmed, but she was denied further information because hospital policy seals patient records even from their families.

She was, however, allowed to question staff who might have known her mother under one of several names: Mei-li Murrow, May Lee, or Madame Psyche, the name she had used as a professional medium. The chaplain, who has been at the State Hospital since 1950, remembered a woman called by these various names "sitting by Lower Lake, usually with a book." He suggested that Joy Meyerlin talk to the hospital librarian.

The librarian, who had been hired in 1958 to open the new patient library, remembered Mei-li Murrow as the donor of hundreds of books to the library just before her death. She showed Joy Meyerlin her mother's name written on the flyleaf of a copy of *The Cloud of Unknowing*.

Then she rummaged through a storeroom where she tries to preserve the writings and paintings of patients, pulling from it a dusty box that had been brought to her by an elderly attendant-volunteer after Mei-li Murrow's death in 1959. In the box were twenty-seven notebooks and a drawing of Mei-li at age nineteen, evidently the only likeness of her in existence.

There were also fragments of a few letters signed by Garin Buddell, the medical author and peace activist. Joy Meyerlin wrote to him and received a prompt reply in which he called her mother "my best friend during my hardest years, an extraordinary woman." Doctor Buddell also sent 108 letters written to him by Mei-li Murrow. He was delighted to learn that the notebooks had survived and urged Joy Meyerlin to publish them and the letters.

I asked Mrs. Meyerlin why she had waited fifteen years before attempting to publish her mother's memoirs and letters. She replied that at first she saw the memoirs as private family history, personal, eccentric, containing facts about her newly-discovered mother which she was hardly able to assimilate, much less publish. Now in her sixties, about the same age at which her mother died, she had reconsidered. "My mother disguised the identity of many people mentioned in her writing. That means she wanted her story to be published."

This book is Mei-li's story as she wrote it in the twenty-seven notebooks and in her letters to Garin Buddell. I made only such changes as seemed essential for clarity. I removed passages of repetition, corrected obvious errors in spelling, and added punctuation where necessary. I then divided the notebooks into seven dated sections representing major periods of Mei-li's life. In the notebooks no division was made, the closely written script proceeding unbroken from the last line of one notebook to the first line of the next.

The transcribed manuscript was read by Doctor Buddell, who corrected my errors of reference or sequence and gave valuable advice on selecting excerpts from the letters which amplify and complete Mei-li's story. Doctor Buddell also suggested the title, in which the term "confessions" is used in its traditional denotation of a spiritual autobiography.

Dorothy Bryant
Berkeley
1986

THE CONFESSIONS

1875–1906

My father's full name was Parker Stanton Murrow. He was born in New York in 1850 to a family I know nothing about. The only communication from them came through lawyers in the form of a small monthly check. Attempts to get more money or to contact the family would, the lawyers said, cut off all payment. My father neither mentioned his family nor endangered his income by trying to contact them.

I learned what little I know about his family from news articles written in the 1920s, attempts to discredit me by identifying me as the "illegitimate daughter of the black sheep of a prominent New York family." These articles mentioned my father's expulsion from Harvard, a brush with French police investigating the smuggling of national art treasures, and hints of scandal involving the daughter of a New York state legislator. At twenty-five he became what the English call a "remittance man," paid to keep away from the family that had given up on him.

My father once said that he ended up in San Francisco while trying the new transcontinental railroad, riding on to the end of the line, never intending to stay. If what he said can be believed (and often it could), he was well received by rich San Franciscans when he came west in 1875. They all knew his name; his reputation had not yet caught up with him. He must have been very handsome and charming. Even during my childhood, when he was already middle-aged, women's eyes followed him. He had good looks, good manners, and some erudition. Despite his early expulsion from college, he could recite passages of Homer in Greek and knew the best literature in English.

Four years after his arrival he was on the brink of marrying a young heiress when she learned he was living with a Russian woman who had already borne him two daughters, my half-sisters Erika and Sophie. The engagement was broken, and the doors of San Francisco society were, as the saying goes, closed to him forever.

He could have done worse. He could have married the heiress if he had been more clever in hiding his mistress Tatania and his daughters. Other men did so. But he was carelessly proud of his little girls, especially the older one, Erika, and let himself be seen with them. The trouble with my father was that he took the virtue of living moment by moment—an admirable and difficult virtue—and turned it into a vice, never anticipating the collision of contradictory acts, never taking responsibility for consequences.

It is not even true that he never took responsibility. He supported Tatania and their two daughters with whatever was left from his gambling. He rented a three-story house for them in the flush of early winnings. Sophie insisted she remembered its glittering chandeliers, though she was hardly more than an infant when his winning streak ended and they were forced to leave its splendor.

It was Tatania who knew Hunters Point, that peninsula of a peninsula jutting from the southeast bay shore of the City into the Bay, where houses were cheap and food almost free. She was the widow of a Russian fisherman who had left her in a rented shack near the drydock while he steamed up the coast to Alaska, returning every six months, until the time he failed to return—lost, boat and all. Tatania made my father sell the jewels, the horse and carriage, and other trappings of their briefly opulent life. She bought a small woodframe house at the southern tip of the Point. Sophie's early memories there, she once told me, were only of the bitter quarrels between her mother and father. A year after they moved into that house, Tatania disappeared. No one ever heard from her again. But there is evidence that she did not desert her family lightly. Before leaving she had the house put in her daughters' names so that their father could never again gamble away their shelter.

So in 1884, at the age of thirty-four, my father was left with two girls, ages seven and six, in a weatherbeaten cabin by the Bay, forty minutes by cable car or horse-drawn wagon from downtown San Francisco. It was a year that both Erika and Sophie remembered well. My father decided to devote himself to his daughters. He resolved to teach them Greek and Latin in addition to what they learned in the schoolhouse a mile away. Erika learned quickly, already showing the talent of the brilliant woman she became. But Sophie could not grasp a scrap of what he force-fed her. He lost patience, shouted, Sophie wept. Whether from natural ineptitude or from the shock of this early forcing, Sophie remained barely literate even in English throughout her life.

Of course, Father's resolution was, like the rest of his life, inconsistent and erratic. When the girls came home from school, he was just rising. If his hangover was bad, they might be sent out to play and to figure out what to do about dinner. After a meal of sorts—on the best days assembled from the vegetable garden of the Portuguese or Greek or Italian family down the road—he and Erika read Greek or did algebra. By nine the girls were in bed and

Father was on his way out, seldom returning before dawn. Sometimes days passed before he came back. Near the end of that year, he hired a woman to care for the girls. She lasted only a couple of weeks, infuriated by their disobedience and his absence, especially on the day he was supposed to pay her.

In early 1886 he brought my mother home. I heard the story from him so many times after her death that I can describe the event as if I had witnessed it.

On a cold, rainy night in January he left the Palace Theater at midnight, then stopped at a nearby saloon where the men were talking about the latest riots against the Chinese, erupting again only that afternoon. The general mood was convivial approval of any means to "drive out the dirty little heathens who take work away from honest American labor." According to my father, he left in disgust (he always felt superior to the men he drank with), walking down Market Street, turning at Third Street, hurrying to catch the last car home.

At this time of night on this street he usually walked near the curb, away from the doorways where a drunken derelict or sick prostitute might shelter, or quite possibly a desperate thief. But this time, because of the rain, he walked closer to the sheltering buildings. Something made him turn toward a doorway—a movement, a rustling, a light moan. He saw what looked like a mound of discarded clothing, a shimmer of silk. Then he heard another moan.

He meant to go right on but took another glance and after that glance took a step closer. Such a small mound, a child perhaps. He bent over the body, then gasped in recognition. It was Dilly, one of the girls from the Jade Palace, a place he frequented in Chinatown. The Jade Palace catered to white men, offering drinking, gambling, and girls. Dilly was unconscious, her clothes torn, the side of her head bloody.

He knew at once what had happened. The mob that had swept through Chinatown had probably destroyed the boot factory above which the Jade Palace operated. The next morning's newspapers confirmed his guess. The whole building had burned to the ground, killing three unnamed Chinese men. How Dilly had made her escape remained a mystery. According to my father, she always insisted she remembered nothing after the first shouts of the mob.

He hesitated, but only for a moment. He could not leave her there. If a drunken, roving gang of white men found her, they might kill her, after making her wish she was dead. If the police found her, they might treat her just as roughly before throwing her in jail. He reached down and picked her up. At first she struggled, eyes closed, like a sleeping child in a nightmare. "It's me, Dilly, it's Mr. Murrow. You know me, Dilly. Parker Murrow." She opened her eyes, stared, and was quiet.

He carried her for half a block. Then she signed to him that she could walk. It had stopped raining. He stood her up. She brushed her skirt with her hand. Then he offered his arm, "and we walked, like any lady and gentleman on Saturday promenade, to the cable car on Mission. And I brought her home."

That was how my mother came to keep house for my father and his two daughters. I know almost nothing about the first ten years of their life together. It seems that they communicated little in either of their languages. My father must have felt no curiosity about her, for in later years he could tell me nothing about her, not even her real name. I have tried to imagine what her life was like. Given the attitudes of the European immigrants who made up the majority on Hunters Point, she would have been seen as barely human by her neighbors, a concubine-slave, a useful disgrace in the house of that seedy American who talked fancy English, a little French, and dead Greek. My sister once mentioned that Dilly sometimes stayed in the house for weeks, as if in hiding. Whether she hid from her neighbors, from immigration agents, from her employer at the Jade Palace, or from her own fantasies of anti-Chinese mobs I will never know. Perhaps she hid from all of them.

In 1894, at the age of sixteen, Sophie married a soldier and went with him to his post in Montana. The following year Erika left to take an apartment downtown on Stockton Street, paid for by an acquaintance of Father's. This man, older than Father and very rich, had met him at a card game and frequently came to Hunters Point for duck shooting. He brought books to Erika, and Father was unaware of his real interest in her until Erika, on her eighteenth birthday (it was like Erika to make sure of her legal right to independence), announced she was moving out. For a time there was some coldness between Father and his rich friend, but gradually Father accepted the arrangement, often staying at Erika's apartment when, after a late night at the clubs, he was in no condition to make the long car ride home.

Two months after Erika left I was born.

Because I lost my mother when I was only eight years old, every shred of memory of her is precious, but the shreds are meager. She brought no documents with her when she fled the Jade Palace. If any existed elsewhere in the City, they were destroyed in the 1906 quake, as was my birth record, which might have given her full name. When I asked her about China, she described a land of dragons and river gods. When I asked how she had come to America, she said that beautiful goddesses had woven her into the corner of a rich brocade which was then rolled up and sent to America. When the brocade was unrolled by an art dealer, she said, she leaped out of it and ran away to Hunters Point, where she found me in a basket of shrimp, swallowed me, nurtured me in her body, and, when I was big enough to nag at her for my freedom, spat me out.

I had been born so beautiful that the water goddess who lived in the Bay was jealous. That was why I must never swim out too far in the water, and that was why I must always obey my mama, because disobedient, beautiful children were easily caught by jealous goddesses who would not let them return to their mama until they had performed awesome tasks.

Instead of being frightened by her story, I was delighted and begged my mother to invent one story after another of my disobedience and capture by the water goddess. The high point of each story was the terrible task imposed by the envious water goddess. The task changed with each telling. Sometimes it was to clean out all the Butchertown slaughterhouses between the tip of Hunters Point and Potrero Hill. Another task was diving for treasure hidden in the hulks sunk in the sand off the Point. One was catching all the flies that swarmed around the tanneries on Third Street. Or swimming across the bay, climbing ashore at Benicia, then walking on a single track of the railroad all the way to Sacramento to bring back a pinch of gold from a deserted mining camp where the ghosts of disappointed prospectors still panned the streams. Or counting all the shrimp laid out by the oriental fishermen who worked on the shore, hauling full baskets from the boats, then boiling the shrimp and spreading them out on broad screens to dry.

In my memory she stands small and thin, with a round, brown face, wearing a long dark cotton dress with a little white collar. I hear her calling me, "Mei-li! Mei-li!" her voice rising on the second syllable to a high note like birdsong. Her wide mouth is always smiling at me or laughing with me, a laugh which turns into a cough she covers with a small hand.

I see her sewing a dress for me or cooking the meals we shared, with a portion laid out for Father, when and if he might appear. I see her working in the garden, planting, cultivating or gathering cabbages or carrots or tiny strawberries. Like all the other families, we ignored boundaries between our yards and railroad or livestock land, planting our vegetables wherever a good spot of open, high ground appeared above the swampy tidelands. My mother's garden patches were among the best, and the secret of her success was no secret: she put on boots and took a wheelbarrow and shovel to the nearest cattle pen, bringing mounds of manure to her plantings.

On Mondays—killday at the slaughterhouses—when the smell of hearty, grassy manure changed to the awful stench of terror and blood, we went down to the shore where the air was better. I played in the sand or climbed on one of the beached ferryboat wrecks while my mother bargained with shrimp fishermen, who smiled at me or swung me up to ride on their shoulders. To these lonely, aging Chinese men, with wives and children (if any) back in China, I was that rare treasure in those years after the exclusions laws, a Chinese child, albeit only a girl, albeit half white.

To add to their delight I mimicked their different dialects, then turned to the men from a Japanese boat, switched to their jargon, then back to English. I did not know that I was speaking separate, distinct languages, and at first I mixed them freely. But I soon learned to match them with the appropriate people. I spoke Italian to our Italian neighbors, Spanish to the Spanish, a variation of this to Mexicans, and other combinations of sounds to the Yugoslavians, Russians, Swedish, French. I did not know that this facility with languages was unusual. It seemed easy and natural, a game like all the other games my mother and I played or she watched me play, ever smiling.

I was almost seven when this fairy tale life began to end. My mother had remained isolated from most of our neighbors, but not too isolated to know that in America all children went to school, even girls. She talked to me about school constantly, telling me that when I learned to read and write all secrets would be opened to me. I could even myself become a teacher. She had seen the teachers at the Hunters Point Grammar School, and they were all, incredible as it seemed to her, women. I did not want to be a teacher. I wanted to be woven into a rich brocade and sent to some exotic part of the world. But I did want to learn to read, and so I went.

I was ahead of my classmates because I could speak English. Only the Irish children could, and they knew no other languages. As soon as the teachers learned that I knew a bit of all the languages spoken at the Point, they passed me around as a translator for the terrified kindergarten children. But the goal was for us all to learn English, and the woman hired to work this miracle was Miss Elva Harrington.

Miss Harrington came from a reformist, abolitionist family in Boston. Her father had served in Congress and had been killed in the Civil War when she was a small child. She was born, she told us, with two passions, "to teach and to travel," and had done so, teaching in a dozen states, Mexico, and several European countries. In 1890, deciding it was time for her to settle down, she had come to California to join the Kaweah Colony, a socialist commune in the redwood forest, but it failed and dispersed about the time she arrived. She came to San Francisco and began teaching at Hunters Point. When I came into her class she was nearing fifty.

I knew these facts about her because her first lessons were built upon each of us telling about ourselves and our families—in English, insofar as possible. She began with her own history to set the example, but hardly ever spoke of herself again. Her interest lay in us, her students.

Under Miss Harrington, I quickly learned to read and write. I remember her patient, expertly planned sequence of adding knowledge, bit by bit, day by day, a most undramatic and difficult art, that of teaching complicated skills so that they seem simple and natural. But most of all I remember the afternoon storytelling sessions when we sat on the floor around Miss Harrington and she asked for the stories we told at home, stories our families brought from far away, "in English, please, so that we may all share the gift only you can give us." During the storytelling, there was no correction of our grammar, only the help of a word supplied as we groped for one yet missing from our vocabulary, only the look of enthralled appreciation on the pale face of Miss Harrington, her sharp eyes intent behind her gold-rimmed spectacles.

I told the story of Mei-li and the water goddess. Miss Harrington said it was similar to a story from the tradition of my Greek classmates and gave me a book of Greek myths where I could read the story of Psyche and Eros. I read it over and over, loving Psyche most when she was disobedient—talking about Eros when he told her not to, sneaking a look at him when he warned her not to. Her abandonment by Eros disturbed me not at all because I was thrilled by the punishments of Aphrodite, which took Psyche to far places and strange adventures. I was less than eager for Eros to rescue her from these adventures, and I asked Miss Harrington why he forgave her when she disobeyed him again, peeking into the box of divine beauty she had brought back from Hades. Miss Harrington explained that the god loved her for her curiosity, for her mind.

I read the story to my mother, who understood English, though she seldom spoke it. She was breathless with pride at my accomplishment. (Her breathlessness had another meaning I did not understand.) I insisted she call me Psyche, as some of my classmates had nicknamed me. She used the name as an honorary title symbolizing my literacy.

I too was intoxicated by my new status, by the excitement of learning, too intoxicated to notice the changes in my mother. Our walks down to the shrimp docks had become fewer even before I started school. More often I ran down alone to get a bucket of shrimp. My mother spent less time in the garden and no longer hauled manure to it. I cannot remember the first day I came home from school and found her in bed. I soon took her lengthening afternoon rest as casually as her more frequent spasms of coughing.

The summer after my first year of school I built a clubhouse on the beach with my school friends. We swam out to half-sunken derelicts, paddling back with scraps for our construction. My brief reign as leader-translator was over. They had all learned English. The only mark of superiority I kept was that, when they were called home for meals, I could go on wandering alone for as long as I wanted. No one called or searched when I stayed out late. I ate shrimp dropped from the drying screens, wild plums from the trees, carrots ripped from anyone's garden.

My sister Sophie had returned home after her husband and three children died in a typhoid epidemic in Montana. I told myself I stayed away from home because Sophie was always crying, but that was not the reason. My father stayed away more than usual too, probably for the same unspeakable, unthinkable reason.

In the fall Sophie somehow got me into shoes and sent me back to school. But now I had a different teacher, one without the subtle skills and deep understanding of Miss Harrington. This one shouted like a martinet for the benefit of the principal but was actually lax, lazy, and ignorant, a pretty girl who was waiting for her fiance to return from Panama and rescue her from this noisy crowd of children. School had lost its magic, and something terrible was happening at home.

I left home each morning but often skipped school, hiding from the truant officer in a little outcropping of rocks on a high slope overlooking the Bay. There I read or played alone. Sometimes I pretended that this was the cliff from which I, Psyche, would be carried by the wind to the beautiful palace of the god. Sometimes I dozed and dreamed that the water goddess had captured me, Mei-li, but would not name the tasks I must complete before I could be reunited with my mother.

As in the dream, our reunion in real life never took place. One day I came home to find Sophie crying more loudly than usual and the house full of neighbors who had never spoken to my mother preparing her dead body for burial.

My first clear images of my father and my sisters date from my mother's funeral. My father at fifty-three was still handsome. He wore a dark, conservative suit and kept his sandy, graying hair and moustache clipped to a more restrained length than the looser western fashion. He still looked very much what he was not, a man of resource and reserve who was to be trusted. He made no expression of deep grief, kept only a distant and dignified solemnity, such as a gentleman might show at the death of a distant relative or a faithful servant. Yet I noticed in his face—around his mouth, under his eyes—a hollow, caved-in look, like the sudden evaporation of tissue that had held his features firm. In his eyes, as he sat near my mother's coffin to receive the guests who never came, I saw flashes, then longer and longer looks of astonished, hurt emptiness. His look reminded me of our older immigrant neighbors, those who had come too late in life to learn a new language.

He had, after all, lived with Dilly for eighteen years. She had cared for his two daughters and had borne him a third one. She had always been there when he chose to come home, had used what he chose to give her, had managed with her garden and surplus fish when he gave nothing. Silent but not subservient, merry as a child with her own child, happy with what he saw as a disaster—a half-breed daughter. Though rescued by him, she had never really depended on him. On the contrary, over the years he had become unconsciously dependent on her. There might even have been between them something my father could never have acknowledged, a spark of real passion bursting through his shell of indifferent superiority, his haughty generosity. In any case, it was at Dilly's death that his drinking changed from a frequent overindulgence to a constant necessity.

Sophie, who wept continually at the funeral, looked much older than twenty-five in her heavy black mourning clothes. She had lost handfuls of hair in pregnancies and in grief. Thin, wispy brown strands fell loose from the roll gathered at the nape of her neck, drifting across her plump, sallow cheeks.

Her naturally soft and sentimental character had been strained almost to the breaking point by the deaths of her husband and children. She came home to Hunters Point when they died because she had nowhere else to go, and her widow's pension was not even enough to feed her. She had nursed my mother tenderly in her absentminded and confused way. She told me over and over, tears streaming, that Dilly had begged her to take care of me, that Sophie had promised, and that I should see her as my new mother. Then she would talk of my mother joining Sophie's husband and children "on the other side," where they would watch over us until we joined them. She tried to tell me stories of her childhood with Dilly, but I refused to listen. I did not want to think of my mother dressing and feeding and playing with Sophie as she had with me. Every time Sophie embraced me, I squirmed loose.

Among these three strangers who now claimed to be my family, and worse, claimed to have known my mother longer than I had, the one who interested me was my sister Erika. She stood tall and slender like my father. Her thick auburn hair was piled high on her head. She had clear, white skin and the blackest eyebrows I have ever seen, sweeping like raven's wings above her large eyes. Her nose was delicate (even my mother, who privately referred to white people as *ai bai* "big nose," would have accepted it) and her pink lips opened to show regular, white teeth, not common in those days even in women of twenty-six. Her dark clothes had the unfussy, unobtrusively good fit that cost money. Among our neighbors she stood out with the elegance of a lady far above our class. She was by that time, of course, a prostitute, and she freely gave the family a summing up of her career.

20

Her liaison with Father's friend had ended after three years. Other men were interested in her, but none had enough money to make her total devotion worthwhile. She accepted an offer from the madam of a famous house of pleasure. "My clients," she said, "are the men they name the streets after."

When Sophie began to fuss and burble and weep, pointing at me, Erika only laughed. "She had better learn early what her mother was and what her own choices are." Then she went on to say that she was making excellent contacts, was saving her money, and hoped by the time she was thirty to start some other kind of business. "Maybe a bookstore." When she was not working, she said, she spent most of her time in the public library. She read in every free moment. During the two days before my mother's funeral, she read the book of mythology Miss Harrington had given me, the only book in our house. When she read the Psyche and Eros myth, she looked at me and said, "A bit erotic for a little girl." She refused to call me Psyche, as Sophie had begun to do in her efforts to win me over. Erika called me May, as my father did.

It was Erika who cut through confusion and made arrangements for my mother's burial. First, she got rid of the two Italian neighbor women who had swooped in like vultures, patting and petting me, their avid eyes gathering material for six months of gossip. She dressed my mother, ordered a coffin, and laid my mother, coffin shut, in the bedroom. "It's not good for May to be looking at that body all day. She knows her mother's dead. That's enough." For those days, when children were less protected from the stark sight of death, hers was an unusual and brave position to take.

No one knew what kind of funeral service to have. Dilly had taken Erika and Sophie every Sunday to the Russian Orthodox church their mother had attended, but after they left home, she had never gone to church again. Was she Buddhist? No one knew. Father went to the nearest church, a Catholic one, but the priest refused to come.

Then Erika went out and returned with a huge basket of flowers to place on top of the coffin. She stood in front of the coffin while Sophie, Father and I sat on the bed facing her, barely room for all of us in the small bedroom. She recited some lines of poetry. Years later I recognized them as Whitman's, the section of "Song of Myself" which begins, "A child said, What is the grass?"

21

We hit another snag when the undertaker said the body would have to go across town to the Chinese cemetery. I cannot now remember how Erika solved that problem, but she did. My mother was buried in a run-down, nearly full little graveyard near the end of Army Street. Then Erika disappeared again.

Our house, on what was then called Gull Road, was a plain plank cabin, all kitchen with two attic bedrooms above. My father and Dilly had shared one bedroom, Sophie and Erika the other, until they left. After I was born, I had their room. Before long my mother was coming to sleep with me, and my father's room was usually empty.

Now he slept in it most nights, and Sophie slept in my bedroom. It was months before I got over the shock of slowly waking each morning expecting to see my mother and instead seeing Sophie. I would close my eyes tightly, trying to make reality go away, until Sophie would prod and shake me and say it was time to go to school.

Then I would quickly dress and eat and leave. Sometimes I went to school, more often not. The first time a classmate asked me, "Did your Mom die?" I ran out of the schoolyard, not stopping until I reached my knoll, my private, hard, silent rocks. On that day, just after a big drive from San Jose, the cattle were in, lowing and bumping each other, herded all around me, uneasy with premonitions of the nearby slaughterhouse. It may have been dangerous to be among them, but I felt safer there than anywhere else.

The depth of my grief, my pain, racked me with shame. Grief weighed on me like a disgrace that must be kept secret. It seemed strong enough to kill me, and I imagined that I could survive the grief only if no one knew. One look of pity, one clear sign of understanding of my suffering, would add a burden I thought would crush me. I must, at all costs, never let anyone see the disgraceful depth of my grief. That was why, on the days I went to school, I was often sent home for being unruly, disrespectful, and a bad influence on others. I didn't go home, of course. I roamed the shore or swam out to a derelict hulk or talked to the tanners or herdsmen or fishermen. Sometimes, when a new herd was in, the Mexican cowboys let me ride double on their horses. The rocking warmth of the horse was the only comfort I could accept.

I purposely came home too late for dinner. By then my father would have left to spend the evening at the Egret, a bar on the edge of South Basin, and my sister Sophie, having put a plate of stew in the warming oven of the wood stove (I hated that soggy, overcooked food—my mother and I always ate crisp sauteed vegetables from a wok which had now disappeared) was off to her nightly seance.

Sophie had found an Italian woman the neighbors called *La Strega* (the witch) and who called herself Signora Renata. She held nightly seances attended by Sophie, who ignored Father's exasperated warning that she was only being "taken for what little you've got, foolish woman!" Since it was customary to give a few cents at each sitting, he was probably right. Sophie came home each night cheerfully announcing that Richard (the youngest of her three dead children) had "come through quite clearly. He says heaven is wonderful, but he does miss the ginger biscuits I used to make for him." That Richard died at thirteen months, when he was able to utter few words, did not faze Sophie. Children grew up at a normal rate in the spirit world.

Alone in the evening, I often sat at the kitchen table with a candle and a brass-handled hand mirror, the only one we had. I would look into the mirror, which, in the flickering light gave back a reflection that looked very much like my mother. I would look at my round face, with its deep, almond-shaped eyes, its barely raised nose, black hair pulled back like hers, and I would whisper to her, smiling and pretending that the reflected smiling face was hers, and that the words I spoke came from her. "Little Psyche-mei-li was a girl so beautiful that the goddess who lives in the Bay was full of envy." I always knew that I was pretending, that my mother was dead and gone forever. I was taking comfort, not the delusions of the credulous Sophie.

But after a while my sittings with the mirror stopped giving me that comfort. My grief had changed, had been assimilated in a way that made this playacting unsatisfactory. I was older, nine, on the outer edge of childhood. Worst of all, my reflection in the mirror was no longer a replica of my mother. My face had lengthened, giving me a pointed chin and a high forehead. My nose was losing the delicate slope of childhood, rising to a narrow ridge like my father's. I was becoming *ai bai*! My hair thickened and began to curl like my father's wiry moustache. The only things left from my mother were my narrow black eyes, my high jutting cheekbones, and my tan skin, even darker than my mother's, since I spent so much time outdoors. I watched myself losing the mother in the mirror, hating the changes reflected there.

Simple Sophie was not completely stupid. "I know you miss your mother," she would say, and I would stiffen to hide the scream which her stab of sympathy threatened to release. "Why don't you come with me to see Signora Renata? Maybe Dilly will come through to you. Why, my Elsie even sent me a flower last week." She would show the brown, dead poppy which had fallen on her in the dark and had since remained crushed in a locket around her neck.

"Stuff and nonsense!" my father would shout. "Get the child to school. Learn sums," he would shout at me, "so you can get a little shop or something, or you'll end up like Erika or a maid to someone like Erika."

"It's Erika who sends money," I wanted to say, "that gets us through the last days of every month." But I did not, for in those days, even a disobedient child like me did not talk back to her father.

I was, however, very rude to Sophie, refusing to speak to her for days at a time or laughing when she told me the latest message from her children "on the other side." I agreed with my father, who shouted at her that if she kept on "like this, you'll end up at Napa," the name of a state mental hospital mentioned often, like a threat of hell, among the people near us. Even the young children taunted the different, the odd, with, "You belong in Napa!" although they had no idea what or where Napa was.

During the day Sophie puttered around the house, mumbling. She was talking to *them,* she assured me, to the spirits of her dead children, who, Signora Renata told her, were with her all the time, though they returned her chatter only through the medium, to whom Sophie went every night. If I shouted at her that there were no spirits, that she was just talking to herself, she would stop whatever she was doing to sit and weep. After a few minutes she would raise her head, dry her eyes, and with a surprised look, as if not remembering what she had been crying about, she would begin to mumble to her spirits again as she picked up her broom and began sweeping. I looked at her with a mixture of envy and fury that she refused to feel a grief as hopeless as mine.

One day, when I looked into the hand mirror hanging on the kitchen wall, I was so enraged at the face I saw—now bearing only my mother's eyes trapped in my new face—that I pulled it off the wall and threw it across the room. Its metal frame clanged against the wall, its glass shattering into a spray of fragments. For a moment I was shocked at what I had done. I heard Sophie upstairs, her weak, high voice asking what had happened, her slow, clumsy steps moving toward the stairway. On impulse I leaped silently over a kitchen windowsill and ran to the outhouse, where I stayed for a few minutes, listening to her calling me. Then I came out, walking back to the house and entering through the kitchen door.

"May? Oh, there you are." She stood near the wall, holding the handle of the mirror, looking at the slivers of glass on the floor. "Look out where you walk. Don't come in yet." She reached for the broom. "Where were you? Didn't you hear me call?"

I shook my head, waiting for her to accuse me, to threaten to tell Father. Instead she looked at me with puzzlement that was becoming excitement. "But if you and me were the only ones here, and I didn't do it and you didn't... then it was Something Else!" Sophie was transfigured, eyes wide, trembling. "Could it be Teddy? He always was full of mischief."

Teddy was her oldest. I understood. Her spirits, she thought, were finally answering back, much the way I did, with infuriated impudence. "No, I..." I had been about to wreck her hopes, but she brushed away my attempt at confession.

"No, it's your mirror, the one Dilly gave you, the one you look at all the time. Oh, May, it's your mother showing you she's here with you all the time. Just the way I said, but you wouldn't believe me. So she had to do it drastic like so you'd see."

"No, no, no, it was...."

"Oh, you're right, it could be a poltergeist. There's good ones and bad ones, but the ones that break things... you know, when I was a little girl like you, I heard things in this house, noises at night mostly, like a footstep creaking the stairs."

This was the first I had heard of her hearing noises. Sophie was simple but inventive. A flock of "memories" gave a continual supply of evidence to support whatever beliefs comforted her.

She began sweeping up the pieces of glass. "Now, I think we won't mention this to Father. He just gets mad, and Signora Renata says we have to be patient with him." She put the glass shards into a paper bag. "But we'll ask Signora Renata what it means. Want to come with me tonight?" I shook my head and ran out, waiting till I was in the wet marshes near the water's edge before I burst into laughter, which I cut off quickly when tears came to my eyes.

That night when Sophie returned from her seance, I pretended to be asleep. I did not want to hear whatever foolish talk had gone on about my broken mirror. But after she was in bed, I tossed restlessly, unable to sleep. I had made myself a toy that day, what we called a slinger, a piece of string tied around a rock, which we then spun round our heads and let go—a forbidden toy because, of course, it could be dangerous. My slinger was hidden under the bed I shared with Sophie. I reached for the string, pulled it up, accidentally jerking it so that the rock hit against the wooden wall with a sharp crack.

Sophie stiffened. "What was that?"

Instantly I saw the possibilities of a new game. "I don't know." At that moment I jerked the string again and produced another rap, this time on the floor.

"What...who is it?" whispered Sophie. "Teddy? Are you trying to call me, Teddy?" I lay very still, the two of us listening together. "Who are you?" We listened. "Is it May you want?" We lay in silence. "May? Is it little Psyche, little Mei-li...."

At that point I pulled the string in a wide sweep under the bed and managed to produce three or four rapid knocks before dropping it. Then, afraid Sophie would look under the bed to investigate, I cried out, "Oh, Sophie, I'm afraid!" and threw my arms around her. It was the first time I had ever let her embrace me. She held me tightly and said, "Don't cry, May, don't cry." I was shaking with laughter which I managed to smother in her large bosom.

So it all began with a joke, a prank, and it grew with one prank after another. I soon found better ways to produce sharp raps in darkness or in the full light of day. There were loose boards all over our roughly built house. By slipping a finger or a toe under the edge of a thin plank, then releasing it to snap back into place, I could produce a "thwack!" that shuddered throughout the house. All I need do was to watch until Sophie's attention was engaged, then a quick flip of my foot, and we were receiving messages from the dead.

In the kitchen, Sophie busy at the stove, an orange might fly across the room and land in the stew pot. By the time she jumped and turned around, I was seated on the floor, oblivious, absorbed in my book of myths, six feet from the fruit bowl. Things disappeared, then turned up in odd places. Once, all of Sophie's freshly laundered underwear was found in the mud behind the house. But to make up for that nastiness, I put her daughter's doll under her pillow. Sophie wept happily as she hugged pillow and doll and fell asleep murmuring her daughter's name.

26

I was careful not to try any tricks when my father was at home, for even when he was drunk, he remained skeptical. But Sophie talked incessantly about her "messages," until Father forbade her to speak of such things to him. "And you..." he said, looking sternly into my face. But then, seeing my mother's eyes staring out at him, he seemed to forget what he was going to say. The truth was that if Sophie's grief absorbed her, so did his, which was as strong, as total as his indifference had been when my mother was alive. Our house was a crazy wasteland of grief.

It was bad enough when Father's monthly check was gone by midmonth. But then his father died (his mother had been dead for years), and by the terms of the will, he was given a final settlement of a few thousand dollars. A few thousand more was to be settled on his issue, if any, but as all the money had to pass through him, we never saw any of it. If Erika had known, I think she might have salvaged some of it, but we saw nothing of her in those days. The money, all of it, was gambled away in six months. After that, Father remained drunk somehow—perhaps he won just enough at gambling to keep him in liquor. All the French and Italians in Butchertown made wine and were free with it, indulgent toward a "gentleman" who probably reminded them of the gentry they had served in the old country.

Sophie and I still grew vegetables and scavenged around the shrimp sheds and slaughterhouses, where entrails were given away free, so there was no danger of starvation. But there was no money for flour and sugar and coffee and for the clothing I was rapidly outgrowing. That was why, during a nasty rainstorm in January of 1905, on my tenth birthday, I agreed to go with Sophie to a seance at Signora Renata's house. I went because I knew that after the seance cookies were served.

In the winter months, the lower lying parts of Hunters Point were flooded. Especially during high tide, some areas were under a foot or two of salt water and never usable as vegetable plots. We were lucky that our crude house had been built on high ground and on piers sunk deep by some unknown fisherman who, understanding the hazards of living near water, had put most of his labor and timbers below the actual house. That night Sophie and I walked on streets (mostly unpaved) like muddy rivers, Sophie in high-top boots,

27

I in bare feet, skirts tucked up, because I had outgrown my wading boots. We crossed to the north side of Hunters Point along the edge of India Basin to a house overlooking the Bay. A wooden sidewalk stretched for a few yards in front of it, and a large awning protected the wooden front door. There Sophie removed her muddy boots, and both of us put on light slippers to wear inside.

Signora Renata was probably only forty (though at the time I thought of her as ancient), very stout and very gray, but with a smooth, rosy complexion. She spoke rapid, broken English in a deep, rough voice, fixing her hard black eyes on me. Sophie, of course, had been telling her about my psychic sensitivity, about the ghosts who now populated our house like noisy boarders. "Ah, *la mezza cina*," she greeted me, and that was what she always called me when we were alone—the half Chinese. She took us immediately to her parlor, a tiny, dim room where everything seemed to be covered. The round table in the center was covered with a red velvet cloth drooping almost to the floor. The two windows were draped in black. One corner of the room was hidden behind thick flowered drapes. The straight chairs surrounding the table were draped with shawls to hide, I think, the stained, moth-eaten plush seats and backs. Signora Renata herself always wore a black lace, red-fringed shawl which almost entirely covered her dress, all the way to the floor.

We were the only people who had ventured out on such a stormy night. The three of us sat down together, Signora Renata and I watching each other suspiciously. I wondered what tricks she would play, yet I half-believed she was genuine. I was worried about the spirits she might call up; what if they came to tell her and Sophie that I had been playing tricks? But nothing like that happened. Nothing at all happened. We sat at the table in total darkness for a long time. Then Signora Renata went behind the flowered drapes for what seemed like an hour.

When she came back, she lit a candle while she grumbled that the spirits had all stayed home out of the rain too. Sophie laughed politely. Signora Renata stared into my eyes for a while, then passed a hand across her forehead, closed her eyes, and began to talk about my mother. She described her, told me how much she loved me, how reluctant she had been to leave me, how happy her hard life had been after she had me, and so on. I no longer remember her exact words but I clearly remember the fury that gripped me as she talked. I remember clamping my mouth shut, clenching my teeth, digging my fingernails into my palms so that I would not cry as I knew she wanted me to do. I knew there was nothing she told me about my mother that Sophie could not have told her. She was playing tricks on me, as I had played on Sophie, using my grief, trying to expose and use the great void of pain inside me. I would not let her. I closed my eyes. I resisted.

When she finally stopped talking, I opened my eyes and looked into hers. There was something like respect in them. She gave me a rough smile, another long look, then asked, "*Ti piace un* cookie?" I nodded. That was what I had come for. She went to the kitchen and returned with a small plate of little white mounds. "*Ossi di morti,*" she said, bones of the dead, sugary white chunks hard enough to break a tooth. "La mezza cina, she have the power, *ma* too shy. Don't be *nervosa*. Come back *con* Sophie. More cookies, eh?"

After that I went to Signora Renata's house at least three evenings a week with Sophie, and after the first night there were always at least three or four other people there. I could hardly sit still for ten minutes, let alone for a full hour of boring "phenomena." Signora Renata sensed my restlessness and began slipping bits of candy and cookies into my pockets at the beginning of the evening, as well as producing delicious almond cookies at the end.

Signora Renata was a shrewd, talented woman, illiterate but intelligent and quick. She had calculated that I would be a valuable addition to her circle. The young, she told everyone there, were closer to the spirit world, and she hinted that a touch of oriental blood made me even more sensitive. She made her clients, who despised all orientals, respect me, almost. These were people who even despised Signora Renata, feeling that their French or Russian heritage was superior to hers, though nearly all were uneducated immigrants like her.

The group would sit in total darkness around the velvet-covered table waiting for raps much like those I produced at home. Sometimes Signora Renata went behind the flowered drapes and produced "spirit music" or gauzy figures who floated out from the drapes and were always instantly recognized by Sophie or someone else as manifestations of loved ones. These figures often dropped souvenirs, a flower or a scrap of paper with a name on it. Sometimes Signora Renata stayed at the table and went into a trance, her convulsed body invaded by entitites which spoke, shouted, sang, ranted fascinating if incomprehensible sounds usually ending with a clear but boring message, "I'm happy in the other world." At the end of the sitting a plate of cookies was passed, then left empty on the table. The sitters would place a few coins on it before they left. It was clear that although Signora had a more regular income than ours, it was not great. She too had her vegetable patch, and I often saw her at the slaughterhouse picking up free entrails just as we did.

After about five months I knew Signora Renata's entire repertory of psychic effects. Most were obvious tricks dependent on darkness and draperies covering the production of a blast from a spirit trumpet or a rap from the table, which might then wobble or even rise an inch or two. Other effects, like the vivid stories told through her by weird entities she called "controls" or her sudden thrusts into unspoken thoughts of sitters, were less easily explained and more interesting to me. But not very.

One warm evening in June, when the licorice with which Signora Renata had filled my pockets was not enough to placate me, I grew bored and brave enough to entertain myself by playing a trick. It was entirely unpremeditated.

Seven of us sat around the table that night; Sophie, Signora, and I were joined by a couple whose three-year-old child had just died of meningitis, a middle-aged widower, and a woman who hoped Signora Renata could find a lost or stolen pearl brooch. It was hot and stuffy in the pitch black room, and the widower was engaged in an interminable and tedious exchange with Signora's table raps, which told him, yes, his dead wife entirely approved of his impending remarriage.

"Someone is standing behind you," I said.

After a brief silence the Signora took over. "Behind who, my child? Tell me, *carina*."

"Him," I said, speaking toward the widower who sat across from me, almost invisible in the darkness. I could hear him shifting on his squeaky chair. The person holding my left hand (we often held hands around the table) dropped it, but Signora Renata, who held my other hand, gave it a little squeeze of encouragement before I defiantly pulled it away from her.

"Is it my wife?" said the widower, his voice apprehensive rather than eager.

I did not know what to answer. The boring evening had suddenly become full of excitement, but also full of danger. These adults were not so simple nor so easy to trick as Sophie. I had started a game I did not know how to play. If I said it was his wife, he might demand that I describe her. "No."

"Who is it?"

"I...I don't know."

Everyone began to speak at once.

"Wait, wait," said Signora, her voice smooth and low. "Now, *piccina,* don't be afraid, I will help you. You others, keep the silence, please, no disturb. You see clear or not so clear?"

"Not so clear."

"A big person or a little one?"

"A...big one."

"Man or woman?"

"Man."

"Ah. Now maybe you tell what he look like." She went on talking for a moment, giving me time to think. I knew that she knew that I saw nothing at all, that I needed time and coaching to imagine and construct the ghost standing behind the nervous widower. "His clothes. You see clear enough to get color? Like his suit, or shirt or...."

As she named things, putting before me an array of choices, constructing the ghost for me—so that I need only answer yes or no—I became resistant. I kept answering no...no...no. I needed her help but refused her authority, determined not to let her take over my game. "No clothes."

There was a gasp of shock all around the table. "*Va bene,*" murmured Signora, "the spirits come in clothes only for the eyes of who needs clothes, but an innocent child sees in purity, the spirit no *in corpo.*"

Again I thought Signora was trying to take over, to extricate me from my place of exciting danger. She was moving the talk away from "my ghost." She even produced a rap or two, irrelevant as they were at that moment, before I interrupted her. "He is tall and naked. There is a strap over his shoulder. It holds a...a quiver full of arrows. On the other shoulder he has a bow. A big long bow." I was describing the picture of a statue of Eros from the book of mythology Miss Harrington had given me. I was about to describe the wings when the widower screamed and jumped up from his seat.

"He touched me! Don't let him...stop, lights! Someone light the lamp! Henry, don't hurt me, I didn't mean it, please don't!"

The lamps were lit and the widower stared at me in terror. "Where is he now?"

I blinked. "Gone." I looked deep into his eyes, the way I did whenever I was lying to Sophie. "Gone."

The man jumped up, threw a dollar onto the table, ran out. I never saw him again. Much later I heard my father say that the widower was suspected of having killed the Indian man for whom his wife had left him. His wife committed suicide. He was never prosecuted for the murder, Indians, like orientals, being hardly considered human. Full of guilt, he had been attending seances. The bow and arrows of my Eros figure had been enough to trigger hysteria even though Henry, his wife's lover, had been a farm laborer who probably never had held a bow.

Both Sophie and Signora embraced me protectively as the others stared at me. I suspect I looked appropriately pale and confused. Sophie babbled about all the psychic activity I incited at home and kept saying, "At school they all call her Psyche." Signora kept nodding at me and patting my shoulder, calling me La Psyche. After passing the cookies and leaving the plate to receive coins, she took a coin from the dish and pressed it into my palm as we left, murmuring, "Don't see too much, *carina*. The ones you scare away, they no come back."

That was how I became a regular feature at Signora Renata's sittings. We worked as a team on my "visions," for I soon saw the wisdom of letting her lead me. In the pitch blackness of the circle she would ask, "See anything, Psyche?" I tended to say no until she had asked me for the third time. As soon as I answered, "Yes," she would begin to question me on what I saw, leading me, and I would generally answer only yes or no.

She explained to the sitters that I fell into a trance that made it hard for me to speak. "So young and shy, afraid of the powers that possess her." Soon the system evolved to allow sitters to ask me questions about a vision, and this made answering easier, for they showed by their questions what it was they wanted me to see, leading me more surely than Signora did. If I began to get into difficulties, I simply "lost the vision." One sitter, after the lamps were lit, asked me to recall and describe a detail more clearly. I was dumb with uncertainty and fear of exposure, but Signora Renata came to my rescue. "She no remember after she come out of trance."

One impressive part of my visions was that they included messages in different languages. If a client spoke broken English, I would identify her accent, then risk a communication from the spirit world in what I guessed to be her native tongue. A sprinkling of foreign words never failed to impress people, even in later years when my clients were more sophisticated. In fact, the more highly educated people considered it indubitably miraculous that an ignorant girl spoke more languages than they had learned in school.

So our act evolved through rehearsal after rehearsal, night after night. Gradually I became more confident and proficient in catching hints of the vision some sitter wanted me to see. Toward the end of the year, when never fewer than a dozen people squeezed into that musty room, Signora Renata made a daring change. She began to leave a lighted candle in front of me on the table, so that I could be watched while my visions came. She judged correctly that a child-like, wide-eyed expression on my face was more effective than darkness, and that I would perform better if allowed to add a wider range of gestures to my act.

She continued to produce her regular phenomena in total darkness, training me to assist her. When Sophie and I arrived, always a bit early, she sent Sophie to the kitchen to do some little chore while she instructed me in the use of levers and props to produce raps or release ghost messages on scraps of paper that floated down over the sitters. When she was behind the curtain, I moved about unseen, giving little pats or strokes to sitters who accepted them as caresses from a dead loved one (or even, with great titillation, from a ghost who was a total stranger). At the end of a good evening, I would get a few extra coins from the money left on the plate, most of which went for food for our table or for clothing. By the beginning of 1906 I was the main attraction at Signora Renata's seances. There was seldom enough room for everyone who wanted to come, including an occasional carriage full of ladies and gentlemen from richer parts of the City, wrinkling their noses at the stench of Butchertown.

The turning point came with a near disaster and exposure. A regular sitter who usually paid well was hoping for some more tangible sign from her dead mother. We gave her ghost music that sent her into hysterical tears. A "spirit drawing" fell into her lap. Under the candle we lit, the scrap of paper showed a pattern that excited her. (It was a hasty scrawl made a few minutes before she came, making no sense at all except what she gave to it.)

The Signora was building to a climax. She doused the candle again and enjoined us to put hands to our hearts and pray. This was the signal that, with no one touching me, I could slip out of my chair and give a few spirit caresses, or spirit drafts from a small bellows hidden behind a window drape.

I was just making a feather-light stroke of the lady's hair when the man who had come with her (I should have taken warning from his sour, skeptical glance when he entered) reached out and grabbed me. Somehow I stifled the impulse to scream. Instead I kicked him as hard as I could while at the same time I jabbed one finger toward his head and, with a lucky thrust, stuck it hard into his ear. The shock loosened his hold, and I was able to squirm loose. As he started to bellow, I dove under the table and back to my chair, drowning him out with my own howls and screeches.

As the lamps were lit, I continued howling, lying back in my chair with eyes wide, in my "vision trance" position. I screamed and screamed, taking all attention away from the sputtering man. Then I let words babble from my mouth, starting with "Fire!" Improvising from there, I yelled, ". . . house falling, the wave, the earth is melting, cracking! Falling, falling, all the world is falling!" I went on screaming anything that came to my head, a composite vision of all childhood nightmares, until I collapsed, shuddering and crying. My tears were real enough. I was terrified that I would be exposed, that I had finally been caught. I imagined that playing so many tricks for so many pennies must bring some terrible punishment.

"*Zitti,* quiet, all right, *stai tranquilla,* Psyche." Signora's broad hands were on my head, then on my shoulders. She looked into my eyes and gave me a little wink. Gradually I stopped shaking. "La Psyche has had some terrible vision. The meaning is veiled even from me. Please, all leave at once. *Andate via.* I must care for the child. At once."

When everyone was gone and Sophie had been sent to the kitchen, Signora Renata chuckled at me. "No worry. You scare them good so they pay no attention to anything he say. Next time, watch out. No more touching. You getting too big." Then she gave me a quarter from the plate and told me to take a couple of nights off.

I took more than a couple. For that was the night of April 17. Before the sun rose again the Great Earthquake struck the City.

34

1906–1914

Although the quake woke me, I had no idea how serious it was. The house shook and shifted sharply, and the bed Sophie and I shared slid away from the wall, then slammed against the opposite wall. I heard a crash of crockery from downstairs and a grinding creak of timbers, then silence. I rolled over and went back to sleep, continuing to doze through several aftershocks. Opening my eyes during one of them, I noticed that Sophie was gone. I dozed off again until it was light.

When I went downstairs I found my father and Sophie sitting at the kitchen table dipping bread in bowls of coffee and milk. Sophie was crying, and father was scowling at her. Everything was as usual except that Father was seldom up this early, though he now came home, eventually, every night.

"Well, she *would* perch the blasted thing on a shelf," my father said to me, but his tone was gentle. I saw at once what had happened. A huge, gold-edged plate with crudely-painted red blotches, which Sophie called roses, had stood on edge on a small shelf above the table, secured by metal brackets. Sophie's daughter had painted it as a Christmas present just before typhoid wiped out Sophie's family. It was sacred to Sophie, and in all my tormenting poltergeist assaults on her, even I had spared this plate. I felt suddenly guilty, as if I had caused it to fall. The pieces of it lay on the table in a heap.

"We can glue it together, Sophie," I said. "You won't even see the cracks. Really." My father watched me, probably thinking that I had hardly ever spoken so kindly to Sophie. No one did, least of all my father.

"I'll bet you slept right through it," said Father.

I shook my head. "I felt it. Did anything else break?"

"The pipe from the well," said Father. "We'll have to haul water in buckets again till I fix it." (He meant until Sophie or a neighbor fixed it; Father was helpless at such work.)

So, what I remember from that first hour seemed quite usual after an earthquake. Our wood frame house had creaked and stretched but returned to place on its strong piers. There were no gas pipes or electric wires to break, and we were used to troubles with the pipe from the well. The metal chimney pipe of our wood stove had come apart, but had been shoved together again by Sophie before she started the fire. As usual, after a sharp quake, we were curious to see and hear about the damage suffered by our neighbors, who always gustily exchanged stories of what they had felt when a quake hit. Father suggested we take a walk down along the shore.

A sudden but slight floodtide that had covered the lowlands with a few inches of water was already ebbing. Everyone was out exploring, as we were. People sloshed about in bare feet, trousers and skirts pulled up, or in wading boots, as we were used to doing in winter. The long pier was gone, slipped off the leaning poles. The shrimp shacks had leaned over, collapsing like a house of cards. Everyone was talking excitedly. A woman ran up to Sophie, looked hard at me, then said, "Did you hear, Signora Renata's house slipped right into the Bay. They say she drowned." I recognized the woman from the seance the night before. Later we learned that this rumor, like many others, was untrue. But at that moment I was filled with dread, not grief, the simple dread of the suddenly unemployed.

I begged to go to her house to see, but Father insisted on walking toward town. So we slogged west on the dirt road past animals—cattle and hogs—freely wandering and looking about, just as the people were. The slaughterhouses, most of them long sheds without foundations, had nearly all collapsed. The animals penned beside them had trampled down the fences, then wandered among the houses. A herd of sheep was gathered, trembling, beside the house of a family whose front porch had collapsed, not for the first time. A young mother stood in the doorway, holding her baby, waving and laughing as people walked by staring at her, then waving back. Her husband was already hammering, putting the planks back in place, and some men stopped to help him.

Father said that when we reached Railroad Avenue we would walk up to Army Street and take the cable car downtown. That excited me and made me willing to push on. I had never been downtown, had hardly gone past the railroad tracks, which seemed to be intact, although people were saying that the quake had ripped up the tracks to the south and north. We were on paved streets now with more buildings, some of them two and three stories, most of them badly damaged, leaning.

Railroad Avenue was covered with shattered glass from broken windows. Two buildings had slid completely off their foundations. Crowds of people stood in the middle of the road. I had never seen so many people. The entire population of Hunters Point and Butchertown was here, but as many more were from the west side of Potrero Avenue. They were the first refugees. Most of them had walked from South-of-Market rooming houses and hotels, which, they said, were in flames. They were full of other rumors. The City Hall had collapsed (true). The Cliff House had fallen into the Pacific Ocean (untrue). The whole city was burning (untrue) and there was no water (true). When I looked toward Potrero Hill I could see, from far on the other side, thin but ominous spirals of smoke.

When I remember the wild rumors of those days, I think of two which circulated some days later. One was that, when the fire swept through Chinatown, it killed the entire population. "Finally rid of the damned Chinamen," said the drunk who passed on this rumor. "Almost worth the fire." Later I learned that the army had evacuated the Chinese to the Presidio to protect them from men like this one. But for a day or two I believed I was the last oriental left in San Francisco. The second rumor was true. Agnews State Asylum near San Jose had collapsed, killing hundreds of mental patients. Survivors had been led out and tied to trees surrounding the ruin. The rumor provoked a dream which recurs even now so many years later—lost souls tied to trees, watching the world fall around them. In the first twenty years of that recurring dream, I was one of them.

At that moment I was more disturbed by another true rumor. Cable cars had stopped running at the moment the quake hit. A few of the people had come in horse-drawn wagons filled with their belongings. Most had walked with whatever they could carry. There would be no car ride downtown.

In the midst of this confusion a small table had been set up. I moved in close and saw, behind the table, Miss Harrington, and behind her a large handprinted sign, BOIL ALL DRINKING WATER. Another sign directed the homeless to sleeping space at the grammar school. Yet another said that a first aid station had been established at the Butchertown Library. The Butchertown Library was entirely Miss Harrington's invention, her personal library plus donations, collected in an abandoned storefront next to a saloon. This was the first I had heard of it and the first I had seen of Miss Harrington since my mother died.

Miss Harrington stood over sign-up sheets: one for people who had space to shelter homeless; one for people who had lost their homes; one for those who could donate food or clothing; one for a volunteer patrol against looters; one for volunteers to cook meals or assist medical workers. "Hello, Mei-li," she called. "Want to help?"

She gave me a few strips of paper, telling me to print BOIL ALL DRINKING WATER on them and nail them to corner buildings. Like other people who had walked near her table, I turned away from it with a calm sense of purpose. Hers was one of the first of the centers of order and optimism which speeded the recovery of the City. The more official committees and edicts—especially the occupation by the army—usually disrupted the order created by people like Miss Harrington.

As I tacked up my last sign, Sophie joined me, saying that Father had disappeared. We walked down Railroad Avenue until we saw him coming out of a saloon. Sophie sighed. But he walked firmly toward us.

"The cable cars aren't running and the phone in the saloon won't work."

"Phone?" I had rarely seen a phone; no one we knew had one.

"To call your sister. To see if Erika is all right."

It was the first time he had mentioned Erika since my mother's funeral, when she told him she was going to work in a brothel. Yet he had evidently kept track of her, even knew her phone number.

Father handed us some bread with strips of beef. "The free lunch from Oscar's Saloon." Then he walked away again. We hadn't eaten anything since breakfast, and it was now late afternoon. We sat on a bench that had been pulled out onto the road, chewing greedily and watching the people walking around. There was more laughter now. For the people of Butchertown and Hunters Point, the damage was slight, little more than might be caused by a winter storm. They could easily round up the livestock, prop up the ramshackle slaughtering sheds, and rebuild the fishing pier. For refugees from downtown, there was plenty of open space. Homemade wine was passed freely. It was like a picnic, or so it seemed to a child like me.

When my father came back he told us to go home. He had gotten a place in a wagon that was going downtown. No, we could not go with him. The fire was spreading. He was not sure how he would get back. We would only be a hindrance. He would find Erika and bring her home with him. We must go home and wait.

He spoke and moved with authority and purpose I had never seen in him. Indeed my father, for a brief few days, became a strong, calm center of rationality, even heroism. Unlike Miss Harrington, whose actions were appropriate to every situation, he came into full possession of himself only during this crisis. I wonder if his life might have been different if he could have lived always on the edge of physical danger, always in a crisis that could have brought him forth as this one did.

That night Sophie and I sat up late looking toward the northwest, where the sky shone red all night. Father did not return. The next day we stayed near the house. Between us, we managed to fix the pipe from the well so we could pump water at the kitchen sink again. We pumped and boiled water, and near the end of the day we had our first request for drinking water from a family that set up camp thirty feet away. We waited up late again that night, sitting outside long after dark. To the northwest that terrible red sky continued to glow. The air was thick with smoke. Our eyes burned. The changing smells told us what buildings were burning. The smell of coffee meant the roasting plant near the Ferry Building was burning. Very late that night I smelled burnt bananas mixed with the bitter stench of burning leather. When we looked east, over the Bay, we saw boats streaming back and forth, back and forth, carrying people to Oakland, while fireboats sprayed arcs of shimmering water to save the docks from the fire.

We put a lamp in the window before going to bed. As I was lighting the lamp I heard some people walking past our house. They stopped. "That's her, that's her," I heard a woman say. I recognized her voice. She was the one who had spread the false rumor about Signora Renata's death. "I was there, I heard her describe it just like it's happening. Little half-chinee, they call her Sy-kee, must be a Chinese name. Look, I was there, and she predicted the whole thing the night before, I swear it!"

My father returned with Erika during the night and fell asleep without waking us, without undressing, she in his bed, he on a blanket on the back porch. They slept until noon the next day, while Sophie and I tiptoed around their smoky, dirty bodies. After they awoke we heard their story. Father had gone to Erika's last address on California Street and found the building burned to the ground. For two days he had wandered through the City alternately helping in rescue work and searching bread lines and refugee camps for Erika. Finally he found her in Golden Gate Park.

Erika described her escape in more detail. When the fire started, she hired a wagon and moved with all her belongings to the house of a friend. But the fire spread and there were no more wagons for hire. She left that house with as much as she could carry, dropping things along the way, until she reached the park with only the clothes she wore and one small bag. She stayed there a day and a night before Father found her. They had walked all the way from Golden Gate Park to Hunters Point. Smeared with ashes from head to foot, she was still beautiful. "It's not the clothes I care about," she said. "It's my books!" A soft look passed between her and Father. In later years, of his three daughters, she was the most impatient with Father's weaknesses. But for this moment, he was the rescuer of the daughter he had taught to read Plato in Greek.

The fires were out, but the smell of smoke stayed and stayed while tents went up all over Hunters Point. It was a good place to be while the City rebuilt. The weather was milder and sunnier than other parts of the City. We were closer to relief supplies. Ships docked just to the north or at the Point itself. Trains from the south ran beside Railroad Avenue. Trains from the east stopped at Oakland, and their cargo of emergency food and clothing was ferried across the Bay to our docks. The animals were slaughtered and cooked as needed and given free to everyone. The shrimp shacks were propped up again, and the boats began bringing in their catch. My image of those days is of lines of wash waving on ropes stretched from tent to tent across what had been open fields. Otherwise, it seemed that the earthquake had actually enriched us, what with all the free food and clothing being distributed.

Less than two weeks after the quake, Signora Renata sent a boy to our house to tell Sophie there was a sitting that night and she hoped we would come.

"Sitting?" asked Erika. "Oh, you're still dabbling in the occult, eh, Sophie? Oh no, not with that garlicky old witch?" She laughed. I loved hearing Erika laugh. The house was always filled with her laughter now. She had decided not to try to move back into town for a while. There was no electricity, no running water, no cable cars. Even though services were being gradually restored, life was dingy and uncomfortable. "I'm due for a vacation. If I don't die of boredom. I've been to a few seances. My friend Hermione used to drag me to them. The credulity of human beings is infinite! What kinds of tricks does your Signora do? Well, if it's the only show in town, I guess I'll go along." Sophie was distressed at the thought of Erika coming with us, but could not talk her out of it. So we set off, walking to Signora Renata's house, which still stood, more or less solidly, on the edge of India Basin.

It seemed as if years had passed since our last visit. We walked around tents, ducking under clotheslines, nodding at groups huddled around cooking fires. Soldiers in uniform eyed Erika, who ignored them. Some of the people stared at us longer than seemed natural as we passed. I thought it was Erika who attracted their attention, but I soon learned they were staring at me.

We passed a larger group than the others, sitting or standing around my no longer deserted outcropping of rock where a man stood, red-faced and shouting, "This disaster is made by the hand of God, which has us ever in His grip...." He shook his clenched fist. "...shaking and punishing the iniquitous ones, the evil city, cesspool of sin, domain of painted women...." Erika laughed her beautiful rippling laugh as we passed. This had become a common scene too, religious harangues which called the earthquake a punishment on a wicked city. Some listeners were solemn; some laughed with Erika.

At Signora Renata's house we were early, but there was already a crowd gathered outside. The Signora greeted me at the door, putting her arms around me and drawing me inside. She shook hands with Erika, and the two of them looked at each other with narrowed eyes. Then the Signora admitted as many people as would fit in a double row around the table, about sixteen. As they came in I noted an important change in her procedure: each of them paid her a quarter before entering the house. To the rest, she waved a hand. "No more room, come back tomorrow."

The seance began as usual, with the Signora pulling the drapes to keep out the fading light of the long day. She made us join hands and wait a long time for a couple of feeble raps. These she had to accomplish alone. I was far too shy in the presence of Erika and so many strangers to take the risk of assisting her, especially after my last experience there.

Finally one of the sitters, a half-drunk man in national guard uniform, said, "I come because I heard about the little China girl."

Signora Renata ignored him, but after answering a question about someone's lost relative, "...safe in Oakland, go and look there," she said, "Now, La Psyche, who comes protected by her two sisters, may be strong enough to let the trance come. We light the candle." She set the candle in front of me, but I sat rigid and silent. When the earthquake came I had been afraid that I had lost my job. Now I was afraid to perform. I was sure Erika would see through it. I imagined her laugh cutting through the room, ripping my act to pitiful shreds. And all these people had already paid. Would they be angry? There was already impatience and suspicion in the voice of the man who had called me China girl. I closed my eyes, not in trance but in terror.

"Understand, my friends, this child has suffered the catastrophe twice, once in the vision, then in truth with us all. See, she trembles in weakness. We must wait with *pazienza*. Calm yourself, Psyche. No harm will come. The vision is gone. We do not ask you to live the horror again. Rest." Her voice was soothing, and her message was clear. She knew why I was afraid, and she was reassuring me. I leaned back in the chair, but I did not open my eyes as I had learned to do for my more dramatic performances. I was too nervous to look into the eyes of any of the sitters.

"Afraid?"

I did not answer.

"*Buona*. Silence means no." She had chosen our easiest system. "You see no visions of fear?"

I remained still.

"You are strong enough now to let the visions come?"

I hesitated, then very slowly I nodded my head.

"But can you speak to us?"

I remained still.

"*Va bene*. You see, my friends, at times she has barely the strength to respond. Silence means no." She had made it clear that she would lead me tonight and my performance would be minimal. My fear eased. "Now the little one is ready, I think, for the questions."

"Will there be another earthquake?" It was the question everyone, everywhere, was asking. Some predicted that an even worse one was coming, that next time a tidal wave would sweep over the City, covering it permanently. I hesitated, not knowing what to do.

44

People hardly seemed to breathe, waiting, I suddenly realized, with as much fear as I felt of them. Some sensible voice inside me told me that, of course, there would be more earthquakes. I nodded, and a gasp went around the table.

"Worse? with tidal wave?" A woman's voice rose in panic.

I sat doggedly silent for what seemed an eternity.

"Not as bad?"

I nodded.

"You mean, *carina,* there will be more earthquakes, but only the usual ones?"

I nodded.

"You see a vision now?"

I kept still, not ready to take any risks. Besides, I thought impatiently, I'd given them assurance of no more big quakes. What did they expect for a quarter? "And was the quake the punishment of God?" It was Erika's voice with a lilt of suppressed laughter edged with sarcasm.

I hesitated again. People were listening to anyone who called them sinful, horrible, under God's wrath. They liked being abused by shouters like the man we had passed. If I learned to shout and scream like him, I would get bigger crowds than Signora Renata could fit into her house. I didn't believe there was a God at all. My father said there wasn't, and so did Erika. Sophie talked about God all the time, but she was foolish. Miss Harrington, whom I respected above all the people I knew, didn't seem to believe in God. She never went to church; I often saw her riding a horse on the beach on Sunday morning.

I took a long time thinking about all this, so long that my silence was interpreted as a "no" answer. I felt Signora Renata pat my hand. I opened my eyes.

"*Basta.* The child must rest. Come back tomorrow night." As we left, she pressed three quarters into my hand.

I expected that as soon as we were far enough away from the house, Erika would sing out her great laugh. But she only smiled, looked at me, and said, "Well, well!" Then she walked on. After a while she asked Sophie, "How long has this been going on?"

Sophie, enormously pleased by Erika's serious attention, talked all the way home. She started from the beginning with the poltergeists, which had stopped for good with the earthquake and which she now interpreted as warnings of the earthquake. Then she went on through my growing participation in the sittings, culminating in my "vision" of the earthquake.

Erika spoke to me only once more before I went to bed. As we entered the house, she asked, "How much did you get?" She held out her hand. "I will keep it for you."

What my sister did the next day stands as a good example of how clever she is. She wrote a letter to William James, the great philosopher-psychologist, who happened to be at Stanford University at the time. Not only did she know he was there and how important he was, but she knew of his interest in psychical research. Her letter was brief. It told him that her sister, "an innocent child of eleven," had predicted the earthquake and had shown other unusual powers. It invited him to come to investigate me. She also sent a copy of her letter to the daily papers, which were putting out a joint edition from Oakland. Doctor James did not answer, but the newspaper printed the letter, which was what Erika really hoped for. "That will bring the fools out," she said, and she was right.

From that night on Erika and I were together all the time. She moved into my bedroom, banishing Sophie to a cot downstairs in the kitchen. She went every night with me to Signora Renata's house, where the crowds continued to grow. At the end of three weeks she made new terms with the Signora. "The main attraction here is my sister. I don't want her worn out or cheapened. She will sit no more than three nights a week, for half the money you take in." The Signora flashed a look of frightful anger at Erika but had no other choice than to agree.

Erika took me to the temporary office of the Bank of Italy on Railroad Avenue where she opened an account in my name, with herself as trustee. "If you want to take any money out, you need my signature. More important, neither Sophie nor Father can touch a dime. We'll give Sophie three dollars a week for the house. The rest we save for your career." As we left the bank, she asked, "Now, where is that library you mentioned?" I turned toward the street where the little storefront stood, dragging my feet as Erika strode forward. What would happen when Miss Harrington saw Erika? Would she turn her back as the neighbor women did when Erika walked past them?

I should have known better. When we walked into the little storefront, Miss Harrington turned from the pile of books she was shelving and firmly shook Erika's hand. "We suffered little damage here because there wasn't much to damage, as you see." She was the same height as Erika, slender and straight like her, with what was called a "good carriage" in those days. "I reshelved the books that toppled out, that's all. But since the quake, the dust raised around here is worse than ever. So many people, relief trains, street repair. My main job is keeping the books clean."

Erika looked around, rummaging among the books, then picked up a thin, brown book. "Oh, good, Euripides' *Bacchantes*."

"Yes, one of our donations from a professor in Berkeley, but I'm afraid it's in Greek."

"Lovely," said Erika. "I lost mine in the fire, and I do prize Beckwith's notes, by far the best in any of these academic editions. May I borrow it?" Her voice was as challenging as when she had laid down terms with Signora Renata, but Miss Harrington did not seem to notice.

"Of course," she said, accepting Erika's erudition as matter-of-factly as she did Erika's profession. "I'm glad to have this chance to talk with you about Mei-li. I'm sure you know your little sister is unusual, even gifted. But she has hardly attended school. That she learned to read and write at all, that she still *can* read..."

"Is a tribute to your teaching and to your continuing influence."

"When the schools reopen, if they can reopen them by fall, there's talk of combining Hunters Point with Outer Mission, but if we couldn't get her to attend school here, how can we...."

"I'm taking over May's education," said Erika. "I'm sure I can do better for her than any school, can protect her from some bad influences and from some of the cruel things that happen to a child of mixed blood."

"You may be right. But there are other influences that do harm." Miss Harrington looked down at me. "I'm concerned, Mei-li, about some stories I've been hearing. There are many superstitious and ignorant people who..."

"Who will pay to have their credulities indulged," said Erika. "What is a harmless diversion for such people must, for people less fortunate than you, be seized upon as their only source of income." Erika was smiling, but her smile made me shiver. I was impressed but not surprised to see that Miss Harrington faced that smile with complete composure.

"I understand that. But I'm concerned about the effect on the child. Sometimes a choice made for immediate survival can, in the long run, bring great danger."

"I think I know that, Miss Harrington, even better than you. What choices does my sister have? With all the schooling you can give her, she will still end up doing someone's laundry. Or if she grows pretty enough, she could take up my line of work, her mother's profession also."

"That is not your plan for her, I hope."

"It is not. My sister has shown some talent in the only other profession in which her race and sex are no barrier."

"Spiritualism," said Miss Harrington, as if she were spitting out the word.

"Many quite respectable and intelligent people are interested in spirit phenomena. Some of our city leaders, in fact, attend seances, especially now."

"I see. You can take advantage of the fear and disorder brought on by this disaster."

"I intend to try."

Miss Harrington shook her head. "Please believe me, I do not judge you. Yet if you turn the child this way and then abandon her when you go back to..."

"I'm not going back. If I wanted to, I would have already. The first businesses to open again were those I worked in. Thriving."

"But you are not going back? I congratulate you."

"Miss Harrington, I am not a stupid woman. I am twenty-nine years old and in good health. I would be a fool not to see that now is the time to direct my energies elsewhere. Would you rather my sister go on with her drunken father and Sophie? Believe me, I have not come back in order to end my days in Butchertown. Together May and I will get out."

Miss Harrington smiled. "Then I hope you will bring Mei-li to see me from time to time, for I will never leave Hunters Point."

"Don't be too sure of that."

Erika's plan for my education was bizarre. It consisted, at first, of reading books she chose from Miss Harrington's Butchertown Library and later from the library and bookstores downtown. I was given books of fairy tales, folk tales, myths (including the collection of Indian tales Miss Harrington had copied by hand from local story tellers). Whenever I finished reading one of these books, Erika rewarded me with a penny, but otherwise made no comment.

Every day, while we walked from one place to another, she recited to me in Greek or Latin, making me repeat and memorize what I heard. She knew several poems in Sanskrit; I memorized those too, the way some people can whistle any tune they have heard once. Her surprised laugh was a greater reward than the penny I earned.

She encouraged my facility with languages by making me speak to shopkeepers and sidewalk vendors, refugees, old men sunning themselves, construction workers, anyone who seemed likely to speak a foreign language. She gave me a penny each time I correctly guessed a native language from an accent and then started a conversation. But she did not let me speak to the same person often enough to become familiar. "The less anyone knows about you, the better."

Then came the history books, not recent history but musty old volumes which speculated on ancient civilizations. We made a game of reciting the names of old cities and making up the adventures of people who lived there, as we sat over an obsolete map in one of the tattered books donated to the Butchertown Library.

The only science we studied was astronomy. At night, we sat on my rock outcropping (the highest point overlooking the Bay) while Erika talked about the solar system and the immense distances of space. She taught me the names of the constellations and how to recognize the ones visible from Hunters Point.

A less interesting part of my education was handwriting. I practiced for half an hour every day, the way some more fortunate children practiced music lessons. Each lesson consisted of copying sentences from a foreign language in a dozen different "hands," each with its own slant, flourishes, and loops.

As soon as newspapers were regularly being printed again, she urged me to read one every day but to ignore the local news and political articles. I was to search for items used as filler—obscure incidents in exotic places.

Certain things were completely missing from Erika's educational program. One was simple arithmetic. I could barely count beyond making change, and Erika deliberately kept me ignorant of the practical ability to figure. Keeping accounts was to be her job. "You needn't trouble your head." Another gap was in those sciences requiring laboratory experiments, which were unavailable to us. Also, Erika was weak or uninterested in the natural sciences. We both knew more, I suppose, about the flora and fauna of Hunters Point than most children know today, but Erika never encouraged my spending time in, say, observing the habits of the many birds migrating to and from the Point in those days.

She carefully avoided books of Christian thought or any other religious thought. This was one area where Erika and Miss Harrington agreed. Whatever poor immigrants Miss Harrington dealt with, at the school or at the library, their religion always seemed to clothe the customs which held them back from better health and more learning. As for trying to give me the religion of my mother, Miss Harrington stated loudly that any religion which existed peacefully within a culture that practiced footbinding could not be any better than the superstitions of the Polish immigrant who made signs against the evil eye every time she saw Miss Harrington cultivating tomato plants in her garden. (I think this must be the only instance of closed-mindedness I ever saw in Miss Harrington.)

Actually Erika's reasons for keeping religion out of my education were less idealistic. I heard her tell Miss Harrington that her research indicated there were two trends in spiritualism, the religious and the scientific. The religious clients could fit almost anything from a seance into their religious system, but the scientific ones might be turned away by any religious talk. Therefore it was best to keep me as ignorant as possible of rituals or gospels of any religion in order to broaden the appeal of my performance.

Poor Miss Harrington, who eagerly supplied books in the hope that, despite Erika's purposes, I would be educated, choked, turned away and said, "You are teaching a gifted child to turn her gifts into lies."

And Erika, through clenched teeth, "I am teaching her to survive, and you know more than anyone how few gifted children have done so!" Then she turned to me and reminded me again that I was never to allow myself to be seen reading, never to speak of our lessons. As far as the rest of the world would know, I had attended school less than two years and was otherwise as ignorant as the seagulls that hovered over the slaughterhouses.

When the streetcars started running—bright new trolley cars with crackling electric wires overhead—Erika took me downtown. I was almost twelve years old, and I had never left Butchertown, never gone further north than Sixteenth Street, never crossed Potrero Avenue, though I had climbed the hill to overlook the Mission District factories and warehouses. My first real view of the city of my birth was a walk through its ruins. First we rode the Southern Pacific train to the Third and Townsend depot, then a streetcar up Third, up Market to the Ferry Building, which stood like a grave marker above the charred wreckage. Since the cable cars were still not running, we decided to walk up California Street.

Much of the debris had been carried away—we had watched trainloads of it being dumped in the Bay off the south shore of Hunters Point—but jagged remains of brick walls were still being pulled down, while in the cleared areas, concrete foundations were being poured. The air was thick with dust and noise, all very exciting for me but depressing for Erika. "That was..." she would say, pointing to a black foundation wall and naming a theater or restaurant or elegant shop.

"We're in Chinatown now," she said, as we crossed Du Pont Avenue through a completely bare, charred wasteland, not one building standing. Everywhere Chinese men were working at rebuilding. They looked different from the men who fished off the Point—smaller, hunched, harried, silent. I had heard about Chinatown from my father and once, from a bully at school who had yelled at me to "go back to Chinatown." For a while after my mother died I had dreamed of running away and finding Chinatown, where, by some miracle, I would find my mother still alive and where I would live surrounded by people who looked like her. Now, looking at these intent little men—Erika towered over them—I felt completely alien to them. I knew that I would never be completely accepted by the Europeans at the Point, but this was the first time I suspected that I might be unacceptable to the other part of my heritage, the part which, as embodied by my mother, I had thought I loved best.

"Look, that was the Towne Mansion. My God." We had reached the top of the hill at Taylor Street, and Erika was pointing to the only thing left standing, a tall marble-columned portico which was the entry to...nothing. We stood there for a while as she pointed to the locations of what had been the homes of the rich. She knew

51

them all, but when I asked if she had been in these homes, she said, "Oh, no. The gentlemen who owned these homes came to visit me, and they will again, May, but only to meet you, to help launch your career." We started downhill. "Tired? We're almost there." I shook my head. I was too excited to feel tired.

Just before we reached our destination, she pointed south toward the black skeleton of the City Hall tower and said, "The house where I worked was down there." Then she briskly turned away from the sight. "Here we are." We had reached Van Ness Avenue, the line at which the fire had been stopped and where, in rented houses and temporary buildings and tents, the shops of downtown San Francisco had set up in business.

During the months after the quake, it was common to see people in ash-streaked formal wear, growing rapidly more shabby and dirty, or in ill-fitting, old fashioned clothes. Many had escaped the fire with only the clothes they wore and could get others only from the donated clothing brought by relief trains. Erika had only the dark blue silk she was wearing when the fire caught up with her, and the underwear she carried in her small case. Around the house she wore only a shift or, on cold mornings, a black velvet, gold fringed robe which my father eyed disapprovingly. Her blue silk was repeatedly aired, sponged, and pressed to keep it as fresh as possible for street wear, but on the rough roads of Butchertown it looked almost as out of place as her velvet robe would have.

The first thing Erika bought on Van Ness Avenue was a hat because "a woman downtown without a hat might as well be naked." The shop woman laughed and agreed, "You're right, Miss Violet." All the shop owners knew her, called her Miss Violet, and all of them she corrected with a menacing look. "You have mistaken me for someone else. I am Mrs. Newland." They nodded gravely. She represented herself as a widow from then on. Of course, all records of her marriage had been lost in the fire. Erika was one of many who snatched a new identity from those flames, it being necessary only to fill out an order for new documents. At the same time that she recorded her "marriage," she obtained new birth certificates which scrupulously recorded the correct known facts. "Never lie without a reason," she told me.

She bought dresses, shoes, gloves, underwear for herself, all in conservative modes and colors, all charged without question. She discarded everything she was wearing, putting on some of the clothes, ordering the others packed in boxes. Now indeed she was

52

Mrs. Newland in a conservative brown suit with a soft green hat that matched her lightly veiled eyes.

Then she turned to the problem of dressing me. I was at an awkward age, almost out of childhood, my arms and legs growing longer but my chest still flat, my waist undefined. I had replaced my outgrown cotton dresses with donated ones. The week before our shopping trip I had tried on one of my mother's old dresses but it was already too small. I had almost gained my full adult height, not very tall, but taller than my mother had been.

Erika bought me two black skirts and three plain white shirtwaists, suitable, the shop woman agreed, for any occasion at which a respectable young girl should appear. Reluctantly I tried on several of the flat, round lids considered suitable hats for girls in those days, but Erika had to agree I looked ridiculous and let me go bareheaded.

Loaded with parcels, we started for home, taking another street car down Van Ness, then out Mission, transferring at Sixteenth. Erika no longer pointed at the blackened squares to tell me what buildings had perished. She seemed quite cheerful, sitting erect, facing the opposite seat where she had piled our packages, occasionally brushing the sleeve of her new jacket with great pleasure. As we crossed the fire line at Howard Street, suddenly out of the ruined area, we looked out the window at little houses with their vegetable gardens beside the Mission District foundries and mills. The streetcar stopped for a freight train whose tracks ended at the cork factory at the foot of Potrero Hill.

"Let's see, we transfer again at Third, I think." Erika peered out the window again, squinted, then reached into her purse and pulled out a pair of metal-rimmed, round spectacles. When she put them on, her face changed completely. Without the glasses, it had been composed for the world to look upon and admire. With the glasses her eyes became more active, restless, avid, less thoughtful, more cunning. From then on she wore her glasses more often than not.

Erika and I took our streetcar rides every week, sometimes shopping, sometimes meeting a gentleman for lunch in a restaurant hastily opened in a house on the edge of the burned district. We even lunched at the Fairmont Hotel when it finally opened on the first anniversary of the quake. These gentlemen listened to Erika, then looked at their plates and talked about their grave losses in the quake. We never saw any of them more than once. I began to dread these lunches as events which put her into a terrible temper as soon as the gentleman had gone and she had put her glasses back on. I was glad when there were no more elegant lunches and no more gentlemen.

I continued to work at Signora Renata's house three nights a week. The long hours Erika spent teaching me showed results. When at a loss for answers to questions, I could babble a few lines from Pushkin in Russian, a Latin chant, or a simple message in the language of the client, who was suitably impressed.

But inevitably, as recovery accelerated, people began to leave Hunters Point. First to go were the soldiers (who had done more to destroy order than to keep it), then the prosperous families, then the single men. One by one the tents and campsites disappeared as people moved back to their homes or to new homes in other towns where they found work. By late 1907 those who were left were, like the usual population of Butchertown, poor families. Attendance at seances began to fall off, and soon Signora Renata could no longer charge an admission fee, but only take shrinking contributions.

"It isn't that people don't want to see May. Her reputation is spreading!" I would hear Erika's voice downstairs late at night after I was in bed, and I could imagine Father and Sophie listening respectfully as they always did now. "That woman who came in a carriage last week, do you know who she was? Her husband is one of the richest men in the City. But he's not going to have her driven out to this godforsaken place every week!"

Soon after that speech, Erika announced that she was moving with me to a furnished house on Haight Street just above Market. Sophie could come along to keep house for us. Father could come too if he promised to keep his drinking under control; it wasn't a bad idea to have a man in the house. "Here, sign," she said to Sophie. She was selling the house at Hunters Point for eight hundred dollars, "More than we'd ever get for this shack if it weren't for the housing shortage. Better get it now." How she managed to get the house on Haight was a mystery. Probably one of the gentlemen had come through after all.

I ran to tell Miss Harrington, who took the news solemnly, sitting me down opposite her in the little library, taking my hand. "Listen to me, Mei-li, and try to remember what I say. Leave Butchertown, yes. Go out into a larger world. But be sure it is larger. You are still

54

a child and decisions are being made for you. In a few years, you can make the decisions. You have great gifts. Promise me you will keep asking yourself for the true answer to how you should use your gifts."

I promised, knowing that I was lying, knowing that Miss Harrington knew I was lying. I ran from the library, ran from any thought, any memory of Miss Harrington. I was moving into the Real City where, Erika said, I would become rich and famous. I didn't want to think about true answers or even true questions. Thinking only uncovered the desperate emptiness which had lain at the bottom of thought even before my mother's death. Plotting and scheming to fool people and become rich and famous—whatever that meant—created an excitement which covered the emptiness.

Our new home seemed an almost unbearably exciting location. We were only two blocks from Market Street, which sparkled and rumbled with trolleys and even an occasional motor car. Haight Street was a double line of two- and three-story houses rising to the northwest, all touching, no space between, windows like huge eyes staring straight into each other across paved streets where wagons rattled and people walked and children played all day long. Actually, by today's standards, it was a quiet street, but compared to the rural spaces of Hunters Point, it seemed the center of a teeming urban world.

The house on Haight Street was actually a pair of narrow flats above what had been a shoe repair shop, empty since the quake. The tiny flat above the store had a square front parlor, kitchen, bedroom and bath. Up another steep stairway was a similar narrow flat. The building—badly built on a brick foundation—had suffered from the quake. Wide cracks opened floors, ceilings, walls. Broken windows were boarded up. But the plumbing worked, and some furniture remained undamaged except for being covered with plaster and dust. The upstairs flat was damaged by rain that had come in through unrepaired cracks in the roof. Erika explained that we had use of the house for three years in exchange for making repairs. She had hired a carpenter, but we would all have to work along with him. We would live in the upper flat, hold seances in the lower flat.

Father suggested renting out the shop, but Erika refused because her plans for repair included certain alterations. Both the floor and ceiling of the seance room were repaired with openings to the shop below and the flat above. A skillful carpenter installed trap doors which were almost invisible. He also altered the back wall of a closet in the seance room so that it would open onto a ladder which went up a lightwell to a window of the flat above. The floor of the closet became a cleverly fitted trap door with a ladder descending to the shop below. He and Erika experimented with tiny levers worked into the woodwork or under the mantelpiece of the false fireplace and attached to metal or wooden tubes which, when the lever was tripped, made sounds echo through the walls. Finally he built a table to Erika's specifications with an underside full of levers and compartments. At the touch of one concealed lever, the center of the table would expel the contents of the central compartment, closing quickly so that, in the dark, with the attention of sitters directed elsewhere, whatever popped out would seem to have appeared from nowhere.

This table, along with replacement of the front windows, nearly exhausted our funds. We had barely enough to buy paint and drapes to make the parlor presentable for clients. Everything else—our broken kitchen stove upstairs, even the leaks in the roof—would have to wait. We slept the first winter on the floor among buckets set to catch the rain. Later we were able to make our living quarters more comfortable. One modern convenience we never added was electricity, Erika maintaining that no one should be able to suddenly switch on a bright light during a spirit visitation.

Father was of no use in all this work. Now that he was living in town again, only a block from Market Street, he was out at the saloons most of the time, usually coming home at dawn and sleeping all day, throughout all the hammering. But it was Father who gave us the answer to how to use the shop.

One foggy dawn in early summer, he appeared with two buckets full of flowers, carried on the streetcar. Setting them down in front of the house, he stumbled up to bed, and the next day he could not remember how or where he had gotten them. (Probably he won them at cards, as he won his drinks.) But by that time Sophie had sold them to passersby, and Sophie was in business. From then on, Father stopped at the wholesale flower market at dawn, buying and carrying home what he could. Sophie's flower shop supported us during those first weeks and remained a small, steady source of income.

When we were ready, Erika placed an ad in the personals column of the *Examiner*. It read, as I recall,

May "Psyche" Murrow
the child who predicted the earthquake
is now holding sittings 9 p.m. week nights
209 Haight Street   Admission $1

She also had the message printed on cards and mailed to some of the people who had attended the sittings at Hunters Point.

I was very nervous on the day of our first sitting in the Haight Street house. We had not practiced using the secret entries to the closet nor the trap doors in the floor or ceiling. "Never mind," said Erika. "We must get started. We won't do anything complicated." She showed me where to press on the table leg to make the central compartment eject its contents. "But don't press it until everyone is looking up to see the flower petals." Sophie was to open the trap door from the flat above, drop a handful of petals (swept up from the shop) and quickly close the trap. "But don't do it until after May blows out the candle, hear?"

How could she induce Sophie to do this—Sophie, who believed in the spirit world? The answer was simple. Sophie believed that the spirits did not come unless the sitters were hospitable, believing, open. A few little tricks prepared the sitters for the real visitations from the other world.

Aside from those two effects, which might make a grand finale, we would do only a few rappings whenever either of us could reach a lever. If I felt nervous, I could stay in candlelit trance with only nods to signify "yes" to some questions. "Remember, just let them lead you," said Erika. "You're a smart girl, May, smarter than they are or they wouldn't be coming to you!" Then she laughed, and her eyes flashed behind the spectacles she wore all the time now.

Just after Father left for the evening, the first people arrived, two old women who had once come by carriage to Signora Renata's house. Then came a pretty young woman who smiled at Erika, but immediately sobered when Erika frowned at her. She kissed me and said her name was Maisie. Then a great many people arrived all at once, and when all seventeen chairs were filled, Erika put a note on the front door saying there was no more room, come back tomorrow. "Come here, May." She took me aside and, pretending to arrange the white ribbon she had tied on my hair, she whispered, "That couple in black lost a ten-year-old son in the quake. His

57

name was Ned and he collected frogs.'' Then she drew me to the table and sat me down with the eight people who could fit around it. The others had to sit in a second circle around us, but Erika was careful not to place any of them behind me.

"My little sister is a shy girl who does not understand the gift bestowed on her. She seldom remembers what happens during a sitting. She always becomes exhausted. For the sake of her health and well-being, I must limit each sitting to one hour. I now ask you all to send your thoughts out toward her to help her in the exercise of this mysterious and taxing gift.'' Having created a solemn silence, Erika put out the gas light and sat on the window sill at the opposite end of the room.

We sat in nearly total darkness and utter silence for what seemed hours, but was probably about five minutes. Without Signora Renata, I did not know how to start. "Perhaps," said Erika, "the gathering is not placed for maximum exchange of psychic energy.'' I didn't know what she meant, but I took her hint and said, "Yes." She lit a candle in front of me and then began moving people about. Three times she rearranged their sitting, then looked at me and frowned. On the third reshuffling, she gave me a slight nod, and I said, "Yes, that's better. I feel...'' My voice trailed off while they waited for me to say what I felt, which was, actually, not quite so scared. I'd had a chance to look at all the people and get used to them. Maisie kept smiling and nodding. The couple in black looked pale and sad with eyes that hardly seemed to see at all. The two old ladies looked kind, and the others, mostly women, looked curious and not suspicious. All in all, a friendly gathering who wanted me to succeed.

I left the candle burning in front of my face while we sat for another eternity. Then Erika produced a rap which seemed to come from midair, and I answered her with one that vibrated the chair containing Maisie, who squealed. With people in the room, the accoustical effect was even better than expected. "Who's there?" I said, and reached out my foot to produce a rap that shook the far end of the table.

A few more raps established the presence of the spirits, and then Erika invited questions. The first ones were still—more than a year after the earthquake—related to divine vengeance and the possibility of recurrence. Then Maisie described a jade ring she had lost, asking me to help her find it. I sat still, not knowing what to say. "Will I ever get it back?" she insisted, and finally I nodded. I waited for the sad couple to ask me a question so that I could mention Ned and frogs, but they only sat, hunched, like stone effigies carved in an expression of grief. People were beginning to cough and grow as restless as I felt. I knew Erika's thoughts as well as if I had been a true psychic: I was losing my audience, and they would not come again unless I did something interesting. But I could think of nothing to do, and the hour had passed.

I blew out the candle and waited for Sophie's shower of flower petals. It did not come. Finally Erika pulled open a window drape, and while all eyes were turned toward her and the moonlit window, I pressed the button and something popped from the center of the table, a small object which rang like a coin dropped from above.

"What is that?" asked someone, reaching for it.

I lit the candle again. One of the old ladies held a small object.

"My ring! my ring!" shouted the girl called Maisie. She took it from the old woman, put it on her finger, and waved her hand about. Everyone turned toward me. Erika had wisely told me nothing about this trick, and I must have looked as surprised as everyone else. It took me a while to realize that Erika had employed another accomplice besides Sophie.

Speaking of Sophie, it was at this moment that she remembered to perform her part, sending a shower of petals over us. Then she snapped the trap door shut with such a bang that all eyes turned upward toward the ceiling. Instead of marveling at the mysterious wafting of flower petals from the spirits, people were scanning the ceiling for what must have occurred to all of them—an opening, from which anything might be dropped, including the ring.

One look at the dismay and fury on Erika's face, and I knew this could be a disaster. The thought of facing her wrath, even though I had not caused this accident, was enough to make me jump up with a scream that somehow I managed to turn into a laugh, as I shouted with inspiration born of terror, "Oh, take your horrid frog back or I won't play with you!" As everyone froze, I laughed again. "You are a wicked boy, Ned, but I like you anyway, frogs and all."

Then I began to mime a series of games with an invisible child. I ran around the room, looking back over my shoulder and laughing, as if being chased. I stopped and shook as if "tagged" and turned to chase "him." I reached into invisible pockets and shuddered at invisible frogs I touched, then laughed and said, "We are frogs too!" and played leapfrog, crouching low on the floor, then rising to jump over my invisible playmate, then took his invisible hands and, circling slowly, sang, "Ring around the rosie, pocket full of posey, ashes, ashes, all fall down," then fell on the floor and lay still. I counted to thirty with my eyes closed. When I opened them and saw Erika's face over me, I knew that my performance had impressed even her. She helped me up.

Ned's parents were crying and laughing and pressing close to me. I gave them a blank stare, letting Erika repeat that I seldom remembered anything that happened during the time when I "crossed over to the world of spirit." Then she hurried everyone out, saying she feared for my health if I did not have absolute quiet and rest. The grateful couple embraced, the woman half-fainting in her husband's arms as they left vowing to come back tomorrow night.

Maisie left last, handing the ring to Erika and taking the money Erika handed to her. "You made those two people real happy," Maisie said to me, as if to calm any pangs of guilt I felt about tricking such helplessly vulnerable people. The guilt I felt was far less than my relief at having again covered a failed trick by inventing another. And I felt the brief, intoxicating thrill of an actor who has held an audience completely in her power.

The next night Ned's parents, Mr. and Mrs. Robertson, came again. Erika stopped them at the door, pretending that we were "already full," but promising them reserved places for the next night. It became her policy that no one be allowed to come every night, lest they become bored by the repetition and begin to look too closely at what was happening. Mr. and Mrs. Robertson did become regular attenders, coming faithfully for the next six years and eventually making possible the advances in my dubious career.

Sophie was the only person allowed to attend every sitting, night after night. After her fiasco at creating psychic effects, Erika decided that the best use of Sophie was as a sitter, a consistently enthralled believer whose credulity was catching. Her other use was as an informant. People came into her flower shop to ask questions about me, and ended up telling the wide-eyed Sophie all about their griefs, hopes, and troubles. Usually, by the time they appeared at a sitting, I knew all about them from Sophie's chattering while she made dinner. She never saw this as cheating. I think she considered it giving me a head start so as to make the most of the hour during which I exercised my "powers."

Over the next three years, while the City was frantically rebuilding, we were just as frantically building my skills. My lessons in writing—I soon wrote in a dozen distinctive hands—continued every morning along with the readings in ancient history and the memorization of line after line of poetry. But that was the least of the work.

Erika took me to see a man named Victor who lived on Eddy Street near Market in a hotel room stuffed with theatrical apparatus. Victor had been a stage magician. He taught me sleight-of-hand tricks which he said I must practice constantly, "whenever you have a minute. You know, the devil finds work for idle hands, and here's some of the devil's work," he laughed. "Now try it again." He taught me to palm small items or to slip things into and out of sleeves. He sent us to another man who sold "occult artists' gear" out of a similar hotel room.

From the second man we bought steel-tipped shoes with a little spring mechanism in the toe. I learned to snap this spring with my big toe, causing a resounding rap to echo through an object in contact with the shoes, which looked almost normal. In those days of long dresses and feminine modesty, no one would have dared to pull my skirt back to examine even my foot.

This man supplied us with wire, thread, and gauzy cheesecloth. With practice, a gauze "spirit" could be "materialized" on wires which made the spirit dance a bit in air before dematerializing up my sleeve. He changed my wardrobe to black dresses, less visible in the dark, with full sleeves and deep pockets could hold any number of things. "Darkness and faith," were our allies, he said. "Darkness and faith, ladies." He sold us fortune cards, astrology charts, and "the latest thing, ladies," a crystal ball. "Better take a Ouija board too," he insisted. "Best to know a little about all these things, cater to the taste of all clients."

That was Erika's theory too. She had set herself to learn everything that mediums did and to teach me to do it better. "You've got to be the best. There's a lot of competition."

On weekends, when we did not hold sittings, she took me to the sittings of other mediums to study their techniques. We found them all below the level of Signora Renata, whom we had already left in the dust. But one of them repaid us for all our wasted time by telling us about "the blue book."

It was not a book at all, but a series of file cards which were mailed periodically to subscribers. Each card carried the name of a person who frequented mediums and psychics, with pertinent details about his or her life and interests. Subscribers were expected to furnish information about their clients, especially those who did much traveling. The fee went to a man—formerly a medium—who collected, printed, and mailed the information throughout the world. Therefore it was possible for someone to consult a medium in New York, then travel to San Francisco and find psychic messages miraculously confirmed by a medium three thousand miles away. This was an expensive service and not one we were sure we could make much use of, but Erika decided to try it.

Maisie and another girl, Rebecca, were frequent helpers. Both girls were actresses who augmented their small income as prostitutes. They were quick, clever, pretty and absolutely loyal to Erika. They came often to dinner, where their part in the seance was planned, and they left immediately after the seance to carry on their other work. Occasionally, when they got parts in a play or musical, we would not see them for weeks.

They were so clever with disguises that Erika often used them as materialized spirits, sometimes as white-veiled presences that talked as they walked around the room, sometimes costumed as deceased mothers or husbands or daughters. Maisie, who was tall and had a deep voice, was quite good in the male parts, while Rebecca, a tiny girl, did children very well. On some nights the two girls did five or six roles each, rushing up and down the closet ladder for quick costume changes while I lay back in the trance which supposedly materialized them. I enjoyed these nights because they were so entertaining. They enjoyed themselves too, saying that they were never given such an interesting range of roles when they appeared on stage.

Then Erika discovered spirit photography, the taking of a photograph during a seance. After Erika took a photo, she would work in the darkroom she had installed in a closet at the back of Sophie's flower shop. By making a double exposure with a shot of Maisie or Rebecca, or sometimes with an old picture of a client's deceased relative, she would produce a fuzzy image of the "spirit" attending our seance.

The spirit photos were especially convincing to men, who considered themselves, usually, to be more skeptical clients. The camera was assumed to be far more objective than it actually was. "The camera does not lie," was a saying believed by millions of people who knew nothing about the variables possible in the processing of photographs. Even my mistakes in the darkroom when I assisted Erika resulted in smudged shapes or whitened areas which clients accepted as auras, astral bodies, or dematerializing spirits who I said had been hovering in the dark.

Our success rested on the fact that most of the people who came to seances were in terror at the prospect of their own death or in deep grief and guilt because of the death of someone close to them. They would grasp at any "proof" that the dead went on living in something like their living form. Their will to believe was stronger than any of our talents for creating illusions. They would identify a smudge on a photo as indubitably the face of their mother. Maisie in a topcoat was a beloved brother. The messages they led me to were miracles, especially messages of forgiveness, which I gave freely. I had only to mention the presence of a spirit for a sitter to declare she felt a cold breeze or the touch of a ghostly hand, or even that she saw the outline of a presence I could sketch in with whatever details I chose from her unconscious prompting. What was even stranger to me was that clients often brought friends about whom they first told Erika a great deal, becoming accomplices in deception, as if they would go to any lengths to support their own faith.

Their credulity did not justify what I did, nor did the fact that I made some of them temporarily happy. It is not true that children have no moral sense. I knew then, as well as I know now, that it was wrong to prey on credulity for profit. At the time my main concern, like Erika's, was that we seemed to clear so little profit.

There were so many expenses. Even rent free, the house cost us money in repairs and upkeep. Subscribing to the "blue book" and other psychic publications cost money. So did the costumes, props, wages for Rebecca and Maisie, the camera, the dark-room equipment. Although we charged a high price for a spirit photograph, we could not cheapen the value of this product by making many. There was even an annual license fee for mediums, which Erika paid with a shrug. "Better than an illegal profession where you are constantly paying off the police." Looking at our situation in 1911, four years after moving to Haight Street, well established in full-time mediumship, I had to agree with Erika that we were lucky to have the income from Sophie's flower shop. That had come to be the one thing we could agree upon, for I had begun to rebel.

63

For five years I had been leading a life rather like that of a child performer, a musician or an actress. Every day there were long sessions of study and practice. I also had household chores to do, including the ongoing repair of the upstairs flat and the maintenance of appliances for the seance room, all those hidden panels and springs which required constant cleaning and oiling to keep them working smoothly. Every evening I held a sitting or attended one. My own sittings bored me only slightly less than the ones of other mediums.

Unlike a child musician or actress, I was not allowed the company of fellow performers. Even if I had wanted to associate with mediums—few of whom were less than twenty years older than I— it would have been unwise to do so. Mediums were always being accused of collusion in fakery. Most of them met only at annual conventions that we were too poor to attend, even if we had wanted to. Erika would not let me associate with any of the children on the block, certainly not letting any of them into the house where they might poke around and discover some of the alterations we had made. Our neighbors, in any case, had warned their children to stay away from the "little half-breed witch." The people nearest my age were Maisie and Rebecca, both about twenty. Apart from the seances, of course, I could not have contact with a pair of "actresses." Nor could a young girl freely roam the streets of the City alone. I went nowhere without Erika, and our few walks always took us to the public library for more study.

My expectation of living a larger, richer life in the City was cruelly disappointed. The opposite was true. I had lost the freedom of Hunters Point and gained only a crowded isolation, like a prisoner in solitary confinement among thousands.

At sixteen, I began to have screaming rages, throwing things, not as a pretended poltergeist but openly. I sometimes refused to sit at seances, forcing Erika to turn people away with the excuse that I was sick. I began to run away, but never very far, because I had no money, not even carfare. Besides, I found Erika's warnings to be true; an unaccompanied girl was immediately accosted by men. I considered going with them, just to spite Erika, but I had heard enough about the realities of street work (neither Maisie nor Rebecca would stoop to that) to stop short of taking revenge on her that way. Sometimes I sat in furious immobility during the whole hour's sitting, while Erika frantically produced phenomena whose effect was ruined by my bad temper.

Once or twice Erika and I had physical battles, she slapping me away from her as I screamed, kicked, bit, scratched, and pulled out handfuls of her hair—while Sophie stood crying and biting her fist and Father shook his head, shaken briefly out of his alcoholic daze. After these battles, I would calm down, contrite, ashamed, and Erika would reason with me. I was an artist, she said, who had to work very hard for a very long time before the reward came. If I stopped now, I would end up scrubbing floors. Being of mixed race, I could not even hope for a job as a shop girl, which was bad enough if I only knew. She was devoting her whole life to developing my career. My unruly behavior could ruin years of work. The costumes and camera were all paid for now, and soon there would be more money.

She offered a compromise. No more attending seances on weekends. "We'll take trips to the country." She actually did take me on the train several times to the Santa Cruz mountains, where we walked among the redwoods and picnicked. The great trees astonished me into temporary calm. I breathed their quiet for a few hours and believed in patience and tranquility.

But as soon as we were back in the City, I was furious and restless again. Once I managed to get to a phone and called Miss Harrington at the Butchertown Library. She listened to my ravings, then begged me to come to see her. But I never did.

One foggy Friday night a man appeared at the door and paid his dollar just like any person curious to see the half-breed girl medium. One look at Erika's face told me he was not just any person. Surprise and delight lit her face for only a second before being suppressed. He wore a mischievous grin as he nodded politely, also pretending they were strangers.

I was struck by how handsome he was. He was about thirty, tall and well built, dressed in an elegantly simple gray suit that made the other men at the seance look like rumpled salesmen. His skin was golden, slightly darker than mine, his facial features regular, his nose straight but thin. His thick black hair was definitely African, as were his full lips, and his voice was that richly deep bass some Negro men have, but without any trace of southern Negro accent. He is mixed, like me, I thought. The Robertsons were there, and I pantomimed a scene of dancing with Ned, but all the time I was dancing for the handsome, dark man who watched intently, then asked Ned's parents how old he was when he died.

"Passed over," corrected Erika.

"Yes, of course, ma'am," he said, and one more brief look passed between them, a look I already resented.

When the sitting was over, he hung back, waiting for the others to leave. As soon as Sophie shut the front door on the last person, Erika threw herself into his arms, and they danced around the room, laughing and mimicking the little dance I had done during the seance with the spirit of Ned. But after a final twirl, he wheeled around and made a deep bow to me. I blushed, hot, confused, pleased, as he introduced himself, "Norman Luther Duclar."

"Let's go upstairs and talk," said Erika. We gathered at the oil-cloth-covered round oak table in the kitchen of the upper flat. Sophie served hot chocolate and cookies, while Erika and Norman talked.

"Is this the first time you've been back since the quake?"

"Oh, no, I was in and out during the first year, covering reconstruction. Then a war in South America. Then Alaska. I thought you were dead. That's what Mrs. Close said. I checked every place I could think of, and no one had seen or heard of you, so I believed her."

"I was out at Hunters Point."

Norman nodded, looked at Sophie, then at me. "With the family."

"And you went back up to Seattle?"

Norman nodded.

"Did you marry Miss Black Society?" she asked. Erika was looking down into her cup so that I could not read her expression.

"I did indeed."

"So you must be father of two or three little..."

"No," interrupted Norman. "No children yet."

"Actually," said Erika, "I did spread a rumor that Miss Violet died in the quake. She is dead. I'm Mrs. Newland."

"Is there a Mr. Newland?"

Erika shook her head. "Mine is the perfect marriage. A respectable title without a man, he and all records consumed in the fire." They both burst into laughter. "How did you find me?"

"You must be joking. How could I not find you? Sooner or later I'd have ended up here. Your sister is becoming quite well known—the mysterious oriental Psyche. That's not your real name, is it?" he asked me.

"No, her name's May," Erika answered.

"Mei-li," I corrected her.

"Mei-li," he repeated, nodding at me. He continued to look at me as he went on talking. "Then I ran into Jessica—she's dancing at the new Gold Slipper—and she told me your new name and your new venture."

"Jessie never could keep her mouth shut."

"Oh, she was very discreet, as everyone else has been. Otherwise I would certainly have heard of your new identity before. Anyway I decided to surprise you."

"And you certainly did." They laughed again. "You'll stay here, of course."

During the next two months Norman Duclar stayed with us while he worked on a book about city hall corruption, of which there was plenty in San Francisco at the time, various politicians having ended up in prison in the political quake following the natural one. He attended nearly every seance, and afterward we sat around the upstairs kitchen table talking, sometimes until Father got home. We all slept late, and I enjoyed a vacation from my lessons and practice. I also enjoyed imagining myself passionately in love with Norman, but only during his absence. When he was with us, talking and laughing at the table, I still found him very handsome and very dear, but close up, a real person, he lost the aura that my imagination whipped up into romantic passion.

On most days Norman disappeared from noon till dusk, gathering material for his book. On Sundays he took us to a play or a concert, though we never sat together. "The nice thing about the places we used to frequent," he said to Erika, "was that we didn't have to worry about race or about rumors reaching my family." So our best times were those spent around the kitchen table, where I learned about Norman.

He was the youngest in a Negro family which had been free for at least two generations before the Civil War and was so mixed that most of them looked white. Few had crossed the color line to pass for white, preferring the proud mixed identity of their family and friends. The family had settled in Washington State in the mid eighteen hundreds, building a fortune in lumber and fishing, then founding a newspaper. They now owned a syndicate of twenty such papers and four monthly magazines, some for Negro readership and some general. Norman had been educated in England, then brought home to work as a reporter along with one of his brothers.

Another brother worked in circulation. Two sisters wrote for one of the women's magazines in the syndicate. Norman traveled a great deal on assignments that took him to San Francisco or Mexico City or Paris. It was assumed that eventually he would settle down and take over management of the newspaper chain from his oldest brother, just as it was assumed that he would marry the woman Erika called Miss Black Society. In one of the funniest sessions we had at the kitchen table, he explained all the social, economic, and racial reasons why he had known from the age of ten (when she was twelve) that she was the only woman he could marry, and that marry her he must.

"Just like royalty," said Erika. I gathered that he and Erika had met during one of his first escapes to San Francisco, just after he graduated from college, when he became one of her first customers. What had started as sex for money had turned into a love affair and then cooled to a friendship. I watched the two of them closely, jealously. Erika showed no interest in resuming a sexual relation with Norman or with any man. She was interested only in building my career.

On the last night before Norman was to return to Washington, we sat up past midnight. Sophie had gone to bed. Erika tried to make me go to bed too, but I refused. "Let's stay up all night. Let's stay up till Norman leaves."

"But you won't be fresh for tomorrow night's sitting."

Norman laughed. "You're a wonder, Erika, a whirlwind of pure ambition!"

"Lucky for May I am. And you could help, you know."

"How?"

"A story about May in the *Examiner*."

Norman shook his head, no longer smiling. "The only thing I could do on Mei-li would be an exposure."

"What do you mean? Hundreds of people believe in her powers. You said yourself that she's becoming famous."

"Yes, and you'd better keep newspapermen away from her. I suspect they're all ready to descend at any minute. And they'll tear her to bits if she goes on the way she's going now."

"If she goes on... what do you mean? I see. You call me a wonder, but you think I'm going about this thing the wrong way? What other way is there?"

"Do you want the truth, Erika?"

Erika leaned her elbows on the table. "Go ahead."

So we did sit up all night while Norman gave his analysis of our situation.

"First of all, I congratulate you on picking up practically every trick of the trade. That's the trouble. It's a standard act, a little of everything, done as well as anyone does it, but just the same old crude tricks."

"They work," said Erika.

"Yes, they work, for now, but the public is fickle. First raps and table tipping were enough. Now everyone wants spirit photos. But how long do you think it will be before people catch on to that? No, don't try to answer. Listen. You know about Palladino?"

Erika and I both nodded. Everyone knew Eusapia Palladino, the great Italian medium.

"I was in New York a year ago when she came. You know what happened to her?"

"I know the papers called her a fraud," said Erika, "but what does that matter? The publicity was good and the people believe anyway."

Norman shook his head. "The newspapers killed her. She's finished. The trouble with you is you read the psychic press, and they still call her 'the divine Eusapia,' but everywhere else, she's dead, just an old woman gone back to Italy, broke and broken."

"That won't happen to May."

"No, not if you listen to me, if you understand what happened to Palladino, what it means. It means physical mediumship is dead. Raps and taps and trumpets and, yes, spirit photography too. The sooner you get out of that, the better. There have already been some prosecutions for fraud, because you see, with a photo, you're selling a product, a tangible thing that can be examined and proven false. Physical mediumship is fifty years out of date. People are still just as gullible, don't get me wrong, but not that way. It's too risky, too easy to find the trap doors or grab Maisie under her spirit veils, or find the levers under the table. All those crude things are on the way out."

"But then what is left?" cried Erika.

"Oh, there's plenty left. Mental effects—with no tangible results but no possibility of exposure as tricks. Like automatic writing. You've trained Mei-li in writing, but you hardly use her skill."

"She wouldn't know what to write."

"Let her try. If she makes mistakes, she still can't be called a fraud. And then you have the trances, when she sees the spirits and talks to them . . . nobody can prove trickery because they don't expect to see what she sees. She should do more of that. More of just answering questions while in trance. Mei-li is a bright girl and she quickly picks up hints of what they want to hear."

"I don't think she could. . . ."

"And she probably ought to have a 'control,' a really interesting one, none of those Indian chiefs or Tibetan lamas, all that has been done to death. Having a 'control' gives range to the act, especially when the medium is young and female and has to act shy and modest . . . except when a control takes over."

"That's just it. May is too young to . . . but I have thought about a control. I just haven't been able to decide. . . ."

"Don't. Mei-li should decide. Mei-li, how old are you?"

"Sixteen," I said. "And a half."

"You see, Erika. She's not a child anymore. And aside from the fact that she's the most beautiful thing I've ever seen . . ." There was hardly a pause in his very matter-of-fact voice, yet a great space opened up, and his words fell into that space and disappeared, buried in my mind for later retrieval. ". . . she's also very, very intelligent. And you don't give her credit for that. You keep too tight a rein on her. Why, the only time those sittings come alive is when something you planned goes wrong and Mei-li covers up, or when she takes her lead from the sitter and acts out a pantomime with spirits. I don't know whether she's a great actress or a great storyteller or what she is, but when she begins to improvise, she casts a spell over everyone, and *that* is what convinces, not the raps she makes with those awful boots. What she has is imagination, which you haven't recognized, Erika, because, clever as you are, you lack it. Well, you asked for it, so don't be angry."

"I'm not angry." Erika looked fierce. "Go on."

"Well . . . those boots. Speaking of her clothes. You've got her dressed up like a child in mourning, a frumpy, fat child with all that stuff in those pockets. Mei-li is a young lady. Get her into some color—a soft blue, I think. You might consider Chinese pajamas, soft slippers—play up the exotic look. It's the only way, I think, of

70

getting her out of the awful styles you women wear now. Don't buy her those straight, baggy pants the women wear in Chinatown. Have some good silk ones made with a fit that shows a neat, uncorsetted body. You know how the clients will swarm in then, Erika. Yet she'll still be quite respectable—in her ancestral dress.''

Erika looked at me, biting her lip thoughtfully. ''I've tried to play down her oriental side because of all the bad feeling against the Chinese.''

''Well, you can't change those eyes of hers. Besides, in the occult, prejudice works in favor of the oriental—the mysterious East and all that.''

''Maybe you're right. Yes, I think pale blue silk trousers with a long coat.''

''And one more thing,'' said Norman. He paused as if to see if Erika had braced herself for a shock. ''You'll have to stop charging admission.'' Erika looked too flabbergasted to answer. ''The medium who charges a dollar a sitting puts herself in a class with vaudeville shows—and movies, which are cheaper and more exciting than jugglers and mediums. But the medium who charges nothing is not an entertainer. She is a lady with a sacred gift.''

''How on earth are we to live?'' demanded Erika.

''On the rich, of course. As soon as you stop charging money, you become more acceptable to the upper classes, who never pay for anything. When the upper class accepts you, the middle class will follow, and they are more likely to give gifts. Madame Blavatsky never owned a thing, but she lived in the mansions of the rich and received gifts. When you charge nothing, you can accept anything. After a few years, Mei-li will meet a rich man, marry him, and retire. Surely that's what you really want, Mei-li. You shouldn't go on with this life any longer than necessary.''

''No rich man will marry a half-breed,'' said Erika.

''Don't be too sure of that. Spiritualists are eccentrics. They tend to be in the vanguard of progressive movements. Don't you read those magazines you subscribe to? I glanced through them. They're against race prejudice, capital punishment, war, and most established churches. So you might find a rich, open-minded man who can appreciate Mei-li. Let him be old fashioned in only one way—that he'll want her to give up her career after marriage.''

''And will want to support her beloved family!'' added Erika.

The next day Erika drew a picture of trousers and a high-collared, long coat, then told Sophie to make me an outfit like it. Sophie made the first set in muslin, then another and another (her mistakes became comfortable pajamas I wore around the house) until she mastered the design. Then she made the first of the silver-blue silk pajama suits that I wore for the next twenty years.

Erika cancelled my sittings for the rest of the month, telling clients I had accepted an invitation to be examined by the American Society for Psychical Research in Los Angeles. Her hastily invented lie added to my credibility, for the only thing worse than being examined by those suspicious and experienced men and women was being ignored by them.

Then she stripped the seance room. Within a week, all our occult trappings were sold: the table, my boots, costumes, various bits of hardware, the camera and darkroom equipment, even the drapes and rugs. She let Maisie and Rebecca go. "If we're careful our money will last a few months." She bought white paint and we re-painted the room, put rush mats on the wooden floor, and stood a Japanese screen in front of the window. Sophie made a dozen pillows covered in black silk, which we scattered on the mats. A few straight chairs we left against the wall. One silver-blue pillow, matching my clothes, we placed in front of the screen. "That's your place," said Erika. "Now let's get back to work and see what happens."

Every time I passed a mirror I remembered Norman's words "...besides being the most beautiful thing I've ever seen...." and I searched the glass for a sign of that beauty. I saw high cheekbones and my mother's dark almond eyes, a thin nose, a pointed chin, and close-cropped black hair whose waves clung as if sculpted to my head. Was this beauty? I had always believed that my Chinese eyes cancelled any possibility of beauty. But Norman too bore the "blemish" of some features of a non-white race, and he was handsome. Even Erika thought so. Was it, therefore, possible to be both different and beautiful?

Norman returned four months later on New Year's Eve. We sat around the table listening to Erika's verdict: the changes had been a terrible mistake. "Attendance has fallen off. People like the Robertsons will come faithfully for messages from Ned, but sometimes they're the only ones here. Even Sophie has lost interest. Thank God for her flower shop. We're almost out of money." Erika sighed.

"People want darkness and candles and mystery. They want something to happen, a spirit hovering over them or a flower sent from a dead relative. They want what we all want, something real to wipe out the truth, that we all die, that death is final and life is meaningless and all our struggle and suffering—meaningless." I had never heard Erika talk this way. Did she too feel that awful emptiness at the bottom of everything?

"So you've lost your ectoplasm customers. No need to panic. I can lend you a little money. Give it time. Now, what are you giving them instead of raps and taps?"

"Not very much," I admitted. "I go into trance and see things. I answer questions. I'm doing more automatic writing, like you said. I use information Sophie picked up or I just let the sitter lead me."

"Fine. A class act. What about a control?"

I shrugged. "We haven't decided on the right one."

"One?" said Norman. "Why only one? You can try out different ones, drop the ones you don't enjoy."

"I thought Cleopatra would be an impressive control," said Erika. "She's read a lot about her."

Norman shook his head. "I'd steer clear of real historical figures. Your new clientele will be more educated, more skilled in trapping you. Your controls should be ordinary, common people mostly, especially if they speak a foreign language. Mei-li has a gift for languages, but what she has picked up so far is not the idiom of the gentry—it's working-class dialect. Any client who speaks another language will notice that."

Norman reached out and put his hand over mine, which was lying on the table. "Trust yourself, Psyche. Don't plan. Improvise. Go into your 'trance,' and then make up a game, a game of becoming a different person. You invent the game and you play, and what I've seen of you convinces me that you will play it masterfully." He kept his hand on mine while Erika sat like a stone between us, looking at our hands, but saying, doing nothing. "Look, it's midnight!" he said, taking his hand away. "Let's open the champagne!" He opened the bottle he had brought and poured the wine into three glasses.

I lifted my glass and said, "To the new year, to 1913."

The second toast was proposed by Erika. "To the real beginning of May's career. And to luck. We'll need it."

"And here's to the rich husband who'll end her career as soon as possible," said Norman.

An hour later we all went to bed—Erika, Sophie and I in one bedroom, Father in another, and Norman in the downstairs flat. I dozed off for an hour or so, then awoke thirsty from the effects of the champagne. I went into the kitchen and poured a glass of water. I drank it, then went quietly down the stairs, through the seance room to stand in the open doorway of Norman's bedroom.

"I'm awake," he said.

I walked across the room to stand near his bed.

"What's this you're wearing?"

"The muslim pajamas. One of Sophie's failures."

"I like them better than the silk."

"So do I." I shivered. He pulled back the covers for me to slide under them beside him, put his arms around me. "I can't be the rich husband, Mei-li. I already have a wife, a good one, and I won't leave her. Soon we'll have children and I'll take over the family enterprises and you won't see me anymore."

"I know."

"When that rich husband comes along, he'll expect you to be a virgin."

"No one, rich or poor, will ever marry me." That must have been the only genuinely clairvoyant statement I ever made.

"You're sure you want . . . you know about sex?"

"Maisie and Rebecca told me what men do."

"No, Mei-li, it won't be like that, I promise you." We kissed and fondled each other, no more, for many nights as I gradually got used to the intimacy which women were at that time taught to fear. It was at least two weeks before we had full intercourse, and Norman took care that I would not become pregnant.

Erika knew what was going on, had given tacit permission. She once said, much later, that Norman made me "more manageable." This only shows again how much more clever she is than I. I began 1913 with my first taste of alcohol and my first lover, and I made the mistake of considering these evidence of adulthood and independence.

I took Norman's advice, experimenting with the invention of "controls" who conversed with my clients. I would babble some nonsense or a few phrases from a foreign language. Then, as sitters asked who was speaking, I would gradually invent an entity, like drawing a picture, improvising. At first the entity was vague, but gradually, in repeated appearances, I would think of details to sketch in, making the image more complex or discarding it if it did not develop well. Of the dozens of controls I invented in those early attempts, I had three favorites: Theophola, a priestess from the temple of Aphrodite in ancient Greece; Jeb, a black slave who was killed leading an uprising in 1820; Benjamin, a weaver who died in the twelfth century massacre of the Jews of York.

I liked doing the men best because, especially in the identity of Jeb, I discarded all the feminine delicacy expected of a girl. As Jeb I sprinkled my southern dialect with French and German phrases which the illiterate slave had learned from two masters. With Benjamin, there was the challenge of reciting some Hebrew phrases and speaking what I hoped would be accepted as old English, a fractured Chaucerian prose which was a challenge and great fun. Theophola spoke English with a few incantations in ancient Greek. She was dramatic in a different way—no shrinking, modest woman. She was a priestess with holy authority, haughty bearing, and a frank sexuality appropriate to a votary of the goddess of love. The men at my sittings were frozen with fascination when I became Theophola. Erika used to laugh and say they all had erections.

It truly was an exciting game, with all the fun of being someone else, someone who spoke and acted in ways forbidden to a girl. Otherwise I answered the same old questions about dead relatives, past lives, and present hopes. As usual the clients led me to giving them the answer they wanted to hear, and after receiving the answer, they enhanced its effect by their exaggerated report of what I had done. They would say, "Jeb knew all about the gold watch my mother gave me," when actually 'Jeb' had mentioned a 'gift' and they had supplied the details with, "Oh, yes, you mean the watch!" When I did automatic writing, they insisted that they recognized the script of a dead friend, and when I saw visions during trance, someone often cried out that, just for a second, she too had glimpsed a spirit.

Meanwhile Norman had written a piece for *The Examiner* that was printed just after he went back to Washington. It was a careful, good-humored description of a girl who seemed to possess some unusual powers which she reluctantly demonstrated for select people, by appointment only, refusing any money, chaperoned by her father and two half-sisters, who were trying in vain to protect her from the growing interest in her powers. Since the newspapers had always ridiculed mediums, Norman maintained a skeptical, amused tone, but he did note the "absence of tappings and tippings that characterize the all-too-familiar displays of the occult." He gave no address, only the post office box that he insisted we rent. Also omitted was a photo of me, in case we might be seen together and connections made between our friendship and his "objective" report. In an impulse of mischief he added that when anyone attempted to photograph me, "something seems to happen to the film." This created a legend which I fostered by refusing, in later years, to allow my photograph to be taken.

During the six months before his return, my clientele slowly grew again, and, as he predicted, was more prosperous, better educated, yet still gullible. These people would have seen through the old tricks we used to do in the dark, but they were inordinately impressed when I gushed a few phrases of Greek or Hebrew or cursed like an outraged black prince in chains. Occasionally someone would begin to ask searching, informed questions of one of my controls, like, "How would you compare the recitation of *kadesh* in your day with present Jewish practice," and at that point Benjamin would begin to fade, replaced by the seductive Theophola. Usually I enjoyed the battle of wits and, one way or another, I won it. My main advantage was that no one believed a young, unschooled girl capable of collecting information and performing as I did. Still, no one offered me the gifts Norman said would come, except the faithful Robertsons, who invited our whole family to spend a week at their summer house near Santa Rosa, a huge mansion on acres of vineyards. In the seven years since the earthquake, Mr. Robertson, a building contractor, had become quite rich. We accepted their invitation, but Father spent far too much time at the winery barrels, and Erika caught a terrible case of poison oak.

During that weekend with the Robertsons I did three sittings, and we saw the advantage of working in the homes of clients. I no longer needed any special apparatus. Besides, it was best not to have our new clientele encounter my father, as they sometimes did, staggering about the house. Furthermore, said Erika, how was I to meet that rich husband if I didn't get into the homes where he lived or visited? So I went to the town house of the Robertsons where, I told them, I could pick up more vibrations, more spiritual presence among Ned's belongings, a sad collection of toys and clothing plucked from the fire. The Robertsons recommended me to others. Soon I was making frequent trips to Pacific Heights, where the rich had built after the quake. I rode in their carriages and occasionally in a motor car. Erika came with me, of course. In one house she bumped into a man who turned pale at the sight of her. "Don't worry," she told me. "He certainly isn't going to tell anyone when or how he knew me."

One of these clients gave me a ruby ring. Another had a long blue cape made for me. "You shouldn't be running around in just silk pajamas in our climate." But the ring had to be worn when I saw these clients, so it could not be sold for cash. I was grateful for the cape which felt cosy in the summer fog.

Norman returned in July and seemed impressed by the progress we had made. He quieted Erika's complaints by giving her more money. While he was in town, we took the weekends off, taking the ferry to Oakland or to Sausalito, then hiring a carriage and riding into the country with picnic food. Sometimes we hired a motor car and drove down the peninsula, again laden with food, for it might be hard for either of us to be served in a rural restaurant. In the City we could not go to fashionable places together because Norman might be recognized, and news would travel home fast on the black society grapevine. In the country we were more likely to encounter prejudice. Finally we found a solution (probably suggested by Erika) in a brothel at Half Moon Bay, a stark, gray hotel standing alone between the ocean and the artichoke fields, where we could spend a day on the beach, a night in a quiet room, and where we ate delicious food cooked by the madam "for my girls," knowing that, for a price, she would be discreet. But within the month Norman had to go back to Washington.

Suddenly the owner of our flats told Erika we would have to leave, having long overstayed the time of our agreement. I could never be sure, but I think our abrupt eviction had something to do with the man who had recognized Erika in one of the mansions where I was now a regular visitor. The owner seemed willing to let Sophie keep her flower shop for a reasonable rent, but I could not see any way that all four of us could crowd into the tiny rooms in the back of the shop.

The Robertsons came to our rescue, inviting me to come to live with them. I refused. Erika pretended to agree with me, saying that

I was too young to live apart from my family. The Robertsons insisted that they meant Erika should come too; there were two rooms and a bath in the west wing of their house, simple but adequate, they hoped, until we found something better. "Please be our guests for as long as you like. It is the only way we can repay you for the comfort you have given us. You needn't eat with us every day. One of the servants will bring you a tray. And certainly we will make no demands on you to conduct sittings unless you want to." The couple were now in their early forties, and, although Mrs. Robertson no longer wore black, she had a gray, grieving look which broke into pathetic smiles during my performances with 'Ned.' Her husband's frantic and lucrative building seemed to be his escape from her frequent depressions.

So it was all arranged over my objections. Sophie and Father would move into the rooms behind the shop on Haight Street. Erika and I would live at the Robertson mansion. On our way there in their chauffeur-driven car, Erika scolded. "This is exactly what we were hoping for, what Norman said could happen. Owning nothing, charging nothing, we end up living in a mansion in Pacific Heights. And you almost spoiled it. Don't tell me you have suddenly developed a conscience. You are not quite able to afford that particular luxury yet!"

She was right. I suffered pangs of conscience, at least where the Robertsons were concerned. They were trusting and kind, frequently telling me that they thought of me as a daughter—not a common thing for rich people to say about a girl of mixed race and dubious family. But my feelings went beyond guilt for my long-term deception of them, went beyond questions of whether or not, as Erika insisted quite logically, they wanted to be deceived.

There had been settling upon me, slowly, like a million separate flakes of snow, the cold weight of the longings of all the people who came to hear me imitate a twelfth-century Jew or a prehistoric priestess bringing messages of eternal life. While feeding their longing, I had become infected with it. But mine was a longing without hope. I knew all the tricks for preying upon the longing of others. I gave spurious meaning to their lives; I knew there was none. I believed only fools, gullible people, held any hope that meaning existed. Yet the longing for meaning grew in me. I could never mention it to anyone, not even Norman. I was too ashamed of it, as I had been ashamed of my grief at losing my mother. All I could do was to try to forget it during an occasional weekend with him. (He would telephone the Robertson house, name a date, and I would drive to Half Moon Bay in a car borrowed from the Robertsons.) Those weekends were the only relief I had until the next big break came, in the person of Willy Knauss.

He called himself Doctor Willy Knuass, though he was not a medical doctor. He was a practitioner of mesmerism and magnetism, a theory of healing based on alleged exchange of electricity as the hands of a sensitive mesmerist were passed over (not touching) a body. This theory was losing followers as more became known about electricity and the word lost some of its magic. (All the houses I visited now had electric lights.) Willy Knauss still believed in mesmerism and considered himself an unusually powerful healer. Persistently mesmerizing and magnetizing at every opportunity, he was ostracized by both medical and religious authorities in his native Switzerland. That he was never legally prosecuted he owed to the fact that his family was rich and powerful, owners of a factory which made instruments for astronomers.

To escape the ridicule (and to the great relief of his family) he began a trip around the world that had lasted more than three years and was now coming to an end. Some travelers search for art treasure or uncharted rivers; Doctor Willy searched for the occult in all its manifestations. He gathered tappings and tippings, keeping a diary of every sound and sight. He collected ectoplasm, pages of automatic writing, spirit photos. He carried on long conversations with spirits through mediums and was especially delighted when the spirit of one of his persecutors (he had already outlived a few of them) came through to apologize for his rational skepticism. He believed everything he saw and heard, and on the few occasions when a trick was so clumsy that even he could not accept it, he forgave the medium. Like Sophie, he believed that only in an atmosphere of faith could the true messages come through. Only in an atmosphere of patience and forgiveness could a medium resist the temptation to cheat, secure enough to wait for the true spiritual message.

He was over fifty when he came to San Francisco. He had already been to New York, Mexico City, Tokyo, Quebec, Sydney, Peking,

Vancouver, Manila, Los Angeles, Salt Lake City, and Lily Dale (a spiritualist summer camp in New York). Everywhere he went he took careful notes for a book he was writing about the work of the great mediums of the world. If his persecutors stopped him from getting a publisher, he would publish the book himself.

Doctor Willy had been married, but his wife had left him and lived alone in Paris. There were no children. He had been particularly fond of a dead sister, Greta. He seemed attracted to boys, but was too shy to make any advances. He drank a great deal of beer, but enjoyed wine, ate well, loved seafood. He passionately hated war and cruelty to animals. He believed that orientals possessed the deepest psychic abilities, but had so far been disappointed in his travels to Japan and China. He believed in reincarnation, yet considered himself a Christian. Christian churches were persecutors of true Christianity, which, he said, expressed itself among the spiritualists who devoted their lives to connecting this world with the next. He spoke German, French, English, and Italian. He had been told by two mediums that in a previous life he had suffered a violent death. He was quite free of race prejudice, and strawberries gave him hives.

All these things and many more I knew about Doctor Willy before I met him because he was, of course, written up at some length in the "blue book," which Erika said might finally reward our investment. He had been in San Francisco for a month, during which his movement from one medium to another had been traced, recorded, transmitted, so that—to use his own words—"the increase of phenomena since my arrival approaches the miraculous."

On a Monday night in late August we were invited to a very grand house where I had held two sittings already. We rode with the Robertsons in their car. They seemed tense. I needed no psychic powers to guess that they had been told Doctor Willy Knauss might be there. It was Doctor Willy's habit to use a false name, then to be astounded when a medium told him things about himself "which she could not possibly know, since she had no idea who I truly was." Of course, every subscriber to the "blue book" had memorized his appearance and his itinerary.

As usual we arrived an hour late to make our high class clients wait for us. We walked through a front garden on a brick path, up three stairs to a wooden door—all these mansions had massive front doors—and were brought into a wood-paneled entry as large as most houses. The sitting would be held in the north parlor, as usual, to our left. I let the maid take my cape. Then, with Erika leading the way, I walked between the Robertsons into the parlor, which was a little smaller than the entry, almost cosy, with thick oriental rugs and a cheerful fire in the marble fireplace.

Beside the host and hostess were about fifteen people I had seen there before. Standing near the fireplace was a round, soft man in a black suit whom I recognized at once as Willy Knauss. He stepped forward, made a little bow, and introduced himself as Mr. Long. He had a sweet smile with a sad droop at the edges. I liked him at once; he was a kind man, I could tell. At the same time I was on my guard because it is not always easy to fool a truly decent, simple person.

I sat cross-legged on the rug in front of the fireplace. Most of the others sat in chairs, except for Doctor Willy and Mrs. Robertson, who took pillows and lowered themselves to the floor with me. We sat for a long time without much happening. It had become my practice never to plan ahead what I would "see" or say, which control would come through, or what message I would give to each client. I had learned that I performed best when I kept my mind blank before a sitting, then spoke whatever came to me, inventing, letting one word lead to another.

That night I was tense, and so was everyone else. All knew that I was being tested, though I wasn't supposed to know. I had the advantage of knowing that and also of knowing that Doctor Willy was not really the rigorous investigator the others believed him to be. Still, he had been run through every trick of the trade dozens of times, and I was determined not to be an ordinary addition to his collection.

After a bit of Greek from my priestess control, I was silent, stuck, and beginning to get a headache. I frowned and put my hand to my head, deciding to dramatize that pain, following my system of making do with whatever came to me. I groaned and closed my eyes.

"What is it, dear?" said Erika, with the protective tone she assumed before an audience. "You're in pain!"

I nodded and groaned again. Then, with sudden inspiration I stood up, opened my eyes, looked around as if puzzled, then closed them again and moved a few steps in one direction, and then another, until I stood in front of Doctor Willy. I opened my eyes, looked at him shyly. I went down on my knees, looked up at him again. "Please, sir," I murmured. "Something tells me that if you would...excuse my familiarity...if you would just touch me...right here." I pointed to my forehead, and Doctor Willy reached his hand forward.

At the slight touch of his fingertips, I bounded up with a smile, giving a great sigh of relief. "Thank you," I said, and moved back to my place in front of the fireplace, smiling as if the pain were gone. It was not; if anything it was worse as all eyes followed me. Maybe I had overplayed. Would he guess immediately that I knew who he was? Or would he be so flattered by recognition of his healing powers that he would suspend all disbelief? The latter, to be sure. As I saw the soft, proud, satisfied smile light his face, I knew that all was well, and my headache actually did begin to lessen.

I reached out my hand for pencil and paper, and I did silent automatic writing for the rest of the sitting. I covered sheets and sheets with anything that came into my head, anything but a reference to "Mister Long." Whenever I stopped, head sunken on my chest, Erika read aloud what I had written, none of which made much sense. Finally I stopped, and Erika announced that the sitting was at an end.

When we were alone in our rooms, Erika praised me for my restraint. "It's important not to overplay, not to give him too much at first. And you don't want to do anything like he's seen before. Don't use Theophola again. He clearly isn't excited by women. I think you'd better...." Erika stopped herself, obeying Norman's advice to let me improvise on my own. "...better think of something because he'll be back soon." She was right. The next morning there was a phone call asking if "Mr. Long" could come for a private sitting that night.

For this private sitting Erika asked the Robertsons to allow us to use the tea house which their Japanese gardener had built at the end of their huge garden. It was a tiny room, bare except for tatami mats on the floor. White shoji screens let in dim light during the day, but there was only a candle to light the room after dark. It was September, a hot, fogless month. The tea house was cool and comfortable.

Erika sat in the corner as silent chaperone (how she hated sitting on the floor!) Doctor Willy and I sat in the middle of the room, only a few feet from her, crosslegged on black cushions I had brought from Haight Street, with a lighted candle on the floor between us. I took a few deep breaths, then let my head fall forward to indicate that I was in trance. A moment later I became Jeb and gave the performance of my life up to that point.

"My friend!" I said, in the deepest, blackest voice I could muster. "Oh, my old friend Victor, how I watched over you these years past, how I tried to come through, how I tried to lead you to this girl who, ignorant as she is, makes the only channel I've found. After a hundred years, to clasp your hand again!" At this point I grabbed his right hand in both of mine and gave it a squeeze that made him cry out in pain. "It's Jeb, your comrade Jeb, but you don't know me. You don't even know you are Victor!" I gave out a thick, deep laugh which impressed even Erika as I let go his hand, then sprawled sideways on the floor in a free, masculine pose, the way a large man would take his ease.

Then I told Doctor Willy, in the voice of Jeb, that he had, in a previous life, been Victor Lawson, a distant relative of many famous families, including that of Thomas Jefferson. He had been born in 1798, the same year as Jeb, who had been given to him as slave and companion. But they had become more than master and slave, had become true friends, growing and learning together, Victor secretly teaching Jeb to read and write, the two of them prizing one another above all others. As they grew older, the family expected their close relationship to change to one appropriate to a slave society. When it did not, Victor's family tried to separate them, but Victor resisted, becoming defiant. So they sent him away, up north to boarding school, where he met abolitionists and, secretly communicating with Jeb, made plans to help him escape, after which they planned to go to Canada where they would make their fortune together. The plot broadened to include other slaves who wanted to escape. They planned a mass uprising and escape, Victor secretly returning to help lead them out. They were betrayed, Jeb was killed, and the other rebel slaves sold south. Victor killed himself over his friend's body, and his family covered up the story, saying that Victor had died of smallpox shortly after being sent north to school. All records of the uprising and deaths had been suppressed.

My invention owed much to *Uncle Tom's Cabin* with traces of *Huckleberry Finn* and Frederick Douglass's autobiography. Probably two elements of my story of Jeb and Victor appealed most to Doctor Willy. One was the extraordinary heroism and loyalty of Victor. The other element was the erotic flavor Willy might find in the relationship, which, of course, I left unspoken. So again I had given Doctor Willy flattery, this time with a pinch of romantic, boyish love, brotherly and otherwise. Tears were running down his pink cheeks when I suddenly slipped out of trance, folded my legs under me, and gave him a shy, puzzled look. He took my hand, told me his true name, and asked if he might return the next night.

I grew very fond of Doctor Willy as he returned night after night. I can still see his rosy face with his neat, white pointed goatee and sparse gray hair sticking up above his large, blue, often wet eyes. He was a very credulous man, very susceptible to flattery, very proud, and very self-pitying. But he was genuinely tolerant and open-minded, which is the better side of being credulous. He loved seeing himself in the role of fighter against injustice; hence I, in the role of Jeb, could endlessly elaborate on Victor's story. He might even have been justified in believing that he had healing powers; there was something soothing in his gentle smile.

Doctor Willy told me many stories about his persecution by authorities, and of his resigning from the Society for Psychical Research, which he found increasingly intolerant of phenomena he believed genuine. Nevertheless, he was considering moving to England, the headquarters of the SPR, because interest in spiritualism was very high there.

It was Doctor Willy who first addressed me as Madame Psyche. Since I was just eighteen when he met me, the title was at first a little joke, an exaggerated bit of courtliness, but it was also a sincere expression of respect. To call an unmarried woman Madame was a recognition of maturity, accomplishment, independence. At one point Doctor Willy said, "You are married to something higher than a mere man."

Night after night, Doctor Willy came to sittings, private or public, and when I refused money, brought gifts which Erika planned to sell as soon as he went back to Europe. At the public sittings he took notes which he said would help in writing the long chapter he intended devoting to me in his book. At our private sittings he laughed and cried with Jeb, who brought him messages from other spirits who confirmed Doctor Willy's healing powers, tolerance, courage, and intelligence. But Doctor Willy also spent time, more and more time, just talking to me directly. At some sittings I did not even go into trance or try automatic writing. I just listened as Doctor Willy discoursed on the meaning of spiritualism.

"We are on the brink of a new era," he would say, "and I may live long enough to see it. Surely you will. The long, cruel history of mankind's crude beginnings is at an end. The old beliefs are being swept away. The churches, those fortresses of superstition, are crumbling. The annihilating drudgery of physical labor is being taken over by machines. The despotic rulers are being swept aside in great tidal waves of democracy. Oh, there is much to do yet, but the trend is unmistakable. We are on the brink of the new age.

"And who will lead us into the new age? You, my dear little Madame Psyche. You and I and all the others who are slowly coming to see the signs of the miracle which is being revealed through you. Yes, the spiritualist movement is the vanguard. For it is we of the spiritualist movement who are bringing together the two worlds, this, and the World Beyond. It is that connection which gives meaning to life, without which, all is chaos. We bring the new gospel, the faith based on evidence, proof that life does not arise and die in senseless repetition but goes on and upward forever. We connect the seen with the unseen. We show that everything is alive, that we have always lived and always shall live, that every atom of every person, animal, indeed of every stone, is precious.

"You are the prophet, the seer who makes the tiny chink of light in the wall between the two worlds. We have always had a few who saw into the unseen, but now, in this age, our numbers multiply. You lead the transformation of the human race, which is about to enter a new era, where there will be no more fear and no more suffering and no more dying. For all will be made clear to us. And glorious. And mankind will at last be free!"

Sometimes after Doctor Willy had left and Erika and I had gone to our rooms, I would mimic him, thickening his accent, wringing my hands as he did, even making my eyes grow wet with sentimental tears. Erika laughed and so did I, but my laughter was a noise to cover shame. I was ashamed of fooling such a nice man. I was ashamed of feeling ashamed, which I saw as weakness. And beneath the shame was despair, for if what I was doing was proof of there being meaning to life, then clearly life had no meaning.

Life had only...a little more comfort than before. We lived in a fine house and ate good food. Mrs. Robertson insisted that we use her charge accounts to buy clothes. I kept to my silk pajama suits, using her accounts only when Christmas came, buying gifts for Sophie, Erika, and Father. I also bought cuff links for Norman, although I knew he would not appear until after Christmas, which he always spent with his wife. We used the Robertson's box at the theater and the opera freely. We used one of their cars for long day trips with Sophie and Father. Except for the private sittings with Doctor Willy, I held sittings only three times a week, usually in other, even more luxurious homes. More and more calls came from journalists who wanted to interview me. I refused to see them, as I continued to refuse to be photographed. Erika and I agreed that there was more to be gained now by being exclusive, even reclusive. Admission to my sittings was carefully restricted and screened, which, of course, increased the curiosity and rumors about me.

In January of 1914 Doctor Willy had been traveling for over three years. "It is time," he said, "to go home and write my book." We took the ferry to Oakland to see him off on the train going east. For once my tears were genuine as I waved from the platform. As soon as he was gone, Erika took his gifts to a dealer and raised a little money.

A few weeks later Norman phoned. He would be in San Francisco for at least a month and had taken a room at the Fairmont. I could meet him there or at Sophie's flower shop. Erika drove me to Nob Hill but did not come in with me. It was a bright, blossoming February day. I had worn my blue cloak and had stuffed its big pockets with toilet articles, for I planned to stay a few days.

I told Norman about Doctor Willy and showed him some letters I had already received from London, where he had settled to work on his book, which he promised would make me "famous around the world."

"Yes, I know you're becoming quite an item, at least here," said Norman. "A reporter friend called me in Seattle, asking how I'd managed to get that interview and did I know you. I pretended I couldn't even remember dong the interview. So we must be even more careful about being seen together."

"But no one knows what I look like," I said. "I still have never been photographed."

Norman laughed, pinched me, and reminded me that descriptions of me in silk pajamas and a long cloak were known widely.

We made love, joked, laughed, read the papers, ate, slept, talked and talked. Norman was especially tender, especially witty, and when he told a joke and watched to see if I was amused and entertained, his black eyes shone so that he seemed more handsome than ever. Yet, several times after we made love, he lay with a still, preoccupied look, until he caught me watching him and made another joke.

On the third day I went back to the Robertsons for a sitting. Then Erika drove me to Sophie's store, where Norman met us, carrying bags of Chinese food. We had a party, and I gave him his cuff links, which I had forgotten to bring to the hotel. The next day we took a ride in the country.

For the rest of the month my brief sittings produced no very satisfying phenomena because I was usually too tired from our parties or excursions. There was something uneasy about our fun, something almost frantic in Norman's laughter. At the end of the month he told me why. "My wife is pregnant. What I warned you about is happening. I'm going to become a family man now. My brother's not well, so I'll be taking over more of the business, staying home, learning to be a real husband and a good father."

I said nothing, but I was desolate. Now I would not even have the occasional visit of Norman to look forward to.

The day before Norman left I received a telegram from Doctor Willy. A wealthy couple was eager to meet me, willing to pay the steamship fare for both Erika and me, and he had plenty of room in his London house to put us up for as long as we would like to stay, a few months at least while he finished his book. As soon as he heard from me, he would arrange for train and steamship tickets.

After Norman's farewell dinner in Sophie's shop, I read the telegram aloud. Everyone expressed an opinion. My father said, "No one is civilized who has not seen Europe." He rambled on, telling of his "grand tour" when he was my age, until Sophie interrupted to say I would surely drown at sea. "Remember the Titanic!" Norman murmured, "They're talking about war in Europe," but Erika laughed, "They're always talking about war in Europe. Can't you all see? Are you blind? This is May's chance. After a few months there she'll come back famous, legitimized, like an opera singer. You know all she needs is a small success in Europe to make everyone here fall all over her."

I said nothing, letting the others argue late into the night. Then we drove Norman to his train. We said our final farewell very briefly in the car so that I would not be seen on the platform. "You're going, aren't you?" he asked.

"Yes," I told him. "I'm going to find that rich husband and marry him and settle down in Europe and never ever do another boring seance!" I was almost shouting so that I would not cry, but at least I no longer felt completely alone, deserted. I had something to look forward to.

On the first of May the Robertsons gave us a grand send-off, hiring a ferry boat to take us across the Bay, toasting us with champagne. Sophie was kept busy stopping Father from drinking all of it by himself. Other people on the party boat included some regular clients and, to my surprise, Miss Harrington. It seems she had gone to the same exclusive eastern girls' school as one of my clients and had often been invited to my sittings. She had always refused, accusing her old schoolmate of "exploiting the poor for your amusement." My clients, who considered her attitude part of the same eccentricity which kept her working among the poor at Hunters Point, invited her as a joke and were surprised when she accepted.

On the ferry she stood silently at the rail watching the water. She was even more silent when we encountered a group of reporters waiting at the train station. I turned away, pulling the hood of my cloak over my head to thwart the cameramen while Erika told the hovering reporters we were bound for "a tour sponsored by the most powerful monarchs of Europe."

It was in that brief moment that Miss Harrington stepped forward and took both my hands. Her grip was strong, almost hurting, and her pale, lined face was set. "This may be your chance to get out of all this, Mei-li. Take it!"

1914–1919

The train was new, clean, luxurious; in the dining car, meals were served on real china with coffee poured from silver pots and sherry served before dinner. The scenery—even the long stretches of plains that came after the rockies—fascinated me. Roaring through some tiny stop where nothing but a dozen wood shacks stood between the track and vast, flat open space was as mysteriously exciting as puffing and grinding through complex, crowded railroad-yard approaches to big cities. The wheel-clacking, shuddering rumbling of constant motion began to feel like a part of me, like the sound of my own breathing night and day, waking or sleeping. Then, when the motion became so much a part of me that I could balance a glass of wine without spilling a drop on the tablecloth, it was suddenly all over. We had reached the end of the line, where my father had started.

We took a large ocean liner from New York. We were traveling second class, and our cabin was an inside one, cramped and stuffy, but the second class deck was pleasant. Many of our fellow passengers were cool toward us, some in response to my race. Others had heard the quickly spread rumors of my profession. A few were intrigued, friendly people who spoke to me in a loud voice with exaggerated gestures until they realized that I spoke English as well as they. (Better, I thought, since San Franciscans do not have the nasal accents of so many other Americans.) Someone from first class came down to our deck searching for the "oriental psychic," and Erika accepted his invitation to tea, where I purposely annoyed Erika by accepting the sherry drunk by some of the men—but none of the other women—instead of tea. I had hoped to be free of my deceptive pose, at least on shipboard, but here I was, confined in it again.

Most of the people at the tea were English. They had attended seances at home in England and hoped they could persuade me to hold a sitting on board ship. They would be happy to pay. The offer was made by an Englishman who said he knew Doctor Willy and other supporters of spiritualism whose names I did not recognize. He was a barrister who had defended some mediums in court. "Our laws are barbaric, I'm afraid, but our movement is the strongest in the world." Erika immediately accepted his invitation while saying (in a choked voice that afflicted her whenever she refused money) that I never accepted payment.

So I ended up doing sittings almost every night. When I complained, Erika said, "Nonsense, it's only an hour a day, and when we dock, scores of people will leave the ship advertising you all over Europe." I argued that the sitting might be only an hour a day, but the identity as a psychic was full time, putting off the young people I would like to meet. Erika did not even bother to answer my foolish hope that I could meet people in any normal way.

We landed at Southampton, then took a train to London, where Doctor Willy met us at Victoria Station. Reporters and photographers had followed him, so that instead of craning my neck to look up at that vast cathedral of trains, or anything else that might be included in my long-awaited first glimpse of London, I was forced to hide my face in the hood of my cloak. Erika spoke brightly and charmingly to the reporters while we walked to a cab followed by porters carrying our luggage. I realized then how firmly she stood between me and other people. I hardly ever spoke to a stranger except during sittings.

Doctor Willy helped me into a closed, horse-drawn cab. He waited until the luggage had been loaded and the cab had begun to move. Then he squeezed my hand and welcomed me. His damp eyes glowed in his round, smiling face as he talked, as if continuing our last conversation, about the coming of "a new, glorious epoch of human love and achievement." He paused only once, to point out the British Museum, which was very near the house where we were to live.

It stood in a long row of identical three-story stone houses behind low wrought-iron fences, older and more austere than the wooden houses of San Francisco, but similar in their narrow huddling line and in their floorplan. On the first floor were two parlors and a dining room. The second floor was Doctor Willy's bedroom, sitting room, and office. On the third floor Erika and I each had a small room, with a third room empty except for a desk and cot. Above us was an attic where two servant girls slept after they had climbed the four flights of steps from the basement where they did the cooking and laundry.

Compared to the Robertson mansion, this house was cramped and chilly, its furniture shabby and stiff, but I liked its plain, indifferent looks. Doctor Willy was renting the house from a distant cousin who had acquired it as payment of a debt. The cousin lived on a grand estate in the country, "... which you will see before the week is out. For my cousin's daughter is to be married, and we are all invited to the wedding. Until then you must rest and gather your energies. You will need them, for many people are eager to welcome you and your divine powers."

92

During the next few days Doctor Willy took us out in an open carriage, showing us the traditional sights of London. We saw Buckingham Palace, Saint Paul's, the Tower, Westminster, Parliament, and a great many parks and gardens. The sun shone brightly every day, the air was close, and the Thames stank like Butchertown. We had left San Francisco shrouded in its usual summer fog and had come to a London heat wave. "Hold your nose and enjoy it," said Doctor Willy, "for soon the long summer days grow short and the winter comes here like... like a dark, soggy bog." We made many jokes during that week about Doctor Willy's soggy bog.

Early on a Sunday morning we were all packed up into a motor car, which Doctor Willy kept in a garage on the outskirts of London, and driven northwest for the wedding. It was about a two-hour drive in the large, slow car on mostly dirt roads. Once through the front gate of the cousin's estate, it took another half hour to drive to the huge house occupied by the family of Willy's cousin, cared for by troops of servants, and still partly supported by local tenant farmers. Seventy people had stayed overnight. Hundreds more—friends and distant relations—drove in as we did for the ceremony and garden reception.

I felt completely out of place. People seeing my silk pajamas thought I was from China. A couple of men in army uniforms spoke to me in Mandarin, which I did not understand at all. Some of the older men just stared fiercely. Later I realized that their disapproval was aimed more at Doctor Willy than at me. They felt he was rather a distant releative to have rated an invitation; to have brought along two American strangers (one of them very odd inddeed) was "a bit cheeky." But when Doctor Willy told them my profession, they relented. One of them spent an hour talking to me about psychic experiences.

The wedding was held in a partially-restored fourteenth century chapel a short walk from the house. It held about two hundred people; the rest of us sat on folding chairs spread over the lawn beyond the crumbled west wall, not yet rebuilt. Sun streamed through other openings in the walls, but the roof was solid with new wooden beams connecting the mossy stone walls. After the wedding we walked back to the gardens south of the house, where servants poured champagne near tables laden with food, surrounding a cake that seemed as tall as I. Everything seemed larger, brighter, warmer than real life. It was like a vivid, golden dream—and in a way it was a dream.

I looked around that park, with its groups of graceful ladies and gentlemen standing under the trees sipping champagne and knew I would be mad to hope that any man of this class would marry me. There was one group in particular which symbolized the hopelessness of my position. Near a gleaming white summer house stood a girl all in pink, maid of honor to the bride, her sister, Stephanie, a special favorite of Doctor Willy. Someone had handed her a rosy parasol, which cast a pinker glow on her skin so that, in her soft, lacy gown, with her golden curly hair piled high, she looked like a fairy princess in one of the old books Miss Harrington kept at the Butchertown Library.

She was surrounded by young men in reserve army officers' uniforms. She held the arm of one of the officers, and from the way he stood beside her, I saw that he was the successful one of her suitors. They were all talking animatedly, and she shook her golden head vigorously as though she disagreed with whatever they said. She laughed, shook her head, talked. They listened, admired, laughed.

I stood watching her and thinking that she was, like me, about nineteen, but that was the only resemblance between us. She had been born to a pink and golden life through which she would glide gracefully, while I stood forever outside doing my cheap, devious little act.

Suddenly Doctor Willy took my arm and pushed me into the group. "Stephanie wants to meet you. You will love each other. She is my favorite niece." Of course, she wasn't really his niece—their relation was too distant and diluted to have a name.

"Now this is the way women should dress," said Stephanie. "Everything I wear is bound tight at the throat, at the wrists, at the waist. I'm locked in, and these wretched skirts are set to trip me if I take one genuine stride!" She shook my hand. "Oh, how I wish I was an American! Women aren't so tied up in knots in your country. You already have the vote in some states, right? Is it in . . . Wyoming?"

"I don't know," and all the young men laughed as if I had said something very witty. They stood at polite attention as Doctor Willy introduced me.

The one whose arm Stephanie held was called Niles, and he explained that Stephanie was a feminist who knew all sorts of facts, like voting in Wyoming. "She's quite right, of course. Our generation is going to break out of all the old prisons. Stephanie's a good deal cleverer than I, you know, and fine artist. She shouldn't have to waste her energy chaining herself to lamp posts. Her painting is extraordinary!''

"Not yet," said Stephanie. "But it will be." She spoke with a simple, straightforward, innocent determination. At that moment I would have given anything for that innocence—it seemed a form of invincible power. "Uncle Willy has told me all about you, or what he knows, but I want to hear it from you. You've led such an interesting life compared to the stuffy, tiresome treadmill women are stuck in here. I do want to get to know you." Her accent was lofty, almost arrogant, and her smile was partly imperious, partly mischievous, as if she saw right through me and was amused.

"I don't think I'll get into the country much," I answered.

"Oh, good heavens, I don't live at Baneful Hall!" That was one of her names for the awesome old estate, which she never called by its somewhat similar title. Sometimes she called it "Chilblains Hall" or "The House of Bane" or "Old Wrack and Ruin." She was always inventing names which scandalized people who were awed by titles and tradition.

"I live in London! I'm studying art there; you can't imagine what I had to go through to get Daddy to agree, and finally Mum moved into a flat with me, to chaperone me properly, ugh! She and Daddy think I'll get it out of my system and come home and marry Niles, but they're wrong. Next year I'm going to Paris to study. Oh, they don't even imagine that possibility. It's going to take a whole year of rows!"

All the young men laughed again, and Niles said, "Perhaps we should marry now, and I'll take you to Paris." Clearly this was not the first time he had suggested it.

Stephanie took her hand from his arm and shook her head. "I wouldn't consider going to Paris with you if we married, though I might be tempted to run away with you and live in sin on the Left Bank." The young men laughed but blushed and looked a bit flustered. Stephanie viewed their confusion with a smile of delight. I had just seen a mild demonstration of her favorite, most characteristic pleasure: saying or doing something which created a silence of embarrassment or consternation. She glowed in such silences, mischief fairly crackling around her.

"Actually," she finally admitted, "brother John will go with me, to satisfy the parents." She tilted her head toward one of the men in uniform, who looked surprised at this news. "But I intend to give him the slip, disappear, and get down to work in peace and solitude, except for the apache dancer I shall take up with.''

She turned to me again. "But first things first. When can you come and pose for me? You're the most beautiful woman I've ever seen. And you're going to be my friend. Oh, yes, you are, like it or not, I'll win you over in spite of my disagreeable, affected, upper-class accent! We all talk that way, can't be helped.'' Now it was my turn to blush, showing that she had read my mind. She shrugged, pursing her lips as if trying to contain her joy at my discomfiture. When I burst out laughing at her expression, she hugged me and declared, in a whisper, that she would be my friend for life, which indeed she became.

In later years, when Stephanie and I recalled that scene, she remembered it as I perceived it at the time—as a fairy tale dream full of innocent princesses and handsome princes.

A few weeks later war was declared. Stephanie never got to Paris, which became an embarcation point for the trenches. Within two years, all the young men who had stood around her laughing were dead.

At first the war seemed certain to be only a brief adventure with slogans and signs and occasional clumps of volunteers marching in cheerful disorder behind a brass band to a train station. As an outsider I saw it as a customary ritual of Europe. It would be over by Christmas, everyone said, and I expected to be home by then, unless weather delayed our sailing till spring. By then I should have built a reputation that would advance my career back home in case a rich suitor did not appear in England. I told Erika my only chance for marriage would be to materialize a rich man at a seance. She did not laugh, only said that I misused my time with Stephanie, learning to be flippant like her instead of going through her to upper class men.

Doctor Willy arranged sittings in his front parlor, and we accepted invitations to other grander houses. Holding seances was more respectable in England than it had been in America. In London alone there were a dozen societies for the protection and advancement of psychics and mediums. The English were more formal than anyone in San Francisco, but they were also, at least in London, more eccentric and more tolerant. A homogeneous people with few immigrants, they smiled upon the few odd-looking people who had the good sense to visit their superior island. For the first time in my life I sensed a lack of hostility toward me as an oriental.

I walked the streets with Erika like any respectable, well-chaperoned young woman; most often we walked the three blocks to the British Museum, where we spent hours nearly every day. Erika had it in her mind that if I simply looked and looked at the thousands of treasures—from the Elgin Marbles to African masks, from Chinese scrolls to Arctic totems—I would enrich my psychic act immeasurably. A bit of automatic writing in ancient runes would be a splendid addition to my act. Eventually we planned that, with Doctor Willy's help, we would get into the reading room and study esoteric documents with which my controls would later season their talk. But even the open collection could occupy us much longer than we expected to stay in England.

Erika enjoyed our walks and our hours at the museum even more than I did. Her only concern was that the excitement of the war would leave people indifferent to spiritualism. She tried to be philosophical abut that, saying at least we would have enjoyed an exciting vacation. The richness of culture revived all her old scholarly instincts. She haunted libraries and second-hand bookstores, tramped through galleries, and, when not attending one of my sittings, sat with her nose in a book all the time. Of course, the more costly pleasures of London were closed to us since we had almost no cash.

For me the real excitement lay in the fact that I had a friend, Stephanie. I began going to her flat several times a week to pose for a series of drawings. We usually sat in her room, a light high-ceilinged place with a narrow bed, two chairs, and one tall window, "not a proper studio," Stephanie complained, but a pleasant room facing south, getting the most of the rapidly diminishing warmth and sunlight. While I posed, she talked about herself, her struggles with her parents to get more freedom, to get an education, her ambivalence about marrying Niles, which had now become complicated by her concern for his safety. Both he and her brother had joined their units in France. She wrote to Niles every day, and sometimes read his answering letters to me. He wrote poetry. So did her brother. About those days in that narrow London room, I most remember Stephanie reading the poetry that seemed to pour out of all the young men she knew.

During moments when she rested from drawing me, she asked me about myself. She was enthralled with my description of Hunters Point. She sighed with envy when I described roving over the wrecks half-sunk off the beach or lying in the sun among the rocks in my hiding place. She had never been allowed to wander alone, to be dirty, to eat what she found dropping from shrimp nets. She had never even been allowed to attend school, though, of course, she had been instructed by excellent tutors in her father's famous library.

She made me tell her over and over again about the earthquake, shuddering with envy at my having been so near the catastrophe. I told her about my mother—as much as I could remember. I cried as I told her, and so did she. Finally I even told her about Norman. She was not shocked, just enormously curious. She knew nothing about the physical details of sex, and when I told her, she laughed and said, "Oh, but how absolutely ludicrous, that's why everyone does it in the dark, else how to keep a straight face! But is it fun? Women aren't supposed to like it, but I bet that's just another of their lies, the bloody men! Tell me how it feels, exactly!" Then she would purse her lips in that mischievous smile while I stammered and blushed.

Stephanie never attended my sittings. She knew I did not want her to. She never asked whether my psychic powers were real. She assumed they were fake, a joke, another piece of mischief that delighted her, especially when she heard that I had attracted clients who were rich and pretentious. She saw no harm in the fraud. "The fools come after it, don't they? It's just too bad not to make them pay. Maybe we could induce one of them to part with the family jewels." Then she would invent an absurd plot for persuading a man (a favorite target was her pompous and rather nasty Uncle Ralph) to become my benefactor. She quite consciously gave me abundant information about the clients she knew anything about, demanding later reports on how I had used it. This information was the only reason Erika let me see her so often. They did not like each other.

In those few months before the end of 1914 she sketched me over and over again, as if obsessed with some secret in my face that eluded her. Once she said, "There, that one's not bad," and gave it to me. I have kept it all my life, the only thing left from those days. I look at it now and try to see what this drawing by a nineteen-year-old girl of another nineteen-year-old girl tells about me. The firm, clear lines of youth tell little. The expression is serious, but not really thoughtful. Sad, in an unconscious sort of way.

I thought I was happy, or as happy as I ever could be. I had made a real friend. I was living in the midst of a great city at an exciting time. My sittings were attracting respectable, learned people who treated me with courtesy. There were even a couple of men whose interest, Erika thought, might make them good candidates for marriage, though they were twice my age. "All the better if they don't last long," said Stephanie, "just so they leave you solvent." She maintained that marriage should be avoided, if possible, and many of our giggling sessions started with her putting up for discussion some ridiculously inappropriate man, often one she had invented on the spot. "And there's always Uncle Willy. He's quite devoted to you, in his way, wouldn't bother you with you-know-what, and is getting on for sixty. You'd be free again at thirty!"

The only unpleasant incident of those months involved poor Doctor Willy. Stephanie and I were in his front parlor one afternoon. She was explaining the enormous effort it had taken to convince her mother she could walk across the park unchaperoned to visit me at her Uncle Willy's house. "And if she knew Erika was out, I couldn't come at all!" It was raining, and she was just setting me into a pose near the streaked window when we looked out and saw a cab stop in front of the house.

A man was helping Doctor Willy out of the cab. He seemed to stagger as if he were sick, then nodded to the man, who, while Doctor Willy was still talking, jumped back into the cab and left quickly. We could hear Doctor Willy's voice rising hysterically, cracking, then turning into a rumbling groan as he began to climb the stairs.

Before he reached the front door, Stephanie and I had swung it open. He was hatless, and his bald head was streaked with filth. His nose was bleeding, the blood covering his mouth. His coat was torn. He looked as if he had rolled in the muddy streets. He clutched his broken spectacles so tightly that the glass had cut his hand. Stephanie brought him into the parlor and stretched him out on a leather chaise while I ran for a basin of water and towels. After I had cleaned his face and head and bandaged his hand, he tried to talk, but speaking made his nose bleed again. Finally Stephanie gave him a stiff glass of brandy, and he dozed off. We sat together, watching him.

When he woke up half an hour later, he was able to tell us what had happened. He had been in Tottenhamcourt Road when the rain began and had ducked into a small shop to buy an umbrella. The shop owner had been rather curt with him, even rude, and when Doctor Willy firmly asked for his patience while selecting an umbrella, the shop owner began to yell at him, pushed him, threw him out of the shop, calling him, "Bloody rotten Hun!" Because of Doctor Willy's accent and continental clothes, the man had mistaken him for a German. A small crowd suddenly gathered, watching and jeering as a few street ruffians kicked and pushed him, knocking him into the gutter. A man in a passing cab had come to his rescue. Doctor Willy had no idea who the man was. He had rushed off as soon as accomplishing his good deed, as if afraid he might suffer unpleasant consequences.

"Barbaric. Uncivilized," he kept muttering. Then he sat in silence and watched the rain streak down the windows. As I watched him I thought of the little speech he had made to me so many times, about the inevitable progress of humanity into a bright new era.

In my memory it seems that this incident came at the same time as our realization that the Battle of the Marne, reported in all the papers as a great victory, had only driven the Germans back a few miles to where they dug their trenches and the Allies dug theirs, and so both sides remained slaughtering each other by the millions for the next four years. In December Stephanie's brother was wounded, and we delayed leaving while he recovered. By that time the German blockade on shipping had been declared, and while we hesitated another few weeks, still expecting the war to end, questioning how safe it was to sail from England, our question was answered by the sinking of the Lusitania. After that, Doctor Willy begged us to take no chances, to remain as his guests until the war—which must end within a year—was over.

Stephanie moved into Doctor Willy's house, into the third bedroom on our floor, where she could be more easily reached by news of Niles or her brother, who returned to the front upon his recovery. Her mother had gone back to their country house which was to be used as a rest hospital for shell-shock cases and convalescent wounded. "At least old Chilblains Hall will serve some purpose before the rotten roof caves in on that wreck," declared Stephanie, as she kissed her mother good-bye. All questions of proper chaperon-age had evaporated. Even women of Stephanie's class were volun-teering as nurses or marrying soldiers in hasty ceremonies. Stephanie's plan to stay with us seemed conservative by comparison.

I would have fought to stay now that Stephanie was with us, but no fight was necessary. Erika was determined to exploit the sudden explosion of interest in psychic phenomena. Even before the reports of the Angel of Mons—a spirit said to hover near the British trenches —there were stories of appearances of dead soldiers. They were sighted in the trenches or in their homes, where they left cryptic signs of their presence, like the poltergeist signs I had provided for Sophie. Erika urged me to invent a "sighting," preferably in Tra-falgar Square. When I refused, she told Doctor Willy's maid that I had seen hundreds of ghost soldiers jeering the speeches of army recruiters there. Erika called this a fraud in a good cause, against the war, actually risky in the militant mood of the country. I for-bade her to repeat it, but within a few days the rumor was in all the papers with "confirmation on the highest authority."

Both servant girls left at that point to take jobs in a munitions factory, and we three women spent a good part of each day trying to keep the house warm and clean. Preparing any kind of food on the coal stove in the basement was a great project. "Serves us bloody right they left us to this old monster," said Stephanie. "Time I knew what working girls go through." She would curse furiously at the old stove, then go upstairs to write the latest incident as a joke in her daily letter to Niles.

The days of that winter formed the view of London that has stayed in my memory alongside my first impression of golden after-noon wedding parties. Pitch darkness covered the City until nearly ten, when the sky grayed. The dim, cold daylight lasted until about three, when darkness descended again. I didn't mind the cold, which was only a little more severe than a winter day near the Golden Gate, and was eased by wearing long woolen underwear. I didn't even mind the walk to the British Museum through biting cold rain or reeking fog—a nasty yellow cloud that settled down like noxious gas, not at all like the bracing fog of San Francisco. It was the long dark I could never get used to. I realize that neither the sunny after-noon wedding nor the endless dark of a winter day truly describes the English climate. But only those two extremes rise in my memory, the dark one more strongly because it was like the war settling down over the country.

My sittings became crowded with people who were hoping for a message from a brother, husband, father, or friend killed in the trenches. People were packed into Doctor Willy's front parlor every night, where I sat knowing that upstairs Stephanie was trying to write something cheerful and uncensorable to her fiance, her brother, and their friends, all now at the front. This was no longer a joke or a game. I did not see how I could go on with it, nor how I could stop.

I performed badly, but no matter. I needed no acting ability, no controls, no exotic messages invented from museum browsings. The crudest automatic writing was sufficient. "I am happy and looking over you. Always beside you. John." There was always someone there whose dead soldier was named John, whose writing was "just like that!" I told myself that people left a sitting with some comfort and that I had not taken any money from them.

Doctor Willy began to revive under the excitement of the broadened interest in spiritualism. He was still careful about going out alone, but as all Germans had been interned, people no longer jumped on anyone with a foreign accent. He began to say that perhaps the terrible tragedy of the war was a necessary part of the world's awakening to the spirit world. He stopped saying that when Stephanie's fiance Niles was killed in late 1915.

His death changed Stephanie. Her girlish rosiness paled. Her slenderness thinned; so did her hair, which also darkened a bit. She was still a beautiful girl who never missed an opportunity to make a joke which made someone squirm, but her face wore the drawn look that comes from prolonged lack of sleep. She made frequent trips to her family home in the country, which she now dubbed, all too appropriately, "Pain Hall," and sometimes "Plain Hell." There she helped nurse wounded soldiers for a few days before rushing back to London, where mail from her brother and other friends arrived more quickly. Stephanie moved into my bedroom, leaving a room free for the many young officers—friends of her and her brother—who came for a hot bath and a clean bed whenever they had leave.

Sometimes Stephanie and I would take these young men to a concert or a show (no chaperones required anymore). They would applaud and laugh at first, but gradually they withdrew into silence, like explorers viewing an exotic rite which has suddenly become cruel and savage. They could not explain their feelings. Only in recent years, when I read true accounts of that war (letters were censored and newspapers published nothing but patriotic slogans) did I understand the look of horror that came over their faces as they watched a crowd laughing at the theater. They had come only a few miles, just across the channel (we could actually hear the guns sometimes) from constant, stupid dying in muddy holes, to find laughter, prosperity, speeches about the glory of war, and complaints about the shortage of servants. The result was that most of Stephanie's friends could not wait to get back to their comrades in the trenches, where, one by one, they died, never uttering a word against the slaughter.

There was a small anti-war movement. Stephanie took me to hear Bertrand Russell speak against the war, but when she quoted him to others, she evoked nothing but fury. Everyone agreed that the only loyal, decent attitude was to support the fighting men. To see that true support for the men would be to stop the fighting was a leap of thought few people could make.

Stephanie made the leap after her brother was killed in October of 1916. She demonstrated with the pacifist Union of Democratic Control. And she drew. She drew the men in hospitals and at train stations. (We always knew that a newspaper announcement of "victorious action" would bring not a change in the war, but only trainloads of maimed and dying men.) She drew exhausted nurses vomiting beside the fallen entrails of their patients. Over and over she drew a still life of the effects of her brother, which were sent back to her. They included a book of poetry and the shirt he had been wearing, still caked with mud and blood.

No public gallery would display her drawings, so the Union of Democratic Control rented a hall and hung them. On the second day of the exhibit the hall was attacked by a flag-waving mob who tore down and destroyed everything. Stephanie drew more, including pictures of the mob tearing down her drawings. These were too satirical to please anyone, even her pacifist friends, who accused her (as usual) of being too flippant about serious matters. "If I can't find something to laugh at, I'll die," she said to me after she had dismissed them with another joke.

More and more men were killed; her friends were marrying the wounded, the maimed. Why? No one knew. It just seemed the right thing to do.

We saw less of each other as the war dragged on and on. She spent more time caring for casualties at "Pain Hall." She wrote me letters from there with drawings of the men and stories about them. "Please write to me, about anything but the war," she said. In one letter I wrote out the stories my mother used to tell me. Stephanie sent back sketches she had made to illustrate my stories, deeply detailed pen and ink drawings of mythic creatures, all in scenes of violent confrontation, all with a jagged look, as if drawn during a sleepless night.

In our letters neither of us mentioned the almost nightly sittings I did, following a monotonous pattern set by Erika. Each day she studied the casualty lists printed in the newspaper, which also gave the rank and home town of the dead. From the lists she copied a few names with details for me to memorize.

During a sitting I would mention the names of fifteen or so recently killed men who were "trying to come through." Often—England being a small country—someone at the sitting actually knew one of the dead men. In that case I would spend more time in "communication" between the dead spirit and the person at the sitting. It was easy to guess what the client wanted to hear. What did any of them want but to vent their grief and to hope for some loophole, some contradiction of the reality—the cutting down of a generation of men.

It was unbearable. Even on the nights when I did only automatic writing, I often froze, unable to continue. Then I was pitied for the great strain I endured, sacrificing my health to maintain contact with the other world, doing so much for the public morale, giving such comfort to those most destroyed by grief. My fame grew. So did my tension and depression. Unlike the strain on Stephanie, which came from doing her best while her world crumbled, the strain on me came from guilt and shame.

How could I do this? What had happened to the rebellious girl who had screamed and kicked at Erika only a few years before? I cannot answer my own question, cannot explain or excuse what I did. Writing of my activities during that war still makes me writhe with the shame that filled me at the time. I was also filled with helplessness, unable to stand against the insane tide that was sweeping lives away. When I asked if we couldn't do something to support the peace agitators, both Erika and Doctor Willy reminded me that we were all three aliens in this country, subject to even fiercer violence from "patriots" than fell on the tiny group of British pacifists. If we supported them openly, we might be lucky to be deported alive.

Then Doctor Willy saw a way that the new interest in spiritualism might be joined to the cause of peace. A rich spiritualist had offered his grand London house (which no patriots would dare to attack) for a party to raise funds for the pacifists and for nursing and rehabilitation at "Pain Hall," which received meager and infrequent help from the government. (Stephanie sent drawings to be auctioned at the party but said she could not leave the huge group of newly wounded.) The grand party arranged for December 18, 1916 would also introduce Doctor Willy's book on his travels among spiritualists, finally published despite wartime paper shortages, with a hastily written afterword on "psychic phenomena in the trenches." After much discussion, Erika decided it would be to our advantage and safe to attend.

The house was set back from the street behind a tall iron gate and walls concealing deep gardens of the sort that used to exist even in large cities like London. Although the main parlors were on the first floor, this house had a large sitting room on each of its three floors. In the top floor sitting room members of a small Italian opera company were singing through concert versions of operas. Below them on the second floor some well-known solo instrumentalists played. The main first floor parlor was large enough to contain a chamber orchestra and an audience of over fifty. Copies of Doctor Willy's book were stacked in the foyer to be given free to all guests, some of whom asked me to autograph one of the pages of the chapter devoted to me. I signed and smiled, always remaining inside rooms where musicians performed, so as to avoid having to talk to anyone. I did not want to be asked yet again for my opinion on the Angel of Mons or the appearance of dead soldiers in a crowd photographed in Whitehall.

I went upstairs to hear a cello solo, then climbed the smaller stairway to the third floor. The cello sounds faded, and I could hear a tenor singing. I opened the door to a smaller room than the ones below. About ten people stood around a grand piano in the center of the room. Along the walls, squeezed tightly together on small chairs, sat people whose faces shone with enjoyment. At the piano a young man was playing and singing an aria from La Bohême. "Che gelida manina...." he sang to a girl leaning on the piano and looking down at him. As he finished singing, he took up the accompaniment for her aria. I circled the room along the wall until I found an empty chair in a corner.

The little group of singers did both the solo and the chorus parts, sometimes pantomiming part of the action after a few spoken Italian phrases set the scene. The small audience applauded the arias and some even joined in, encouraged by the man at the piano.

He played all the orchestra parts, sang the tenor lead, and conducted the other singers, giving rhythmic nods, bright smiles, agonized frowns (during the sad songs) bouncing up and down to give cues or encourage applause. Yet with all this playing and grimacing and bouncing, he did not take attention away from the other singers. Instead he seemed to communicate energy and joy that inspired singers and audience. In my now more than two years in England I had not seen a group of English people enjoying themselves so exuberantly. But, of course, I had spent most of my time in seances in the formal, respectable homes into which Erika had worked so hard to gain entrance.

The young man was small, hardly taller than I, with a slight, almost delicate build. He wore a white shirt open at the throat, with a bright blue scarf tied around his neck. His mobile face was the epitome of Italian good looks—long, with an aquiline nose, large black eyes, a small black moustache above pink lips, a full head of curly black hair. Even in my corner chair I was close enough to see the beads of sweat form on his brow as he sang and accompanied the opening duet of the final act. I could also see that he had no score in front of him. As he pounded away and hit an occasional wrong note, he raised his eyebrows in my direction. At the next wrong note, he blinked and smiled at me. And, it seemed to me, during Mimi's death song, though he played faultlessly, solemnly nodding tempo with the singer, his eyes were fixed on me. At the end of her singing, he stood to speak the curtain line of Rudolfo, then crashed the final chords on the piano and bowed to a standing ovation.

When the applause died down he spoke in Italian, thanking the little audience, introducing each of the singers. Then, pointing toward a servant now standing near the door, he suggested that we partake of the supper which was about to be served.

We all walked downstairs to the first floor. The chamber orchestra continued playing in the main parlor, but a buffet had been set up in the second parlor. Guests were filling plates with food, then walking away into other rooms to sit at little tables. As I took a plate, I noticed the little dark singer talking with Doctor Willy. I wandered until I found a room at the back of the house, near the stairway where servants were running up with platters from the basement kitchen. This room was little more than an alcove which I entered through the library. A tiny niche with a window seat, it reminded me of the illustrations in the books Miss Harrington had shown me, in which a clean little English girl in a pinafore sat reading. So it was true that such a window seat actually existed outside of fairy tale books! I settled myself on it and began to sip a glass of punch that had been liberally laced with gin.

I had not been here very long when Doctor Willy came, followed by the singer. "Ah, here she is, our little Madame Psyche. My dear, Signor Gentoro is a great admirer of yours and has asked to meet you. *Signorina Murrow, posso presentare Carlo Gentoro.*"

The singer bowed to me. I smiled and said that I also admired him and had enjoyed his singing. *"Ah, parla italiano!"* *"Pocchino,"* I shrugged. He spoke rapidly, telling me that he had attended two of my sittings about a year apart and had longed to make my acquaintance, but was on the road with the Franze Opera Company most of the time. It had been such a delightful surprise when I walked into the room where he was performing. This time he would not miss the opportunity to pay his respects.

And so on. I could see that Doctor Willy was becoming a bit stiff, a bit disapproving of the Italian effusiveness, the operatic manner of Carlo Gentoro. He hurried off when someone came and said he was wanted in the main parlor.

"Permesso?" Carlo sat down beside me on the window seat. We sat in silence, watching some people who were moving about and talking in the library a few feet away. After those people left the room, a deeper silence fell. Up close Carlo looked very young, very boyish. There was something mischievous in the smile he turned toward me. Suddenly he winked. "Is it true you're from San Francisco?"

"You speak English?"

"Shh...." He looked around in mock operatic apprehension of being found out, although no one was anywhere near. "I'm an American, like you. Had you fooled? It's harder to fool the Europeans. Doctor Willy is a real feather in my cap. Oh, the people in the company know I'm not Italian, of course, but by now they've almost forgotten it."

"You look Italian."

"Polish, actually, Polish Jew, from New York. My real name is Karl Goldman. But nobody ever launched an operatic career in the United States with a name like Karl Goldman. I came over here six years ago. I thought I'd be back home by now, with my new name and Italian identity, but I like the life here, and with the war making travel pretty risky...well, you know."

I was puzzled. "Why have you told me all this? Aren't you afraid I'll expose you?"

"No. And I won't expose you either!" He winked and made such a comical face that I had to laugh.

Suddenly Erika appeared, dressed in her coat and carrying my cloak. "I've been looking all over for you!" She was very annoyed and did not soften when Karl stood and bowed and flashed his charming smile. In rapid Italian he asked permission to call on me. When she looked puzzled, he pretended her silence was assent, thanked her effusively, and hurried away. As she led me through the crowds to the front door, she scolded me. "Look, May, you don't have time to waste with some third-rate singer in a road company. They're like vaudeville players back home. No future. That rich husband won't come around if he sees you sitting with some little Italian street singer!"

Karl came to the house the next day and almost every day after that. This was my third winter in London, and it seemed, like the war, endless. Karl and I did not talk about the war. He sang for me. He would sit at the piano and announce an opera (usually Italian, sometimes Gilbert and Sullivan), playing and singing all the parts, jumping from one to another during duets and trios, singing women's parts in a light, pleasing falsetto. He also knew dozens of English music hall songs that sounded—as Erika said—like vaudeville.

Between songs Karl talked about himself. He had been born in New York City. His parents were immigrants who worked in factories for a while, then opened a shop. They were orthodox Jews. He was the youngest of seven children, six sisters, then Karl. He was petted and pampered, given all the education his family could afford until they saw that he wanted not to be a cantor, but to sing gentile opera. They threatened to disown him. They refused support for his musical studies, then relented to give him help, only to react again in condemnation of his ambitions and withdraw the help. He worked his way, came to Europe to begin his career. He hoped by the time he was ready to go home his parents would be resigned. Then his mother died suddenly, and he father berated him

108

for not being there. Relations with the family were worse than ever, almost non-existent. "Meanwhile I'm getting used to living here. Maybe next year I'll go back home for a big American debut that will bring my father around. I say that every year."

This was only his third visit to England. Usually the Franze Company confined its tours to the continent, it being too difficult to transport all their gear across the channel. But since the war started they had been unable to enter Austria and take their usual route through Germany and Switzerland. This fall Karl had brought half the company to England to perform concert versions of their repertory. The others, including several children, had remained in Maestro Franze's home village near Turin along with their props and costumes, their theater tent and their best instruments. In January the company would reunite to tour Italy until spring. Perhaps by then the war would be over and they could follow their old route through northern Europe.

Erika and Doctor Willy were amused when they realized he was American, Doctor Willy saying that indeed all successful American opera singers had adopted Italian names. Erika waited till Doctor Willy had left the room, then bluntly told Karl her plans for me. "So don't get any ideas that May is going back with you to applaud your Metropolitan debut, if you ever make one. She will go back either on the arm of a rich, preferably tone-deaf husband or as the queen of the occult, married to the higher aims of the world beyond!" After this outburst she was friendly, even singing along, laughing and calling Karl a "clever mouse." He did not mistake her manner. "It only means she does not take me seriously." He stayed in London working as an extra church organist during the Christmas holidays when the rest of the company scattered to spend the time with their families. And he came to see me as often as Erika would let him.

In mid-January he was gone with the company, touring war-free zones in Italy. He wrote me nearly every day. His letters were like his singing—lyrical, varied, amusing, loving. They were also honest, revealing what he felt I should know about him.

First of all, he said, there had been a marriage back in the States. A young singer became pregnant and they had married quickly (another blow to his family; she was a Catholic) but she had lost the baby. They separated, and he had no idea whether the marriage still stood legally. He had not heard from his wife since he came to Europe six years ago.

He was older than he looked, almost thirty. Perhaps Erika was right about him, he said. It was time for him to have had good roles at major opera houses in Milan, Salzburg, London, time for him to have gathered up his European experience and headed home. He said he stayed because of the war but maybe (he wrote) he was afraid to go back. He was clever, had an excellent ear, an extraordinary memory, perfect pitch, and boundless energy. But his voice was a bit light, and his drive not strong. "Perhaps I am what your sister says I am, superficial. Perhaps even my father's judgment is correct."

I preferred his less confessional letters. He wrote long descriptions of the towns in which he performed, amusing stories about all the things that went wrong—costumes lost, car breakdowns, leaky rooms, sick horses and children, quarrelsome singers. "But we are like a crazy family that goes on somehow. I wish you were with us."

My letters to Karl were short notes of a few sentences. I had no time to write. As Erika had promised, my career was reaching a new height in the early part of 1917.

By this time everyone in Britain had lost someone close—husband, son, brother, father, friend. Many, like Stephanie, had lost almost every young man they knew. Where there had been talk in the beginning about being "home by Christmas," now people spoke of the trenches as of a permanent part of life. Stephanie wrote to me that she had dreams in which she was very old and the war was still going on, the young boys still being sent off to die, Britain occupied only by women and cripples. Without any warning, she had quietly married a friend of Niles, the only survivor of their group. He had been blinded and had somehow survived other wounds which kept him in continual pain. They went on living at "Bane Hall" where Stephanie supervised the nursing. Every letter began with her saying that she needed a change and would come to London soon, but she did not come.

So many desperately grieving people were turning to spiritualism that we could no longer contain all who came to Doctor Willy's house or to even larger houses, even with nightly sittings. Twice in the middle of a sitting I collapsed. Of course, said Doctor Willy, the physical strain of using my psychic abilities so often was too much for me. Erika and I knew better. The main reason for my collapse was gin.

Erika had been giving me a drink or two before a sitting to blur my disgust and blunt my rebellion. Soon I was drinking heavily. By the time she realized her mistake I had found ways to get liquor without her help. She begged me not to drink. I refused to work sober. "You'll forget the casualty list!" I answered that if I did, I'd just pass out. I might pass out anyway. She begged me not to spoil everything. There were big plans. Doctor Willy had hired a hall for my next sitting. She promised me fewer sittings for larger crowds.

The hall was a wide, drafty, dimly lit place upstairs above a row of shops but centrally located near Saint Paul's. Erika took me there through pouring rain in a carriage at about eight in the evening early in February of 1917. She gave me my last quick swallow of gin and breath mint, then took me into the hall.

We entered from the back and walked the center aisle between folding chairs set up in all the empty space. There must have been about four hundred seats, all occupied. Along the walls a line of people stood. Others were being turned away as we entered. As I walked down the aisle, silence fell. Ahead of me was a platform with three chairs, one for me, one for Erika, and one for Doctor Willy, who was to introduce me.

The plan for this evening was set. I had memorized the latest casualty lists. I would go into trance, then would say that I saw men coming down the aisle, each of whom marched up to the platform, gave me his name and then disappeared. In other words, I would recite names for one hour. That was all. "That's enough," said Erika. "That's all I ask. Do it."

The hall was cold. Even with all those people, even with the thickest wool underwear under my silk pajamas, there was a dank chill on that platform, so I kept my cloak on. I would have kept the hood over my head, but Erika pulled it back, with a gentle smile as she whispered, "If you let me down now...."

I sat behind a small table, Erika on my right, within arm's length but removed from the table. On my left, Doctor Willy stood making his introduction. "This strangely gifted young woman from San Francisco, where orient meets occident, already titled Madame Psyche by clients who out of respect, nay awe, for her astonishing powers...." When he finally finished, Erika stood briefly to say that I would go into trance and see what would happen, but that perhaps nothing at all would come.

I remained seated, closed my eyes, rested my elbows on the table, clasped my hands, and let my head droop forward. In this way I felt less exposed to the audience, hidden from them, not looking into their sad, hopeful faces. I stayed this way until Erika made a hissing sound at me. Then I raised my head, opened my eyes, and looked down the center aisle.

"Men are coming. Young men," I said dully. "Men marching down the aisle. Come forward. Give your name. Homer Blodget from Kensington. Rodney Graves from Wales."

"Can't hear!" someone shouted from the back row.

"Rodney Graves was the name," said Erika, and after that she repeated the names that I mumbled.

At the mention of one name, a woman screamed and sobbed. "Where? Where is my James? Is he here? Will he stay with me? Where do you see him now?"

Erika looked at me. Everyone looked at me, and I would have told Erika to make up her own answer, but Doctor Willy was listening, and I was not rebellious enough to disillusion him. So I said that I only saw the men walk up to identify themselves, and that then they faded away.

I went on this way for another forty minutes, then let my head fall forward onto my hands. Erika stood. "My sister is exhausted." The meeting was over. A few people came to the platform, but Erika kept them at a safe distance, pulling my hood over my head before reporters with cameras could get close, and rushing me out the side door.

"See, that wasn't so bad," she said, when we were back in our bedroom at Doctor Willy's house. The people had been a blurred crowd. I had no close contact, learned no names, spoke to no personal questions. It was much less painful than my usual performance. It was also, I thought, less effective. Perhaps the sheer boredom of the audience would release me from this farce.

I was wrong. Before we went to sleep, Doctor Willy knocked on our door with the news that a rich merchant had offered the use of a larger, better hall, free twice a week for as long as we wanted it. And, although admission had been free as always, some people had insisted on contributing to defray expenses, including one very generous check. Erika took it all, saying it would go toward buying our tickets home. She was always talking about going home, then agreeing when Doctor Willy said it was too dangerous. Now she sounded more resolved to go.

"Surely you will not attempt a voyage until the war is over? People are saying it could be another four years."

"America is on the brink of joining in," said Erika. "When she does, it will soon be over."

The next morning, the newspapers carried articles on page three, with photos of the rapt crowd. My dull, drunken monotone had been most effective. The truth was it wouldn't have mattered what I did. Psychics were beginning to attract mass audiences all over, for doing just what I had done, reciting casualty lists. I was more exotic looking than most, and charged no money. That, and those terrible times, were the secrets of my great success.

There were never fewer than a thousand people at the mass sittings I held twice a week during the next three months. It was said in news reports that I not only gave the name, rank, and home of the dead soldiers I "saw" but that I also told facts about them which "were completely private to all but closest family members." I don't remember giving any facts, but then, I remember little about these mass sessions, having downed at least a pint of gin before each one.

The incident which crowned my success was my arrest near the end of April 1917. In the middle of my recitation of the latest casualty lists (slightly scrambled, of course, by intention as well as by alcoholic confusion) half a dozen policemen marched down the center aisle. Another dozen held back the crowd which began to shout against them. I was led away to court where I was charged with fraud under the Witchcraft and Vagrancy Acts of 1735, which were still being used against mediums and clairvoyants in England. In fact, one of Doctor Willy's activities was raising money for the ongoing campaign to repeal the act.

For several days after my arrest (I was released on bail) the papers were full of the story and full of furious editorials which all but demanded the death penalty for me. All the newspapers were against psychics, but their attacks on me aroused widespread defense of me by thousands of people who wanted to believe that they had not lost their dead sons, husbands, and friends forever. They wrote letters. Money for my defense poured in. All the desperate grief of those murderous times seemed to gather into an effort to declare me innocent, honest, authentic, true.

My most powerful champion came as a complete surprise. Unknown to me, Arthur Conan Doyle had been in the auditorium when I was arrested. He published an article in which he came out for spiritualism (his son, too, had been killed early in the war) and said that his questioning of people who knew me convinced him that I was an authentic clairvoyant. A friend of his, an eminent barrister, would handle my defense free of charge. Several support rallies were held.

By the time we came to arraignment, two other factors weighed heavily in my favor. One was that I had never charged admission (Erika was finally happy about that) which weakened the charge of fraud. The second fact was that the United States had just entered the war, and it might have seemed unfriendly to the new ally to prosecute an American who, many prominent English people stated (signing a letter circulated by Doyle), was performing "great service to the gallant people of Britain." The charges were dropped.

When Karl returned to London near the end of May, he found me free, famous, and drunk. We became lovers then, for Erika stopped trying to chaperone us, having decided that Karl was preferable to gin. He did keep me sober when he was in London, but I still drank too much when he was away, as he often was whenever he could drum up work for the few members of the Franze Company (only five this time) who came to look for summer work in England.

News stories of my mass sittings, my arrest, and my endorsement by Conan Doyle had reached America. Soon we were receiving cables from psychic groups asking when I would be coming back to the States, offering to sponsor a series of sittings. Erika replied that as soon as travel seemed safe, I would return, appearing under the sponsorship of whichever society could make the most generous arrangements for transportation and expenses, "Madame Psyche being entirely without funds and dependent on the generosity of friends." She set the groups one against the other, competing for me.

By then I was drinking all day, moving indifferently through a hazy world. Conan Doyle quietly dropped me from the list of psychics he endorsed. Even Doctor Willy could not ignore the signs of alcohol, but as always, he was charitable. "The poor young woman, under such a strain. It is not unheard of. The Fox sisters destroyed themselves with alcohol. Let us be grateful it is not opium, and do what we must to cure her." He suggested sending me to a spa in Switzerland which specialized in curing alcoholism, but Erika refused to let me go. It would use up all the money she had collected, would take me away at the height of my popularity, and might reveal my drinking problem to the public.

When Karl was in London, I drank less, so Erika did not discourage him, though she did not want us to be seen in public together. The solution was to let him stay at Doctor Willy's house when he was in town. Doctor Willy blinked at that too. He convinced himself that Karl was a homosexual (perhaps because he was himself secretly attracted to Karl's delicate good looks and sweet nature). Hence our relationship was "pure." I might be alcoholic, but in Doctor Willy's eyes I could be nothing but virgin and would remain so, priestess of the new religion that he still hoped would save the world.

As for Karl, he played and sang to me, made love to me, told me funny stories about the town he had last performed in. I know that he attended two of my public sittings, because I saw him sitting in the back of the hall. But he never mentioned them to me, nor did he ever talk about our future. It was I who insisted on asking what we would do when the war ended.

"You'll go home, I guess," said Karl. "Erika is working night and day on your triumphant return."

"And what will you do?"

"What do you want me to do?"

"You could come home with us, I suppose."

"I could go home, but not with you. Erika would not allow that."

"If you were my husband, she would have to."

"A proposal? This is so sudden!" We were lying in bed, and Karl bounced up with delight. "But there is the matter of my first marriage. I might need a divorce. So it would be best if I went home alone, got that cleared up, and then we could marry. If you want me. Whatever you want, Mei-li. Is that what you really want?"

I wasn't sure. I tried to draw a mental picture of our future in America. He would pursue his musical career. I would quit the psychic racket. "Once we're married...."

Karl looked doubtful. "You know, your career is already far beyond what mine will ever be in music. In fact...let's face it, May,

I will never have a first-rate career at home or anywhere else. I'm not good enough, and there are not many little touring companies at home like the ones here. We'd be poor."

"I don't care."

"And discriminated against—a Jew and a half-Chinese. In most states we probably couldn't get legally married!"

We both laughed at that, but when he left for a week of work in Ireland, I thought about our alternatives, and the next time he was back in London, I asked him if he really wanted to go home.

He hesitated for a moment, then shook his head. "My family has disowned me. To my father I'm dead. One sister still writes to me, but secretly. I would only make things harder for her if I went home."

"Especially with a half-Chinese psychic," I added.

He did not laugh. "There's nothing in America for me. I like the life here, the older, denser culture. I like the Franze Company. We're like a family; we take care of each other. Some of them are third-generation with the company. Maestro Franze and Madame are like a mother and father to me. Their two daughters sing with the company, their son is prop manager. As long as my voice holds out— the Maestro has a vocal method that has preserved his voice, he's almost seventy, and he's coaching me. Some day he'll retire in Langero, near Turin, where he has a bit of land and a few students he coaches when he's there. Some even come from Turin to study with Madame who teaches violin and piano as well. Maestro has led a good life. I would be content with such a life."

"So would I," I said.

The Franze Company's fall tour of northern Italy had been cancelled. There was heavy fighting at Caporetto, near the Dolomites. Many had been killed and the Germans had advanced far into Italy. A new line held them, but no one knew for how long. Milan and Venice were out of the question. Even Verona might not be safe. Maestro and Madame were in Langero. They sent word to the others to remain where they were until it was certain that Langero was safe. Madame would contact everyone before the end of the year.

Karl stayed with us, and Erika tolerated him because my drinking had stopped altogether. Karl and I planned our escape. If I had been a devious pretender before, I now became doubly devious. I prepared carefully for the mass sittings and gave as good a performance as I could. I continually discussed with Erika the proper time for my return to America. I granted several interviews (photographers banned) with reporters who fleshed out their articles with material from Conan Doyle, who had himself borrowed liberally from Doctor Willy's book. (It is easy to trace almost everything written about me back to that one chapter written by the most credulous of men.) Talk of peace was in the air. A group of believers in New York had offered to put up the steamship fare whenever we were ready to return. Erika began to plan a cross-country tour ending in San Francisco.

In December I wrote to Stephanie, telling her of my plan to escape with Karl and remain in Europe. I knew she would be glad to see me desert my career and that she would like Karl. Our plot, which depended on her help, revived her spirit of mischief. She quickly sent the letter I asked her for, inviting Erika and me to come and help make a happy Christmas for the wounded.

Erika responded exactly as I had hoped, saying she was too busy to go to the country at any time. Besides, the trains were always late and jammed and the roads nothing but muddy tracks at this time of year. I agreed with her, saying I didn't want to give up my last Christmas with Karl to go and sit with the walking wounded. But I did want to see Stephanie again before we went back home. Could I spend a week with her after the new year when Karl left? Erika agreed that I needed and deserved a rest.

On January 2, 1918 Erika saw Karl and me off on the train to Crewe, where Karl supposedly would join members of the Franze Company. I would bid Karl good-bye and continue northward to Stephanie's estate. Or so Erika believed. At the next stop we changed to the boat train, and we crossed the channel that night.

Madame Franze had written detailed instructions for taking a series of local trains through unheard-of villages which ran well to the west, away from battle lines. These little trains were late and slow, our route often doubling back upon itself. Nor did I see the French countryside, for it rained constantly, the grimy windows almost opaque with streaked soot. Of course, none of this dampened the high spirits of our adventure.

Only on the main line train which took us through the French Alps were we sobered by signs of the war. Most of the cars had been commandeered for wounded and sick soldiers being taken to a new hospital in Turin. Those well enough to sit up were jammed into a car where we sat, some of them sitting on the floor. Every time we went through a tunnel one of the men began a wheezing sob which was really an attempt to keep himself from screaming. I heard one of the soldiers say that he had been trapped underground for hours with ten dead men when a dug-out had collapsed.

We came out of the last tunnel, swept around a steep peak, then saw rolling, forested hills, and below them a broad plain. "There, you can see Langero from here," said Karl, "or you could if the fog lifted." We swerved around two more hills, then veered eastward to Turin where we would have to change trains, taking a local that would double back to Langero. The local train was nearly empty. We rode for over an hour, past eight tiny train stations set between cornfields and vineyards, until we saw the station marked LANGERO. We got off alone and began to walk across empty fields.

The first building we passed was a factory, a long brick and stone building which Karl said manufactured cotton thread. It and four others like it were set in the midst of corn fields between Langero and the next village. Nearly all the villagers worked in the factories as well as cultivating small plots of land. We followed a road past small chapels and roadside shrines, and two rather grand houses that Karl explained were summer dwellings of factory owners who lived in Turin most of the year. A third, even larger white stone house was surrounded by a wall enclosing formal gardens. This was the home of the owner of the largest factory, Maestro's uncle, who had given him a row of houses in the village and some farm land to the north.

We reached the edge of the village, about three miles from the railroad, and faced curving stone walls, the backs of the outmost houses. All the houses, Karl said, were built the same, in an attached row of six or seven narrow dwellings on a packed dirt floor with a ladder to wooden sleeping lofts, then another ladder to an unwalled attic stuffed to the tile roof with corn husks and hay to feed the animals roaming in the courtyards between the rows of these three-story apartments. The rows of houses huddled around each other in seven or eight tightening cirles rising toward the center and heart of the village, a tall, rosy-gray church that could be seen looming above from almost every yard and pathway.

The row of dwellings inhabited by the Franze Company stood just below the church, and the barns across the courtyard contained props, costumes, wagons, and two automobiles. We found them by following the sounds of music and hammering echoing through the quiet streets (all the other villagers were at work in the factories).

Two separate rehearsal groups were playing and singing as we arrived. Others were working on props and repairing cars or wagons. Maestro Franze was giving a singing lesson. Madame was feeding lunch to the children. When she saw us, she clapped her hands and said, "You're here! You're safe!" and threw her arms around me as if she had always known me. "We were afraid we would have to leave without you. Oh, Carlo, she is much more beautiful than you told me!" Within a few minutes she had introduced me to everyone, sent Karl to help the smaller rehearsal group, turned over the feeding of the children to me, and gone to work on finishing the cleaning and packing of costumes. By the end of the day, I felt as much a part of the Franze Company as if I had been with them for years.

Madame and Maestro Franze had sung together as children in the much grander company of his parents. They married in their teens and formed their own company, which had become known and respected all over Europe. Nearly all the best musicians in Europe had traveled for at least a year or two with the Franzes. The war had been hard on the company. By 1917 it had shrunk to fewer than twenty adults and their seven children.

Madame was a plump, bright-eyed woman with a round face, quite wrinkled. But in makeup at twenty paces its pretty, youthful look prevailed over any signs of age. She played piano very well (everyone in the company played well enough to accompany a fellow singer) and violin even better. Her vocal range was wide enough that she could sing either soprano or alto in chorus parts. The natural strength of her voice lay in its low notes; when she took a contralto solo, everyone stopped to listen, even in rehearsal. It was said that she could have joined one of the great opera companies of Italy but had refused in order to stay with Maestro.

Madame was the heart and head of the Company. When anyone spoke to her, she turned to listen with animated expectation, as if she had been hoping and waiting for only these words. She coached all the singers, conducted many reheasals, sang along with any chorus section that needed help, handled advance publicity, and kept the books. Sometimes I wondered if she ever slept. She was always smiling, making each performer feel that anything was possible, even easy. I never saw her angry; her worst expression was a pained look of disappointment when anything really terrible happened.

Some of her great energy went into supporting Maestro Franze, who was, like her, short and ruddy though not plump. The Maestro had a fine head of curly white hair. His smile and eyes shone like an imitation of hers, but with a hard-edged glint to them. He was capable of terrible rages or of dark, brooding silences that Madame usually headed off by whisking everyone away with little sweeping motions, as if she held a broom. The Maestro still sang many lead parts, though these rotated among most of the singers, and he had the final say on all artistic decisions. He held everyone to a high standard of performance and, like his wife, made performers enjoy doing their best, but their best was never enough to satisfy him. Nothing could satisfy him. He was a deeply disappointed man, a composer of dissonant music that no one, least of all his own company, could profitably perform. He became, Karl told me, truly happy only when he was with other composers, playing, comparing, arguing about each other's music, but since the beginning of the war he had been cut off from most of the ones he loved and respected.

Usually the stay in Langero, where all the villagers knew him and respected him for his talent as well as for his relation to the "padrone," refreshed him. But now the war was coming close even to Langero. Many of its young men were at Caporetto. Each day brought news of the death of another, as well as conflicting reports about the Germans—they were near Milan, they had been pushed back, they were moving west, they were retreating. Whatever they were doing, they were much too close to Langero.

It was Madame Franze's idea that we head south. "We will be safe as long as we stay west and on back roads. We play first in Vipetro." Where? No one had heard of the place. "Near Genoa," she said. Already eight other small towns had telegraphed confirmation of booking. Other bookings could be arranged from towns along the way. "We'll go as far as Rome, then see what happens." Maestro nodded gravely as he always did when she decided on a course of action. Within the week we were on our way to our first engagement, rumbling off in three wagons and two automobiles.

At first it seemed impossible to find work for me. I could neither sing nor dance nor even read music, an inexpressibly sad handicap to these good people, almost as bad as blindness. The children read music as soon as they read words. Madame Franze told me I would surely learn from them—it was as easy and natural as breathing.

Meanwhile, there were chores I could do willingly, if not very well. Maestro insisted that even my cooking was fine when washed down with plenty of wine. I could help take care of the children and of the smaller props. After seeing my handwriting, Madame also gave me work copying parts, which I did accurately without knowing how to read the notes I copied.

That winter was fairly mild a few miles inland from the Mediterranean. We performed for a small fee plus room and board with families in villages slightly larger than Langero, clustered around a church on a steeper hill, and surrounded by somewhat richer farmland, but no industry. Maestro was restive in these "godforsaken rock piles without even a train track near," and insisted we head for the coast and the larger port towns. But Madame was saving the coast for summer when it would be hot and everyone with money spent it at the shore. Through careful planning Madame kept us sheltered, fed, and busy till June in tiny villages where there were no signs of war. Then we went to the coast and began inching our way from the outskirts of Genoa southward.

By that time I was loosening the drawstrings on my pajamas while everyone in the company made jokes about the growing evidence that I would add a new member to the company. "We need another soprano!" Karl was ecstatic about my pregnancy, and I felt proud. Finally I was going to accomplish something worth doing.

Every few miles along the coast were the villas of rich people who spent their summers on the water. We performed as often in these villas as in theaters. In one unusual piece of luck we were taken up by the widow of a recently deceased industrialist who had made a great deal of money in the war. She had the whole company transported on two barges to her villa on Isola Giglio, where we went through our repertory twice. We were on the island for a month, bathing and sailing all day and performing at night. She paid little, but fed us well.

We tarried on the coast outside Rome as long as possible, Madame Franze insisting that the fever season was not really over till November. She did not like Rome, called it a disorganized, unhealthy place. But the others could hardly wait. All had friends in Rome, admired performers, former teachers. All expected to find mail waiting for them. So did I. I had been writing regularly to Stephanie.

There was a letter from her waiting when we drove into Rome at the end of October. It contained a clipping from a London newspaper which reported Erika's statement that I had gone to Tibet.

My sudden disappearance was "an act of spiritual forces" sending me to follow intense study with a guru hidden in the mountains. Erika could not say when I would return, but I surely would return soon, "guided by the spiritual forces which summoned her." Stephanie had enclosed a caricature of me sitting on a mountaintop wearing nothing but an idiotic grin.

About a week later the war finally came to an end. My first sight of the Spanish Steps was as part of the crowd of musicians who gathered there on the night after the Armistice to sing the Verdi *Te Deum.* Hundreds of singers filled the steps and spilled over onto the Piazza di Spagna where instrumentalists stood playing, their music held up for them by anyone who wasn't playing or singing. The concert master of the Rome Opera conducted from the stone boat in the middle of the fountain (dry since the second year of the war). People carried candles, embraced each other, wept. No one had organized the concert. It had just happened, the way things did in Rome.

The end of the war did not, however, automatically solve the problems of the Franze Company. Everything was still unsettled in the north. Recovery would be slow. One of the yachts that had come to Isola Giglio while we were there was owned by a Sicilian prince who had invited the Company to visit him, promising lodging and many opportunities to perform. "Probably a good place to spend this winter," concluded Madame Franze, "but no place to have a baby." Better for Karl and me to stay in Rome where there was a good lying-in hospital. After the baby came we could either wait to be picked up by the Franze Company in the spring or, "if you can't stand this anthill on the ruins" (Madame Franze's name for the Eternal City) we could go up to Langero to wait for them.

Friends recommended Karl for a temporary job as rehearsal pianist in their opera company. They also offered us a room in their apartment on the second floor of an old palazzo that had been partitioned again and again into smaller and smaller apartments, housing mostly musicians. Our room was about ten feet square with grayish-brown flaking stone walls, one of them containing an alcove housing the stone bust of some stern ancestor of the original owner. From another wall jutted three steps from a grand staircase, cut off by partitions, and on the ceiling at least fifteen feet above we viewed the lower half (the rest lost in partitions) of what Karl's friends said was a very old, very bad Salome dancing with the head of John the Baptist, which dripped blood across their ceiling. The room was bitter cold until Karl bought a tiny brazier in which we burned coal throughout that winter.

Our daughter was born the day after Christmas. We called her Joy. Karl chose the name, saying it was a happy English word that had a Chinese sound to it. Joy's eyes were round and brown with thick, black lashes, like Karl's. She was blonde at birth, but her hair quickly darkened. Karl thought she looked like his mother. We gave her his mother's name, Rebecca, as a middle name.

With her birth the world changed completely. Perhaps I should say it became her. There was only this new creation, this Joy, this part of me miraculously lying beside me, outside me, an invisible network of nerves still connecting us. I could lie forever, it seemed, unaware of the Eternal City or of anything else, watching her, holding her, listening for her breathing. With her at my breast we both were nourished, and neither of us needed anything but our connection.

Of course, I was weak in the first two months. It had been a hard birth, and my languor was part of my slow recovery. Karl insisted that before long I would take interest in other things—the mothers in the Franze Company sang with as much intensity as anyone—but at the time I could not believe that I would ever care about anything else again. Part of me was outside, apart from me. The best part, better than what was left of me, better than I had ever been, and from now on I must watch and guard it. How could I want to do anything else? If I looked away, I might miss the sudden yawn that stretched her little mouth, or the stare of her wide eyes suddenly fixed, focussed, following my moving hand, or the sudden quivering smile that made me burst into tears.

But Karl was right. Gradually I was ready to move with her beyond the walls of our narrow room. By March I was taking her almost daily to rehearsals, where Karl played piano all day and sometimes worked as prompter and understudy for tenor soloists. He also sang in the chorus during performances. For all this work he was paid barely enough for rent and simple food. I helped by doing a little music copying. I did not suggest going to Langero because, despite having to work so hard for so little, Karl was happy to be with other musicians.

We spent Karl's few spare hours marveling over our baby. He carried her on our long walks when it was not raining, singing to her. His voice instantly silenced her crying. We were sure that she would become a musician like him because of the way she remained quiet during rehearsals, sometimes sleeping but sometimes with a serious, intent look in her eyes, as if she were listening to the music.

In April influenza came to Rome, and someone was always sick. Karl sang almost every night. A member of the chorus died of flu, and Karl was offered a permanent job with the company. We turned it down. The Franze Company was due in Rome at any time, and Karl was eager to travel with them again. "Besides, the flu is getting bad here. I think we're safer on the road."

In early May we were with the Franzes, heading north again. For the first time in five years, the company would follow its old route through the Austro-Hungarian Empire, now divided into small states with new borders. Karl had played only one season on this route before the war, but the others had toured many times, had favorite towns and friends they had not heard from since the start of the war. Madame and Maestro had German relatives on both sides of their families, a network of musicians that went back generations. Wherever we went they welcomed us with tears of joy. They sheltered and fed us, arranged and publicized our performances, joined us in performances and in endless discussions of music. That was the happy part.

The sad part was the destruction. For the first time I passed through battle zones where large areas of towns had been burned. The loss of life was even worse than in England. In some villages all of the young men were gone. Wherever we went, Madame Franze would ask about this or that boy she had watched grow up—in one case, a boy she had helped bring into the world. Dead, was the usual answer. Furthermore, behind the hospitality of the Franze's musical friends was stark hunger.

Maestro's oldest friend, a composer like him, shook his head and said that the days of the traveling opera company were ending. The war had changed people, brutalized their taste. "I used to think that the motion pictures were just a fad for the tone-deaf, but now I think all the young people go to see them. This war generation... they want shadows, not flesh and blood, just silent, dead shadows flickering in the dark."

124

We saw more and more people walking about on the streets wearing gauze masks as protection against flu. Their eerie appearance was unnerving. People began to stay out of crowds, away from public performances. One provincial weekly paper printed a list of local influenza deaths on the page where they had printed war casualty lists.

After a third week of poorly attended performances, we sat down to discuss our prospects. We were living on the emergency fund usually saved for bad winters, and winter was yet to come. Strangers were less welcome now in little towns that used to welcome the return of the Franze Company. It was believed that strangers brought the flu.

The best thing to do was to go back to Langero. We could all help with the harvest and settle in for a while. If conditions improved, we would go south in the fall. If not, we would stay in Langero, away from the large centers of population, where the epidemic was the worst. Some of us might get work in one of the factories. Maestro, Madame, and Karl might take a few pupils. In any case it would be better to keep the children in Langero until conditions improved.

We began to pack up, everyone moving slowly. I had never seen them so depressed. "During the war," said Karl, "we thought we were suffering as much as we could. But there was excitement in our pain, in our fear, even in our horror at the destruction. Now the war is over, the excitement is gone, but the dying goes on. We expected things to go back to the way they were before the war. But they never can, never again."

After making that little speech—so unlike him—to me privately, he began singing as he packed. Madame instantly joined in and soon had the others singing. Joy, who could now sit up alone, sat on a blanket in the midst of all the bustle and singing. She waved her little arms up and down, making long "Ah-a-a-ah" sounds, her way of singing along with her father. Whenever I think of her—as I do every day—I remember her that way. And I remember Karl winking at me, nodding his head sideways to show how the others were cheering up, then starting up a new song, his eyes bright and his face flushed.

It was not until the middle of that night, when I woke to find him moaning and burning in delirium, that I realized his eyes had

125

been bright with fever. Karl had caught influenza. Decisions were made instantly. We would drive straight to Langero, which we might be able to make in a day. Karl and I were given the smaller of the two cars. I would drive with him stretched out on the back seat. The others crowded into the other car and the wagons, taking Joy with them. Sudden weaning would be better than exposing her to Karl. After leaving the others in Langero, I would drive on to the hospital in Turin.

I led our procession of cars and wagons. The others were never out of sight, but came nowhere near me except to help pour gas into the car, and once to change a flat tire. Whenever we stopped, I could hear Joy crying. She usually stayed with other in the Company quite happily, but she sensed that something was wrong, and she wanted to be with me and her father. As I drove, Karl talked and sang incessantly, but the songs were minor-keyed chants and his talk was a ceaseless argument with his father, sometimes in English, sometimes in Yiddish.

When we arrived in Langero, I put more gas in the car and went on, telling the others I would return as soon as I knew Karl was out of danger. The only sound that answered me was Joy's incessant weeping. The adults stood silently waving to me as I drove off.

Before they were out of sight in my rear-view mirror, I felt the first wave of nausea and trembling.

During the last hour of my drive to the hospital, I held the road only by sheer will as fever phantoms danced in the road ahead, their hideous humming ringing in my ears. I drove onto the hospital grounds and through a couple of flower beds before the car came to a stop. The last thing I remember was getting out of the car and taking a few steps on a soft lawn before the cool green tipped up to meet my blazing head.

1919–1926

That day was August 27, 1919. The rest of that year is lost to me, except for brief glimpses of figures that glided through my nightmares. I saw my mother, but before I could take the hand she held out to me, Erika's voice said, "She's stopped breathing again." At the sound of that voice, my mother retreated, I sobbed at losing her again, then breathed. Signora Renata floated by with Miss Harrington and the Robertsons and Doctor Willy, who had joined the Franze Company. There were strangers too, women and men dressed in white, who judged me, then ordered punishments. And always Erika sitting and watching.

Sometimes I knew that some of the people were real and others were not, that a white-robed judge was really a nursing nun, and that the figure sitting in the corner really was Erika. Then everything merged again into insane fantasy until I awoke one morning to church bells, snow lightly clouding the window, and the sight of Erika dozing in a chair in the corner.

How gray her hair had become, gray at the roots, the first inch, then abruptly auburn. How long had she been dyeing her hair, and what had made her suddenly forget to do it? I slid away from that question. I did not want to know why she looked so pale, why she was here, why I was here, where "here" was. When she opened her eyes and saw that I recognized her, she stared for a moment, then nodded slowly. Then she got up, came to the bed, took my hand, and kissed me lightly on the forehead. She left the room; when she came back, a nun was with her. The nun was younger than I, a girl with a wide grin and plump, rosy cheeks. *"Buon Natale, Signora,"* she said as she touched my forehead and took my pulse. I closed my eyes and drifted back to sleep.

For the next three weeks, I asked no questions, and no one volunteered information. I ate and slept, sat on the edge of the bed, took two or three steps from it, leaning on Erika, then sank back into exhausted sleep. One morning in January I finally let Erika tell me.

"Karl's dead, isn't he?"

"Yes."

"And where is Joy?"

No answer.

"Dead."

She nodded.

Karl had died only a couple of days after we were admitted to the hospital. Then flu struck the Franze Company. Joy and two of the other children were brought to the hospital, but the adults stayed in Langero, the well ones nursing the sick. Erika did not know their fate. One of the children had recovered and been sent back. The other and Joy had died. Erika had received a cable from Madame Franze and had come to the hospital where she had been ever since, renting a room nearby.

When Erika arrived I had already been given last rites, in case I was Catholic. For several days I was expected, hourly, to die. Erika stayed with me night and day, giving me care that none of the nurses had time to give, care that barely kept me alive. Pneumonia had set in. The doctors gave up on me. Even if I miraculously recovered, they said, the virus had affected my heart. The slightest exertion would probably prove too much for it. That verdict gave me comfort, made me cooperate with Erika's efforts to get me up. I believed that in the midst of some quick movement my heart would stop as the doctors predicted. It made some interesting flutters and skips—as it has throughout the years ever since—but missed only a beat or two before starting up again.

Letters came. One began, "By the time you are able to read this, I will be in South America." It was from Claude, son of Madame and Maestro Franze. Both had died of the flu, along with two of the children and one woman. The rest had recovered, but the Franze Company no longer existed. Members were taking jobs wherever they could find them. Claude was selling the property in Langero and emigrating. He understood that my sister had arrived and would take care of me. He wished me a speedy recovery and better luck in the rest of my life. It was clear from the tone of the letter that he had not really expected me to live to read it.

There were letters from Sophie and from Father, the first from them since 1917 when the undependable mail from the States had stopped almost entirely. They were concerned but puzzled about our delay in coming home. Clearly they knew nothing about the events of the past year. There was a stack of letters from Stephanie, who had come to see me when I was unconscious, but after a week had to return home. Her husband was very ill, and the flu epidemic had decimated the war survivors at "Pain Hall." Her letter acknowledged the deaths of Karl and Joy with no false note of comfort. She knew too much about death to offer easy words. One of her letters added a death which Erika had not mentioned to me. Doctor Willy too was dead, from a heart attack which struck him while he was recovering from flu.

Erika filled in the details. He had died before she left London. At his death his family allowance was cut off. He had had no money of his own, his family taking care to see that none of their fortune would find its way into the hands of spiritualists. Even if we wanted to go back to London, there was no place for us. Erika adamantly refused an invitation from Stephanie. As soon as I was well enough to travel, we were going home. Then suddenly she smiled. "Poor old Doctor Willy. It seems that he has come through to at least six mediums already, even becoming the control for a very boring woman in Liverpool. He would certainly be finally cured of his acceptance of every occult murmur if he knew the banalities he is supposed to be saying through these amateurs!"

Then a wire came from Norman, in a code I felt too weak to decipher. ALIVE THANK GOD STOP PSYCHE'S BEAUTY ATTRACTING WIDEST ATTENTION STOP MARRIAGE TO THE MONSTER TIMELY STOP BRING FORTH THE BRIDE STOP ORACLES PROMISE EVERYTHING STOP. Erika said he was simply urging us to come home and take maximum advantage of public interest in spiritualism and in me.

It was only then that I realized my illness, the death of Karl, the birth and death of Joy—all, all had been kept secret. So far as the public knew, I was in Tibet. Erika tried to show me some clippings from the newspapers, but I brushed them aside. What had happened to me was terrible enough. To have hidden it all—to deny it—seemed as cruel as another death. "I'm not interested," I told Erika. "I'm going to die. I'll never survive the trip home."

"Yes, you will!" insisted Erika. "You're only twenty-five years old, May, with a great career still in front of you. It's just as well..." I think she had been about to say I was lucky to have lost my child, but wisely did not. "...that I'm here to salvage it. You *will live*!" As usual Erika looked determined but, for once, not convinced she was right.

At the end of January Erika took me to a sanitorium in Spain and left me there. The place had been a convent and was still run by nuns who observed silence. Most of the next two months I spent in a walled, sunny courtyard, not speaking much even to the other patients, mostly tuberculars who, like me, expected to die soon.

From another walled courtyard we heard mental patients, crying or screaming.

In those days doctors believed that heart patients should avoid exertion; I was warned that I should sit or lie down as much as possible. I disobeyed orders, walking constantly during the times when I was not forced to be in bed. I marched, pushing myself round and round that courtyard with the only hope left to me, that of causing heart failure. It was probably the best therapy I could have had. By the time Erika returned in early May, I was better in spite of myself. I even woke some days able to think for a few moments of my baby, enjoying a memory before it turned sharp and slashing, tearing at my feeble heart which somehow went on fitfully pumping.

Erika returned laden with baggage and with plans. She had had new clothes made for me: two new sets of blue silk pajamas and a cloak. She had tickets on a ship to New York, leaving from Portugal in a week. "Norman will meet us in New York—along with, I suspect, reporters from every major newspaper."

"I won't talk to them."

"Right. I've already put out word that your spiritual masters in Tibet impose a vow of silence regarding their teachings. Now, we have invitations from a dozen societies in New York, and twice that many across the country."

"I won't do any seances."

"We'll think about that."

"I won't."

"Plenty of time yet. I promise you a quiet sea voyage. Only six passengers on a cargo ship where no one will have heard of you. After some time..."

"I'm through with all that."

Erika sighed. "While we're on our way home, I want you to think about something. All the money we made during that last year of the war went into your doctor and hospital bills. I sold everything but the clothes on my back to get new clothes for you. I borrowed our steam ship fare from Norman. I'm forty-three, too old to find a husband or even to go on the street. We could find work scrubbing floors, but you're too weak even to do that. Maybe you'll die, and then all these problems won't matter to you. But while you're alive, you can't just go on letting me think about them alone. Now, here are the latest clippings. You can read them on the train to Lisbon."

There was a thick stack of them, nearly enough to keep me reading throughout the train ride, all from American newspapers, all saying the same thing. The famous Madame Psyche, whose occult abilities had become legendary in England during the late war, who was authenticated in writings by Conan Doyle and the late Doctor W. Knauss, who at the height of her fame had withdrawn to the East to subject herself to deeper occult disciplines, had reappeared in Europe and was now on her way to New York. In only a few of the articles was there an ironic tone or a qualification like, "who is said to have been in Tibet during the past year...." I was being reported like a baseball game—of interest to a great many people whose favorite sport was not to be disparaged by those who did not share their enthusiasm. After skimming through a few of them, I put the rest aside and let myself be lulled into a doze by the motion of the train.

It was true that no one in our ship had ever heard of me, nor did they care to. The crew was Portuguese. Three other passengers were Sicilian men who spent most of their time sitting in a lifeboat playing cards (quite comfortably, on cushions, an overhead tarp sheltering them from sun and wind) and hardly speaking even to one another.

I spent my time pacing the deck in only my silk pajamas, hoping for pneumonia if not heart attack, but Erika chased after me with my warm cloak; the weather was, in any case, mild. The sea air and exercise continued to strengthen me in spite of myself. On the second day out, the sixth passenger, who had also been pacing the deck, avoiding the card-playing Sicilians, approached Erika and me and introduced himself.

"Guido Altieri. Despite my Italian name, I am from Lucerne originally and have much Austrian blood on my mother's side. With such a mixture I am a true American. Yes, a naturalized American citizen, but in my heart a citizen of the world, of all humankind, voting socialist like any man of decency and intelligence. You are Americans, of course. Have you read *Looking Backward*?" When Erika nodded, he declared the utopian novel was his bible, but Erika cut him short by saying the book was, "...a nineteenth century dream of a nice man, but we do not live in the world of nice men."

133

"Too true! The war. The barbarism. Mr. Bellamy never dreamed."
Guido Altieri rolled his eyes, then nodded slowly and sadly. But
he was incapable of looking sad for more than a moment. The brief
pursing of his mouth relaxed into a wide smile, and his eyes sparkled
continually with enthusiasm for what the world might be, never
mind what it was now. I could not have met anyone whose outlook
and mood were, at that time, more opposite to mine. Like the fresh
sea air, his presence conspired against my will to die.

He was a small, portly man, about forty years old, neat and
quick-moving. He had thick, rather long, black hair which stuck
out as if electrified by his enthusiastic talk. Bright blue eyes shone
through his tiny round spectacles. He wore a deep gray suit so im-
peccably tailored that Erika at first took him for a rich eccentric
until she learned that he was a tailor. "Also an automotive mechanic.
In today's world an auto mechanic can always earn a living, as can
a good tailor. Reality, Mrs. Newland," he stated, bowing to Erika.
"Plain food, high thoughts, a good trade, and a man can live and
still have his dreams."

This was his ninth trip from Europe since he had come to America twenty years before. He had traveled over much of the United
States and Central America. He was a master at both of his trades,
but he never worked for long, saving his money for travel, living
among different people until he ran out of money. "I want to see
how people live. And, you know, they live badly. "Yes, 'you live
badly, my friends!'"

"Chekhov," said Erika, and he looked at her with respect.

"Indeed, Chekhov, and he was right. I visited the Soviet Union
too. There they are changing, since the revolution, but..." He
shrugged and smiled. "I'm going to stay home now for a while, in
the States. Politically it is unwise to leave the country if you are a
progressive person. They might not let me back in one day. You
should have heard the interrogation when I came back from the
Soviet Union, where I had also worn out my welcome. Best to stay
at home. Plenty to do at home."

At that point Erika decided that we were talking with a man whose
politics could only taint us. She began to avoid him as much as possible on such a small boat and warned me to do the same. But I
liked Guido Altieri. He had a lively mind and a good heart.

He began to pace the deck with me, telling me of his travels, of
his looking for a place where people "live well. The good life, the

golden mean, a sane mind in a healthy body." He was an avid reader of only the best literature. He hated moving pictures and churches and popular newspapers which "made the people stupid." He had never married, "Thank God," though he did not believe in God, he quickly added. "I will tolerate the mention of God only for the sake of hearing Bach." He did not believe in marriage and the family. He quoted Shaw, "The home is the girl's prison and the woman's workhouse." There must be a better way to live, he kept saying.

He asked me about myself. I said I had been caught in Europe by the war, that my husband and child had died of influenza, and that I did not want to talk about it.

He tactfully avoided questioning me, and my silence did not inhibit him. He talked about everything from the Oneida Community in New York (he knew their whole history) to the intricacies of fine tailoring. He even offered to improve the fit in the shoulders of my cloak. He suggested deeper pockets for my pajama suit, which he greatly admired as rational and healthful clothing for women.

After a couple of days, Erika made a stronger effort to get rid of him. She told him who I was. She knew that, with his strong convictions, he would be appalled. He was appalled, but not repelled. His blue eyes dulled, rolled once, then fastened kindly on mine as he spoke his now familiar verdict, "There must be a better way to live."

He was full of suggestions. Opportunities for women were better since the war. I must go to school and learn typewriting and book-keeping. Nursing was a good trade. Hard, but always in demand. He warned me against marrying. "The only good men, those who respect the freedom of a woman, are like me, and I don't marry." He even offered to lend me money to go to school, to get out of the life I was living. "You want to be with the people. You don't want to be on the side of the ones who eat them!"

"If it's eat or be eaten," Erika said breathlessly, catching up with us on our fifth lap around the deck, "I'd rather eat." But Guido and I ignored her until she gave up and went back to our cabin.

Later I overheard her berating him in a sharp, angry, hissing voice. "My sister is going to die, do you understand? It's a miracle she is still alive. It's only a matter of time before her heart gives out. It could happen at any moment. If you want to bring on that moment by exciting her...."

So, for the last three days of the crossing, Guido Altieri and I talked about tailoring, car repair, the climate of Rome, marriage customs in El Salvador, and the San Francisco earthquake. I described for him what I could remember, telling him that damage was still visible when we left for Europe. "But my sister Sophie writes that everything has been rebuilt."

Guido said that he had never been to San Francisco, but planned to work his way there eventually. He imagined it would be a fine place for an auto mechanic. "All those hills, all those brakes to repair. Good for a tailor too; the people there like to dress well. It may be just the place for me. I will look for you when I come to San Francisco."

I assured him I would be glad to see him again. Erika remained stony.

The night before we were to dock in New York, we took one more turn around the deck. Guido said he hoped my health would improve and I would find a good life. Then, just as I turned toward my cabin, he burst out, "You won't die, my friend! Break out of this. Make the good life. You can do it!"

Erika heard him and came rushing out to drive him away, as if he were a stray, barking dog.

We docked in New York at five a.m. on June first and took a cab to the hotel where Norman had booked rooms for us.

It was when I saw Norman that, for the first time, I began to cry. He led me to a couch and sat holding me while Erika sat across the room watching, no doubt wondering if this were the emotional episode which doctors had warned would put an end to me. Norman assumed I was crying out of grief, but my feelings were more complex. Seeing him made me realize how much had happened in six years. He looked different to me, older, heavily middle-aged. He had straightened his hair and plastered it down with some kind of shiny grease. His skin looked lighter than I remembered, as if age had faded him. "You are more beautiful than ever," he said. Then he told me to rest because there would be a press conference in the afternoon.

The reporters came—without cameras, as Erika ordered—to our hotel suite. About twenty of them crowded in. They stayed for about an hour of heavy silences interrupted by questions and quick, desperate filling-in by Erika. (Norman was not there; we were back in America, where a black man who was not a servant had best be invisible.)

"Were you really in Tibet for a year? There's no proof of that, no record of your going there."

Silence.

"Tell us about Tibet. What did you do there?"

Silence.

"My sister was required to take a vow of silence on all that has passed between her and her Tibetan masters."

"Are you ill? Rumors are that you were in a sanitorium in Spain before coming home."

Silence, then Erika again. "The other-world contact she has maintained with the countless numbers of souls passing over during the war put a severe strain on my sister. It could be said that, like any of our soldiers, she nearly gave her life in the war."

There were no other questions about the past year. Evidently Erika had been successful in hiding all but the fact that I had been in the sanitorium. In later years, no other reporter came up with the facts, and if any survivors of the Franze Company heard of me, they kept the secret of the year I spent with them.

"Why will you not allow pictures to be taken?"

Silence. Erika and Norman had argued about that. Erika felt it was time to allow pictures, even motion pictures; a minute in a newsreel would soon spread across the country. Norman believed that the short-run gains of publicity would be less valuable than playing up the mystery of my appearance. I sided with Norman, and Erika gave in. Actually she had won, because in losing this point she had gained my consent to see the reporters.

"What are your plans now that you are home?"

Silence. I felt less at home in America than ever before. These men all seemed raw and rude, though they were no worse than the British press. I would soon get used to their ways. If I lived. But I didn't intend to live, so it didn't matter. Erika stood. "These are the cities where my sister will appear on her cross-country tour." As she passed out the sheets of paper, one young reporter made a final attempt to get me to talk by making me angry.

"Good money in the psychic trade?" I almost smiled at him. If only he knew how little profit we had made in the psychic trade!

Erika hastily spoke, as if she sensed that I might finally say something—the wrong thing. "My sister has never taken one cent. Hers is a sacred gift which she bestows freely and at great cost to herself. As you see, she is very tired. Please go now."

Both Erika and I believed that Norman's work had been wasted —the press conference was a failure. We expected either to be attacked or dismissed. Instead we were handled almost respectfully in the papers, with references to Conan Doyle and reports of my having contacted legions of dead soldiers. So it was true that, like any performer who had had even a moderate success in Europe, I had gained stature at home in America. No opinion on the authenticity of my powers was offered. Instead there were lengthy descriptions of my "pale and fragile beauty...hints of Asiatic mystery in her eyes."

Norman claimed credit for the last phrase. He had suggested it to one of the reporters, a friend who had helped to keep the mood of the others friendly and tolerant. "Now I've done all I can for you, and I'd best get back home."

"To your family," I nodded. With a twinge of envy, I asked, "How many children are there now?"

Norman looked even older as he shook his head. "None. The first was born dead. My wife has been pregnant twice since then, but lost both."

This had not been the only catastrophe in Norman's life. The war had brought great changes to the Northwest, including competing newspapers backed by big business interests who were not above using race against their competition. The era in which the Duclar family could enjoy a friendly relation with the white majority was over. White advertisers and white subscribers had been drawn away. Norman had been forced to sell out. He still had the chain of black papers, but their condition was always perilous, bringing in little money and demanding that he travel around to keep them going. "That's how I happen to be here to meet you, that and the radio station. I came to New York to pick up some pointers on what to do with it." With what? With the radio station he had bought with the proceeds of the sale of the newspaper. "You don't mean to tell me you've never heard a radio?"

To Erika and me, radio was something that carried messages between ships. We knew people could buy devices that received messages sent by radio and that some people had sent music as well as messages through the air. But it seemed a thin way to listen to music.

Norman explained that anyone could apply to buy a frequency on which to broadcast. Some of these broadcasts went as far as a forty-mile radius. People were buying receiving sets. "Soon everyone will have one." Norman became excited as he explained, almost like his old self. "If I can..."

Erika cut him off. We had more serious things to discuss than the latest American fad. "May had better rest again."

Norman could do no more for us, at least not now. Within a couple of days he was on his way back across the country toward San Francisco, where he often stayed now. Erika packed up and rushed us on our way. She seemed anxious to leave New York although we had received many more invitations from psychic groups right in Manhattan.

Our first stop was Pittsburgh, the first of nearly thirty cities across the country, all of which now merge in my mind. The pattern was always the same. We were invited to stay in the home of a family active in local spiritualist activities. Our accommodations were always comfortable, sometimes sumptuous. We stayed an average of two weeks in each place, and were always urged to stay longer, even though I held only one public sitting and a couple of private ones, mostly remaining in my room and refusing to talk to anyone. The sittings were uneventful. Erika, doing her usual thorough research, coached me or nagged me with information, of which only a small amount remained in my mind. I did not bother to invent a "control." In my still weakened condition, I often felt faint, closed my eyes, spoke softly, if at all. Sometimes I alarmed Erika by rambling on about the pain of grief, and a couple of times I started crying and could not speak at all.

I hoped that the disappointment of clients would put an end to my mediumship, but it seemed that I could do no wrong. As we moved from one city to the next, the newspaper coverage grew as did the crowds for my one public appearance in each city. The less I did, the more awed were the reports. The more I refused private sittings on the grounds of weak health, the more requests came. My fame had nothing to do with what I did or didn't do; it grew regardless.

This slow movement across the country enabled me to get used to Americans again. While I was in Europe, I had little sense of being with a different sort of people. Like an infant, which I was in a way, I merely accepted people as they were. Now that I was back in the States, I was struck by the difference in the people. There was something too open about my countrymen, too revealing. Every thought and feeling was on the surface, popping out on their faces the moment it arose. Call the Europeans secretive or reserved, it did not matter. I would have called them—now that I was used to them —more restful to be with. I also understood why European clairvoyants had so easily made great reputations in the States. Reading minds was no trouble àt all here at home. Every thought marched across the face playing its theme like a brass band.

In Minneapolis, a woman who had attended one of my public sittings (the hall, seating 2500, was full) told reporters that during the sitting she had suddenly been cured of a migraine headache. I insisted Erika tell reporters that I claimed no powers of healing, but the story spread anyway. After that a few people in every group insisted that my presence had healed them.

Crowds doubled and tripled. Reporters swarmed. By the time we reached Denver, I was refusing interviews, then refusing public sittings, then refusing anything but a silent trance during private sittings. In other words, I was doing nothing at all—after which a client would invariably give a newspaper interview in which she described astounding visions or healings induced by sitting near me while I was in trance. Offers of ridiculous fees—thousands of dollars— came for brief private sittings. Erika wavered, but I was firm. Not a penny. I hoped to discourage her, to make her give up hoping that she could make anything of my career. All I did was to increase my credibility and my fame. Soon, letters from Sophie were saying that reports were regularly appearing in the newspapers at home. By the time we reached San Francisco, I could be sure of a royal welcome. I stayed longer and longer in each place, trying to delay, to slow the building momentum.

The fourteen months we took crossing the country was the first of the five or six truly hopeless years of my life. I was tortured not only by the loss of Karl and Joy but by the seething of my own thoughts. For fifteen years, from before the time I was really capable of thinking, I had been playing with the most deeply felt needs of others. I had exploited their grief. Now I knew what they felt. I knew the depth of pain that turns people to spiritualism or back to the religion of their childhood. Yet I was immune to the appeal of spiritualism, and I had no childhood religion to fall back on.

Other people led normal, working, family lives which kept them busy except for the dark times in the night, when they might wake to ponder their secret griefs. I lived constantly with questions about the meaning of life and death. My livelihood itself stimulated a hysterical clamor for false answers to impossible questions. And I saw no way out. My new triumph had become my punishment. There would be no husband and family, no other work that could rescue me from this terrible deception at which I was now, no matter what I did, so successful. My one hope of escape was the one expected by those grave doctors at the sanitorium—the very oblivion my clients feared, the oblivion which the next skip of my heart might announce. That was all I had to hope for and wait for.

I almost believed the wait was over when our train reached Oakland. I had one of my breathless, heart-thumping sweats (so routine I have since learned to ignore them) and was taken by ambulance to the ferry and then to Sophie's house, confounding the reporters and inflating news coverage of my "mysterious re-entry into San Francisco." I was left in peace because no one connected me with Sophie or even knew where her house was.

Many changes had taken place in the six years since I had seen Sophie and Father. Sophie was still in the flower business, but her business had changed. She had moved out of the Haight Street shop and set up two outdoor flower stalls downtown, one on Powell Street and one on DuPont, now called Grant Avenue.

In 1916 a tunnel had been cut through Twin Peaks, providing trolley car transportation to the west side of the City. Sophie had saved enough money to buy a house on 43rd Avenue south of Golden Gate Park, an odd brick and log structure cut up into eight tiny rooms, surrounded by sand dunes. Not far from it there stood one short row of new stucco houses like the ones that would gradually cover the dunes during the next few years. But during the time that I lived there the house stood alone, fog-shrouded throughout the summer, wind-swept and abraded by the sand that Sophie was always sweeping out the front door. The ocean surf made a constant muted roar only a few blocks away. Norman guessed that the house had been built originally in such a remote place for some illegal purpose—gambling and prostitution—like the few others spotted among the dunes. Sophie had bought it for the most virtuous of reasons, to keep Father at an inconvenient distance from downtown bars.

She also kept him busy in the flower business. Each morning at dawn, except when it rained, she and Father took the trolley car, which ran between sand dunes then through the Twin Peaks Tunnel and straight up Market Street to the Ferry Building, a trip that took nearly an hour. From the Ferry Building they took a cab to the wholesale flower market, filled the cab with flowers and rode up to their stalls.

Father manned the stall on Powell, while Sophie took the Chinatown stall on Grant. They were there all day. After the offices let out, some workers making the last purchases of the day, Sophie closed her stall, walked to Powell, closed Father's stall, and the two of them walked down to Market Street to take the trolley car back home again. They were usually asleep by eight. Their routine had done wonders for Father. He was by no means a teetotaler, often slipping into bars on Powell Street during the day. But he could not leave the flower stall for long, and actually did not want to. He had become a well-known character on the street, with regular customers. He dressed as carefully as the bankers who stopped by his stall to hear him discourse on the financial news or on Plato. He was now in his seventies and looked better than he had at any other time I could remember.

Sophie's stand was up near Broadway, where Chinatown merged with the Italian settlement of North Beach. Neither the Chinese nor the Italians bought flowers, but the tourists who came to look at them did, stopping to get directions from Sophie the Flower Lady, possibly the only person on the street who spoke English. She no longer went to seances, or talked about her dead children. She had grown very fat and, in her way, very capable, managing much better alone that she might have with Erika and me.

Sophie had prepared one of the little rooms for me, and one for Erika. Norman also rented a room from her. He now spent more time in San Francisco than up in Washington. Since there were no children and—doctors surmised—never would be, he and his wife had gone their separate ways, though she wanted to keep the marriage for the sake of appearances. She told her friends the truth, that he had to be in San Francisco often to oversee the operation of his radio station.

So after all that had happened, here we all were again, everything the same, everything changed.

For a few days I lay in bed resting, Erika watching over me like a nurse or a prison guard. Sophie and Father were at their flower stalls all day. Norman was in and out, delivering monologues about radio, to which none of us really listened.

On a quiet Monday I sneaked out and walked the five blocks to the ocean, where I sat in the sand. Wasn't it Samuel Butler who wrote that watching large bodies of water is healing to the sick soul? At the time I had never heard of him, but I instinctively sought his recommended cure, although I did not want to be cured. I wanted to die.

When Erika and Norman found me, she was frantic with worry, but Norman pointed to the spot of color in my cheeks and suggested more outings. In addition to my walks on the beach, Norman took Erika and me on drives around the City. We saw no sign of the earthquake anywhere. Norman took us to see the remains of the buildings on the fairgrounds where the 1915 exposition was held— during the year I had begun memorizing casualty lists. We drove downtown and he pointed out new buildings. Everything was bustling and crowded and new, yet, in a way, completely unchanged. All I could think of was Stephanie as we drove through this optimistic, busy town which had not seen war. That night I wrote to her for the first time, and after that I wrote at least twice a month, needing this contact with someone who admitted the reality of death.

Only Hunters Point, which we skirted briefly during one ride, was unchanged, except for the addition of more clanking, smoking, smelly foundries and tanneries. There was no reason to stop; Miss Harrington was no longer there, but she was alive, probably living in a downtown hotel. Sophie saw her at least once a month when she stopped to buy a flower and to talk. "She always asks about you, May."

Finally Norman took us to see his radio station, a tiny square shack, hardly bigger than my bedroom, perched on top of Twin Peaks under a huge tower and beside noisily humming, metal-sealed machinery. Inside the shack a man sat surrounded by dials, playing a record of one of the popular tunes of the day. "Tonight, there'll be a jazz trio here. And we'll add another studio next year. Range is poor. This is a tough radio town—too many hills. But there's no better location. Sometimes they get our signal in Oakland!''

I had been back in San Francisco nearly a month and no one had found me. A brief article in the *Examiner* asked, "Has the mysterious Madame Psyche pulled another disappearing act? Is she off to Tibet again? Maybe she has gone to Southern California, where talents like hers are accepted with more credulity." From that tone, I could tell what I was in for when the newspapers found me.

In fact Erika had considered taking me to Los Angeles or San Diego, but decided against facing the competition there. She liked the stability of the quiet home Sophie provided. But she was at a loss as to how to proceed.

"Frankly," she said to Norman one evening, as if I were not there, "I don't know if her heart can take it. She can't exert herself to put on any show. People upset her, and when she gets upset, there's every chance she'll just...pop off...just like that." Erika snapped her fingers without looking at me. "More than once when we were coming across country, I thought I'd lost her. The doctors all say the same thing. She could pop off tomorrow or go on for years, but she'll never be any better. So what do we do, live off Sophie? I suppose I could operate a third flower stand for her." The thought of Erika selling flowers made Norman and me laugh. "Well, at least she can still laugh. You'd never know it from the way she acts, as if she wishes she *would*...." Erika always stopped short of acknowledging my suicidal urges.

"I have a better idea than that," said Norman. "Radio."

Erika sighed. She always stopped listening whenever he began to talk about his obsession.

"Thousands of people in San Francisco own radio receivers. And they have to listen to my station—there isn't any other, though that can't last much longer. Mei-li, you wouldn't have to see people. I'd just drive you up to the station, you sit in front of a microphone for an hour, then go home. Easy."

"But what would she do?"

"Talk, of course. Mei-li has a lovely voice, haven't you ever noticed? I think it would broadcast well."

"Yes, but what would she say?"

"Come on, Erika, you have enough brains to figure that out. Give her some typical questions, like the ones she's handled a million times. Pretend you're a client. No. No, I think—letters. Say that she has a letter from someone, someone who asks...."

144

"I won't pretend to bring messages from the dead," I said, realizing that I had, in this denial, agreed to let them put me on radio. I was indifferent. It didn't matter what I did while waiting to die.

"Oh, what's the point?" asked Erika. "You can't pay us anything, you're going broke just keeping the silly thing operating. Why should clients pay anything, if they can just turn on a radio set and get May for free?"

"You haven't been listening to me. I told you last week about the store that gives me fifty dollars just for mentioning them between numbers that the jazz trio plays? Listen, let's just try. May, I'll drive you there and bring you right back here again. No one to see, no reporters, all quiet and easy."

And that was how I entered my final phase as Madame Psyche.

Norman put an ad in the *Examiner* stating that my health did not allow public appearances but that I could be heard on Radio KXO that night at ten. Norman chose that time, he said, because, "By ten, the children are in bed, in case the churches or schools object."

In those days, the time of a program was approximate. There was always trouble with equipment, and programs started when they could, were changed without notice, or canceled and rescheduled. The miracle of sound traveling over the air was enough for people who patiently tuned to the frequency which might or might not bring sounds, usually through ear phones.

That night, September 8, 1921, we finally got started at about ten twenty. I wasn't nervous at all. The truth was, I couldn't really believe that speaking into the microphone (which looked like a huge, plucked, dried center of a sun flower) would carry my voice beyond that little hilltop shack, or even if it did, that anyone would be listening to what I said. Our problem had not been whether or not I would feel able to speak, but what I would agree to say.

Erika kept showing me letters from people who had attended sittings during our trip across the country, suggesting that I take up one of their questions. I only repeated that I would not pretend to carry messages from the dead. At the last minute Erika gave in, deciding to cancel the program, but Norman insisted on driving me to the station and sitting me down in front of the microphone. Up to the moment the engineer pointed at me, I had no idea what I would say.

During a long moment of silence, the thought of the Robertsons came to me, and the thought of Joy. I spoke of what it meant to lose a child and how many people came to me because they could not bear life without a sign of their child. Then I said that no one could bring a grieving parent anything like what she already had in memories of her child. I began to describe an infant—Joy, of course, though I did not name her or identify her as my own—recreating her in words, remembering and describing a happy gesture, a look, a sound. "No medium can give you anything better than that memory and the love awakened in you by it."

I had spoken for nearly half an hour, had refuted whatever I was supposed to stand for, and had enraged Erika against both Norman and me. I was satisfied. That would be the end of my career.

The next day brought two hundred letters to the radio station. The following day there were three hundred more. Total mail on that first broadcast reached nearly nine hundred, an unheard-of response at a time when only a few thousand people in the City owned radio sets. Some of the letters contained money, and Erika said firmly that we would keep it. "We won't ask for money, but if it comes, I'm going to keep it!"

Norman only laughed. "That's peanuts compared to what I think I can get." He took stacks of the letters to show to downtown merchants and offered to mention their businesses, at no charge, during the next month of broadcasts by Madame Psyche. If at the end of the month they noticed an improvement in sales, they would begin to pay a monthly fee. Most agreed to try it.

I broadcasted at ten p.m. one night a week, Norman beginning and ending my talk with a quiet announcement that "the following merchants have made it possible to bring the valuable message of Madame Psyche to you. Support for these merchants would be appreciated." The following month the merchants, pleased with a sudden increase in sales, began to pay. This part of my story sounds obvious in these days of commercial radio and television, but in those days, commercial financing of programs was not taken for granted, in fact was hardly thought of.

Norman's radio station was one of less than a dozen throughout the entire nation at the time. Only a year later, there were hundreds, with hookups to long-distance phone service, which carried programs further and further from the original narrow radius reached by a local signal. In those first days, Noman took a share of the money for maintenance of the station and turned over the rest to Erika, who paid rent to Sophie, covered our few expenses, and banked the rest. Later, radio performers were paid fixed (often very low) salaries, but our original arrangement with Norman continued, so that as commercial sponsorship increased, our income did too.

Once again, life settled into a routine. Every day Erika and I worked on the mail. Or rather, Erika worked. I skimmed a few letters until I found several which I thought I could discuss on the radio. The rest of the letters Erika answered personally, signing them Madame Psyche. (I have never signed that name, and if there are letters signed with it still in existence, I never wrote them.)

Erika also had a printer make up copies of what Doctor Willy and Conan Doyle had written about me. Whenever reporters contacted the radio station requesting an interview, they were sent copies of these articles. Summaries of them appeared over and over again, reminding the public that I possessed "uncanny powers verified by respected investigators."

In my radio talks I made no such claims, never mentioned occult powers. I chose letters which described problems, then talked about the problem, offering no solution, but only sympathy. The only fraud I practiced was to pretend to read character in the handwriting of each letter, always seeing noble traits of character that would help the writer to transcend problems.

Nevertheless, within a short time we were receiving letters claiming that the sound of my voice over the radio had healed someone's longstanding illness. Other letters said the writers had heard of my healing someone in Cincinnati or Phoenix during the year I spent crossing the country, and requested a healing by radio. Erika showed me articles about a man on a radio station in Mississippi who claimed to heal with the sound of his voice. Listeners were told to just put the afflicted part of their body near the radio—he had a special day for the liver, another day for arthritis, and so on. She suggested I follow his example. I refused, and she did not press me. Things were going well enough.

By 1923 my program was being carried by long-distance phone to more than two hundred radio stations across the country, seven of them owned by Norman. At least once a month came an invitation from a New York station, offering ten times the number of listeners we now had, and at least triple the amount of money Norman could pay us. To my surprise, Erika refused to consider moving to New York. She said the California climate was better for my precarious health. She sounded evasive, and I thought there might be another reason, but it didn't matter to me. Nothing mattered to me.

I was, to my growing public, the mysterious, disembodied voice of a woman who was said to exist on a plane beyond ordinary life, in a precarious, etherealized state where any disturbance might destroy my thin ties to life on this worldly plane. My listeners would have been surprised to know what the life of the mysterious Madame Psyche actually consisted of.

The broadcast day, Monday, began with a light supper cooked by Sophie when she and Father came home from their flower stands. About nine Norman and I drove to the Twin Peaks radio station, which now had added studio space. I began speaking at ten and spoke for a full hour broken into three segments by commercial announcements. By the end of the hour I was tired but too tense to sleep. Throwing bags of received mail into the back of the car (another week's work for Erika) Norman would drive in and out the little streets winding around Twin Peaks until he was sure he had lost any reporter hunting for me. Then we drove to an all-night movie house on Golden Gate Avenue. About three a.m. we drove home and went to bed, where I might sleep through the next day, awakening to find Norman gone.

From Tuesday to Saturday he would be traveling to one of his other radio stations. Erika worked on the mail. I took long solitary walks on the beach, which was usually so cold and foggy that I had it almost entirely to myself. In 1924 I bought a car and often drove alone for hours, around the City or south on El Camino, sometimes as far as San Jose, especially in spring when the orchards bloomed. Only once did I cross Potrero Avenue again to drive toward Hunters Point. I wanted to find and visit my mother's grave. But the cemetery where she was buried had disappeared, covered by a two-hundred-foot-high natural gas tank built by the power company.

I wrote descriptions of the gas tank and other sights in my letters to Stephanie, but on the subject of my reviving career I wrote nothing. Neither did she care to write about her barren life with her invalid husband. The main subject of our letters, as I remember, was Charlie Chaplin movies, which we both loved as only very sad people can.

By the end of 1925 Norman's predictions were coming true. The first network of radio stations was about to hook up, coast to coast. His radio stations were being bought by the network, and he would be paid in stock as well as being hired in an executive position. He was working on a ten-year contract for me. There would be a real producer, a well-paid position for Erika as my manager, a staff to handle the mail, and a generous budget for advertising.

While Norman and Erika exulted, I looked ahead to the next ten years as a flat, dusty road on a treeless plain leading nowhere. I had been ready for an early death, but not for the indefinite prolonging of this life. Was there no way out? Several times, when I felt the onset of breathless pounding in my chest during walks on the beach, I tried to run. But I only fainted, then woke a few minutes later, cold and wet, my hair and mouth full of sand. Dying was not so easy as those doctors had led me to believe.

It was during those weeks of contract negotiations that I reached the crisis point toward which I had been moving all my life. It was while I was planning another suicide attempt that the change came. My new plan was simply to walk into the ocean. Suddenly, at the instant when I decided upon this method, I knew I would not do it. I lacked the energy, the courage, the determination. My suicide was a fantasy, a comforting delusion I had held before me as my clients held delusions of spirits.

For the first time I gave up expecting imminent escape by death or by any other means. The question was not how to die, but how to endure life until it chose to leave me. Like all the people who listened to my voice on radio, I felt weak, unable to cope alone. Too weak to be distracted by fame and vanity. Weaker than anyone I knew. Weaker, it seemed, than thousands of people I didn't know.

My father, now seventy-five and still pontificating from his flower stand near Union Square, was beginning to be a bit senile. He tended to repeat quotations from his favorite philosophers. One of the quotations played over and over like a broken record was a saying by Voltaire that he roared to his sidewalk audience whenever he saw a passing pair of nuns. "If God did not exist, man would have had to invent Him!"

The quotation, which I had been hearing all my life as a preface to one of Father's attacks on established religion, suddenly seemed a simple, instructive statement of fact. Yes, I thought. Quite true. Yes, that was what I would have to do. Invent myself a God. How silly, ridiculous, humiliating. I could never admit this need to anyone, but fortunately I wouldn't have to. It would be my simple, stupid secret to help me deal with my simple, stupid weakness. Since, just as Voltaire said, I could not go on alone, I would have to pretend some god did exist, though I very well knew it did not. I would pretend. I would invent. I had invented hundreds of spirits for other weak-minded people. Now it was my turn.

I said all that to myself; then I forgot about it.

A couple of nights later, as I was going to bed, I remembered. Making sure my door was shut and that everyone else was asleep, I sat on the edge of my bed, hesitated, then went all the way—I knelt on the floor. I whispered a few awkward words: "Hello. You. I don't know any prayers, but you know what I need. I am glad you are with me. And you won't ever go away. Thank you." I said a few more words in the same vein before getting up and slipping under the covers. "Thank you for listening," I said, then giggled. I sounded as if I were giving the sign-off of my radio program! I turned over and fell asleep.

When I awoke, the sun was shining brightly through my window. We had had several weeks of fog, which is usual in that part of San Francisco, and I was glad to see the sun again. I got up and went to the window to look out over the soft dunes. Then I remembered my invention and murmured, "Oh, a sunny day. That's nice. Thank you." That comment set the pattern for the rest of the day. I did not kneel again or try to invent any sort of prayer. Instead I kept a silent conversation going, as if the god I had invented were a companion, respected but familiar, to whom I would comment on what I was doing and thinking.

That night, when I did my radio program, I kept mentally checking with my "companion," inwardly asking, "That's all right, isn't it? That bit of advice won't hurt anyone. That old lady just needs a friend like you." And so on. I felt foolish, but, to my surprise, feeling foolish was not as painful as I expected. At the end of the program, I inwardly said, "This time I did no harm. Thank you."

I began to say a polite, friendly, silent "thank you" to my invented god each time something pleasant happened. If something difficult presented itself—an unpleasant memory or Erika's insistence that I look over a detail of the contracts with her—I asked my companion to "help me with this." When I was alone I actually spoke quietly. If anyone was near, my constant conversation with my companion was inward and silent.

One morning I awoke to an empty house. Norman had left on one of his trips. Sophie and Father were at their flower stands. Erika, said a note on the kitchen table, had taken the car to do a number of errands and would not be home until dinner time. The sun was shining ("thank you, another nice day"). I decided to pack some fruit and cheese and walk down to the beach. It was a mild day, yet always crisp near the ocean, so I wore my warm cloak, carrying food in a brown bag, mumbling all these plans to my companion, then shutting my mouth and communicating only inwardly as I walked down the road between the sand dunes. Although a few scattered rows of stucco houses had been built in the past three years, there were seldom any people on these streets, yet I did not want to get into the habit of mumbling in public.

It was about noon, and there were only a couple of people on the beach. One man was fishing, wearing hip-high, black rubber wading boots and standing in the surf. Above the black boots he was all brown—brown shirt, brown hat, his broad back turned to me, stolid, still, as his arm reached back, then forward, flicking his rod toward the water. Perhaps he was only practicing fly-casting. On the edge of the water where the sand was dark and wet, two children, warmly sweatered but barefoot, were building a sand castle, helped by a woman about my age, their mother, I suppose. Besides these two I saw only a large dog, far to my left, which ran into the water to retrieve a stick, swimming back with it, then shaking and barking as if both enjoying and protesting the game. Whoever repeatedly threw the stick was hidden behind a rise of sand. I could not even really see the stick thrown, but knew it was when the dog rushed, leaping against the waves to catch it.

I kept back against the sea wall where the sand piled up and grew warm in the sun, sheltered from the wind. I spread my cloak on the sand, then sat on it, leaning back on my elbows to watch the fisherman, the children, and the leaping dog. I was at such a distance from them that I heard only the rushing and heaving of the ocean.

The sky was a clear blue, and the ocean glistened white on blue, so dazzling that it hurt my eyes. "Beautiful," I said.

There was a twisted, scrubby bush growing out of the sand above me and to my right. I moved slightly so as to shade my head a little from the hard brightness. As I looked up, positioning myself, I saw how the sun's rays pierced between the leaves of the bush. The leaves shook and waved in the wind, and the light behind them rippled through like a white-hot fire shooting thread-thin rays of heat. "Oh, now that *is* a nice effect," I said, with a casual little laugh of congratulation for my companion. "Thank *you*."

What happened then, I realize, was not a unique experience. In the past few years I have read many attempts to describe it. But at that time I had read nothing in the literature of such experiences, I am glad to say, for I know that it was not stimulated by any reading nor suggested by any of my false occult invention. It was like nothing I had read about or heard about before it happened to me. But it was nothing new. What I experienced had always been there, unknown until this sudden opening revealed it.

The light that I had watched piercing in shifting darts through the leaves above me suddenly fused with invisible light all around me, igniting an explosion, no, an exposure, a revelation of light. I seemed suddenly to perceive—no, to become part of—the world as physicists explain it—as energy in varied rates of motion, creating shifting forms. I now saw this energy as light in everything, in the leaves of the tree, in the sky, in the sand, in the people standing near the water, in the water itself. The light was like water in the way it flowed through everything, like fire in the way it flamed, a brilliant glow of power at the core of everything. Everything was only a part of that light, a form of that light, all the same, all one.

I too was part of the shining waves of light flowing through me like a sexual orgasm. There are sexual orgasms which are especially complete, felt all the way to the toes, to the roots of the hair. My feeling as I merged into this light was like that kind of orgasm multiplied infinitely, over and over, a hundred times stronger, the repeated waves strengthening me for the next wave and the next, as the energy moved and shone through me and everywhere around me—there being no longer any boundaries between me and everything else. Yet there was never at any time a sense of loss of myself. In this feeling of oneness with the light I was more myself than I had ever been.

The beauty of everything stunned me. The dog at the edge of the water, shaking himself, the drops of water bursting from the animal in dazzling spray. The precious children bent over their mound of sand. The thick, booted fisherman stolidly throwing out his line and reeling in. Seeing nothing but the outline of his lumpy shape, I knew him to be beautiful. His casting out into the sea, reeling in, casting out again, was full of meaning.

As was everything else. Just as each grain of sand was suddenly beautiful, each was also full of meaning, each carried a message that as we were all like grains of sand, so were we all full of that one light. The children intent on building something that would be swept out by the next tide were a lesson in concentrated, disinterested effort. The dog leaping and paddling toward the floating stick was a teacher of simple joy. Now I knew that there was no end to meaning, to the messages dropped everywhere, glowing from everything. The entire material universe, everything, right down to the nail on my left little toe was a poem, a metaphor, a shifting expression of reality, full of more meaning than I would ever comprehend.

My glimpse of this incomprehensible meaning filled me with humility, with a sense of being nothing. Yet it was a delicious, liberating humility, and contemplating it sent more waves of lightning orgasm through me. This nothingness was greater than anything I had ever imagined, this being a tiny, ephemeral expression of something greater than I had ever hoped for or was even capable of imagining. How paltry were the greatest hopes I had ever heard any person voice, compared to the reality. How little had my clients asked for, seeking nothing but the ghost of another human being.

The state I have tried to describe lasted for about half an hour at its greatest intensity, then gradually faded, though for a long time, simply by thinking of it, I brought back faint orgasmic waves. Although it faded, I never saw it as a temporary flight from reality. It was the opposite, an experience of hidden reality which I have never doubted. Whatever its fleeting manifestation, it left me permanently changed by what I then knew and what I know still and will always know.

I knew better than to say anything. Erika and Father would think I had gone mad. Sophie would get my experience all mixed up with her old occult fantasies. Norman would be puzzled and worried. And Stephanie—if I wrote to her about it—would turn on me the scathing hilarity she kept ready for all "holy blather." Besides, I felt a strong inner prohibition against telling anyone, least of all anyone who would listen sympathetically, even if I knew such people, which I didn't. I knew no one.

Erika remarked that I looked rested. A few days later she said she was glad to see me looking so happy. "The best days are coming, you see it now. Once you sign those contracts our worries are over."

I did not want to talk about contracts. I wanted only to talk to the nameless reality which had revealed itself to me. And I wanted to listen, to see, to touch its messages to me. One of the letters from a listener quoted from Whitman, the same passage that Erika had read over my mother's coffin twenty years before. Its appearance now seemed to me a miracle, not a coincidence. I no longer believed in coincidence. Everything had meaning. Like the poet, I saw infinite meaning in a blade of grass. And in everything else.

I even saw meaning in the biblical quotations and other religious sayings my listeners wrote to me. What had been superstitious dogma suddenly was revealed as metaphor invented, no doubt, by others who had seen the same reality which had dazzled me. No longer contemptuous of religion, I felt the truth behind all gospels, all rituals. I felt that I could have happily worshipped in any kind of temple, in all temples, or in none at all. I chose none at all. I doubted that any fixed set of metaphors and rituals, taken literally by its congregation, could contain my new sense of reality. Containment might have been just what I needed, but I did not know that yet.

I knew only that I must quit all lies and pretensions. The sense of peace which had followed my first ecstasy was fragile, shaken whenever I said or did anything unworthy of the reality that had touched me. If before I saw no escape from my life of deception, now I saw no way of staying in it.

When Erika and Norman came to me with the completed contracts ready for my signature, I told them I had decided not to sign, would not talk on radio any more, would not be Madame Psyche anymore. I was quitting, and Erika could keep whatever money we had made.

154

I was naive to think I could satisfy Erika with that money. It was a good amount, but nothing to what we were likely to make in that first decade of network radio when the talking box became the dominant voice in almost every home. For Erika this was a repetition of my earlier betrayal of her. She had worked to build my career, and I had run away when we were on the brink of success. She had literally saved my life and nursed me back to the best state of health I could hope to reach. She had rebuilt my career with little help from me. And now, when she saw us within reach of success and security, I was running away again. Why? Erika was shrewd enough to know that I was concealing my reason for quitting, but she could not imagine what that reason might be. The more she raged at me, the more certain I became that it would be futile to try to tell her the truth. She would think me insane. I said only that I would give her a month to replace me. Then I was through.

During that month Erika tried every argument possible—my health, my lack of training to earn a living, my half-breed status, my age, now over thirty, my complete lack of experience in ordinary life. She appealed to Sophie and Father, who agreed that I was ungrateful and unwise, but clearly determined. Each of them decided to explain me to Erika. Father pointed out how narrow my life had been, that I might as well have lived all this time in a convent. "May needs people," he said, waving his arms in a slightly drunken flourish then subsiding quickly as Erika gave him a murderous look.

Sophie's theory was different. It was not unusual for a person to have supernatural powers at some time in her life but then to lose them. Obviously, since my return from Europe mine had waned along with other vital forces. Perhaps it was time for me to retire. She ended by offering me a job. She was thinking of opening a new flower stand at Fisherman's Wharf, which was beginning to attract tourists. I could take over the Chinatown stand. Erika turned on her, grabbed her, and shook her until she cried.

Through these noisy scenes Norman said nothing. Finally, when we were alone one night, he admitted I might be wise to get out of radio now. "There's nothing in it for you but money, and that only for a short time." Programs like mine would soon be forced out by professional entertainers. Before long the network would find a way to break their contract with me and drop me. And yet, he said, Erika was right. I lacked the training or even the physical

155

stamina to support myself. "You might think about coming to New York with me."

As the networks swallowed stations and pushed aside pioneers like Norman, there was still a place for him in New York, in Negro programming. There was a great irony in this, none of it lost on Norman. He had grown up in a time and place temporarily freer for a few of his race. In the past decade his family had scattered to wherever they could best cling to the shreds of their affluence. His bold leap into radio, when others were dismissing it as a passing fad, not only had made his financial future but had now put him in a position to profit from the segregation his family used to believe they were gradually overcoming.

The separate culture, music, manner, and taste of the segregated Negro minority were reflected in radio programming on stations aimed at Negro listeners. The network which had absorbed Norman's radio stations was willing to let him develop these stations. But to do that, he would have to live in New York, where there were Negroes in sufficient numbers with money to spend, so that a station could attract commercial sponsorship. His parents dead, his wife in Mexico City, writing only when she needed more money than the regular allowance he sent, there was nothing to keep him in California. "Come with me, May. We're good together, both of us not one thing or another. I don't seem to be able to relax with women who are one color or another or think they are. There are things I don't have to explain to you. There are things you and I don't ask of each other."

Surely Norman had asked little of me, not even sex, which one doctor had said might kill me. "You're not an old man yet," I said, though he looked older than forty-five and had been advised to decrease his smoking, eating, and work because of high blood pressure. "You need someone who can be a real woman to you."

"Let me be the judge of what I need."

I told him I was unsure, but that if I decided to go with him, I would follow him to New York within the month.

He looked at me as if he knew he would never see me again. "Okay, within a month, but no longer. I'm not a man to stay alone, you understand. I won't wait for you."

156

I made my last broadcast in November of 1926. Erika had tried to take over the program, but the network wanted Madame Psyche or no one. She opened the third flower stand. I am sure she never forgave me the fact that at fifty she had to go to work for Sophie.

Erika wrote a meticulous accounting of the money we had, a little over twenty thousand dollars. She sat me down and forced me to listen and to look at her figures. Then she handed me a cashier's check for half of it. "If you refuse it," she said, "I will be put to the further trouble of opening an account and depositing it for you, a procedure it is time you learned to do for yourself. For this sum of money I buy the right never to hear from you again. I do not want to be called and told when you are sick or broke, and this amount of money should assure that you will, for some time at least, have no reason to call me."

Other than bitter, formal statements like these, Erika no longer spoke to me. Norman had already left for New York. Sophie and Father told me I could stay as long as I wanted, but I knew my presence made them awkward and Erika furious, so I left as quickly as I could. As I left she said something I have never understood. "Never mind. I have my revenge."

1926–1930

I put my clothes into the car and drove over Twin Peaks, then down Dolores Street, which became El Camino Real, the road cut by the Spanish conquerors over the old Indian trails, the only road in those days which ran down nearly the whole length of the state from San Francisco. I followed El Camino for three hours, stopping only for gas and food, a bag of apples and winter pears bought at a roadside stand.

Below San Jose I turned up into the rough roads of the Los Gatos hills and on to the Santa Cruz mountains. I wanted to see the redwood trees again. I had it in my mind that the reality I had touched was expressed most clearly by these living columns thrusting their top-sprouted leaves into bright light while their clustered height made a shadowy quiet of the ground where they had stood firmly rooted for centuries.

Fortunately we had had almost no rain yet, for the roads leading into the redwood forest were mostly gravel or dirt. The broad asphalt quickly narrowed to thin, winding dirt roads that climbed and climbed in narrow curves between deep, green chasms. At the summit I stopped to let the car cool off before beginning the descent through the deepest forests, which would eventually lead out to the ocean at Santa Cruz. I had seen no other car on the road, not one. In the summer, there would have been a few vacationers who did not take the train, but during the winter the mountains were virtually deserted, sometimes cut off from both inland San Jose and coastal Santa Cruz when the crude roads washed out in the rain.

It was dusk when I stopped at Felton, which was made up of a gas station combined with a bar and grocery store near a huge redwood-log restaurant (closed for the winter). It took a while to find the man who put gas in my car and looked at me curiously when I said I was driving on up to Boulder Creek. "All the resorts closed this time of year," he said. "Nobody up there."

The resorts were clusters of tiny wooden cabins, about two dozen to each group among the redwoods near the San Lorenzo River, which trickled gently down to the ocean during the summer but rose and roared gushing right up to the cabins during rainy winters. From June till September families rented a cabin for their two-week vacation, sitting under the redwoods, fishing and swimming in the river, playing games and dancing at night in the social hall that sometimes stood in a clearing around which the cabins were built.

I had seen them during our brief visits and had envied them this simple and unexciting respite from their working life.

"There's one place here," I told the man at the gas pump, "with a swinging bridge suspended over the river, where the banks are high, maybe fifty feet above the water in summer." He only shrugged. "Lot of those bridges built, washed out, built again. But there's nobody up there now," he repeated. "Except the Ankers down in the Garden of Eden." He nodded his head toward his right, away from the road to Boulder Creek. "They're the only ones left. Everyone else gone back to San Jose for the winter."

He pointed me south on a narrow road that curved into suddenly thick woods, telling me to watch for a sign about two miles in. I felt a rising thrill of familiarity as I wound slowly along the twisting road. Even before I saw the sign, I knew that this was the place where we had taken that ride years ago, when I had snapped a picture of Sophie and Father on the bridge that swung high over the river. When I saw the wooden sign GARDEN OF EDEN, crudely painted in white and nailed to the thick trunk of a redwood tree, I noticed that a smaller FOR SALE strip had been nailed diagonally across it.

I turned left onto an even narrower dirt road, hardly more than ruts between thick trees that scraped and brushed against the car, making raspy moaning sounds across the roof and clinging, dragging rushes of sound along the windows as I bumped up and down in well-worn ruts and holes. I let the wheels feel their way. There was nothing to do but follow this "road" wherever it led. I could not have turned back if I tried.

After less than a mile the road opened suddenly into a small clearing, where a large redwood log building stood, live trees rising through its roof into the darkening sky. This would be the social hall of the Garden of Eden Resort. All around were shadowy, tall trees. I could see a faint light coming from a small cabin, a lean-to attached to the big social hall. This must be where the Ankers lived. A dog had begun to bark, a light moved, and I saw a man standing outside the lean-to pointing a flashlight in my direction. I got out of the car and walked toward him.

"You lost? Car trouble? I got some gas here and a tire pump, but I can't help you. I got a bad back." I couldn't see his face clearly in the dark, but his voice sounded old, as did the woman's voice that called out, "Who is it, Simon?"

"My car's all right, but I'll get lost if I try to go further. Can I rent a place for the night?"

"We're closed for the winter."

"Just for the night, the nearest cabin."

"We don't provide bedding."

"I'll just wrap up in my cloak."

He hesitated. "You alone. Cost you three dollars," he declared, as if that fact would get rid of me for good.

I handed him three bills before he could change his mind, and he pointed to a cabin half-hidden behind a tree growing up through its front porch. I turned and walked to the cabin, climbed the few steps to its porch, opened the unlocked door. I was in a room barely large enough for a brass double bed covered with a moldy-smelling mattress. A doorway opened into a kitchen with a cast-iron stove, a table and two chairs, and a small sink. Beyond that, a thin door opened to a tiny cubicle containing a flush toilet, obviously a new addition. I was grateful to find it there and use it before stepping outside onto the porch, where I found a seat cut into the thick trunk of a live redwood tree.

I sat down and watched the stars come out over the tops of the great, dark trees, which seemed almost to reach up to touch them. Every branch was still. Now that the dog had stopped barking and the man had gone back into his lean-to quarters, everything was quiet. It was the quiet I had been looking for, the quiet where at last I could be alone and still with the new reality I had found, the reality to which I still talked, as though to a person, since I knew no other way. "Here we are," I whispered into the stillness, and an orgasmic ripple, like an echo of the experience on the beach, silenced me. I sat there all night. I was not cold. I found that by gathering memories of that day on the beach I could induce a flush of body heat that kept out the damp chill of night under the redwoods. That ability gradually left me too, but during that first winter I was able to switch it on like an electric heater.

The next morning, as soon as it was light enough to move about, I walked around the property, not straying far beyond the clearing. There were fifteen tiny cabins hidden among the trees, some of them built around a tree, all arranged so that looking from one cabin, I could not see any other. Each cabin had a little sign tacked over the door, giving its name. The cabins were named for birds: the Oriole, the Bluebird, the Chickadee, the Sparrow, the Robin, and so on. Behind the big social hall was a flat area of brush and tree stumps littered with old bed springs, rusty pipes, cracked barrels, and other trash. This open area ended abruptly at more tall redwoods which surrounded it. Following a faint sound, I walked to my left, across the clearing and back into the trees, where I found a narrow trail that led to the high bank of the river. I could see the swinging bridge only a few yards away.

I hurried along the bank to it, then walked out on the rotting planks, holding the ropes on either side of me. The bridge trembled, creaked, and swung from side to side. Halfway across it, I stood about thirty feet above a clear stream about twenty feet wide and no more than a foot deep. The stream twisted immediately out of sight. I could see no more than one hundred yards, but I knew this was a tributary of the San Lorenzo River, which eventually reached the Pacific Ocean. As I swung over the river on the rusty old iron cables and rotting wooden planks, I heard an improbable sound coming from the redwoods downstream. A train. I was not so cut off from the world as I imagined. Train tracks ran along the river down to Santa Cruz.

When I got back to the clearing, I found Simon Ankers outside chopping wood. Smoke was coming from the small chimney of the lean-to, and I could smell coffee. The dog gave only one short bark this time, then rushed up to me to be petted. It was a small black scotty, a breed common in those days.

"This is a beautiful place," I said. Ankers glanced at me, then gave a sharp swing of his axe, splitting a chunk of wood. "Such a huge area, a whole forest of your own!"

"Our place is only seven acres," he said. "Narrow strip from the swinging bridge up to the back of the Oriole. The rest is State Park. Can't expand, can't build more cabins, can't touch the trees, can't . . ." At that point I heard the thin voice of his wife calling, "Simon!" He turned and walked slowly into the lean-to. He moved as if he ached in every joint.

When he came back, he carried a cup of coffee which he handed to me. "My wife says have some coffee." He looked intently at my face as if just noticing it, then down at my legs, where my pajamas showed through an opening in my cloak. He was small and thin, with a red face and thin gray hair, almost white. Two or three days' growth of beard sprouted white from his creased cheeks. He picked up his axe and frowned as he split another chunk of wood.

164

"It must be lovely to be able to live here all year round," I tried again.

He kicked the piece of wood to one side. It flew to strike the wall of the social hall. "Yeah, great for redwoods. They live a thousand years on dirt and sun. Folks can't."

"I'd like to stay here for a while."

"We're closed in the winter. No one comes here in the winter."

"I'd like to rent a cabin, the one I stayed in, the . . . the Canary," I said, remembering the name I had seen over the door in the early light.

"We only rent to white people here. You a Jap?"

"I'm half-Chinese."

"Worse yet. White only here. I'd lose all my business if I let in non-white. Nothing personal."

I smiled, absolutely sure that I would get my way, that whatever I wanted must come to me. "There aren't any other whites here to see me. I'll rent just for the winter."

"I can't have a bunch of Chinamen moving in."

"I'm alone." I laughed. "I don't even know any Chinamen."

"This place is miserable in winter. Wait till the rain starts."

"There's a stove in the cabin."

"I'm not chopping firewood for you!"

"Is fifty dollars a month enough?"

He said nothing, and I took his silence to be agreement. Before he could change his mind, I turned to walk back toward my cabin. "Hey!" he called. When I turned, he said, "That one leaks like a sieve. Better put you in the Cuckoo." Then he turned and picked up another block of wood, muttering loudly enough to make sure I heard, "That's where she belongs, wanting to stay the winter." He gave a breathy wheeze I took to be his laugh, then repeated, "The Cuckoo, that's where she belongs," quite pleased with his joke.

So I settled into the Cuckoo of the Garden of Eden, an irony whose full depth I would not know for years, and Mr. Ankers could not begin to suspect at the time. His own life was crammed with as much irony as he could handle.

Originally from Canada, Simon and Miranda Ankers had lived in San Jose for over thirty years, where they had owned a small prune ranch, which was not quite enough to support them. Both of them worked in the canneries four months of the year in addition to caring for their own orchard: spraying, pruning, picking, drying.

They worked hard and lived simply; with any luck they would have managed.

But they had no luck, Simon Ankers told me over and over as he swung his axe down on blocks of wood. Miranda had spells of suicidal depression. She had been in and out of Agnews State Hospital for over twenty years. Yes, she had been in there when the big quake came and the building fell down, killing many patients. She had helped take care of the injured, had calmed the violent. They had sent as many patients as possible home, but she stayed for weeks after the quake because they needed her. The new hospital was built better, but it was still a hell. She had begged him not to send her there again.

Their only child had been "wrong" from birth, withdrawn like his mother in her worst spells and, unlike her, sometimes violent. It was something in the family. Her father had killed himself. So had her brother. Whatever money they had went to doctors, who were no help at all. The boy had died at Agnews when he was barely twenty, said to be a suicide. But his mother had seen how, during restraint of violent patients, accidents happened. She knew certain attendants were hardly less violent when provoked than the most violent patients.

His death in 1916 had caused one of her worst spells. Simon had managed to keep her home during that one, but the orchard had suffered neglect; he was afraid to leave her to tend the trees or work in the cannery. After that bad year, they never seemed to catch up again. To make matters worse, Simon had begun to suffer from arthritis and could no longer do the heavy lifting in the packing sheds. Miranda tried to go back in as a cutter, but was often too ill. She began to be afraid to handle knives, afraid of the conveyer belt, then afraid to leave the house at all. She often spent the whole day in bed.

Simon had tried to lift her spirits by taking her on the train ride through the redwood forests, alongside the river to the coast at Santa Cruz. The motion of the ride soothed her, and she loved the redwoods. That was how the idea came to them to sell their prune ranch and buy the Garden of Eden Resort. It seemed an ideal solution. The vacation season was only three months, from June to September, when Simon would simply check people in and out and make sure they didn't light fires in the wrong places. The rest of the year they could live quietly on the place, which would be good for Miranda, quiet, peaceful, and beautiful. When the owner accepted the amount they got for the prune ranch, they believed they had finally gotten lucky.

During their two years in The Garden of Eden, they learned how mistaken they had been. They had estimated their income on the basis of all cabins full for the three-month season. A vacancy at the high summer weekly rental rate was a serious loss, and, although the resort had a steady clientele, there occasionally were one or two cabins vacant. Taxes and repairs to the pretty but flimsy cabins cost more than expected, even with Simon doing all the work. He had to buy tools. His Model T truck was wearing out; it had just broken down again. He had been led to believe that he could rent trailer space in the logged-out clearing behind the social hall, but it turned out that there were numerous restrictions on the use of the land. Moreover, Simon was not a sociable man. Three months of vacationers, with all their children and dogs, were a terrible ordeal. For Miranda, the three-month season was intolerable. She hid in the lean-to and shuddered as the noise of dancing and singing reverberated through the walls of the social hall at night. She said it was like being back at Agnews.

Then winter came, heavy rains alternating with short periods of damp chill. Simon's arthritis flared up and Miranda's depressions fell on her like stones crushing her. Other resort owners and managers left during the winter, taking other jobs or going to their homes inland, where they lived on a pension. Simon and Miranda had no other home now and no other income. The Garden of Eden had become their prison. During their second winter the road had been impassable for three weeks. Now, going into their third winter, Simon was still trying to find work in Gilroy or Los Gatos, anywhere he and Miranda could stay through the winter.

I gave him three hundred dollars, six months rent in advance, suggesting that he might be able to use the money to get away for a month or two when the rains came. He tried to refuse the money. "You won't stay that long. Only a fool...I won't refund a penny if you change your mind!" So in the midst of his refusal he accepted me.

I spent the last two months of that year in a state of intoxication. I took walks, I sang or whistled, I sat alone in some little spot of sunlight between the trees, happy to be alone because I knew that from now on I was never alone, that I never really had been alone, that I was immortal and indestructible and loved and safe.

I sent the address of the gas station in Felton to Erika and Sophie in case they wanted to reach me. Erika retaliated by having all my mail forwarded, all the letters that continued to come to the radio station. George, the man at the gas station, looked at me curiously, but since no radio signal penetrated the mountains at that time, he had never heard of Madame Psyche and read the name on the envelopes as "Mez Pish," when I picked up the mail.

I opened all the letters, sent back any money they contained, but read no letters unless they were addressed to me by my real name. In the whole great pile of December and January letters, there were few to read. Sophie sent a Christmas card. Stephanie's usual monthly letter came. There was a letter from Miss Harrington, who heard that I left the radio show, questioned Sophie at her flower stand, then wrote to congratulate me. Mrs. Robertson, in whose mansion I had lived in 1913, also wrote to me. She had just returned from South America, where her husband had held an ambassadorship until dying suddenly of a heart attack. The most surprising letter came from Guido Altieri, the man I had met on board ship. He had finally arrived in San Francisco. He congratulated me on becoming an honest woman. Like Miss Harrington he said, "I could see you had it in you to do something better. *Corragio!*" In my replies to these letters I did not mention the experience on the beach, but my prose was, nevertheless, extravagant. I wrote that I had rediscovered a place I had visited when very young, a place which lived up to its name, the Garden of Eden. I described the giant redwoods and said I hoped to live a better life among them.

In January, after a full two weeks of heavy, incessant rain, Simon Ankers decided to take Miranda to Gilroy and use the money I had paid them to rent a room in a boarding house for the winter. I offered to drive them in my car; Simon agreed. "Danged Model T probably wouldn't make it over the summit."

I saw Miranda for the first time when she came out to get into my car. She was pale, tiny, thin, like a child with the face of a haggard woman. Her hair was dyed deep black, which made her frightened old-child face look even more pale and lined. She smiled sweetly at me, and her fear flickered out for a moment before flashing on again in her eyes, on her twitching lips. She never spoke during our drive, never looked out the car window. After leaving her and Simon in Gilroy, I returned to the mountains with enough rice, dried fruit, and canned goods to last me another two months.

The rain stopped, and the rest of the winter was unusually dry, with cold nights, dewy morning mists, and hard, bright afternoon sun cutting through the tall trees to reach patches of ground for only about four hours a day. I set a chair in an open spot behind the social hall where I could sit in the afternoon sun. In the cold mornings I hiked miles along the river bank or up and down the wooded hills, wearing out my shoes in the first week. George sold me some boots for a dollar, a pair his son had outgrown. At night I made a fire in the cast iron stove, lit the kerosene lamp, and wrote letters which speculated on how perfect life in the Garden of Eden would be if shared with a community of congenial souls.

Guido Altieri answered enthusiastically, saying he would come to see my Eden as soon as he was fired from his present job, which should be soon, as he was trying to organize a union. He showed up in February, walking out of the forest from the railroad track, where he had hitched a ride on the freight train that kept a winter schedule, chugging through twice a week. He was wearing the same suit he had worn on shipboard four years ago. His wild hair was a bit more gray, but his wonderful smile was the same, wide as his eyes, anticipating something new and wonderful. I was sitting in the clearing behind the social hall, taking my afternoon sun, when he appeared. "You found me without any trouble?"

He nodded. "You described it so well, with such love. When I saw the swinging bridge, I jumped. The train ambles so slowly through here—and I am used to jumping on and off trains." He looked around the clearing, then said, "Of course, all these stumps must come out before we can plant vegetables."

That afternoon he silently followed me as I showed him around the place. He looked into every cabin. He paced the length and width of the social hall, a wooden platform about four feet off the ground. In the center was a huge fireplace, built into a redwood stump at least six feet in diameter. Sprouting up through the floor were seven fairly young redwoods, less than a century old. The walls and roof, Guido said, had been added later, enclosing what must have been an open dance floor. "See where it leaks all down the trees, but with some caulking here and there it could be a little less damp in winter."

That night we ate rice and beans for dinner with dried apricots for dessert. We sat up by a kerosene lamp talking, till Guido yawned, got up, and marched off to choose a cabin for the night. "Have you no eagle cabin here? Only small birds? Very well, I shall rest in the nest of the Sparrow, the least of the creatures of the earth.''

Each morning Guido hiked with me. In the afternoon we dozed in the sunny clearing, and at night we sat up and talked. By the end of the week we were talking as if we had always had plans for a community here. With two or three to a cabin, there was space for at least fifty people. Decisions would be made democratically at meetings in the social hall, which would also be a school, a concert hall, a theater, a place for recreation of all kinds. We could grow our food in the sunny clearing behind the social hall. In the beginning we might have to ask people to contribute some money, but after a year or two we would surely be self-sufficient, making a little cash on outside jobs, all of which would go to the community. Guido, for instance, could repair autos for our neighbors or vacationers. Other members of the community would contribute a few weeks of skilled labor to earn cash for taxes. Everyone would work, and would share according to needs, which would be few in this simple setting. The housing was already here. We could keep goats for milk. "They eat anything," Guido exclaimed. By the end of the week we were arguing over what kind of education to provide for children born to the community.

When it was time for Guido to go back to San Francisco, I walked through the trees to the tracks and waited with him for the slow freight. As he waved good-bye he shouted over the puffing of the engine, "Remember, all you need do is acquire the land, and plenty of people will want to come."

From then on my letters were full of plans for a new way of living. I invited all my correspondents except Stephanie, though I kept her informed of my plans. Miss Harrington replied with cautious interest in seeing the place when and if I should somehow acquire it. Mrs. Robertson wrote a six-page letter, enthusiastically offering to come, to contribute, to do "everything to help your brave and true venture," but her letters disturbed me because she made references to spiritualism as a guide to communal living, despite my insistence that I had no occult powers. Perhaps I should have confessed to her at that point that my mediumship had always been false. But that seemed unnecessarily cruel. At the time it seemed best to let her assume, as Sophie did, that I had lost my occult powers.

In early March I drove to Gilroy to pick up more supplies. But first I went to the boarding house where Simon and Miranda Ankers were living. Simon had found work as a handyman at a nearby winery. The landlady took me up to their room where, she said, "Mrs. Ankers will be in. She's always in." I knocked on the door and the landlady called, "You have a visitor," then turned and went back down the stairs. After a long silence, the door opened a crack, and Miranda Ankers looked at me with frightened eyes. After recognizing me, she slowly opened the door just wide enough to let me in.

It was a tiny room with a high ceiling peeling in tan strips. Wallpaper full of blooming orange poppies and hovering bluebirds seemed to close in on the room. But Miranda had managed to squeeze an arm chair into the space between the bed and the wall, beside a window where the sun shone brightly. There was a board, crayons, pens. Papers were strewn all over the wooden floor.

Miranda was writing a book for children. It was the story of a snail brought against its will to the New World, a shy, frightened creature, despised as ugly and repellent, hiding in its shell. It discovers that it has been imported in order to be ripped from its shell, grilled, and eaten. It cannot run from its captors, can only withdraw inward waiting for its shell to be broken and its soft, exposed body devoured. But it is saved by its own ugliness. No one wants to eat the snail. The men responsible for bringing it abandon it. It is free, ignored, left to produce many, many snails who eat whatever is grown by men.

The drawings were lovely whirls of shells. When heads did poke out, they invariably had dark, frightened eyes like Miranda's. I was impressed that the story was not only whimsical and adventurous but, as Miranda explained to me, accurate historically, recounting the importing of snails to California.

Miranda looked almost happy that day. She was used to their room. It was cozy and quiet, and she felt safe sitting in the sun behind a window. The landlady even let Simon bring her dinner upstairs so she didn't have to sit at the table with other people. She dreaded going back to the Garden of Eden. When she spoke of it, her face became tense and haunted. She was convinced that one of "those giants" would fall and crush her. Seeing me made her cry, reminded her that she would soon have to go back. "Maybe not," I said as I left her to find Simon.

I found him washing gallon jugs in a stone outbuilding of a winery half a mile from the boarding house. After his initial shock at my question, he told me he had paid forty thousand for the Garden of Eden and had put another four thousand into improvements. He would be happy to get his money back and get out. I offered him nearly all I had, about nine thousand, as a downpayment if he would carry the loan—I was sure no bank would lend money to me. "Get a lawyer to draw up papers on the terms of the sale, and I'll be back in two weeks to give you the money and sign the papers." We shook hands on it, and I went back to the Garden of Eden, laden with a sack of raisins Simon insisted on giving me (a by-product of the winery) and the provisions I bought at the store in town.

In lengthening days of the next two weeks, I kept a delicious solitude and silence, not even opening the mail I picked up only so that George would know I was alive and well. I was back in an intoxicated state of bliss, like the first moment on the beach, as I walked around what I was sure would soon be my heaven of redwoods, my Garden of Eden. Of course, we would keep the name.

On April second I drove back to Gilroy to sign the contract, hardly glancing at it in my excitement.

I wrote to Guido, to Mrs. Robertson, to Miss Harrington, telling them I had bought the Garden of Eden and that they and anyone else who wanted to come could help me build a new way of life. I even put an ad in the *Examiner* inviting "all who want to work and share in creating a new way of life" to join us. They could write me for a map. Simon Ankers came to collect belongings he and Miranda had left in the lean-to. He left behind the Model T and some tools included in our deal.

Within a few days Guido arrived in a huge hired truck, carrying his tailor's sewing machine, his automotive tools, his clothes, and a trombone. Also packed into the truck with their belongings were seven people Guido had persuaded to come with him, telling them to bring plain clothes and linens, tools, and "instruments of creativity," like his trombone. There were several musical instruments unloaded and another sewing machine. But there were also some household goods unlikely to be useful, or even to survive in the rough, often damp cabins—a tiny antique writing desk, a silver tea service, a radio, useless in the mountains at that time. Their owners laughed as they carried these items to cabins, admitting they simply could not give them up.

I happily walked around watching the unpacking, not thinking about the fact that when it was done, there would be ten very hungry people to feed. When they finally finished, it took a couple of hours to get a good fire going in the social hall, find a large pot, combine the right proportions of rice and water, cook it, add cans of beans to warm up in the rice—while everyone waited, plates and spoons in hands, shivering in the early evening chill.

It would have taken much longer if I had not been helped and instructed by Edward, who had also driven the truck. Edward was a fairly tall man with sandy blonde hair (later a beard which came in spiky red) and a fair, thin skin covered from head to toe (as I learned later during swims in the river) with freckles. He was about twenty-five, and, as he told us after dinner when we sat on social hall benches introducing ourselves, he had grown up in an orphanage where he had learned to cook large quantities of plain food. He had worked as a cowboy, had panned for gold, had served in the army. He and Guido had met at the auto shop where they all expected to be laid off next week, so Edward had decided to try group life again.

"Well, this won't be like the army or the orphanage," I promised.

"No, Ma'am," he answered shyly and blushed. I soon learned that he blushed whenever a woman spoke to him or even looked at him.

The third single man in Guido's group was Jack, a deep-brown Negro, the tallest man I have ever known. Jack was large-boned and thin, not skeletal, yet I was always conscious of his massive skeleton as he moved, slowly but not lazily, rather as if every movement was thought through and directed by his ever-alert brain. Jack had been part-time janitor at the auto shop where Guido and Edward worked, the best job he could get in San Francisco, where a Negro could check into the Palace Hotel with no trouble, but could seldom find work except as a domestic servant. Jack and Guido had become friends because they were the only two in the shop who read and talked about books.

Jack introduced himself as a poet. To celebrate our coming together at the Garden of Eden he had written a poem which he read aloud to us as he sipped from the jug of wine he had contributed to our dinner. It was a very tight, compressed poem which I found hard to follow, full of words I did not understand, and allusions to authors I had not read. His voice sounded strange. His accent was not the southern one of most Negroes, nor the clear, unaccented coastal speech of Norman. Jack's accent seemed to have been invented and imposed over his original speech. It was terribly precise, hard-edged, full of broad a's, like the accent Karl had sometimes affected when he entertained us with Gilbert and Sullivan.

The other people Guido brought were two married couples who had been members of a reading group with Guido. This group had grown out of the leftovers of old "Bellamy Clubs," groups of people interested in utopian ideals and literature. Orin and Jean were the older couple. Orin was a retired army officer, and Jean was a nurse. The second, younger couple, Paul and Ralda, were happy to hear of Jean's occupation because they were soon to have their second child.

Their first was a four-year-old boy so fair that his hair was almost white, his skin pale and soft. With his blue eyes and quiet attention, he had that angelic look some boys hold for a few years before it is suddenly invaded by manhood. His delicacy came partly from his having barely survived what doctors now call an allergy crisis. He had nearly died before someone had dared to withdraw the sacred food of American children—cow's milk. He was eager to "go fishing and never have to go to school." When his parents looked at him, laughing with the rest of us, the fear still haunted their eyes. Jean called him an angel, and the name stuck.

Angel's mother was barely twenty years old. She had given birth to him at sixteen. She was thin, with soft brown hair long enough to sit on. When she introduced herself, she spoke at length about her great hopes for our community. Her voice was soft, the kind which swallows words back into the throat and which seems to get softer as listeners lean forward almost holding their breath to hear. This was a trick that I had sometimes used in seances, but in Ralda's case I believe it was done unconsciously out of shyness and poor hearing. She explained that they had been hunting for over a year for a community, a better place to raise their children.

Paul was no older than Ralda. He wore his dark hair to his shoulders and had let his beard grow thick and black. Both he and Ralda wore rough-woven clothes they had bought on a trip to Mexico. They looked strange. Jean used the word "Bohemian" to describe them. Today perhaps they would be called "Beat." Every few years the name changes, but I suppose the non-conforming young arise in fairly constant numbers. The difference between this couple and the other non-conformists of those years was that Paul and Ralda's rebellion had nothing to do with illegal alcohol, fast cars, or literary pilgrimages to Europe. Paul said they wanted to help form a new kind of human being, starting with their own children.

It was time for me to introduce myself. Everyone there knew about Madame Psyche. I told them that my entire career, now ended, had been based on trickery. Everyone seemed to be waiting for me to go on, to tell why I had come here. I hesitated, searching for words that would explain the experience which had changed my life. But I found no words, so I said I had put a down payment on the land, that I wanted to live a simple, quiet life based on loving and sharing, and that anyone who wanted to join me was welcome. "We will all live and work and learn together," I said.

"From each according to his ability," said Guido.

"To each according to his need," answered Jack, cutting the air with his sharp consonants.

Jean frowned, Orin smiled, and we all ducked as a small bat suddenly swooped down from the ceiling and glided across the room. We never did manage to clear all the bats from the upper rafters of the social hall where they came on cold nights when the higher branches of the redwoods were covered with frost.

The next morning at dawn I awoke to loud blows and shouted curses. "Cock-sucking son of a bitch!" Crash. "Motherfucker!" Crash. "Bastard!" Crash. I rushed out of my cabin expecting to see a murder in progress, but it was only Edward behind the social hall already at work chopping and digging out stumps. For all his shyness, he swore constantly and joyfully while working, and never censored his speech in the presence of women or children. The oaths burst from him like healthy sweat.

Angel soon joined him, digging with a small shovel around the roots. His parents slept while Jean and I made breakfast over an open fire, and Guido, Orin, and Jack sat in a shaft of sunlight in front of the social hall arguing about whether there would be assigned work or if all tasks should be taken up voluntarily.

After breakfast we named things that needed to be done and let people volunteer to do them. That morning everyone volunteered to do more than each could, but at the end of the day, when we reported our progress after dinner, we had accomplished a great deal. Those two daily meetings—for planning and for reporting results—became a regular part of our life at the Garden of Eden, as did the two meals a day which accompanied them. After dinner that first night, Ralda took out a flute and began to play. That also set a pattern. From then on we had some kind of entertainment every night for at least an hour before going back to our separate cabins.

Three more women arrived at the end of the week, two whom I knew and one stranger. The stranger was Gertrude, who had seen my ad in the paper and had written me a letter accusing me of "abandoning your occult fraud in order to make fools of people in another way." I had written back telling her that I had been a fraud but hoped I no longer was. She came, she said, to see for herself, and she stayed.

Gertrude was an extraordinary woman. Only twenty, the daughter of a poor French family in Oakland, she had already completed her BA at the University of California, working her way through as a live-in maid in the homes of her professors. She was beautiful, with thick dark hair and blue eyes which drooped a little at the corners, as if her great effort had made her permanently tired.

The next to arrive was Mrs. Robertson, who hoped to find the security she had lost with the death of her husband and the peace that had eluded her throughout the years when she had attended my seances. She was in her sixties now and seemed more physically robust than she had been during the years when she brooded over the death of Ned and kept me as her resident psychic. She immediately asked when we would have a seance, and I immediately responded, "Never," but she smiled as if she did not believe me. I found her presence disquieting, but could not stop her from joining our community, especially when I remembered how long I had lived on her misplaced generosity.

Finally came Miss Harrington, Elva Harrington—I had not used her first name before. She arrived with one small bag. "A few books will come by parcel post. Am I too old for your foolhardy experiment? The Kaweah Colony died upon my arrival thirty-five years ago. I hope I won't jinx this effort!" She was in her late seventies, "on borrowed time, past my biblical allotment of years," thinner than ever, but erect and firm except for a slight tremor, an almost imperceptible wobble of her head when she sat listening and watching intently during our evening meeting on the day of her arrival. To Angel and his pregnant mother she said, "I might still be a pretty good teacher. I thought I'd be dead by now, but since I'm going to live a bit longer, I'd like to do something interesting with the time. 'Made weak by time and fate, but strong in will, To strive, to seek, to find, and not to yield.' "

"Tennyson," said Jack.

Elva Harrington looked up at him. "Another teacher?"

"No, rather a scholar," said Jack. His broad "a" sounded like "rah-ah-ther." He began to name the universities and colleges he had attended, though never as a registered student. He had worked as a janitor in a dozen institutions, auditing classes during his off hours, "defeating the caucasian conspiracy to withhold education from me."

A guilty, sympathetic silence was broken by Gertrude. "From the amount of work you did here last week, I'd suspect you spent some of your on-duty hours sitting in classes too." He glared at her, but she only glared back.

Miss Harrington turned to Angel and asked, "Just what work is being done, and who is doing it?"

Angel looked around the room. "Edward digs god-damned stumps." His parents winced. "Guido is making a kitchen here in the social hall. All us men help Edward and Guido. Mom cooks, and May helps her. Gertrude can do everything. Jean just sits or drives around, and this lady doesn't do anything either." He pointed to Mrs. Robertson.

I hastily explained that Jean kept our financial accounts and drove out for supplies, and that Mrs. Robertson was paying for supplies until Guido and Edward found some paid work.

"That reminds me," said Elva Harrington. "I have a small pension, a monthly check which I'll sign over to you each month. That should help." She pulled a check out of her purse and handed it to me. "Now, I don't know about the rest of you, but I go to bed early. Assign me a cabin."

The next morning Angel's parents came to see me and handed me a check. They had been shamed by Miss Harrington into telling me that they were not so poor as their rough gypsy clothes made them seem. In fact they both came from wealthy New York families.

Ralda's parents were divorced. Ralda had been educated in progressive schools in Europe as well as in New York. Her father was a famous violinist, and a great many well-known artists were people she had grown up calling Uncle Giuliano or Aunt Kirsten. Ralda herself had been a prodigy, reading at two, playing the piano at four, exhibiting water colors at seven.

Paul's family was more conservative, Episcopalian, frowning on divorce and contraception (he had six brothers and two sisters). He had been rigorously tutored, then sent to boarding school at ten. He, too, was a brilliant student, had been put ahead twice, had completed high school at fifteen. He had been about to enter Harvard when he and Ralda met at a Sunday afternoon jazz session in the apartment of a famous author. Both Paul and Ralda had been brought by their parents, who believed they would benefit culturally from the experience, and were appalled by the result. "Instant pregnancy," smiled Paul. There were "solutions," but the young couple chose marriage and a nomadic existence which stopped in San Francisco with Angel's illness and Ralda's second pregnancy. "We'd almost given up, but now we think we've found what we're looking for," Ralda concluded. "From now on we'll throw in part of our allowance too." She handed me a check far larger than Miss Harrington's pension. I passed it on to Jean.

Four days later we ran out of coffee, and at our evening meeting, Gertrude proposed that we buy no more. She cited the expense, the temptation to sit idle over a cup of coffee, the health effects, which she explained with medical references. "Even if it had no bad effects, we should give it up, just as we've given up meat, because it's not necessary, and we have more important things to do with our money. Giving up one bad thing leads to giving up others. Without the coffee, we can skip sugar too."

Jack, our biggest coffee drinker since running out of his wine, snorted, then drawled, "Too, too convincing and characteristically puritannical. Gertrude will end up either a college professor or a minister."

"Not likely," retorted Gertrude, "both being closed to women. Negro men have no monopoly on frustration." They were glaring at each other again.

"Well, with both beauty and brains," said Orin, trying to mollify her (everyone knew by this time it was impossible to mollify Jack) "you'll make a grand wife for a university professor."

Gertrude turned her glare on Orin. "They are the worst, as I learned working in their kitchens. I don't intend to spend my life baking cookies for faculty teas. Which brings up another point. It's not fair for the women to always do all the cooking and cleaning up." It was becoming clear that while Gertrude made a point of facing up to Jack (as the rest of us never could), she really did not like any of the men. Her anger had roots in a reality the rest of us did not admit. Since gaining the vote five years before, women were assumed "equal," and any talk to the contrary was considered quaint or tiresome. Gertrude's reminder of the truth was heard but ignored as childish or shrewish. As if to pacify her, rather than admit the justice of her complaint, we agreed on a compromise. Women would continue to do the cooking, but everyone was responsible for cleaning up afterward. Even Gertrude agreed that the only man capable of cooking—Edward—did more than his share outdoors and could not be spared for work in the kitchen.

The following week was a grumpy one. Some of us had headaches; others were listless, depressed, irritable. Gertrude explained that these caffeine withdrawal symptoms would last only a few days, after which we would feel better than ever. She was right. I remember an evening a week later, just after Miss Harrington's eight boxes of books arrived. She and Gertrude and Jack, smiling in complete harmony, rummaged through the books while Guido showed Ralda and Paul some fine points of tailoring and Edward carved little wooden figures for Angel. Orin read aloud from some utopian tract while Jean worked on the accounts and Mrs. Robertson mended her stockings. There were many evenings like this during that first spring, quiet with drowsy companionability after the day's work.

It was Gertrude again who declared our drowsy evenings a detour, "delaying decisions that must be made." At what became a very long evening meeting she said we were making a great mistake in putting off discussion and agreement on a set of principles to guide our community. The first thing we needed was a voting procedure, a process by which to agree on other policies. Guido replied that voting was devisive, that all decisions should be made by consensus as the Quakers did.

"What?" said Jean. "You mean we can't even agree to vote on voting?"

"I had enough rules in the army," said Orin, while Jean flashed an impatient look at him, but said nothing.

Ralda and Paul said probably rules and policy should grow out of situations as they arose.

"By then it's too late," insisted Gertrude.

"I agree," said Miss Harrington.

Edward nodded, but as usual said nothing.

Jack withdrew to a corner, saying he had a poem coming and must not "drown inspiration in pointless discussion."

Mrs. Robertson turned to me, saying I could find answers to all problems with my psychic powers.

"I cannot!" I insisted. But then I added that our totally new experiment must be given a chance to create totally new questions and answers growing out of each other. I really did believe at the time that no serious problem would arise unaccompanied by a solution.

And so, sitting between the apprehensive frowns of Elva Harrington and Gertrude, we put off planning and began to let things happen. We had, in a sense, declared thought unnecessary.

Some thought of the contract I had signed would at least have prepared us for the arrival in July of vacationers who had booked cabins the previous year. When the first family drove in with their four children and large dog, Mrs. Robertson told them they had made a mistake. There was no mistake, they replied. They had been coming to the Garden of Eden for the first two weeks in July since the first cabins were built, "back before the war." They had made their reservations as usual when they left last year, with a deposit, and here was the rest of the money. They would take the Cuckoo as usual. It was easy enough for me to move out of the Cuckoo and into Elva Harrington's cabin for a while.

Throughout the rest of that summer, people with reservations arrived, probably three dozen families in all. By doubling up we were able to accommodate them in the cabins of their choice. These were respectable working class people with well-behaved children, just able to afford an annual two weeks in the mountains, doing their own cooking, enjoying simple pleasures like fishing and hiking. Some of them brought home made wine and beer, legal in those years of Prohibition, and no one drank to excess. In the social hall they found the boxes of Bingo cards and games behind the fireplace, where they had stored them last year. Someone was always able to play an accordian for singing and dancing.

These people had a wonderful collection of lore about the Garden of Eden. It had been operated as a resort by various eccentrics, one wildly alcoholic, another politically radical, one stingy and mean, another a cat lover whose scores of pets, gone wild, had had to be hunted down and shot after the pack had attacked a child. There were stories of huge fish caught in the river, of hilarious falls from the swinging bridge (when the water was luckily high enough to break a fall), and of the ghost of the social hall.

180

Unfortunately, Mrs. Robertson was there when the ghost was mentioned. She suggested that I should bring it back and find out who it was. I took her aside and begged her never to mention my previous life, but it was too late. Some of the people there had heard Madame Psyche on the radio and realized who I was. No one asked me to call up any ghosts, but there was a definite change in the way they looked at me.

There were other ways in which their presence changed the place, diluted the unity we were trying to build. Some of the men pitched in to dig out stumps, just for the fun of the group work, but most of them, of course, were there for a rest. (Their wives worked as hard as ever, cooking and caring for the children.) Their mood, even their pleasantries, their friendly questions about our plans for the place, interrupted the work. Edward went on digging stumps without ceasing, but often Guido and Orin would sit with a group of men whose questions had set off a lecture on the search for community and the good life.

The most difficult disruptions were little things, like wine, which they offered freely to us. Guido found it hard to refuse a glass of wine. "We should refuse because we cannot offer anything in return. But to refuse a glass of wine is almost an insult!" Worse than the wine for most of us was the smell of coffee brewing in the morning, and the smell of steaks on barbecue grills at night. Our simple diet was adequate but hard to maintain cheerfully when our nostrils were filled with old satisfactions. Angel's parents were upset that the other children gave him candy, and their parents were upset that we did not keep candy for sale on the place.

Miss Harrington and Mrs. Robertson held story hours for the children (during one week there were twenty-eight attending) and Gertrude took them on long, strenuous hikes, which kept them out of the way as we tried to get on with repairs. Jean set up a small store, since vacationers were accustomed to having milk and bread supplied on the place. Only Jack withdrew and brooded, and I could not blame him.

For all their good qualities, these people were very prejudiced against Negroes, and when they realized that Jack was not a servant but an equal member of this odd community, they showed their disapproval, mainly by passing rumors. Children told Miss Harrington that their parents intended to leave or to refuse to use the social hall or to swim downstream in the river—since plates Jack had eaten from were washed in the river—and so on. They never took any of these actions, but continued to buzz and rumble with hostile threats.

Jack retaliated by scandalizing them further. He waited until quite a few were out in the clearing after dinner, tossing horse shoes and visiting in the waning sunshine. Then he walked deliberately over to where Angel and his pregnant mother happened to be standing, her long hair hanging forward over her face as she bent to say something to Angel. As she straightened up and smiled at Jack, he put his arm around her and stood talking to her and Angel. They stood this way for no more than two minutes, but in those two minutes a deadly chill fell over the scene, a silence in which everyone went on doing what they were doing, but all action lost meaning, vibrating with outrage. I heard a door slam as one of the vacationers turned and went into her cabin, her children with her, as if to protect them from the sight of something unspeakable. Then Edward, bless him, appeared with a tool in his hand and asked Jack to come and help him.

"He didn't have to provoke them," said Orin at our next meeting.

"Possibly I provoke certain other people," retorted Jack, pronouncing the *p*'s of these words like little spitting explosions. No one answered him. The truth was that some in our community felt uncomfortable at the sight of Jack touching a white woman.

It was Gertrude who finally spoke, for once in support of Jack. "He only exposed bigotry, which is indefensible," she said flatly, "and contagious." The real lesson of this incident, she said, was that we must find ways for us to spend more time apart from the vacationers to protect ourselves from regression to their values.

Gertrude had found a sunny but isolated section of the river where we women could bathe and sun ourselves in privacy. Past a shallow bend in the river and beyond a clump of rocks topped by fallen logs was a deep pool for those who could dive and swim several strokes to rocks on the opposite bank. Thick brush and tall trees lined the banks. On warm days when we could spare an hour from work, we walked down there, took off our clothes, bathed, then lay on the rocks in the sun.

It was in one of those warm, lazy hours that Jean told us about Orin and herself. He had joined the army at seventeen, had risen in the ranks, been sent to officers' training school, and during the Great War had attained the rank of captain. He had come back from the war, his first taste of actual combat, a confirmed pacifist. He had seven years to go before retirement and no way to earn a living outside. Ostrasized for his outspoken anti-war views, broken to the rank of lieutenant and assigned to a routine job in supply, he spent the years reading history, trying to understand why men made war and how they could be stopped. He had not found final answers, but he kept searching, his search mostly taking the form of arguments in which he told, again and again, with sickening detail, what it was like to be under gas attack.

He was still under forty when he retired with a small pension. It was hard to imagine how he had ever chosen a military career. A loose, broad man with thick, coarse black hair inherited from his grandfather, a full-blooded Navaho, he was a mixture of warm affection and incredulous impatience. Crying easily, he swung from high expectation to deep disappointment, then back to euphoric hope again.

Jean was his opposite, an even-tempered, controlled woman, tall and blond and orderly, with hair smoothed back in waves from which wisps never strayed. She wore neatly buttoned dresses that wrinkled less than other people's, and spoke in cool, controlled tones, her lips hardly moving. She was the daughter of a widowed school teacher who had struggled to get a good education for her. Jean had graduated from a mid-western university and had been accepted into medical school. Then her mother suddenly died, leaving two smaller children. Jean left medical school, became a nurse, and took over the support of her family. She had met Orin, who was six years older than she, during the war and had married him.

During the ten years since the war she had lived on army posts with him, hating their life as much as he did. The other officers' wives treated her with malice, were twice as hard on her for her husband's pacifist talk as their husbands were on Orin. Shifted around constantly from one uncomfortable post to another, Jean had found it impossible to work and unwise to start a family. But she had been staunchly loyal to Orin, whom she saw as a man of great passion and vision accidentally put down in the wrong place at the wrong time. Everything would change, she told herself, when he retired. Still in her early thirties, she would be able to have children as well as help Orin find a good place, perhaps start a business.

A few months after his retirement, Orin announced that they were going to the Garden of Eden with Guido. It would be best to defer having children. For how long? "Orin doesn't say. He hasn't consulted me on any of the choices he's made for us lately." Her voice remained quite cool as she made this indictment of her husband. She might have been reporting the latest figures in her account-keeping.

"Oh, but you're perfect here," said Ralda, who was sunning her huge belly as if the baby inside would benefit. "You and Edward."

Jean stood up and put her clothes on, quickly buttoning her neat dress as she said, "Yes, useful, I know. I try to be. But that does not change the fact that this is not the place where I want to be."

"And therefore," said Gertrude, in her relentlessly probing way, "recognizing Orin's 'passion and vision' is no longer enough?"

Jean turned without answering and climbed up the bank. I wanted to forget what she said, wanted to believe that she was beginning to love our life here, and so I did forget and believe for as long as I could.

Since vacationers filled the social hall every night, we took our meetings out into the clearing behind the hall, where we sat in a circle on tree stumps, the moon lighting our dozen faces as we discussed our daily routine, our plans, and what to do about the vacationers, who seemed to disrupt both. None of them openly protested my ownership of the land or our plans to turn it to another use than as a vacation resort. They all spoke of this vacation as their last one at the Garden of Eden. But our community did not hold private ownership so sacred. Buying the land had only been a necessary expedient in starting our commune. "Some of these people," said Miss Harrington, "have been coming here since they were children, and now they are bringing their children."

"Their time is past," Jack said, in clipped tones.

"We can use the money they bring," said Jean, whose milk and egg business actually showed a small profit.

Angel said he liked having other children come. But his parents disapproved; Angel had picked up some language and attitudes from these children which were not in keeping with our ideals. Guido felt that we might continue to take vacationers who would fit into our way of life, though our way was far from being defined, Gertrude pointed out, since we had refused her suggestion to define our principles. To Jack's statement that he hadn't joined our group in order to expose himself to racist visitors, Orin replied that it had done some of them good to have to be polite to Jack, and that was part of changing the world to make it safe for our way of life. Edward said nothing, as usual, except to mention that he needed a new axe handle. Mrs. Robertson suggested that I should go into a trance and try to get an answer from the other world.

Finally we agreed that we would take no new vacationers, but those accustomed to coming here every year could keep coming, either paying rent as always, or joining in the work of the community during their stay. Our discussion had taken three hours.

I had continued writing to Stephanie, giving her full reports on the progress of our life among the redwoods. That fall she wrote that her husband, long bedridden with gradual breakdown of his damaged body, had died. She was set free from what had become (she admitted in her letters) an empty sacrifice. But set free for what? There were no men of her generation to marry even had she wanted to, which she did not. She was not rich enough to restore and maintain "Bane Hall" as a residence even if she wanted to, which she did not. The property had come to her, now nearly empty of war veterans, "an albatross round my neck, my House of Usher, may it crumble." She would hate an idle life, yet the only work she knew was nursing. "And I'm sick of sickness, of pain and death. I must begin to paint again, but can't seem to start. I'm like a dancer in a bloody graveyard, all motion paralyzed."

My suggestion was one I never expected her to take seriously— come to our Garden of Eden and make a fresh start. To my surprise she booked passage on a ship taking the South Atlantic route, coming through the Panama Canal and up the West Coast.

Her ship docked in San Francisco on September 20. On that day I rose at four in the morning to drive up to meet her, a trip of three to four hours in those days, if I was lucky and the car did not break down on the way. I was lucky, but the ship docked early and the passengers were already coming down the gangplank when I arrived.

I did not recognize Stephanie until she called and came toward me. The golden, rosy girl of 1914 had been long gone, of course, but so was the wraithlike, grieving nurse of the war years. Just over thirty, like me, Stephanie looked older. Her hair was streaked with gray and she still wore it long, against the fashion of the twenties, yet not pinned up in the pre-war style either. It was drawn back from her face and fastened with a clip at the nape of her neck, from which it hung to her waist. She was dressed in heavy English clothes, but again, there was nothing traditional about them. She wore a wine-colored felt skirt, full and long, with a baggy tweed jacket and a long, multicolored knit scarf that circled her neck, then hung down like her hair, both in back and in front. On her feet were soft boots that she had had specially made. They reminded me of elfin boots from fairy tales; probably they were, aside from my sandals, the most comfortable shoes any woman dared to wear in those days.

Fashion in women's clothing is strict, and women who ignore fashion are either pitied, ignored, or stared at with suspicious fascination. Stephanie's deviation was the kind that evokes stares. Furthermore, she had gained over twenty pounds since I last saw her. She had a solid, sturdy look that, along with her clothes, said quite clearly that she did not care what people thought of her. We must have made an odd-looking pair walking arm in arm away from the dock, I in my cape and muslin pajamas, Stephanie with hair, scarf, skirt flowing out from her in the sharp wind.

During the long drive south Stephanie talked constantly about each thing that caught her eye. As soon as we were out of the City, driving along the marshes and salt flats of the Bayshore, she asked about the tides, the birds. She groaned at the sight of the dry, brown hills, which I assured her would turn green with the first rain. As we went on, passing the miles of fruit orchards, she demanded the name of every crop, and at one point she laughed, "Well, of course, it's Italy, isn't it?" She laughed often as she talked, not in the mischievous, light, pre-war giggle which had long ago left her, but in a full, deep series of coughs, like a warm, funny refrain at the end of a verse. Like her added weight and her arresting dress, it was a decisive and decided laugh—a choice she had made.

When we turned at Los Gatos and began the ascent into the first redwoods, she fell silent. There was nothing like this in Italy or anywhere else in Europe. For the full hour along winding roads to the summit of the Santa Cruz mountains, she and I gave the redwood forest the proper tribute of silence. As we began the descent toward the west, winding through thickening groves, I told her something about what we had accomplished so far, what we hoped to have done by spring, when we could begin to plant our own food. She listened until I finished with, "Any questions? Well, you'll see when we get there. Won't be long now."

"You've changed," she said. I could feel her watching me, measuring each angle of my profile as if seeking the right line to trace on paper. "Something's happened. I don't know if I like it. Is it a man? Are you in love?"

I shook my head.

"Well, you don't have to tell me...look at that tree!" She went on talking and laughing as we turned off the road and into the Garden of Eden.

She knew everyone by name, identifying them from the description in my letters. That night after our communal dinner, she stabbed at the group with a tougher form of her old mischief. "All right, let's cut the idealistic chatter and tell me what's really expected of us intrepid utopians!" Guido began a discourse on freedom and love, quickly interrupted by Gertrude and Miss Harrington, who said, "No, Guido, tell her what we *do*." Frequently interrupting each other, the group gave a kind of report to Stephanie.

Theoretically we all contributed four to eight hours of manual labor. (Edward actually worked extra hours digging away at the stumps.) We rotated the preparation of meals, but cleaned up after meals together. Miss Harrington and Gertrude had been teaching and supervising children, but now that the vacationers were gone, they had only Angel left. His mother was expecting her baby any day, so she and Paul had moved to San Jose temporarily to be near a hospital. Angel preferred to stay with us. I helped on all tasks that did not involve fast or strenuous movement, for at least eight hours. Mrs. Robertson spent most of the day gathering berries, herbs, and other edibles. Jack worked sporadically, saying that when a poem was coming, he could not desert it to dig stumps or repair roofs. Jean had become the central administrator, keeping track of supplies, handling the money. Her husband Orin spent most of his time assisting whatever Guido was doing. In the evenings Miss Harrington and Gertrude were working together on a study of progressive experiments in education for children. There were plans for more music in the evenings, now that the social hall would not be full of vacationers.

And what financial contribution did each make? Stephanie wanted to know. None at all from Gertrude or Jack, who had no money, nor from Mrs. Robertson, who had millions. Jean read aloud her report, which listed some earnings of Guido and Edward, who had repaired cars for vacationers. Miss Harrington and Orin were contributing most of their monthly pension checks, a sum matched by Ralda and Paul. Earnings from summer rents and food purchased by vacationers had gone toward mortgage payments. We would need, said Jean, who was obviously glad of this chance to discuss our financial situation, all our cash contributions just to keep up those payments.

Stephanie said she would pay a monthly sum slightly larger than Miss Harrington's pension check and would work a maximum of four hours a day at whatever Jean assigned her; the rest of her time was reserved for her art. We all agreed that this was a splendid arrangement.

Throughout our discussion Stephanie had been scribbling rapidly at what I thought were notes on a pad. But now she ripped the sheet off the pad and handed us a sketch of the whole group. Gertrude was a fussy hen. Jack had been caricatured in clerical garb with a nasty, self-righteous expression. Orin and Guido teetered on a soapbox while Miss Harrington stood listening with clear displeasure. I was drawn with an insipid, smug smile on my face, its stupidity rivaled only by the worshipful smile with which Mrs. Robertson looked at me. The only people who escaped looking ridiculous were Edward (dozing in polite, exhausted boredom), Jean (adding columns of figures) and, of course, little Angel.

Our laughter was a bit strained as Stephanie's eyes roved the group with their old glint of mischief. Nevertheless we pinned the sketch to the wall of the social hall. It remained there for a long time, seeming more or less funny depending on how things were going at the point one happened to notice it.

Stephanie spent her first night in my cabin, and since the nights had suddenly turned quite cold, it was a comfort to have two bodies to warm the bed. Of course, the comfort of having Stephanie with me went far beyond bodily warmth. She and I had lived through a time of unrelenting sorrow that the others had not known so intimately. I followed her example and never mentioned the war, but I think it helped each of us to know what the other knew.

188

The next day she surveyed the cabins, then asked for the lean-to attached to the social hall. With one large window, it was lighter than the cabins. Recently added, it was more tightly built and drier, safer for her materials.

A few days later, she and I drove north again to San Francisco and returned loaded with paints, canvas, pads, charcoal and a variety of tools. Edward built an easel to her specifications. She hammered up some shelves for herself, and within three weeks had created a good studio.

During this time she continued to sleep with me, and when her quarters were complete, there was hardly room for even a narrow cot. It seemed the most natural thing in the world for her to continue to sleep in my cabin. Everything about the change in our relation seemed to come naturally out of what had been and what was. We became lovers just as if we always had been. The comfort of our warming each other in bed became caresses of soothing pleasure. There was no "falling in love." We had always loved each other, had always been dear to one another.

Stephanie had been loving women, she told me, since her marriage. Among the survivors of her set in England, love between women was accepted as a rational adjustment to the deaths of all the men, accepted so long as it was discreet. As for me, the mystical experience which had changed my life had not made me less human, did not subdue normal physical appetites. What it did was to make sacred any expression of love. My sexual relation to Stephanie was the last I had with anyone, and the best.

That fall and winter brought a sudden influx of people, more than doubling our numbers. My memory of these and later arrivals who came steadily, especially in the winter, is dim, except for three who became especially important members.

One was Mas, a small brown Japanese man whose few words of English were harder for me to understand than his Japanese. He said little in any case. He and Edward were like brothers in their sparse talk and their devotion to long hours of work. Between them they made our stump garden bloom, Mas insisting that much could be planted before all the stumps were dug out. It was Mas who brought real knowledge of growing food, of enriching the soil by composting, of controlling raids by insects and animals. That we fulfilled to any extent our plan of growing our own food is entirely to Mas's credit.

The other two were the remarkable Isabella and her twenty-five-year-old son Ramon. Isabella was an actress, singer, dancer and musician. She had sung minor roles with the San Francisco Opera, and she had appeared in plays in theaters up and down the West Coast. She played adequately nearly any instrument put into her hands, and was truly proficient on piano and flute. Isabella was nearly fifty when she came to us, too old to get any but a few poorly paid character roles with minor companies on grueling tour schedules. She had become quite round, but still had long black hair and amazingly soft flower-petal skin, which she protected from the elements by wearing a huge, floppy black hat, day and night.

At first it seemed that, despite her creative talents, Isabella must either leave us quickly or destroy our experiment, for she talked incessantly. Incessantly. I never saw her not talking, though, of course, I never saw her completely alone. Often, and increasingly, I saw her becoming alone. The only way we found to "stop" her was to interrupt or to walk away. Someone was always walking away from Isabella.

Yet everyone came to admire her, for she overflowed with ideas for concerts, plays, recitations, spontaneous dance that the rest of us thought impossible, and then, under her direction, performed. It was no good expecting Isabella to rise before noon (gradually we became grateful for the silence before she awoke), but from late afternoon onward she worked steadily on whatever creative project she planned for the evening. It was Isabella who made our long, wet winters endurable, who succeeded in making Mas sing Japanese songs with her, in making Edward dance, and Gertrude laugh. It was Isabella who, during our bad times, would sit alone at the piano she had brought with her, doors of the social hall wide open, filling the air with Mozart. I cannot hear Mozart today without imagining that I smell the redwoods and without remembering Isabella saying, "When the angels play for God, they play Bach, but when they are disporting among themselves, they play Mozart."

Isabella's son Ramon was as different from her as could be. First of all, he was several shades darker than she, probably resembling his father, and his appearance made Isabella's Mexican origins clear. In fact, his features were so classically Indian that he could have been the model for the broad-faced pre-columbian statues museums were beginning to collect at that time. He was very quiet in a brooding way which women often find attractive, sensing (not always correctly) a smoldering sexuality behind the sullen, passive look. If people were always walking away from Isabella, women were always drifting nearer to Ramon.

I never thought to ask why he had come with his mother and why he stayed, when it was clear that he approved neither of her nor of us. Only last year, reading an interview of him, I learned that Ramon had been arrested with a marijuana cigarette, had jumped bail, and needed a place to hide until the statute of limitations ran out on this offense—three years, I believe. This was the only way to avoid a sentence of many years in prison. Ramon was an accomplished jazz pianist, and during the three years with us, he suffered horribly from isolation from other jazz musicians. But his suffering had its good side. He is now a successful performer, and in that interview he referred to his years at the Garden of Eden, saying that the period of isolation from his colleagues forced him to develop an individual style which contributed to his later success.

Ramon, like his mother, was used to late hours, and he often sat up in the social hall playing all night, but with the doors closed, so that only faint syncopations drifted out into the dark. Resistant to any daily routine, he was not unwilling to work. He finally won his independence from our work schedule by taking over the horrible job of the laundry, which had defeated us all. With old industrial machines repaired by Guido and set to work with gas motors, he did all our laundry once a week, in a twenty-four-hour stint, then lay in the shade or sat at the piano the rest of the time, frowning and shrugging at whatever woman had made some excuse to join him. All of the women who came and went that winter flirted with Ramon, and some went beyond flirtation. They left just as often out of jealousy of their rivals for Ramon's attention as out of dissatisfaction with our way of life.

Of course, many of the people who came were "winter Edenites," as we called them, who suddenly found other places to go and things to do when spring—and the heavy work—began. Probably that first year we attracted the fewest of those who came only for temporary shelter. The problem increased as time went on, for we never could agree to turn anyone away. There was one man—I have forgotten even his first name—who appeared three years in a row with the first rain, vowed to say for good, and left when the first wildflowers bloomed. If we had bought coffee, wine, and sugar, no doubt many more winter Edenites would have fed off us, but Jean was adamant about not spending any funds this way, and Ramon, who rode to town with her to get supplies, supported her. He soon stopped riding to town with her, no doubt to avoid being seen, but usually sat playing the piano near the desk where Jean worked on accounts. Her cool presence kept at a distance the women who were always following him.

Ralda and Paul's new baby was a girl, and they named her Eden. She was a strong, healthy baby whose name and presence were a statement of hope for our community.

Other events of that first winter were not so inspiring. First of all, as if to compensate for the very dry winter of the previous year, the winter of 1927–28 became one of the wettest on record. It began raining in late October and it never seemed to stop. The rain pattern in central California is a three-day pattern: three days of rain, sunshine for another three days, or a week, or a month, then another three days of rain. That year the pattern was reversed. It rained steadily for three weeks, misted over for three days, rained for another two weeks. The sun shone brilliantly for three days; then we were back in a steady downpour. All the cabins leaked, roads washed out, and the river rose to touch the rotten boards of the swinging bridge. Isabella kept a fire going day and night in the social hall so that the piano would not be ruined by dampness and cold, and most of us huddled in there, sleeping on the floor.

In November everyone but the baby fell ill with dysentery. Jean and Stephanie, who had had experience with dysentery patients, suspected the water, and a brief consultation with a local doctor told us what any of the locals—doctors or not—knew. The water supply, piped from mountain springs, was safe, but the beautiful, fresh, clear river had long been polluted; no one drank from the river. Except us. The piped water was a slow trickle which often shut off. We were in the habit of washing our dishes in the river, of scooping up a bucket of water or of leaning down to cup and drink in our hands. It was a miracle, said George at the gas station, no one had gotten sick sooner.

A few recent arrivals left. The rest of us began boiling drinking water and slowly recovering. During any dry spell, Edward led a group of men up the mountain to the spring to repair the pipes and improve the flow of pure water. Nevertheless, we had other outbreaks of dysentery and soon made it a permanent policy to boil our drinking water.

During rainy days we all worked in the social hall to build a kitchen that could feed at least fifty people at tables and benches made from redwood planks. Then, shortly after our communal Christmas dinner, Isabella insisted that we build a proper stage at the other end of the social hall, near Stephanie's studio. Of course, there was no money. Everything had gone into the kitchen stoves, and we were behind on the mortgage payments. Mrs. Robertson came to the rescue, caught us up on the mortgage, and paid for materials to build a stage, complete with blue velvet curtain and two tiny dressing rooms. The piano was lifted to the stage, and by the time the worst of the cold and rain were over, we had our theater. But our frequently voiced gratitude to Mrs. Robertson was not enough. She repeatedly asked me to hold a seance, hinting strongly that she would be more generous yet if I began regular sittings. I refused. Later I did not even answer when she asked.

By the end of that winter, the social hall was a fine gathering place. At one end, large quantities of simple food could be cooked, to be served at the tables and benches gathered around the fireplace in the center. We sat at those tables for our meetings or, by turning to face the other end of the hall, to see and hear someone perform on the stage. Moving the tables and benches out to the walls made a large open space for dancing or, during the long rains of that first winter, for sleeping. From the rafters hung bouquets of fragrant herbs, drying for later use in making tea.

As soon as the rain let up a little, Edward led a stump-digging crew. The water had loosened the shallow-rooted redwood stumps. Working together, the crew could dig out at least one stump a day, cutting and covering it to dry out for next winter's firewood supply. But Mas pronounced the soil leeched by pine and redwood; to get started on a good garden we would need some top soil and fertilizer. After a two-hour meeting, we decided to fall behind on the mortgage again and buy the necessary soil and tools. Edward fidgeted silently throughout the meetings, and no one needed to ask what he was thinking: two hours that could have been spent digging.

193

But others—like Guido and Orin—enjoyed the long meetings, the talk, the very process of sorting through all opinion to reach consensus. Meetings became longer and more frequent. Sometimes, during the work hours, everyone stopped (except Edward and Mas) for an impromptu meeting on how to proceed.

I remember one incident which showed us at our worst. Most of the men were digging stumps when Mas mentioned that next they must build a fence to keep out the deer. Jack offered to set up watches to shoot the deer and add them to our food supply. Guido protested that our vegetarian diet was adequate and more humane. Within a few minutes all the men except Mas and Edward had stopped working and were debating the "deer question." Jack stood apart, neither speaking nor working, a superior smile on his dark face. It was laundry day and the pipes had broken down again. Gertrude, Ralda, Stephanie, and even Isabella were hauling buckets of water to Ramon's washing machines. Miss Harrington and I stepped out of the little chicken shed we had just stocked with a dozen hens, in time to hear Gertrude shout angrily, "If you haven't anything to do but talk, you can help us haul this water!" The men ignored her and went on talking. Nevertheless, she had made her point and, for a while, there was less talk interrupting work.

By the spring of 1928 the social hall functioned well for meals, meetings, and entertainment. The clearing behind was half dug, fertilized, and planted in vegetables. We were all healthy again. As soon as the rain abated we began work on repairing the cabins. We had the material, the skills, and the will to make sure that before the next rainy season, all cabins would have tight roofs.

Money remained a problem. Guido and Edward had found some outside work but, as Jean reported at each meeting, materials, tools, and food used up much of our income. We were now paying only the interest on the mortgage. Fortunately, Simon Ankers was not eager to foreclose and take back the Garden of Eden. The expected summer renters did not begin to appear in May. We knew we would miss their money. But we did not ask ourselves why they had not come. We were too excited about some ideas we were developing.

We had discovered that many more people lived in or near the mountains than we had thought. There was still some logging going on and several active quarries. There were some dairies and even patches of farm land, above the rich Santa Clara Valley land, but still arable. Workers in these industries lived below the mountain vacation cabins, closer to paved roads and schools. And, of course, many families came to the other mountain resorts in summer.

Isabella and Stephanie proposed that they offer free lessons in music and art to the children of these people. We put ads in the local paper and left notices in shops and gas stations. Nothing happened. Finally, George, at the gas station, told me that people were suspicious of us. Edward went to talk to him—the only time Edward acted as our spokesman. I don't know what he said, but he convinced George to send his son to us for trumpet lessons. After George's son came a dozen other children, transported by George in the back of his Model A truck. When vacationers began arriving in the mountains, word spread quickly, and children were dropped off for classes every day for two weeks, then would disappear to be replaced by other two-week students. There were even some children of dairy workers and pickers in nearby orchards.

At first we wondered if they should learn some garden skills, learn to use tools, participate in all our activities. But that idea died when Gertrude pointed out that our students were children of the working poor, including vacationers. Most would leave school soon to work at manual labor. What was missing from their lives, and might always be missing, were music, art, poetry, even dance, except for a few folk dances which were themselves dying out as the youngsters became locked into the popular couples dances of the day. "They are losing their own folk culture and gaining no other," said Miss Harrington. "The old story," she murmured, looking very old at that moment, and very tired.

So it was decided to offer instruction in singing, in every musical instrument we had, in free-form dance (Isabella was a friend of Isadora Duncan) and, of course, in drama. Gertrude offered to write a play. Ramon would set parts of it to music, Edward, Orin, and Paul would build sets designed by Stephanie and painted by Mas, with volunteers under him. Jean and Ralda would make costumes under Guido's direction. I would copy out parts as I had so long ago for the Franze troup. Everyone volunteered to do something, including Mrs. Robertson, who would pay for the materials. The most excited volunteer of all was Angel, who had been promised other children to play with during the summer. He also wanted "a big part" in the play, which Gertrude promised to write for him.

Isabella became the creative director of the project, with Miss Harrington as managing director. Miss Harrington spent the morning preparing for the children, many of whom would have to be fed lunch, while the rest of us did our regular work (and Isabella, of course, slept). In the afternoon the children arrived, twenty regulars and a constantly changing group of another twenty or so. One way or another we were all involved with the children for three hours in the afternoon. When they left, we ate our simple meal, then had a meeting or worked on individual projects for an hour or two before going to sleep, all except Miss Harrington, who went to bed right after dinner.

In an explosion of energy beyond even what she had hoped for, Stephanie did hundreds of sketches. Sometimes, in dreams or in daydreams, I see those sketches with a strange clarity. Isabella, her pudgy body under her floppy hat, giving a nevertheless heart-lifting kick as she demonstrates a dance step. Dozens of little children, alone or in groups, dancing or gesticulating. Guido reading aloud from some classic of utopian thought—as he did at least one evening a week while we sat around him making costumes or repairing tools. Edward and Mas, always with tools in hand. Mrs. Robertson sitting at a table alone, eyes closed, body rigid—she had begun to try her own seances in the evening, but no one joined her.

Two brooding figures appeared again and again in drawings: Ramon at the piano, eyes closed, leaning into the keys on strong, stubby fingers (Jean sitting nearby, bent over her bookkeeping), and Jack, standing, leaning against a tree or a wall, his dark, bitter eyes sharply alert. Gertrude and Miss Harrington were always in sketches with children. Ralda was drawn over and over again with Eden, a laughing Madonna and Child. Orin and Paul huddled in groups of other men, gesticulating, arguing, perhaps around Guido, pictured with a book. Stephanie's sketches soon covered the walls of the social hall.

During that summer we gave half a dozen recitals in which children played or sang or danced or recited something, no matter how brief or elementary, for the audiences of parents. But our major effort was aimed toward the musical play performed by over thirty children on the first Sunday in September, the Labor Day weekend which officially ended the vacation season.

It was a great success, the social hall packed with people from all over the area, some who had children in the show, many who came out of curiosity. After the performance Mrs. Robertson served herb tea. Stephanie invited performers and audience to take a sketch as a souvenir. They left us bare walls, exhaustion, and a feeling of unity approaching the ideal we aimed at in all our talk.

The only false note in our harmony came from a member of the audience, a free-lance writer who interviewed several of our members including, unfortunately, Mrs. Robertson, who spoke of my "contacts" with her dead son. This led the writer to looking up old newspaper reports about me. The resulting article, published in the *San Jose Call* was titled "Psychic Garden of Eden" and gave as much space to my former career as to the accomplishment of our children's performance.

But we were too busy to react or even to care what any newspaper said. We were gathering a fair harvest, more tomatoes and carrots than we could eat before they would spoil. Our first crop of chard, which Mas assured us would grow all year round, was thick. Squashes were swelling on the ground, and beans that had been allowed to dry in the pod would give us many substantial dinners, as well as providing seed for a larger crop next year. We all worked at canning and drying, preserving whatever we could. This required a substantial cash outlay for jars and preservatives, but Jean approved this one-time purchase of materials for years of putting by food. And so we faced the winter with a sense of accomplishment and a good supply of food.

Then came the first results of that writer's mischief. A sudden influx of people came with the first rain, people who had read or had heard about the article in the *Call*. Some came expecting to sing or dance while their mundane needs were provided for. Some came expecting seances. Some had physical ailments they presented for an occult cure—they remembered my radio program and the rumors about the curative power of my voice. Many had less visible ailments, deep mental problems which had made them restless wanderers looking for a kinder world than the one in which they were now lost. Some were criminal, some alcoholic, and some cheerfully parasitic.

In my memory they are a crowd of dozens with shifting faces. Some stayed only a day (including the thieves, who left with whatever they could find of any value), others a week or a month. A few stayed for the whole winter, but none stayed beyond spring. One visitor stayed less than one hour—Mrs. Robertson's brother, who had seen her quoted in the newspaper and had come to urge her to leave with him. When she refused, he clamped his jaw shut, looked around, then rode out in his chauffeured limousine.

They came and went throughout that winter while Edward cursed all newspapers in a steady, subvocal mumble, and the rest of us argued about entrance requirements. The same old sides opposed each other. Those who said we must impose requirements and screening for newcomers were led by Gertrude. (Miss Harrington spent a great deal of time in her cabin now, and joined few discussions.) Those who were adamantly and idealistically for free entrance were Guido and myself. Guido believed that the test of our virtue as a community, in fact our very definition as something better than existing society, depended on our accepting all people and working to overcome whatever problems arose. My position was the classic one of pride tempting God—I was sure that the force of love which had opened itself to me would overwhelm all problems. Stephanie, Ramon, and Isabella retreated into their arts. Edward and Mas silently dug out stumps, with little help from new arrivals. Jean presented weekly reports on what it was costing us to feed everyone. The debating circle around Guido, who stopped work more and more frequently to chew on a philosophical point, grew and grew, swelled by ever-new arrivals replacing the ones who quickly left, tired of our plain food and high-minded talk.

None of these problems bothered me as much as the constant nagging requests that I hold a seance during the long, damp nights that were upon us again. Before, it had been only Mrs. Robertson who said she hoped for a glimpse of my "former powers." Now there were daily requests from the newcomers, some of whom left with my first refusal, only to be replaced by new people with the same request. I gave them the same answer that I had been giving Mrs. Robertson—the reality of life was more exciting than any effect ever gained at a seance. "Then show us that reality," some said. I answered that I couldn't, that it was all around them but they had to see it for themselves. Often they argued with me, accusing me of withholding some secret, and I would be on the brink of telling them, of describing the sights and feelings I had been bursting with ever since that day on the beach, nearly three years past. But always, on the brink of telling, I stopped, warned by a silent but very strong prohibition. Only a great shock and loss could have loosened my tongue, and that loss came.

Miss Harrington had been spending longer and longer hours in bed, had grimaced though never complained with chest pain. "Just gas," she dismissed it. We began to take her meals to her cabin. I noticed that we carried most of her food away again, but was not very concerned because I usually found her reading in bed, ready to talk about something new she had just discovered in one of her beloved books. I encouraged her to rest and avoid the abrasive scenes among all the strangers coming and going.

Then one night I went to her with a bowl of soup, anticipating a few minutes of balanced, focussed conversation. I found her lying with her head thrust backward, her eyes half open, her mouth loose and wide in the dropped-jaw collapse of death. I was unprepared for the wave of grief that hit me. I had believed that, after my experience on the beach, I would view life and death with equanimity and love, all as part of the changing aspect of the reality I had glimpsed. But it was not so. I still knew that reality, but I felt the loss of Miss Harrington no less strongly, felt it as a loss of part of my own life.

I grieved for the little girl of great promise, the one only Miss Harrington saw and believed in. I grieved for the loss of Elva Harrington herself, for what I knew her to be and for all that I had never learned about her and now never would. Her death brought on the first heart-stopping faint I had experienced in nearly a year.

Guido made a coffin while Edward and Mas dug a grave beyond the clearing, over our property line, near a tree where Miss Harrington often took children on hot days to sit in the shade and tell stories. We did not mark the grave because we were breaking the law by burying her here, but we reasoned that no one would be likely to disturb the grave in government parkland. We even tried to believe, as someone said at her simple burial service, that burying her here planted us and our hopes more firmly. (No one mentioned evidence for the opposite conclusion, that Miss Harrington's pension died with her, leaving us short of money for rice.)

In that December of cold, long nights we deeply missed the austere good temper of Miss Harrington, the invisible, ignored strength and balance she had given us. We became more impatient with our problems and with each other. Everyone could see that we were moving toward a crisis.

Upon Mrs. Robertson's third request that I hold a seance to contact Miss Harrington, right after a meeting that turned into a bitter quarrel between Jack and two new men, I asked everyone to assemble in the social hall the next night. "You're not going to do it!" said Stephanie. No, I had no intention of holding a seance. "Then what will you tell them?" Only the truth. Stephanie watched me, but when I offered no further explanation, she asked no questions. Her minimal participation in meetings had shrunk almost to the total withdrawal it soon became.

That evening I stood in front of the group with a mixture of dread and joy. I planned to tell them that I could not bring Miss Harrington back, but that I could inform them about better things than contacting the dead. I still felt a deep, irrational prohibition against my saying anything to anyone. Yet I had been longing to speak, to share my knowledge, so that everyone would know what glory lay just beyond the petty problems we were now experiencing. I thought it possible that my fear of speaking out was only that—fear of embarrassing myself, of being called crazy or illogical or religious. In truth, I may have been trying to strengthen my own sense of the deeper spiritual reality which had been, if not destroyed, almost mocked by the effect on me of Miss Harrington's death.

There were about thirty people in the social hall that night, shivering because a cover had blown off the firewood and had not been replaced; the wood had become wet in the last rain, and we were having trouble keeping fires going. (Responsibility for this problem had been the subject of quarrels the previous night.) Everyone looked uncomfortable and tired, not at all like the people who had ended our summer so jubilantly only a few months before.

I began by saying that I possessed no occult powers and never had. I spoke of how I first knew Miss Harrington, and that led me to telling about my own life, including how I had begun my career as a psychic. As I spoke, movement in my audience ceased. Gradually people became completely attentive. By the time I came to what I wanted to tell, they were watching me almost hypnotically, the way some of them often gazed into the fire on cold, rainy nights.

I began by describing the despair I had reached that day on the beach. I tried to keep my voice simple and objective as I described what had happened to me. But the memory of it, spoken aloud for the first time, brought over me a feeling like an echo of that initial ecstasy. I stopped trying to control my voice or my choice of words and let myself be taken up into the feeling. I did not rant or gesticulate; it was nothing like that. All I did was to come out of disguise, stop acting as if I perceived the world as everyone else did. I let out the fiery energy which had come into me, let it blaze in my voice and my eyes, let it shine on the people who listened to me.

When I finished, there was an even deeper silence, then a sob from one side of the room. People were crying. They also were smiling, beginning to stand up, to embrace one another. Some came to embrace me. Others began to talk about why they had come to the Garden of Eden, what hopes and fears they had, how determined they were to make our community work. "I know now," one man said, "that I will find what I am seeking. You have shown me. I have it within me to do it." Isabella began a song, and everyone joined in, even Jack. Then Edward suggested it was time to go to bed, since there was plenty of work to do before the next rain.

Stephanie had said nothing, during the meeting or after. That night in bed I asked her if she thought I should not have spoken out. "I don't know," she said. "I don't know what this is all about, what you're getting at." Somehow I was surprised; I had assumed she knew. If there were other people who had had the same experiences as I, and there must be, many of them must be artists like Stephanie. But she denied it. She did not understand what I was saying, and furthermore she didn't like it. "Do you know the feeling," she said, "when you are ill, feverish, and everything around you begins to drift outward, away, until all the old familiar things have moved out to some immeasurable distance from you? That is how I felt, listening to you talk about . . . that thing. That you were drifting outward, getting further and further away, and smaller and smaller, disappearing."

"I'm not," I said. "I'm closer. There's more of me with you, right here, because I've spoken."

"What do you want? Am I supposed to do something different because of . . . that thing?"

"No."

"Good. And I'll thank you to tell that thing to keep its bloody paws off me."

I didn't say that I was sure she was always quite firmly gripped in the paws of that thing because she clearly would not have appreciated the compliment. She kissed me and twined her feet in mine as we always did on cold nights. In a moment she was asleep, having accepted what I said but taking no interest in it. If she was thinking of anything as she dropped off, it was probably of the mural she planned for the walls of the social hall. These were the only comments she ever made on the "secret knowledge" I had told. We hardly ever spoke of it again. When anyone mentioned it, she said, "Oh, that thing." I decided that was as good a name as any for the unnameable, and I have used it ever since.

The next day everyone (except Isabella and Ramon, of course) was up early, cheerfully working. There was much laughter, much sharing of tools and advice, a feeling of love I had not seen for months. In the afternoon, Jean came to me with extraordinary news. Mrs. Robertson had asked her how much the mortgage was, and then had handed her a check for the full amount. After what she heard last night, she knew, said Mrs. Robertson, that she would never leave the Garden of Eden. She wanted to safeguard ownership of the land by our group.

We waited a week, to make sure Mrs. Robertson did not change her mind, then announced at a meeting that our financial worries were over. With the land secure and no payments to meet, we could get through this winter and would soon be able to supply our needs with our own produce, some outside work, and whatever contributions people cared to make. Jean would contact a lawyer about putting the land into a trust to be held for the benefit of the community. We selected a few people to oversee the trust. Jean herself refused to be on this committee and asked for some help in handling the money. "Someone should be familiar with all this, in case . . . ." We waited, but she did not finish her thought. Gertrude offered to help. Then everyone gave a cheer for Mrs. Robertson, who stood up, smiling and crying, moving closer to me.

She embraced me, then whispered, "You have finally regained all your powers and more. Whenever you're ready, let's contact my dear boy again, and his father." She saw the shocked look on my face, backed off, repeated, "When you're ready," and moved away to accept the gratitude of others. That was when I realized she had not understood a word I said. She had heard what she chose to hear, had even managed not to hear my confession that my mediumship had always been fake.

She was not the only one who had misunderstood. Guido told me that despite the improved morale of the group, he, as a dedicated atheist, felt threatened by my unsuspected religious leanings. Was I planning to hold religious rituals? Gertrude also made a short, quiet but disturbed comment to Stephanie, who passed it on to me. Was I declaring myself some kind of holy figure like those cults in Southern California? Their criticism did not bother me as much as the questions of new people about my "method" for reaching the illumination and ecstasy I had described. When I told them I knew no more than I had said, they began to argue among themselves about the best "method," often stopping work in order to do so.

Nevertheless, the euphoria of the group carried us through January. Twice during the month I was asked to speak to the whole group again, to clarify what I had told them. All I could do was to repeat again my description of what had happened to me, and that seemed to suffice to inspire them again. The most rapt listener was Mrs. Robertson, and she was the one, I think, who still heard the least. Hardly a day passed without her referring to the "powers" she expected me to be ready to use again soon.

February was mild. Already some of the winter Edenites were leaving, but it had not been a bad winter. All the stumps were gone from the clearing. We were getting ready to plant twice as much as last year. Conflict among us had not ended, but would be eased when malcontents left with the usual spring exodus.

Then two things happened which I now realize marked the beginning of the end for us. A couple had arrived in January with a child the same age as Angel, about five. The little girl was already suffering from whooping cough, though we did not know that at the time. Angel and his baby sister caught it. Jean gave advice on caring for the children, and we all settled down to rotating nursing as they went into spasms of choking, vomiting, coughing to the point of strangulation and exhaustion before managing, with a pathetic whoop, to get a breath of air.

At the worst time, when the coughing had already gone on for six weeks, the little girl's parents disappeared, leaving their sick child with us. When it was clear that they were not coming back, Jean insisted on taking the child to the county hospital in Santa Cruz. She was weak, and Jean was afraid pneumonia would set in.

Jean returned from the hospital escorted by police, who were investigating complaints from hospital authorities (who feared blame if the child should die) that our care had been negligent. The police even muttered about kidnapping charges. Finally they left, convinced that no criminal negligence had occurred, but their open contempt for us was upsetting. And they would not leave until they had taken the names of all the people on the premises.

Ralda and Paul announced they were leaving, taking the children to San Francisco to be near the best doctors, then, when they were well enough to travel, back to their families in the East. They had decided that the Garden of Eden was not the best place to raise their children. No one contradicted them, but everyone silently mourned the loss of Angel. Aside from catching whooping cough—which could have happened anywhere—he had led a happy life among us and had given us much happiness.

The second and more serious blow came with Ramon's decision (after giving a false name to the police) to leave immediately. His announcement was a time bomb which blew apart our community. "Jean goes with me." Suddenly exposed was a situation everyone had known about—everyone but Jean's husband Orin, and me. Jean, nearing forty, was pregnant by Ramon, twelve years her junior. She and Ramon had been planning to leave. That was why she had asked Gertrude to take over some of the bookkeeping. The police had only speeded up the inevitable. Ramon had contacted a band in New York. A job was waiting for him. Jean would manage Ramon's career and bear his child, a more fruitful use of her energies, she said, than our community offered.

Orin was stunned, then furious. When he shouted at her, out in the clearing where everyone heard, she shouted back that he had dragged her here, had refused to have the children she wanted, had done little but talk while she pitched in to keep the place going as long as it had. Now she was through. And, shortly after this uncharacteristic diatribe, she was gone. Orin's bitterness increased and spilled over to cover us all. We had allowed Ramon to join us, had not told Orin what was happening between him and Jean, had not supported Orin when he shouted curses after them when they left. It didn't help that Isabella looked a little pleased at the prospect of becoming a grandmother. Or that Stephanie viewed the whole affair as pure farce. I tried to keep her away from Orin because whenever she looked at him, she was unable or unwilling to suppress a grin of high glee.

Mrs. Robertson begged me to talk to the community again to try to restore the feelings I had evoked before. I tried. I described my experience again, reminding everyone of the reality which should be remembered whenever we needed a light to fade out the darkness of troubles like these. But there was something stale in my words. Used up, trite. The words were losing force. This was not the last time I told my story, but at each telling the effect on my audience was less, like a drug to which they built up tolerance after each dose.

Somehow, with the silent pushing of Edward and Mas, we managed to plant. More people came. Some brought liquor. We had a long meeting about the danger posed to our community by breaking prohibition laws. Someone said that everyone in the mountains drank bootleg liquor. Yes, said Gertrude, but the police were not looking for an excuse to raid those people. She was convinced that local opinion was rapidly turning against us—partly because of some of the people now being attracted to our community—and she was right. That meeting ended with no conclusion, no answer, as usual.

There were other meetings, more and more frequent ones, until we were haranguing each other almost every night. Disputes arose over work; the volunteer system had broken down, and we could not agree on a system for assigning work. Isabella wanted to make plans for another summer of drama and art classes, but others said we had too many problems to solve without another infusion of summer children. (We could have saved our breath. After the visit by the police, rumors of child abuse had erased the reality of what we had done for the children the previous summer. There would be no children applying for art and music classes again.)

Because of these same rumors, Guido and Edward were having trouble finding paid work in the community. We no longer had mortgage payments to make, but we still needed cash for some of our food. Even when they did find work, they were missed, for Mas had more and more trouble getting a full day's work out of other people, who were coming and going at an ever accelerating rate.

Any suggestion that we keep newcomers out for a while provoked another long, inconclusive argument. During these wrangles Stephanie silently painted her mural on the wall. Mas, Edward, and the few others who had been up at dawn, dozed off. Gertrude stayed in her cabin working on the accounts turned over to her by Jean. Jack argued with the newcomers. Mrs. Robertson talked about "signs" that Miss Harrington was among us, which led to rumors that the Garden of Eden was haunted. Isabella's post-midnight Mozart on the piano in the social hall added to rumors of "hauntings."

In June a process server drove in and handed me papers which informed me that I was being sued by Mrs. Robertson's brother and by the trustees of her late husband's estate. That was how we learned that there were strings attached to her money, that her expenditures were subject to approval by trustees, and that her brother had convinced the trustees that I had "seduced or coerced" Mrs. Robertson into giving me money. Gertrude and Guido went to a lawyer, who informed them that all moneys given by Mrs. Robertson were frozen, attached, which meant our mortgage was unpaid after all. Now there were legal fees, which we paid by borrowing on the equity I had in my downpayment on the land.

The story of the suit broke in the newspapers at the same time as a series of articles about us. In late April a young woman had joined us, staying for about a week, following people around, talking as she tossed the bright red hair which streamed over her often bare shoulders. She had a way of asking apparently innocent questions which divided everyone into factions. She walked about half dressed, asking men to rub ointment on the resulting mosquito bites on her thighs and chest. At our Saturday night meeting she complained that men tried to take liberties with her. Next morning she was gone.

She was a reporter for the most sensational of the San Francisco dailies, much of whose stock was owned by the Robertson trust. Her "exposé" ran five days during the last week of July. Among the "facts" she reported were these: members of our community were required to engage in "free love," including misegenation and homosexuality; members were starved into submission by a meatless diet which had already killed one elderly woman and nearly killed a child rescued by authorities; Madame Psyche used mass hypnotism during nightly meetings; members had turned over to her all their assets, more than a million dollars of which was in secret bank accounts in her (my) name.

The charges of homosexuality were based not on any knowledge of the relation between Stephanie and me, but on that first summer when we women gathered at the river to swim and sunbathe. We had been seen after all. We were described as a "lesbian coven" indulging in nude orgies and plotting seductions of men to be enslaved in "Madame Psyche's Sin City." For the first time we realized that even the friendly vacationers who came during our first year had spread rumors which had nothing to do with what they knew to be the reality of our daily life.

The old members of our community laughed at the idea of my having taken in millions, but newer arrivals were suspicious. They became reluctant to give anything at all—money or labor—to help us survive. Nothing shook the faith of Mrs. Robertson, who insisted on staying no matter what pressure was applied by relatives and their lawyers. But her faith was based on her stubborn belief in my psychic powers. Anything she said to recent arrivals only made the worst rumors sound true.

It was one of her relentless requests to "try your psychic powers again" that provoked an incident worse, in my mind, than any of the disasters of that year. I turned on her. I did not shout or call her names. I did not even raise my voice. I dismissed her with a brief indictment of her life-long credulity and stupidity, delivered in clipped tones of cold rage. She shrank from me with a look of terror. I doubt she had listened to my words any more than she ever listened to me. What she responded to was the blind, violent fury projected by my voice and my look.

She could not have been more stunned than I was a moment after I spoke. She shrank away, leaving me sitting under the tree near Miss Harrington's grave, a setting we all saw as symbolic of the highest spiritual peace and love. What had just come out of me expressed an inner scene that was quite the opposite.

That inner scene was full of rage and grief at the failure of our hopes. It was the same rage as had been expressed by Orin, except that his was honest and conscious. Mine had been submerged and denied—for how long?—under a stubborn, iron-willed faith that somehow all would be well because I had seen the light of that thing, and it had changed me. But it had not changed me. Whatever I had experienced had not automatically made me a better person. My knowledge of that thing was only that—knowledge—nothing more. It did not make my enterprises sure to succeed, it did not free me from all the faults of human kind. It only gave me less excuse for indulging them.

I was still a fraud, even to myself. I had convinced myself that I would no longer feel petty human emotions. I had suppressed ordinary mean human feelings until they were ready to boil over. Then I had relieved the pressure by pouring them over a foolish, harmless old woman who could not retaliate. In my arrogant self-delusion I had been no less deluded than Mrs. Robertson.

I said nothing, not even to Stephanie, about my sense of shame at the way I had failed all of them, failed the meaning of that thing. To make such a confession would only be another self-indulgence, a demand for comfort and sympathy from people who had barely enough energy to get through each day of the slow death of our community.

Throughout that summer, when the mountains were full of vacationers and the roads and trains full of people going to or from Santa Cruz, we were subject to sudden midnight attacks. Usually it was a car full of drunken men who probably decided on the spur of the moment to drive down the road into the Garden of Eden, shout some obscenities, throw some bottles, then skid around and drive out before we quite knew what was happening. Those of us who walked out from our cabins near the railroad track were likely to suffer the same kind of attack from a train—shouts and garbage thrown at us, sometimes even by children. After each attack a few more people left, until it seemed we would soon be down to the eight who remained from our beginning, plus the invaluable Mas, and Stephanie.

We worked hard to bring in and preserve the fine crop of food we harvested that fall. We did not plan anything beyond storing our food for the winter. We did not talk about the future. All of us knew that our community had no future. Perhaps that was why, during those last months, we were so kind to one another, almost recapturing some of our early good feeling.

We needed all the kindness we could muster after our final catastrophe, the burning down of the social hall. We never learned just how the fire started. The fireplace, built into the old tree trunk, was lined with stone which might have broken, letting hot coals drop into the wood. Vandals had screeched through the place that night. One of them might have thrown a bottle containing an incendiary. The fire might even have been started by one of us. Guido had seen Orin go into the social hall very late; he remained convinced to the end that Orin had taken his revenge on us all by destroying our one tangible sign of success. He never confronted Orin with his suspicions. Their philosophical discussions had long since ended; Orin hardly spoke to any of us.

Though the social hall was lost, a heavy fog had made the nearby trees dripping wet, keeping the fire from spreading. Again, for a day, we were overrun by police and rangers. When they left, we had to face the worst loss. Not only had we lost Stephanie's murals, a full year's work, but everything in the studio attached to the social hall. Stephanie shrugged and said she would buy more supplies. But the days and weeks went by, and she did not suggest a trip to San Francisco.

The destruction of the social hall put an end to our communal meals. As the winter rains began, we huddled over the little stoves in our cabins, cooking in small pots at odd hours of the day and night. Mrs. Robertson caught a cold with an alarming cough, and we insisted that she leave. She went back to her home in San Francisco in November, the day after the stock market crash.

Jack went with her, driving her car, carrying with him only the box in which he kept his poems. He had been hired as her chauffeur. Since he had said so often that he had never been a white man's servant, I must have looked surprised, and he answered the look on my face with, "I think we're in for times when only the rich will eat well, and I'm going to eat with them." His speech had lost some of its "British" edge, as if he had begun softening it to suit his new role.

Within a month Stephanie received word from England. The crash had had worldwide effects. Her funds would soon be restricted. She had better come back to England. "You were ready to go anyway," I told her. She nodded. The Garden of Eden had been good for her, but in the long run she would do better work at home, now that she had started again. "Your country has more open space, but not for the mind."

"So I'm going to lose you again."

"You needn't. Come with me."

"I wish I could."

"Has that thing told you not to?"

I shrugged. "It hasn't told me to go with you. You understand."

"No, I don't!" she shouted, startling me. I hadn't realized that she was barely containing her fury or grief or love or whatever it was that erupted, pouring over me from then on.

Day after day she bombarded me with attacks on my "delusions." Some days she used her most wicked humor, calling me Saint May and giving a lopsided, hilarious genuflection as she asked whether we were to say grace over some leftover chard and raisins. Other times she contemptuously quoted from accounts of masochistic and bizarre behavior by people who claimed some sort of revelation. Then she would become quiet and kind, reasoning with me, pointing out that we had all learned valuable lessons at Eden, she would not have missed it for the world, but it was time to move on. When I gave no answer, she said harshly, "The people you love die soon enough. You don't leave them for a dream." She did not cry. I had never seen Stephanie cry, not even during the worst of the killing during the war. Instead she switched back to ridicule, giving an impersonation of "that thing" as a thunderbolt-tossing Jehovah or a mealy-mouthed crucified Christ. The worst thing about this time was that it showed so clearly and widened so impassably the gulf between us. She was the closest person to me in all the world, but she hated what was even closer to me.

When she said, "You have become a person of no human feeling. You care for no one," I broke down. Once I had begun to cry, I could not stop. I was still in the grip of that thing, but its grip was no longer ecstatic, nor even warm. It felt like a cold, stern master whose nature I had completely misunderstood. I cried as that glacial hand shook me, knowing it would never let me go, no matter what I wanted or what Stephanie wanted.

She became frightened that my sobbing and trembling would bring on trouble with my heart. But gradually I was able to regain control, and the strain on my heart never went beyond one of the usual pounding episodes, which I tried not to let her see, breathing as quietly as I could.

She still did not understand, but at least she knew that she was wrong to call me unfeeling. She stopped taunting me. We talked quietly and concluded that I would stay until the suit was settled and then would probably follow her to England. The word "probably" meant we both doubted that I would.

Stephanie, Isabella and Gertrude left on the last day of 1929. Stephanie took her leave casually, saying she would see me in two or three months, probably. Isabella was going to join Ramon, Jean, and her grandson. Gertrude would go to Montreal, where she had found a job in a girls' boarding school. (Gertrude is now the president of a famous women's college which has gained even greater stature under her firm control. Recently I saw her picture in a newspaper. She was part of a delegation to the White House on National Education Day.)

Orin left the next day, telling no one where he was going. With his pension gone, there would be no more cash.

There were only four of us left—Guido, Edward, Mas, and I. Ownership of the land was still disputed, and Guido guessed rightly that the lawyers would drag things on until any claim I had to the land was absorbed in fees. It may even be that one of our lawyers (we fired the first two, staying with the third only because no one else would take our case) instigated the government action that suddenly took the land, absorbing it into parkland. However it happened, we were abruptly informed that by a hastily passed state bill, the land we were on now belonged to the state, which had paid off our mortgage with Simon Ankers, and we were trespassing.

A ranger posted the trespassing notice, but made no move to evict us. There was still food left, though it was going fast. We were feeding new groups of winter Edenites, different from the ones who had come during our first two winters. These ate, talked about places where they might find work, then left. Some were people who had rented cabins in years past. They had been suddenly laid off their jobs, could not meet rent payments, had been evicted. They had only one piece of advice for each other and for us—find relatives, family. "Your family has got to take you in. Else you starve." Mas followed their advice and went to his brother's farm near San Diego. Now only Edward, Guido, and I were left, and they obviously were staying only for my sake. With their skills they might find work in San Francisco. I urged them to go. I had plenty of food, plenty of time to decide what to do. I would write. We would keep in touch. They left together in the Model T.

A month later Guido wrote that Edward had worked pumping gas for a week or two, then had hitched a ride to Sacramento, where a large hospital was said to need a general maintenance man. He had promised to write, but Guido had heard nothing. Guido had a job in a pants factory, where he would stay only long enough to save money for a ticket to France. A friend in Paris had written that there was no depression there and plenty of work for a good tailor.

I stayed on for another day, and another, and another, assigning cabins, distributing food to the homeless who passed through in this final phase of our experiment in communal living.

1930–1940

On a bright day in April, when I had just calculated that I had enough food left for a week, the forest ranger showed up. He was a nice man about my age, the father of one of the children who had attended art classes the summer before our last. He said he had no intention of forcing me to leave, although he had been ordered to do so. I told him I had no intention of forcing him to disobey orders. I would be gone within two days. I traded him a couple of tools for a strong canvas backpack that would hold my wool cloak, a change of clothes, toilet articles, a few letters, Stephanie's old sketch of me, a pot made by Guido from a World War helmet, a soldier's knife left by Edward, and the few dollars I had left.

The next day I threw the pack into the car and drove to George's gas station. For the first time, George and I shook hands as I asked him to hold any mail that might come for me and suggested he take anything he could use from the Garden of Eden. Then I got into the car and headed inland.

Once over the summit of the Santa Cruz mountains, I coasted downhill, eastward into the Santa Clara Valley, onto Blossom Hill Road. As far as I could see, the rows of fruit trees stretched in long lines of snowy puffs, white and pink. This was a ride I had taken with my sisters before the war, and later with Norman, the spring ride down the peninsula to see the orchards in bloom.

I turned off Blossom Hill Road onto a narrower road running between orchards. Now the white puffs were above me on either side, dropping their blossoms on the grassy clods of earth beneath the narrow tree trunks, each with a neat band of white painted around it. Why? This was the first time I had ever been curious about the purpose of the familiar mark. Driving past the trees I experienced a strange optical illusion. The evenly spaced trees at first seemed to stretch in straight lines perpendicular to the road, then suddenly to shoot off in straight diagonals at all angles from the road, angles which shifted with the movement of the car, almost making me dizzy.

I was enjoying this effect, remembering it from past rides, thinking I might just continue north through miles and miles of orchards all the way to the edge of San Francisco, when suddenly the motor gave out and the car coasted to a stop. My first response was disbelief. This was the car that had driven up and down Twin Peaks, throughout San Francisco, down these roads and back again. It had carried people, wood, tools, and food up and down the mountain roads near the Garden of Eden, never requiring any attention beyond a change of tires or some minor repair done by Edward.

There was no reason to believe that the car would not break down eventually, yet its sudden stopping on this narrow road between flowered orchards was like the pulling out of yet another rug of illusion I had stood upon. Without this machine, which like me was aging and in precarious health, what would I do? I did not know the most elementary repairs to make on it, nor even how to discover what needed to be repaired.

I pressed the starter, sat down for a few minutes, then pressed again. It sounded weaker the second time, and I was afraid of running down the battery. I was also getting warm. I got out of the car and looked up and down the unpaved road. Not another car in sight. Nothing but thousands of identical little trees running in dizzying diagonal lines in all directions. I sat down on the running board to wait for a car to come past.

I waited a long time, but no car came. I was on one of those side roads used only by farmers, who might not come this way at all except for pruning or harvesting. I could sit here, I thought, while the blossoms fell and the trees leaved, and the fruit ripened. I could sit here and die.

Then, quite suddenly, a man appeared. He must have come through the orchard. He wore shabby jeans, dirt-spattered from boots to knees, a plaid lumberjack shirt, and a broad, floppy, dusty hat. Thick straps crisscrossed his chest. From one strap hung a conical basket hamper. The other secured a blanket wound around lumpy belongings hanging from his back. I recognized him as a fruit tramp, one of the migrant workers Norman and I often saw in our summer rides and sometimes picked up, if Erika was not with us. ("Dirty, smelly winos," she would say when she saw them on Howard Street in San Francisco, where they spent the winter in cheap hotels.) This one was a white man with wrinkled, weathered skin and a limping, shuffling gait. Yet his smile and his voice were young. He might be not much older than I, or he might be over sixty. Some tramps lived to an old age, but most of them only looked old and worn, from too many cold nights outdoors, too many hours at stoop labor, and too much wine to ease the aching chill. Yet, every fruit tramp I'd ever seen was cheerful, sociable, well-mannered, if mildly light-fingered, as Norman put it.

This one tipped his hat before pulling up the hood of my car and peering into it. He talked while he peered and poked, telling me that he had "come to pick cherries for Berelli." He was early, of course, but these days you had to get there weeks ahead of the others if you wanted to find work. He thought he might be able to repair drying trays for Danzel or even thin onions—though he hated that, it would break his back yet—till the cherries were ripe. At least he could count on sleeping in Berelli's barn; they were nice people, even fed him now and then if he ran out of cash. This past winter had been a bad one, with people losing work everywhere. He'd hardly had a few day's work the whole winter up in the railroad yards where he used to work through the rainy season. Too many master mechanics out of work, willing to do "anything for six bits an hour."

He frowned, stepped over to the car window, put his head in, then pulled it out, smiling a boyish, gaptoothed grin. He invited me to look at the gas gauge, then smiled again and said he suspected I could solve my problem "easy enough." No, he was not sure where the nearest gas station was. Pretty far, he thought.

Then he turned around, seeming to peer down one diagonal of trees far into the distance. "Old Dona Ceresita lives over that way, if she made it through another winter." He pointed, saying we were on the property of an ancient lady who might have some gas at her place. I took a gallon can from the trunk of the car.

"Better take that too." He pointed to my pack in the back seat. "Never know about people, whoever might come by."

I slung the pack over my shoulder and started walking along the line of trees he had pointed to, at a slight angle northeast from the road. The white blossoms were beginning to fall, drifting across my face, whitening the ground. When I turned and looked back, the tramp was standing there, waving at me. I looked back once more and could still see him standing there, watching.

I must have walked for twenty minutes, crossing two more narrow dirt roads, keeping at the same angle along a row of trees, before I came to a long, low adobe house, stained and chipped, crumbling at the corners. One end of the building had completely collapsed into lumpy, melting blocks covered with weeds. I had seen buildings like it before, sometimes out in a field or woods, sometimes in the middle of a town, next to a factory or hamburger stand. Leftovers from the Spanish days of California, they were used as overnight shelter for tramps or nested by small animals. Recently I have heard about efforts to preserve or restore the few remaining. In 1930 they were being allowed to crumble to dust, melting like sugar cubes in winter rains.

This one still had a roof on it and windows, but otherwise looked neglected. The bushes and flower beds around it were overgrown, weed-choked, dusty and littered with broken pots, papers, and rusty parts of broken tools. A few large cracks in the adobe walls gaped, unpatched. I saw a narrow road on one side of the house, but no sign of a car or any source of gas for my car. I thought of the tramp waving at me through the trees and imagined that the smile on his face had been less cheerfully innocent that it seemed. I set down my can and turned to look back the way I had come. As I looked down the long straight path I had taken along the row of trees, the gap narrowed, then closed in the distance.

"*Aqui estas, mala!*"

The voice—high, hoarse, imperious—came from an open window and went on berating me in Spanish. "The whole place will go to ruin with your neglect. Must I tell you everything? Must I stand over you and force you to do your work?" The voice faded, then came on clearly again as the heavy wooden door squeaked open and I saw a woman standing in the doorway. She wore a long black dress that reminded me of the widow women of my childhood. Through the thin black veil that covered her head and part of her face I could see sparse white hair and a deeply wrinkled face. She was, as the tramp had told me, very old. Probably her eyes were bad, and she had mistaken me for someone else.

"Get to work at once. Clean up this garden. If you stand there another moment, I'll have Juan take the whip to you!" As far as I could see, there was no Juan or anyone else to carry out the threats and orders that continued to pour from her in a mixture of Spanish and English and some other language I could not identify, but which might have been some Indian dialect. My attempts to interrupt her, to introduce myself, only enraged her and made her jumble of words—the conglomerate language of one who had lived in California for many, many years—pour out with more shrill fury. She did not fall silent until I set down my can and obeyed, stopped to pick the trash and papers out of her flower beds.

I worked until the sun was touching the hills and tinting the orchard blossoms orange. Twice she had brought me a cup of water. Now she appeared in the doorway and summoned me to eat.

I followed her into a small, cool kitchen, totally dark to me for a few seconds until my eyes began to adjust. A huge, black wood stove almost filled the room. It was cold, unused. A few open shelves on the wall held dishes above a deep sink in which more dishes lay. Between the sink and the stove stood a small wrought iron table with a tiled top and two stools. On the table was a bowl of fruit and two small bowls of milk. I was very hungry, but I waited for Dona Ceresita to sit down and wave me to my stool with a mumbled warning that this was the last time she would provide a meal for me; it was high time I took over the cooking. She glared at me. Whoever she thought I was—perhaps her last servant—argument was futile. I lifted the bowl of milk to my lips. The milk was canned—and a bit sour. As I drank it, I gradually uncovered a gold leaf design with a large family crest set with what looked like rubies at the bottom of the bowl. I glanced at the sink, covered with dirty dishes, and the shelves above. The dishes matched, a set of about twenty gold leaf pieces studded with precious stones. I learned later that these were the remnants of family treasures that Dona Ceresita had been allowed to keep. The rest were in museums or had been sold to private collectors by her many descendants.

After we had eaten, the old lady left the room. I washed the dishes as best I could with a bar of soap and cold tap water in the sink, dried them, and put them on the shelf. I found a broom and swept the tile floor, opening the door to scatter the dirt out in the garden. Then I went back inside and through the doorway which led to the main room of the house.

It was too dark to see much. Dusky light came from two high, narrow windows facing east. I sensed a long room with a high ceiling, a tiled floor, a few pieces of furniture covered with small objects whose shapes were unclear to me. The old lady summoned me to the center of the room, warning me not to be "clumsy, watch out there, you'll break something!" She was seated in a stiff, high-backed chair. Beside it was a stool which, clearly, she expected me to sit on. "Well . . . light the candle," she said impatiently, but I could not find candle or matches. "Never mind, never mind," she said with weary impatience. As soon as I was seated on the stool, she began to talk as if continuing a conversation with invisible people, in a nearly incomprehensible tongue.

I hardly heard a word she said. The strangeness and confusion of the day had exhausted me. I was drowsy and dull. The shadowy objects cluttering the room surrounded us like living presences, listening to her.

After a while she abruptly said it was time to go to bed. I helped her out through the kitchen and down a path to the outhouse and back, helped her wash at the kitchen sink, then helped her back into the large room. Her bed stood against a door that had led to the collapsed bedroom at the far end of the house. I undressed her and helped her into the woolen nightgown which lay on the bed. It took a few moments of fumbling in the dark to find the step stool she used to climb up into the high bed. She scolded in a steady, hoarse monotone until she sank onto the pillow.

By the time she was settled, I could see well enough in the dim room to make out a large chest at the foot of the bed, covered with a straw mat. I assumed correctly that this was my bed. I took my woolen cape from my pack, wound myself up in it, and curled up on the chest.

I awoke in the morning as the sunrise spread light through the room, and now I could see the shapes of the objects which filled it. It was like the storeroom of a museum.

There were three tables and two chests whose tops were covered by small objects: carved figures, candlesticks, bowls, baskets, vases. The walls were covered with religious objects: paintings, woven hangings, shapes carved from wood or stone. Most of these objects were Christian, depicting the Virgin Mary. But these Virgins varied widely from any Christian art I have ever seen. Some of them looked quite fierce. In boxes scattered on the floor were baskets and bowls, odds and ends of wood carving and pottery. The chests (this I learned later when I removed dozens of objects to open the lids) were full of hand-embroidered linens.

"What a disgrace! How you've neglected all my things. No more of that, I'll see to it. No more laziness. You'll learn, my girl, you'll learn!" The old lady was awake and scolding again all through breakfast, after which she told me to get my rags and start cleaning. She sat in her chair and fell into a doze after I started dusting the figures on one of the tables.

Dona Ceresita slept most of the time. Sitting up for meals, walking to and from the outhouse, and sitting up in her chair talking seemed to take all the strength that flickered in her old frame. Between eating and scolding, she dozed, giving me time to go outside (she never left the dim house except to go to the outhouse) for a rest, a breath of air, a short walk.

She seemed to be quite alone in the midst of orchards that stretched beyond sight. Yet the trees were cared for, the ground cultivated. The kitchen cooler held cheese, smoked meats, and canned food. Most important, there were tire tracks in the drive leading from the house to one of the side roads.

She could not have been alone for long. Despite a huge pile of dirty laundry, she had some clean underwear in bureau drawers. She needed help in dressing and bathing, yet she did not look neglected. Her level stare as she scolded me had been all bluff; she was nearly blind. That was probably why she never went outside. In less familiar surroundings she would be lost. Even here, left alone, she would be lost. She was furious at me because she desperately needed me to take care of her until someone showed up. It was not as if I had anywhere else to go or anything else to do.

The blossoms fell quickly, puffing out in clouds with every light breeze during the next two weeks as leaves began sprouting around hard, green fruit buds. I cared for the old lady, cleaned for her, scrubbed clothes in the kitchen sink, listened to her scolding and her ramblings. At the end of two weeks, at dawn, I heard a truck drive up to the house and stop. I hurried outside to see a girl jump down from the driver's seat. She was about eighteen, with thick auburn hair bursting out of the waves sculptured to her head by some hair dresser. She had a sturdy, rounded body like that of a mature woman, and very white skin. She was followed by two boys, who began to unload crates from the truck, stacking them at the edge of the clearing under the first rows of trees.

"Oh, another new lady? I'm glad they found someone. I'm Angelina. I hope you're going to stay, Miss . . . Mrs. . . . you speak English? Gee, I don't know any Japanese, if that's what you are."

"I speak English, but I wasn't hired to stay here. I ran out of gas, came here, found her quite alone. It didn't seem right to leave her. My name is Mei-li."

"Glad to meet you, Mrs. Lee. How is she?" Without waiting for my answer, Angelina hurried into the house. A moment later she was in the doorway again, calling to the boys to bring in the groceries, mostly boxes of canned goods.

While they were unloading, Angelina siphoned a gallon of gas from the truck into my can and began walking with me across the orchard. She seemed to know exactly the road on which I must have left my car, though I was no longer sure. As we walked she told me what she knew about Dona Ceresita. "She must be about a hundred years old, honest. My father started leasing land from her before I was born, and he said she'd already been there for years and years. There are these trustees or something that come down from the City and argue with her every once in a while. She owns a thousand acres— old Spanish land grant. Or the trust does. She won't leave the old adobe, and it'll come down on her in a good rain storm, my mother says. There are dozens of grandchildren and great-grand nephews, but I've never seen one. They're just waiting for her to die. They don't care. She needs someone to take care of her, but no one will stay, except in the winter. As soon as there's other work, they leave. That's why we come by whenever we can just to make sure there's food in the house. I was sure glad to see you. I'm always afraid I'm going to come here and find her dead. She's gotten so weak this past year."

When we reached the road, there was no sign of my car. "Probably that tramp stole it the minute you were out of sight. We got some of those men picking for us, and you have to watch them. When I'm in San Jose I'll report it to the police. If he's still around here with it, they'll get him fast. They know all those guys."

On the way back to the house Angelina told me she had one more year of high school and then would go to San Jose Normal School. She would be working in the canneries again this summer to save money for her college expenses. She would be the first in her family to finish high school, let alone go to college, and she was going to become a teacher. Her parents had emigrated from Italy. They had their own five acres of prunes and many more acres of peaches on leased land. She and her four brothers worked on the ranch and in the canneries. They also worked in their own drying sheds, but they hired pickers. "My father says that's work I don't have to do," she said proudly, patting her wavy hair, which immediately sprang out again into wiry ringlets. Her white cheeks had turned rosy pink from the quick walk, and she looked beautiful and fresh and young. It startled me for a moment to realize that she was only a few years older than my daughter would have been. "I have to hurry, I'll be late for school. Don't leave yet, please!" I promised to stay until some other help could be found.

I was willing to stay a while, serving the old lady. I needed time to think about our life at the Garden of Eden, and I thought of it constantly. That is, I thought about our failure and all the reasons for it.

There were good reasons to believe that our community could never have survived in a society so hostile to anything different. Still, the main reasons for our failure lay within ourselves, and in hindsight they were clear. We had refused to select or screen applicants. We had no clear set of principles or purposes, no standard against which to measure our actions, no means to ensure that necessary work would be done. We had unrealistic expectations of self-sufficiency and few people with the skills necessary to reach even more modest goals. And all these faults sprang from the deeper reason for our failure, my stupid pride. I had believed that because I had glimpsed a world behind, within, beyond the world of everyday life, that I could live wholly in that world, that thing, and that the material world would conform to my new, half-formed, dazzled view of its latency. I had forgotten that I was still a human being and that, whatever my mind and heart were taken up into, my feet were still on earth.

In those long nights when I lay at the foot of Dona Ceresita's bed, I thought about the night I had brought our group together again temporarily by telling of that thing. The more I thought about it, the more convinced I became that I had violated a promise, a prohibition against speaking. No one had understood what I had told them. The more often I repeated my story, no matter how inspired my listeners seemed to be, the more clear it became that they could not understand what I meant by what I said, no matter how many different ways I tried to say it. Telling was not the way to express that thing.

By breaking my silence I might even have caused the breakup of the world we were trying to make. Or was that thought only more pride? Was I again thinking that my knowledge of that thing gave me some special power to make things happen? These variations of prideful thinking were a habit I must break, along with the habit of speaking out. The old lady was right. I had a lot to learn.

I was at least free of any trace of intoxication from my experience of that thing. During the four-year attempt to create a Garden of Eden, all the orgasmic thrill had eroded away. I knew it would never come again, not in that way. I did not doubt the reality of that thing, but I had learned to doubt my assumptions about its nature and meaning.

I had begun with a great mistake. I had mistaken my experience for an end instead of seeing it as a beginning of a long journey. If I were to take even the first step on that journey I would have to learn to listen for directions, watch for signposts, feel the way on the path. That thing would draw me back to it. I had only to let it.

Did I know at the time how deceptively easy the word "only" can seem? I think I began to know, and that was progress.

Suddenly the peaches were ripe. Angelina's brothers came in two trucks, one loaded with ladders and crates, the other with pickers. Most of the pickers were single men like the one I had met in the road. The oldest were a couple of Filipino men and one Japanese, who was delighted that I could speak a few words in his language. From the Filipinos I picked up a few words of Tagalug, and they laughingly pronounced my accent "not bad." The white men were somewhat younger but still over thirty. One had been a fruit tramp since boyhood, but the other four were men who had worked in factories in San Francisco until they had become too ill or too slow to keep up with the younger men. Then, as one said, "it was either take whatever seasonal work you can get, or starve."

They were all good workers, agile and fast, starting at dawn and hardly stopping except to take a drink of water and a siesta after lunch. Providing plenty of water was a task I could take on, and whenever Dona Ceresita was settled for another nap in her chair, I walked around the orchards, bringing water to the men. They were grateful for the service, and I enjoyed talking to them. At the end of the day, they were loaded into a truck and taken back to the family ranch where Angelina's parents allowed them to sleep in a shed.

On the third or fourth day of picking, the truck was followed by an ancient, rattling, puffing car containing the Lopez family. The father, Emilio, a tall, handsome man in his forties, seemed to understand English but refused to speak anything but Spanish. His wife Wanda was much younger than he. She had four children, each about a year apart, and was expecting another. She tried very hard to understand and speak English. Angelina's brother asked me to tell the family they could pitch their tent at the far end of the clearing. It would be easier for the family to stay here, near where they worked.

224

Wanda picked peaches alongside her husband though she often felt dizzy on the ladder and fell once, though not far enough to hurt herself or her unborn child. She often stopped to nurse her baby, shaking her head and sighing that since she was pregnant again, her milk was no good. The three-year-old and four-year-old worked too, sorting and stacking peaches in the crates. The two-year-old lay quietly on the ground—too quietly. Wanda told me he was sick, feverish, probably had a cold.

Then he broke out in spots, and Wanda diagnosed measles. The other children had had it. She knew. There was no money for a doctor, no time to stop picking, and the child must be kept away from the infant, who would surely die if she caught it. I took the sick child into the house, using a peach crate and some of Dona Ceresita's old linens to improvise a bed. For about ten days he lay red and hot and gasping, too weak to cry, eating little but fruit and diluted canned milk. Then the fever broke and the rash subsided. Dona Ceresita seemed not even to notice him, even when he was well enough to cry a bit. She was almost as deaf as she was blind.

During all this time the father, Emilio, remained stiff and hostile toward me, arguing with his wife against letting me care for the child. She argued back, demanding if he wanted "this one to die too?" So there had been still another baby who had not survived.

The day I brought the child back to Wanda's tent was the last day of picking. It was Saturday night, and Emilio had driven into San Jose "to drink with the other men" leaving Wanda with the children. She worried about his drinking prohibition liquor—they knew a man who had gone blind from bad whiskey. At least here in San Jose he could go to the back door of any Italian home and buy a jug of homemade wine that was probably all right. We sat outside the tent on a rough blanket, the children curled up asleep around us, except for the smallest, held in Wanda's arms while we talked.

Wanda was a thin, very dark woman with a long, determined mouth rarely curved into a smile. She and her husband came from a village near Guadalajara. When she was a child, he was already a man. He had carried her on his shoulders, like all the other children, before he left to seek his fortune up north. Fifteen years later he had come back, looking for a wife, driving a car, rich by the standards of the village. He wanted the prettiest girl in the village, Wanda. As for her, at seventeen, she had no future in the village but hunger and premature old age. And she had always idolized the handsome Emilio. They married and drove north.

The work was no harder and the pay a little better than at home. But their life seemed harder because of seeing all the others who were well off, like Angelina's family, who looked down on them. Worst of all was the constant moving, never having a home, a village, a community. From here they would go to Gilroy for prunes, maybe tomatoes. After that was lettuce in Salinas, then cotton. What she hated most was going south to pick oranges. The further south you went, the more Mexicans there were, and the worse they were treated. Then too, the Mexicans themselves held you down, stayed in a group, refused to learn English. Your own people stopped your progress. "Progress" was a word Wanda used often and reverently like a prayer.

She and Emilio disagreed about that as they did increasingly on other things. He would say they had to move or starve, and she would counter that if he didn't drink, they could save enough to stay near San Jose through the winter. She insisted they must learn the American language and American ways. He hated all Americans, including all immigrants from Europe. Americans included everyone but Mexicans and Negroes, whom he looked on as hardly human, and Filipinos, whom he despised even more. Every time he saw a Filipino with a tall, blonde woman, he would say, "There's another whore found herself a houseboy."

He was not the man she had thought she was marrying, not the man she remembered from her childhood. He had followed the crops for too many years, saw too many bad things, drank too much. He had become cruel and hard and angry. You couldn't talk to him. He had hit her once, but only once. She had taken a stick and beat him when he was asleep, drunk, helpless. He awoke bruised from head to toe and never dared to hit her again. But he drank more, became more stubborn and silent and bitter. Old and hopeless, almost. And Wanda was young—only twenty-three—with ambitions for her family.

First of all, to make this baby the last, no matter what the priest said. A woman had told her what to do. Also, she was saving money, unknown to Emilio, hidden. When she had enough, she would buy a piece of land. There were lots east of San Jose you could buy for almost nothing. A few Mexicans and Filipinos had built there, little shacks of scrap wood and metal, even cardboard, but their own, on their own piece of land. Once you had a fixed home, you might make it through the winter—maybe send the men south to pick cotton or oranges, but the kids could stay put, stay healthier, maybe even go to school. The height of Wanda's ambition was to see her children in school and herself working in a cannery.

I told her I had no doubt that she would achieve her ambition. She told me she would never forget that I had saved her son's life. We embraced before I went back into the house. The next morning she and her family were gone.

The picking was done, and I was alone with Dona Ceresita again. Angelina was a faithful visitor, showing up at least once a week. She was working in a cannery, which she left for an hour or two. "The boss's son is sweet on me, so I come and go as I please." She wore a white net over her hair, required for women workers at the cannery and hardly removed during the season, she said, except when she went to bed. When she drove me into San Jose to shop for groceries, I saw the streets full of women in white hair nets, rushing about shopping before or after their ten-hour shift. A hectic, festive atmosphere pervaded the town, as if these women in lacy white caps were all brides in some frantic ceremony.

Everyone, Angelina explained, came in the summer to work in the canneries. Everyone. All the women, kids fourteen and over (and under if they looked old enough), students from the college, teachers from as far north as San Francisco. It was hard work, and you had to be fast, but it was fun, too, and at the end of the day the girls would walk arm in arm down the streets, singing, flirting with the boys, dropping off at their homes, one by one. The only trouble was that the pay was lower this year, and Angelina wouldn't be able to save as much for college as she had hoped. But she was lucky— some of the girls weren't hired this year at all. Next summer would be better, after this slump was over. That was the important canning season, coming just before she would start college.

The people on the streets reminded me of those I had known in my childhood at Hunters Point, the older ones chatting, laughing, calling out to each other in Italian or Yugoslav or Swedish, the younger ones aggressively "American" with short hair and short skirts. Often during these drives into town I kept an eye out for Wanda and her family, but I never saw her or any other Mexicans. "They have their own places," Angelina said. "They like outdoor work."

Summer ended and the hot fall days shortened. Angelina said to me, "I come every week, afraid you'll be gone and poor Dona Ceresita will die alone." She was devoted to the old lady in a way I have rarely seen in young people, who are usually repelled and frightened by the toothless, hairless infirmity of old age. And the old lady was devoted to her. She accepted services from me as her due, but when Angelina came, the old lady came to life. Deaf to anything I said, she heard Angelina's softest words, laughed at her little jokes, agreed to change her dress or eat a bit of soup after having adamantly refused my attempts. Angelina would lovingly brush the few hairs on the old lady's head, rearrange her veil, pin a flower on it, and sing a few bars of "Ramona" (from the movie she had seen eight times) as the old lady giggled.

I promised Angelina I would stay until the lawyers sent a real nurse or until I was not needed anymore. Dona Ceresita could not live much longer. She hardly moved anymore except for her response to Angelina and her slow, painful walks to the outhouse.

I did what I could for the old lady throughout that winter, which was especially wet. The orchards were flooded, then the roads, then, for almost a week, the town of San Jose. The rivers always overflowed, said Angelina, but this year was worse than usual. I kept the old stove going night and day with wood brought by Angelina, but the place was always clammy and damp, the walls actually dripping water through open cracks.

I strained a thin gruel, like food for an infant, which was all Dona Ceresita would touch except for coffee. She liked it strong, and I added thick condensed milk to give her some nourishment. When she could no longer walk to the outhouse Angelina brought a commode to keep beside her bed. Sometimes she soiled herself before I could get her to the commode. Cleaning her was a long, sickening chore, humiliating, yet never so humiliating for me as it was for her. So humiliating that it would break her anger and she would mumble, "Enough, enough, I want to die." But the next day she would wake a little better, in control of her bodily functions, though even when clean she smelled stale as if her body were already half dead. By December she was eating almost nothing. She was all bone, her skin so thin that washing hurt her. I smoothed her skin with oil, as I would bathe a new baby. On Christmas Angelina brought a small tree that she decorated as she had every Christmas since she was old enough. For the first time, she said, Dona Ceresita took no notice of the tree.

I had plenty of time that winter to answer letters which had been forwarded to me by George from Felton. After discarding those addressed to Madame Psyche, what I had left were mainly letters from Stephanie. She was living in a small flat in London, painting huge canvases of redwood trees, trying to figure out what to do with the old country house, which had been greatly damaged during its use as a war hospital and had stood empty during her years in America. She had neither the money nor the will to restore and maintain it. She hoped someone would buy it to use as a school. Everything was so uncertain. The United States' economic troubles had spread to England, but Paris, during a brief visit she made, seemed unaffected. She hoped for economic recovery in the spring.

Had the U.S. papers carried news of the last German election? The Nazis, led by a vile, stupid man, Hitler, had suddenly risen from total political failure and won over a hundred seats in their parliament. Stephanie's family was split between admiration for Hitler and abhorrence. Stephanie hoped that the spring economic recovery ("we constantly refer to it as something which simply *must* come") would plunge Hitler back into obscurity for good. I took little interest in this comment at the time and probably would have forgotten it completely if I hadn't kept the letter, reading it over with others until I lost it about ten years later. By the time I lost it the name of Hitler was no longer just an item of news from Stephanie.

From Guido I received a Christmas present, two pairs of overalls from the factory where he had worked since leaving the Garden of Eden. They were a small size, with minor defects, so employees had been allowed to take them. He thought I might find them useful, since I preferred pants to dresses. He had lost contact with Edward. He had his ticket to France. He promised to write from Paris, but I never heard from him again. I wish I could have written him later to tell him how useful his gifts proved to be.

In late January, while a dozen Filipino pruners were trimming the trees, we had a brief hot spell of the kind that often precedes a windy, rainy spring. One or two of the trees actually responded by putting out a couple of blossoms. I plucked one, which fell apart in my hand, but I brought the petals inside anyway, held them up to the old woman. She could not see or hear, but when I touched the petals to her cheek, she smiled.

After that day she mostly slept, and many times I thought she had died, so long a gap would come between her breaths. But she went on for one more day, then another, then another.

The blossoms had sprouted and fallen when the end came. She had insisted on getting up to sit in her chair. I went to the kitchen to make her coffee. When I came back with it, I found her sitting upright, her head turned to one side and resting against the back of the chair. She was dead.

Angelina's brothers were in the orchard, bracing the heavily laden branches, unloading ladders and crates in preparation for the pickers. I went out to tell them, and they discussed the best way to tell Angelina. She was at school, and this was her graduation day. To telephone would be too cruel, even if she could be reached. They were all leaving now anyway to attend her graduation. After the ceremony they would tell her.

I went back into the house, changed the bed, washed the body, dressed it in a clean nightgown, and lay it on the bed. I sat with it until Angelina and her family came. Angelina was wearing a white dress with a white, wide-brimmed straw hat and red roses at her waist. She cried a little as I pulled the sheet up over the face; the mouth had fallen open and rigor had begun to curl its edges. Then Angelina called the lawyers who told her to take care of the funeral and send the bill to them.

Angelina arranged what must have been the grandest funeral seen in San Jose for many years. The body was moved to a large funeral home, where a rosary was said that night. The next day a procession followed it to the huge Saint Joseph's Church for the requiem mass. The church was full, partly because people were curious about the old lady who had been an unseen legend for so many years, and partly because the town was filling up with cannery workers who had heard that free food would be served to mourners on the church grounds after mass. (There would be no procession to burial; the body was to be taken to the family plot near the Presidio in San Francisco.)

The day after the funeral a huge truck drove up to the adobe and three men began emptying the house, loading everything into the truck. They were down from the City and their instructions were to move Dona Ceresita's effects to a storage warehouse. They took everything but the kitchen stove, which was too heavy and ash-laden, and one gold-leaf, ruby-studded cup, which I managed to hide and keep for Angelina.

(The adobe stood for at least another decade, slowly crumbling. Pickers refused to sleep there, calling it haunted. But I sometimes found it a good hideout during the troubles that came in the next few years.)

When I gave the cup to Angelina, she kissed it. Then she kissed me and asked what I would do. I could only shrug. "Well, what do you want to do?" I knew no way to explain to this girl that I wanted to learn what that thing wanted me to do. She frowned and bit her lip. "I start at the cannery tomorrow. I don't know if they'll hire an oriental—this isn't Alviso! I'll try. You took care of Dona Ceresita, so I won't leave you in the lurch. I'll tell Gino if he wants to take me to the dance, he has to put you on. That's a sacrifice, I'm telling you—he has two left feet. But you'll get on at least for cherries. You know how to pit cherries? No, I guess not. I guess you don't know how to do anything." She was right. I was thirty-five years old, and I was about to apply for my first job.

"First of all you have to put on a dress. You can't go in there like that, looking like a Chinaman. Maybe one of my mother's will fit you—she's small. And pull your hair down like this a little around your eyes, so they don't notice the slant. If anyone asks, tell them you're Russian. A lot of Russians have a little slant like that. You speak some Russian? Never mind. You don't want to overdo it and sound like you're just off the boat. All the girls talk American, except at home for the old folks. I got a bunch of hair nets. You can have one of mine." She actually pulled one out of her pocket and put it on my head as if conferring a new identity on me. "There, now you're a canner—well, a cutter anyway."

It turned out that finding me a place to live was harder than getting me hired at a cannery. There were cheap hotels and rooming houses all over town which catered to transient workers, but these hotels were for single men. Only bad women (Angelina looked away when she said this) rented rooms in these hotels. Respectable working women lived with husbands or with parents, never alone. It might be possible to rent me a room with a family but that could be difficult because of my mixed race. I suggested that there might be a Japanese or Chinese family with a room to rent. "No," she said firmly. "You can't stay over on that side of town." Finding no other solution, Angelina took me home with her.

She and her family lived in a sprawling but crowded wooden house on five acres of prunes. One of her brothers had just married and brought his bride to live with them. All the bedrooms were full. Angelina slept on a couch in the parlor. I offered to sleep in the shed, but that was out of the question. The fruit tramps, four men, were out there for the season. I saw a tent beside the shed and asked if Wanda Lopez and her family had come back. No, this was another family. Wanda usually showed up later. Finally we decided that I should sleep on the front porch.

I gave Angelina's mother a dollar for one of her cotton dresses and three more for one week's room and board, "porch and board," she joked with a strong accent and richly rolled r's. I laughed and made some remark in Italian, and that won her over, even though I had spoken in the Langero dialect, "*quasi francese.*" In a few days I had picked up enough of her Genovese dialect to make her even more comfortable with me.

Angelina's father was a large, morose, sickly man, tubercular. Her four brothers all looked like her mother, slight, with sandy brown hair and dark brown eyes, but, like her, they were wiry and strong. Angelina, with her white skin, rich dark hair, and full-bodied beauty, seemed an advance on the whole family, combining her parents' looks into a body which expressed American optimism. Her parents were proud that she would go to college and become a teacher, but they were also proud of their own accomplishment. Teaching was nice for a woman, until she married, but working your own prune ranch was real work, tangible as the earth itself.

There were nine of us (including the new daughter-in-law) at the dinner table that first night, and it would be our last night of eating together. Everyone would be working long overlapping shifts during the season. We four women and two of the brothers would be dropped off at the cannery tomorrow at dawn, the women to pit cherries, the men to haul boxes to and from the packing sheds. Then Angelina's father and her two other brothers would drive back to their ranch, gather the pickers and drive them to leased land to pick more cherries. They were almost finished. Next would come the peaches, which looked early this year. The "boys" might have to pitch in and pick too. No, said one of the brothers, there were plenty of people dying to pick, coming in hoards every day, whole families, some even white. But with what the canneries were paying this year, said another brother, was it worthwhile to pick at all? "What?" gasped Angelina's mother. "You mean let good food rot?"

"Oh, we have this same argument every night, every night," said Angelina. "I'm sick of it," and she began to talk about the new Jean Harlow movie coming to the San Jose Theater.

"Won't have any time for movies," mumbled her father as he leaned back. His wife stared at his full, untouched plate, a sure sign, Angelina told me later, that his TB was "coming up again."

The next morning shortly after six I was seated at a huge table (one of a dozen tables in a vast chilly room) with over twenty other women, all of us in our white nets and cotton dresses, most covered by a homemade muslin apron. One of the women looked at me and muttered, "Next they'll be hiring Mexican," but otherwise everyone smiled and nodded when Angelina introduced me as, "My good friend, May."

She and her mother sat on either side of me to show me how to pit cherries and to cover up for my slow incompetence by doing some of my work for me. The cherries were brought to us in pans by boys who stopped to flirt with Angelina or with the other young girl seated opposite her, a blue-eyed blonde with a pink ribbon on her hair net. We were to sort the cherries as we worked, putting soft ones into the "pie pan." The firm ones must be slit just so, near the stem, and the pit extracted without gouging out the meat of the fruit or pulling out the stem. We used thin, hook-blade pitting knives brought from home. The cherry must look as if whole and untouched, Angelina explained, for these would become maraschino cherries to decorate ice cream sodas or the new Manhattan cocktail. One of the girls had actually tasted a Manhattan, but the others were silent as she described its sweetness. Women who drank at all, let alone in a bar where such things as Manhattans were served, were considered "fast."

Most of my first efforts ended up in the pie pan. Angelina and her mother alternated between their pans and mine, so that when the floor lady came by, she would not see me as a total failure. The floorladies dressed in white, with white caps instead of nets, and roamed the huge room like suspicious nurse-teachers. Conversation died when one came near, but otherwise it was as constant and rapid as the quick hands of the women, which never stopped, even when nicked by the sharp blade and bleeding bright red onto the pink Queen Anne cherries. It didn't matter, Angelina whispered when I tried to wipe my blood away from the fruit; the cherries would be dyed bright red anyway.

Angelina's mother was not the oldest at the tables. One of the women was over sixty and had worked every canning summer for nearly thirty years, "since the first cannery opened." More of the women were my age or a bit older, with husbands and large families, six or more children. Angelina and the blonde girl were not the youngest at our table; there was one fifteen-year-old. This was her second season. Last year she had done only peaches, but she hoped to apply for each crop "all the way to fruit cocktail," which was canned in the fall, assembled and cut from gallon jugs of inferior fruit saved from each crop. It seemed that workers were hired for one crop at a time, then had to reapply for the next as it came. Unless I showed fast improvement, I could see it was unlikely that even Angelina's influence could get me rehired for the next crop.

The atmosphere at the table was cheerful, as Angelina had promised it would be. The boys carrying pans back and forth made jokes and stopped to flirt with the young girls. The older women teased them both, talked about their children and grandchildren. They gossiped about the young girls who had shown up wearing lipstick, and about the handsome pan boy who last year had been a mere child, nearly a foot shorter. They complained about the college students and teachers who always got the best jobs. "That snotty girl just watching jars on the belt, when I been cutting six years and never got a chance at it." The young blonde girl said that maybe Angelina would act snotty too next year when she got into college, and everyone laughed, but the two girls exchanged a look that was not friendly. The tension was dispelled when someone mentioned the floorlady; everyone could agree on disliking her. "I knew her when she was a cutter, worse than May." Laughter at me, with me, was safe and friendly, and some of the women threw a cut cherry into my pan to help, then went on laughing when the floorlady rushed to our table and said we were not working fast enough.

"You tell those boys to bring us some good cherries, and we'll work faster," said the blonde girl, whose name was Helena. "These dinky little things are all pit and skin." Silence. It was dangerous to talk back to a floorlady. This floorlady acknowledged that "the whole shipment is like that, and if you don't like it, you know what you can do," and stalked away to another table. But she had provoked a chorus of complaint. These cherries were a miserable lot. It took forever to do a pan. At two bits a pan, they'd be lucky to make a couple of dollars a day. "May will be lucky if she makes two bits a day." They laughed again, but their laughter had a tired sound. They were resigned. The floorlady's threat was not an empty one. Anyone who offended her during cherries might not be hired for peaches. With all twenty-six canneries running full, said one older woman, there should be work for everyone. But crowds of unemployed stood around outside, waiting with the hope of even one day's work. Any of us could easily be replaced.

"Yeah, but can they do the work? The fruit'll rot before they get it out."

"Yeah, like May's pan will ferment into cherry brandy before she finishes it." They laughed again, but then gave out a cheer; I actually had finished a pan. "Now yell, 'Pan Boy!' and get yourself another," said Angelina.

Except for a half-hour lunch, we worked steadily until almost dark, more than ten hours. Some of the women turned in chits for a dozen or more pans, but I had done, with help, only five, and the floorlady said I would have to do better if I wanted to stay. "She will, you'll see," said Angelina, with her most charming smile. "May's a nurse, took care of rich ladies, her last one just died. She's smart, catches on fast." The floorlady seemed impressed at being told I was a nurse (not an unpaid servant), and Angelina kicked me to make sure I would not correct her. Perhaps this title put me almost in the category of the privileged college students and teachers, despite my ambiguous race. The floorlady frowned, then shrugged and agreed to give me a few more days.

During the next two days my work improved very little, but the floorlady seemed to have forgotten her threat to let me go. Aside from complaints about the bad cherries, the women remained cheerful until at the end of Saturday—payday—we picked up our pay envelopes and discovered that we were being paid, not the twenty-five cents a pan which had been last year's rate, but only ten cents a pan. Even the fast, competent pitters had earned hardly more than a dollar in each ten-hour day.

One of the older women burst into tears. The others counted their few bills and coins in silent shock. Then Helena, the little blonde girl from our table, shouted at the manager, who stood behind the paymaster, who stood behind the thin bars of his window. "You told us two bits a pan, same as last year."

The manager, a stout man with a tiny striped bow tie that seemed to choke him, glared at the defiant girl. "I told you nothing." Then his face flushed as he shrugged and turned away from her glaring eyes. "The retailers just dropped their price again; we got to follow if we're going to stay in business. You don't like it, don't come back Monday." His voice had fallen to a sullen mumble, full of anger and shame.

Helena opened her mouth again, then closed it, seeing she was on the brink of being fired. She turned and walked out with the rest of us. As soon as we were outside she said "See, I told you what would happen if we don't get organized. Look, we got tonight and all day Sunday to do something."

Angelina pulled her mother and me away from her, rushing us across the street to where one of her brothers waited for us in the truck. "What'd they pay you?" she asked him as she pushed her mother up onto the front seat and slammed the door.

"Same as last year, two bits an hour."

"They put the women down to ten cents a pan."

"Jeez."

We climbed up onto the truck bed, and Angelina's brother drove off. After a silent ride of several blocks he turned toward their house, about another mile into the orchards. "Keep away from Helena," Angelina said to me. "She's a radical. If the floorlady catches you even listening to her union talk, you'll lose your job. And so will I, so will all the family." She was quiet for a while, waiting for me to answer. When I said nothing, she spoke as if I had disagreed with her. "May, the only way I'm going to get through college is to work my way, and that means the canneries. That's all there is. I can't afford to get blacklisted. Cherries are only another two weeks. Then we go over to Libby for peaches. I already signed us up, you too. I know a floorlady there, my mother's cousin."

The next morning I went to mass with Angelina, her mother, her married brother and his wife. The other men had "no use for priests." And there was always work to do at home. Angelina dressed herself in a lovely flowered silk, wore high heels, and tripped about light as a dancer, as if she had spent the week resting. She lent me another of her mother's dresses and a scarf to cover my head.

Saint Joseph's church was full of families, the older women in somber, mostly black dresses, the young women in gay colors, and all the men, young and old, in neatly pressed suits. I recognized a couple of "pan boys," stiff in collars and ties.

236

The crowd was restless, especially during communion, when many remained in their seats. The priest's sermon seemed unnecessarily stern, almost angry, as if what sounded like a simple, traditional recommendation of patience and peace had some other more immediate meaning. As I looked around at familiar faces of women from the cannery, I saw clenched jaws, eyes which did not look up at the man in the pulpit. I realized that his words and their silent resistance to them had something to do with what I had seen yesterday at the cannery. Everyone knew there had been another drop in wages. The priest's sermon was only a repetition of Angelina's warning to conform. Yet even she looked down into her lap, her face flushed with anger, when he spoke.

As we rose to leave, I noticed that the back row was full of dark people, Mexicans. I looked among them for Wanda and her family, but recognized no one.

Outside, the girls showed off their bright dresses, standing in laughing clusters, very conscious of the boys nearby. Their parents gathered in other groups, overseeing the flirting between boys and girls. Across the street the Mexicans gathered, their skirts even brighter shocks of color. Neither group seemed aware of the other.

Angelina stood surrounded by four boys while I stood on the edge of the group of older women with her mother. They were discussing the new reduction of wages in all the canneries. I heard one of the women say to a man, "Sure, they always cut the women first, and you don't care, but wait till they hit the packing sheds. Wait till you get laid off and only your wife is working!"

At that moment I felt something stuffed into my hand. I turned to see the back of Helena's blonde head as she hurried away. I was pretty sure she had not been in church, but she was out here in a fresh, full-skirted blue dress and white shoes, moving among the groups of people, laughing and flirting, and surreptitiously stuffing crumpled scraps of paper into their hands. I looked down at mine. It read, in scrawled pencil, "Union meeting tonight 7 p.m. Thomas Hotel Room 347." I decided not to show it to Angelina. Should I throw it away? If I dropped it in front of the church, someone might see what Helena was doing and report her. I looked around and saw a perfectly clean sidewalk. Others were either planning to attend the meeting, or were, like me, protecting Helena by not publicly discarding the message. I kept it clenched in my fist until we got home. Then, while helping prepare the big Sunday lunch, I dropped it into the stove.

That night Angelina and her brothers went to a dance. The following morning one teased the other about dancing so often with Helena. So, if there had been a meeting, Helena had gone from that to a dance. How hard these young people worked and how hard they played!

On Monday there was little laughter around our table except when the floorlady was near and Helena described the dance. When the floorlady moved away, Helena talked about the union meeting, which she and two of the other women had attended. There would be another meeting next week. Helena urged all the women to come. The oldest woman at the table sighed. "Been a union off and on ever since I started working. Never did anything but collect dues and call meetings. I stop going to meetings, stay home and get the wash done instead. By the time people agree on anything, the season is over."

Helena disagreed with her, patiently, respectfully, and so earnestly that I did not see how anyone could resist her. There were only a few bosses, and many workers. If all the workers acted together... then a quick glance warned her of the approach of the floorlady, and she began to tell a joke, ignoring the floorlady's warning not to talk so much. For all her talk, Helena was the fastest worker at the table. Even pitting a handful from my pan, she kept ahead of all the others, who were themselves quite fast. They needed to be. The cherries were pouring in, suddenly ripe, yet even smaller than the earlier ones. Our shifts had been extended to twelve hours, and a night shift had been added. Every hour was precious in the race against spoilage of the hateful little fruit whose meager meat seemed hardly enough to cover the pit. "I wonder where they're sending the good cherries," Angelina complained.

It was on Wednesday that Helena proposed her "baby strike." "Listen, you ladies don't have to do anything. I'll call the floorlady and tell her we ought to get at least fifteen cents a pan for these lousy little cherries."

"She'll tell you to go to hell," said Angelina.

"And I'll tell her we are going to just sit here until we get fifteen cents a pan."

"They'll fire the whole table," said Angelina.

"No, they'll fire me, that's all." Helena tossed her head and laughed. "We're the best table in the place. You ladies know your work, and the boss can't afford to let these cherries sit. Look at them, rotting in front of us. They're not going to lose these cherries for a few pennies. They'll give in, and then they'll fire me, as an example! How about it? You don't have to do a thing but stop work when I say."

"I can't risk it. I need the job."

"You think the rest of us don't?" Helena glared at Angelina.

"I can't afford to get blackballed. Troublemakers don't get hired for the next crop."

"You're not going to be called a troublemaker, only me."

"What good will it do? So we get a little more for cherries. They'll be done in a week anyhow."

"The good it does is that the bosses think twice before they cut wages again. You think they don't all plan together? Why do you think the rate for cherries dropped in all the cherry canneries on the same day?"

At that point the floorlady drifted by again, and both girls fell silent. None of the rest of us spoke, even after the floorlady moved away. The argument had become a struggle between these two girls, so similar, both young, both pretty and spirited and intelligent, both looking as if they ought to be always in flowered dresses, flirting outside church and planning their next dance.

"We go on like this," continued Helena, "and by the time we get to fruit cocktail, we're making less than pea pickers."

"I won't be here for fruit cocktail," said Angelina.

"No, you won't," said Helena. "You'll be a college girl then, won't you? We won't see you till next summer when you come back and they put you watching cans on line because you're too good to be with us cutters. But what about Lina here, or Mrs. Fedorat? They got kids and husbands out of work. They're not chopping their fingers in these lousy cherries to go to college, but to feed their families. When you got your teacher certificate and a good job, and all the fruit stains wear off your fingers, we'll still be here for ten cents a pan, or maybe five cents, or three cents!"

Everyone was quiet. Helena had hit a sore spot. Angelina's mother sat with her head bowed, hands trembling so that she cut herself again (she had dozens of thin white scars on her hands).

"But we all stick together, and nobody loses but me, not Angelina, not the rest of you. Look at these cherries. They can't afford any delays. They got to get them done right now." Helena smiled around the table, even at Angelina, who refused to look at her. More silence. "If no one says anything against it, I'm going to do it. Going going..." she said, like an auctioneer, while one or two of the women faintly smiled, "...gone!" Angelina had opened her mouth, but did not dare to speak against the silent vote against her.

A few minutes later, when the floorlady was near our table again, Helena stood up and said, "I want to talk to the manager."

"He's not here."

"I saw him down in the office when we came in."

"He's busy. Talk to him after your shift."

"He'll be gone then. I have to talk to him now." Helena stood straight and firm facing the woman, who was about my age but very tall and heavy, with a fierce frown she wore like a weapon.

"What about?"

"About these cherries. They're so small, we ought to get more. We want fifteen cents a pan." Helena had raised her voice and could be heard at most of the other tables. Silence spread over the room swiftly.

The floorlady froze, her frown deepening into a shocked look that was less menacing. For a moment she stood speechless. Then she said, "You sit down, girl, and get back to work." Helena sat down as the woman swung around, almost full circle, sweeping the rest of the room with a hard, warning glance, then walked away.

About fifteen minutes later, she was back, walking silently and slowly, keeping her head turned away from our table. This time Helena did not get up but kept working, throwing over her shoulder, "You tell him?"

"What?"

"You tell the manager to give us fifteen cents a pan?"

The floorlady ignored her.

Helena looked around at all of us, meeting the eyes of each woman with a glance which, while not menacing like that of the floorlady, was just as strong. Then she raised her voice as loud as possible and said, "I speak for all the ladies at this table. We are going to work another fifteen minutes. If the manager isn't up here by then, we are going to stop working."

The floorlady stiffened in outrage. "Are you letting this girl tell you what to do? Mrs. Celini? Mrs. Lamoski? You going to let this girl get you into trouble?" She waited through another silence. "I didn't think so." She laughed and walked away.

Exactly fifteen minutes, later, Helena put down her knife. One by one all the women followed. Angelina was the last, but finally, with all the others watching her, she put it down, and we all sat with our hands folded in our laps. The floorlady was there in an instant. "What are you doing? Get back to work. I'll have you all fired. Get back to work!" A few hands trembled as if they would reach for the knife again, but no one did. The floorlady stomped away. Within a minute she was back, followed by the breathless manager, his red face puzzled, almost smiling.

"What's all this? You ladies have a problem?"

Helena stood. "These cherries are hard to work on. We want fifteen cents a pan. We're not going on until we get fifteen cents a pan."

The manager walked up and down behind the women sitting hunched over their clasped hands. He threw out his fat belly, swung his arms, opened his mouth several times, then closed it again. Heads remained bowed except for Helena's. She met his glare steadily. Work at the next table slowed, then stopped. The manager snorted impatiently, sighed, cleared his throat. Then he looked around, shrugged, and put on a forced smile, the self-pitying smile of a patient man. "All right, ladies, all right, fifteen cents." A cheer went up from a table on the other side of the room. He wheeled around, silencing the cheer. Then he swung back again.

"But you!" he yelled at Helena. "You're fired! Get out. Right now." Helena only smiled as he shouted to make sure the women at the other tables all heard his threat. "And..." He turned and looked around the table until he came to me, then glanced at the floorlady, who nodded. "You too. Out." He looked around the table again. "And...." The others stiffened. Helena had promised that only she would be fired. "And...the rest of you get back to work, and I don't want to be bothered again!" He was glaring at the floorlady as he strode away.

Helena pulled off her hairnet and waved it silently at everyone in the room, no one daring to look up at her as she took my arm and walked me out. "Smile," she whispered between clenched teeth, turning a broad, triumphant, beautiful grin on everyone who glanced at her, especially at the floorlady, who looked furious and frightened.

As soon as we had crossed the yard and were out the gate, she threw her arm over my shoulder and began to cry. "Oh, I'm sorry, May, really, I'm sorry. I was sure he wouldn't fire anyone but me!"

I tried to reassure her. "He was getting ready to let me go anyway. He did it this way to scare the others. I couldn't have lasted more than a day or two. I just wasn't fast enough."

"That's true, May, you're a lousy pitter." We both laughed, and she dried her eyes as we turned down Market Street. "But he didn't scare them, or not as much as usual. They've had a little taste of the power of acting together, and that's something to build on. We're trying to build a union here, May, and more people are starting to see that's the only hope we have, the way things are going. This valley is ours, and they act like...."

As we walked arm in arm, Helena talked about her union organizing. The union had so much working against it, mostly the seasonal nature of the work. The AFL wouldn't bother with them, called them migrants who couldn't even pay dues. "We're not migrants, we live here, we own a little land, we scrape by somehow in the off season. The way they dropped the wages, some people could lose their homes. I guess they'd like that, then we'd have to drift in and out like the fruit tramps." But that wouldn't happen. The union would get strong, made up of workers who had a little house, a little orchard, proud and independent people "settled here long enough to get together and make the canneries do right!" Before she turned off towards her family's little orchard, she told me the address of the union office again. "I'm going to tell them they have to help you because of what you did." Of course, I hadn't done anything; my incompetence had accidentally made me her fellow victim.

I walked to Angelina's house, which was empty and strewn with dishes and clothes the men had used during the day. They worked hard too, but the women cooked and cleaned for the men in addition to their own long hours in the cannery. I washed the dishes, scrubbed some clothes and hung them out, then started dinner, picking greens from the garden for salad, and adding some canned vegetables to the rabbit stew left from last night. By the time I was setting the table it was dark, and the family was drifting in, being told how I had lost my job.

The conversation that night—as various family members drifted in to eat, trading places at the table, slumping in exhaustion over their plates—was about unions, about Helena, and about her family. There were strong similarities between the two families. Angelina's father was Italian, Helena's Portuguese. Both had emigrated to work as miners in Colorado. The difference was that Helena's father was a socialist, a union organizer even in the old country.

"He was blacklisted there," said Angelina's father, "and blacklisted again in Colorado. Well, we both got married and had children, all around the time of the bad strikes, the Ludlow Massacre. Only one thing we agreed on, it was a good time to get out of Colorado. He showed me a letter he got from a cousin out here. It said, if you can work twelve hours a day on your own five acres and a few more you lease, and your boys help after school, and your women and kids all work summers in the canneries, and you raise your own chickens and rabbits and vegetables—then you might just barely make it out here. So we came. So my sons don't grow up to be miners."

Like Angelina, Helena had four brothers, two older than she, and two younger. But Helena's mother had died, and her father's lungs were worse than those of Angelina's father. Helena had left school at thirteen to keep house for her family. The children of both families had gone to school together, and the boys got along well. But the girls, Helena and Angelina, did not, and their conflict reflected the political differences that had separated the families.

Helena was like her father, a socialist from the cradle, "always talking union." She was bright, and their house was full of books. This fact was mentioned with faint suspicion and followed by a darker verdict; Helena had gone communist. It was because she had had to leave school, explained Angelina. She would never get off this treadmill of hard work. She was a fanatic, and it was all envy, envy, because she had "no mother and no chance to better herself."

The rest of the family was not quite so harsh in their judgment of Helena, but they agreed that radical politics and unionizing only brought trouble. Experiences in Colorado had convinced Angelina's father; strike and you lose, and you never make back your losses. Join a union and you get blacklisted. Even Helena's brothers, regular enough fellows and not bad workers, had trouble holding jobs because of their sister's activities. Their own anger at Helena probably would break up her family as soon as the father died, which wouldn't be long now. There was a brief hush of sympathy as everyone nodded. The breaking up of family was a tragedy. Family took care of one another. Who else would? The best—the only thing to do was to work hard, take care of your own, and stay out of trouble.

"Yeah, well, but it was Helena got you fifteen cents a pan to pay for your fancy education," muttered Angelina's middle brother, the one who had danced most with Helena last Sunday night. There was a tone of resentment which made it clear why Angelina would have to work her way through college. None of her brothers was bookish, none wanted to go to college. But neither did they believe in putting hard-earned money into a college education for a woman.

I kept quiet during this discussion and the argument it turned into. It was clear that this boy was more attracted by Helena's blonde beauty than by her politics, and repelled by some of his sister's strengths. Even if I had felt free to take sides, I could not. Both Angelina and Helena seemed to me to be generous, brave girls, working and struggling with honesty and honor and conviction which I had lacked at their age. I wondered if, no matter which path each took, they would both end by losing their families.

I still had enough money to continue paying Angelina's mother for my room and board. I proposed that for the next two weeks I could keep house and cook while all of them worked in the cannery finishing cherries. Then peaches would be ready; I was still signed up for peaches.

During the next two weeks I managed to be the first one up, cooking breakfast and packing lunches as I had seen the other women do. During the day I cleaned house and washed clothes, even did a little outside work, feeding the chickens and rabbits, watering the vegetable garden. Angelina's father was cleaning trays and boxes to be used when picking started in the orchards still leased from the estate of Dona Ceresita. These peaches would go to the same cannery where we would all be working. The cannery price had just been put down, and Angelina's father had told the waiting pickers that he would have to pay them less accordingly.

Every day someone brought home rumors that the canneries planned a twenty percent cut in wages, not only inside the cannery but in the packing sheds. Rumors were announced but not discussed. The family was reluctant to discuss the growing discontent among their fellow workers, and too tired to do much but eat and fall into bed.

Of the four men camping in the shed, two left when they learned what their wages would be; they hoped to do better elsewhere. The day after they left, two Mexican families drove in, and the day after that a family from Oklahoma. Angelina's mother shook her head. "I see white men picking, but never a white family. Mexicans, yes, but no white family traveling like gypsies, no place of their own." Since both my English and my Spanish were better than hers, she asked me to explain to the three families that they could pitch their tents in the leased peach orchard or could use the adobe house. I walked across the driveway and past the shed to tell the family from Oklahoma. They had parked as far as possible from the Mexicans, although, despite shouts and threats, they could not keep their children from playing with the Mexican children. There were more than a dozen children playing beside the shed, but they made little noise for so many children, a sure sign of long-standing hunger. When I went back across the driveway to speak to the Mexican families, I asked if they knew and had seen Wanda's family. One of the women knew Wanda but said she had not seen her for a long time. "I think they went back to Mexico."

Cherry canning ended, and there was a gap of a few days before the picking and canning of peaches. During those few days, the women worked long hours at home, getting ready for the July fourth picnic. This was as big a holiday as Christmas, with a parade, a rodeo, and many picnics, celebrated not as a particularly patriotic holiday, but as a pre-harvest festival. After the fourth, Angelina's mother said, there would be no rest again until Thanksgiving—that is, if they were all among the lucky employed to process and preserve the harvest.

On the morning of the fourth everyone was up at dawn, the men rushing through outdoor chores while the women started cooking. Later, Angelina's brothers went to the parade, while the women continued cooking. By eleven, they were home again to load the food and us into the truck and drive to Alum Rock Park, where Angelina's father had gone early to reserve a picnic table and barbecue pit. The park lay across a canyon on the east side of town between low, wooded hills. It was named for the natural mineral water springs that trickled from huge rocks into which drinking fountains had been built. Angelina's father said that the sulfurous waters helped his lungs. All the older people drank the water, claiming it cured many different ailments.

Hundreds of people crowded into the park that day. The women stood over tables and pits, still cooking. The men threw or watched horse-shoe games. The young people swam in the new, enclosed pool. After a huge mid-day meal, the men napped while the women cleaned up. Then the older couples strolled across the broad lawns, stopping to sample the water at each fountain, until the dancing began.

Everyone converged on the wooden platform. Everyone danced at least once, from the oldest grandmothers to the smallest toddlers, standing on their grandfathers' feet. Then the older people watched while the young married couples and teenagers held the floor, dancing, dancing, stopping only for a drink or a light snack as the sun went down. After dark there were modest fireworks, handled with care because of the surrounding dry, brown hills. Children ran around with sparklers like elves waving magic wands. The women sat slapping at mosquitoes while the men loaded everything back into the truck. Then we climbed on and rode home. By ten o'clock we were all in bed, except for Angelina's older brothers, who were allowed to stay out later.

The day after the picnic I put on my white hairnet again and rode to the cannery with Angelina, her mother, and three of her brothers. Along the way we picked up walkers, until the back of the truck was full of girls in white hairnets and bright cotton dresses, laughing and teasing Angelina's brothers.

The laughter died as we got down from the truck and walked into the cannery yard. The crowd of people standing around, unhired, watching glumly, was larger than the crowd that streamed into the cannery in the dim dawn light. Underneath the chatter and the busy movement and the flirting with box boys seethed an undercurrent of anger. Angelina groaned at the sign posted over the cashier's window: CUTTERS 5¢ BOX, CANNERS 20¢ HOUR. Both cashier and manager were absent as if to say, take it or leave it. Angelina's disposition did not improve when she saw we were assigned to a table where Helena was already at work. Somehow, perhaps because she was such a good worker, perhaps because blacklisting was not yet very efficient, Helena had slipped through and been hired.

Peaches were easier than cherries. We took a peach from the box left beside each of us by a boy, cut it in half along the seam, dropped out the pit, and placed the peach halves in a pan according to the degree of softness or the number of blemishes, so that cutting and sorting proceeded together. Much easier than pears, Angelina told me, which would come next month. Pears were harder to pit and had to be peeled, while peaches went through a lye bath which removed the peeling. Her only complaint about peaches was that they gave her a rash; after an hour of work I could see her hands beginning to turn a sore, raw red.

The main disadvantage in cutting peaches was that we worked standing up, risky for me after an hour or so because I tended to grow dizzy. I worried that if I grew faint a company nurse (I had heard there was one but needn't have worried; she never appeared, if she existed at all) might take my pulse and have me fired lest I drop dead on the job. I saw that a few of the older women were leaning against stools. No one said anything when I took one and perched on it, but I could see that I had, in a sense, declared myself old. In fact, among these women, with their many children and unending labor, thirty-six *was* old. It seemed even older when the box boys brought "good" boxes (those with the largest, firmest peaches) to pretty young girls like Helena and Angelina. But resentment of that favoritism was routine, and tolerated. The new resentment, over the drop in wages, was more serious and universal.

The women talked openly and bitterly about it as they worked. The older ones had seen the pay drop every year from its height of seventeen cents a box only five years ago. "And that wasn't so hot." Even the fastest cutters could finish little more than three fifty-pound boxes in an hour. When Helena mentioned a union meeting taking place that night, no one answered or even looked at her, but later when a box boy whispered the same news, I heard someone whisper, "Where?"

At lunch that day there was more union talk, and when I went to the washroom I saw a scrap of paper stuck to the mirror over the wash basins announcing the place and time of the meeting. Later that afternoon the floorlady passed our table and looked suspiciously at Helena. "I pulled down signs in the ladies' room four times today. If I find out who keeps putting them back up . . . ." No one looked up at her, but a muffled snicker was heard. "Who's laughing there?" Silence. But the silence was defiant, angry. One of the older women looked up at the floorlady, narrowing her eyes, and the floorlady looked uncertain for a moment, then walked away. Of course, I knew better than to ask Angelina if we were going to attend the meeting.

The next day Helena told everyone at our table about the meeting. It had been attended by workers from every cannery in San Jose, all twenty-six of them. The workers were not going to stand for this wage cut. They were renting a hall for a larger meeting to plan action. Apparently what gave new force to the discontent was the pay cut of the canners. These were not temporary summer workers. Skilled workers, both men and women, paid by the hour and working nearly all year, they earned almost as much as floorladies and supervisors— or they had until now. Now their pay would be little more than what a good cutter might earn. "They're hopping mad," whispered one of the box boys.

Despite the smoldering anger, the larger meeting, Helena admitted, did not attract more people. Probably everyone was too tired at the end of days that sometimes stretched to twelve hours of work as the quickly ripening fruit poured in. More cutters were hired, very young ones, some children who swore to being fifteen, while Helena insisted they were no more than twelve. "They're passing up the experienced cutters," she said, "because these kids are easier to handle, glad to earn a few pennies." Two of the children who joined our table laughed and sang, and the floorlady did not scold them, perhaps because their antics diluted the constant, open discussion of the wage cut.

Yet weariness and need might have kept everyone under control if it had not been for the arrival of the first apricots in the last week of July, when cutters on the apricot tables were told we would get three cents per box. The cannery always paid less for apricots than for peaches since "cots go, pits and peels and all, right into the can," presorted by growers who held back the ripe ones for drying. But, 3¢ BOX IS SLAVERY someone wrote with lipstick on the mirror in the women's washroom. Voices were raised in complaints and not lowered when the floorlady looked threateningly at the speakers.

Of the glowering women around our table, only Helena looked bright, almost happy. "Some of you ladies pitted cherries with me last month, and you remember what happened when we all acted together. Now it's not just a few tables, not just one cannery. It's all of them. Come to the meeting tonight and you'll see." Her blue eyes were bright, her cheeks flushed, her blonde hair thrusting little curly ringlets like a golden halo bursting through holes in the white net covering her head.

That was on Thursday. I did not attend the meeting because, of course, Angelina drove us straight home, saying only that, at this rate, she must get more hours. She hoped they would need a night shift and she could work a double shift. Otherwise, she could not save enough to get through the college year, and if she had to drop out, the college would fail her in all subjects, giving her a grade average so low that she could never go back. She did not want to talk about meetings or unions; she needed sleep. Dawn would come tomorrow at five.

The next morning Angelina's father drove us as far as Fourth Street, dropping us off to walk the rest of the way, as he would need the truck. We joined the streams of women walking toward the canneries, but when we reached our cannery yard, we saw that there were already dozens of people standing in front of the doors, not unemployed hoping for jobs (they were out near the fence) but workers carrying signs and shouting, "Strike!" The signs demanded TEN CENTS MORE PER HOUR and FIVE CENTS MORE PER BOX. Helena was in the center of a group of picketers. She had tacked her white hair net on the edge of her sign where it fluttered when she waved it but otherwise hung limp in the warm, hazy dawn. "Don't go in," she shouted. "Stay out for a decent wage!" Arriving workers were stopping in groups, and some of them cheered when Helena waved her sign. "Union! Union!" chanted a large group.

Above them a door opened, and a man in a dark suit stepped out onto the raised porch. "Get away from there, get away." But the picketers did not budge. "Anyone wants to work, come in, otherwise leave." He gestured toward the lineup of people near the fence. "You want work? If these people don't want to work, we can use you." Some of the people moved forward, then stopped, hesitating, as Helena led a chant, "Scabs, scabs, scabs!" and signs were waved in more menacing motions.

Some of the people moved forward again and were pushed and jeered at by the crowd, but they got through to the door and disappeared inside. "That's fine," yelled Helena. "Those people will have one day's work, but when our union wins, they won't work again. That's a big price for one day's work!" The other people hesitated, hung back again. But Angelina gripped her mother's arm, and my arm, and began to move forward. As she reached the crowd of pickets, she said, "Is anyone here coward enough to touch my mother?" She gave her mother a little shove, and her mother walked through the picket line, through the small doorway. Then Angelina tried to pull me forward.

I could not move. I had no idea of not moving, no idea one way or the other until that moment when I simply could not move forward past Helena, past the group of picketers. Angelina turned to look at me. In one glance, she understood more than I did. "Don't be a fool," she whispered. "There's no real union, and there are ten people looking for every job in there. The strikers have already lost—a few hours waving signs and they're out of a job, that's all. We can't afford that." She pulled at me again, but I could not move. I looked up at her fresh young face. She was as white as her hair net. I felt as frozen as if I were looking at the Medusa.

"May, I got to! May, don't let me down."

I felt the ache of tears rising in my throat. I didn't want to let Angelina down. I didn't want to join the strikers, and I didn't want to cut apricots. I didn't want to be here at all. But my orders were clear. I had subdued myself, trained myself for over a year to let that thing lead me. It had led me here, and now had come the strongest, surest order, like a weight of ice freezing me. If I disobeyed, if I wrenched myself forward out of this paralysis, I would be back at the beginning again.

Angelina let go of my arm, turned her back on me, and marched through the crowd to the front door. As she reached it, Helena spat on her.

Suddenly Helena was beside me saying that she was head of a committee and had to check out some other canneries. Would I come along? "You speak Russian? Italian too? How about Yugoslav? Great! I might need you to translate to some of the older workers."

We walked down Fourth Street, Helena chattering happily. "I never thought we'd do it! It was those cots did it, brought all the cutters and canners together. Before, we were all divided, as far apart almost as the canners and pickers. Now we're going to bring them in too, bring all the unions together, make a whole new union of all the agricultural workers!" Helena's mission was to cheer on the picketers at seven of the canneries, and to remind them to come to the meeting that night where organizers from San Francisco would help plan a mass rally in the park for the next day.

At each cannery we found long picket lines being crossed by new workers escorted by police, who were jeered at by crowds of workers drifting up and down the street. Men in the crowds came to Helena with news, confirming her best hopes. "We've hit every one of the canneries, all twenty-six. The Frisco office couldn't believe it. They always said the canners were hopeless, would never strike. I guess we showed them!''

Her next job was to drive to San Francisco and pick up speakers for tonight's meeting and tomorrow's rally. She got into a borrowed car and offered me a ride back to Angelina's house. I was glad to accept it; the walking and the crowds, the angry excitement, had been very tiring. For Helena, of course, the stimulation had the opposite effect; she glowed with energy, excitement, and hope. When she dropped me off in the driveway, she said, "Look, May, if anyone warns you about me, says I'm a radical, a dirty communist, well . . . ." She laughed. "They're right!" She drove off with all the excitement of a young beauty rushing to meet her lover.

When I went into the house, I found Angelina's mother. She had left the cannery at lunchtime and had not gone back. There was really no work to do. The boys were home too, cleaning trays with their father. The cannery supervisors were acting as if work was going on as normal, but it wasn't. There were inexperienced cutters messing up the fruit, no box boys to bring it in, and some of the belts weren't operating. The police were escorting a few workers in and out, and fights had broken out. She was afraid. She shook her head. It would all blow over quickly, but there would be hard feelings between old friends, old neighbors, old *paisani*. It was best to stay clear of it, stay home for a day or two; plenty of work to do here. "The first prune drop . . . already."

I asked if Angelina had come home too. No, Angelina had been put on a capping machine. They were paying her by the hour for as long as she would stay, all day and all night, whether or not the machine was kept running. She had made the manager promise to keep her permanently on the capping machine. Angelina's mother said no more, made no comment as I folded my clothes and put them into my pack. Both of us knew that, no matter how the strike turned out, I could no longer stay with them.

That night I attended the meeting held in the big dance hall. Several hundred people were there listening to speeches made by men and women introduced by Helena. When the speakers read their list of demands—union recognition, wage increases—the audience listened attentively, cheered, then voted unanimously for them. But speakers who began more general talks about "the worker in a capitalist society" were ignored, and some people shifted restlessly, pulled out pocket watches, then yawned and walked toward exits. Helena took the floor, announced a rally in Saint James Park for the following day, Saturday, and the meeting was hastily adjourned while there were still some people present to hear adjournment announced. Helena rushed out as soon as she had made her announcement; she and the steering committee would be meeting all night.

Some of the organizers from San Francisco had brought bed rolls and were spending the night in the hall. When I wrapped myself in my cape and lay down in a corner, no one took any notice of me. I lay in the dark listening to the voices of others who could not sleep, voices firm with idealism and purpose. Unlike them, I was uncertain and afraid. They whispered about the invincibility of truth and justice while I thought that since committing myself to truth I had moved from one defeat to another. I could not think of any way I could have avoided being where I was now, and I would rather have been almost anywhere else. But—I reminded myself—I don't really want to be where I want to be. I want to be where that thing sends me. And with such thoughts of unconvinced conviction, I finally fell asleep.

The next morning I slept past dawn for the first time in many weeks. When I awoke, I counted five bodies on the floor, stirring, then jumping up, young men with no aches or stiffness after a night on the hard floor. One of them went out and brought back bread and coffee. They all knew each other—students who had met at meetings. They asked who I was—an older organizer sent from "party headquarters?" When I explained that I was—or had been—a cannery worker, they were respectful and friendly, asking me questions I could not answer. I explained that I had helped Helena by translating her messages to some of the workers, but that I was here only because I had nowhere to sleep. I offered to clean up our breakfast remains so that they could go to the park and help set up for the rally. I would come along later. Actually I had no plans to attend the rally. It might be better for me just to leave town, though I could not think of where to go and, of course, I had no car. I thought that if I could be alone and quiet for a few moments I would receive some clear summons, some direction, a reasoned, clear idea on how to proceed from here, not a sudden, irrational urge like the one which had made me freeze before the picket line. (I have been a long time giving up that comforting expectation. First come the sudden urges, followed eventually by clear, rational reasons.)

Three hours later I found myself walking down First Street toward Saint James Park, a green, tree-shaded square, surrounded by century-old buildings put up in the days when San Jose was the state capital. Over the park that day hung a hazy, smoky smell of burnt wood and plaster, paint and varnish. Only a month before, the old county courthouse—the grandest building in San Jose, a deteriorating leftover of those days, with broad steps, tall columns, and a huge dome—had burned. The brick walls were still standing, but the dome had fallen inward on the gutted building. Angelina's family had barely mentioned the fire at the dinner table, considering it no loss, only hoping the town would not use tax money to restore it. The times were too uncertain to spend money restoring useless relics. Most people had enjoyed talking about the drama of the fire, hardly noticing or caring about the dusty mess and smell they passed on their way to work.

But on that last day of July 1931, as I approached the park, the blackened, dead building looming over it, the acrid smell filling the hot, still air—suddenly I thought of ruined villages I had seen in Austria after the war, full of the smell of destruction left in the wake of an army.

For an army was here too. Police. In cars, on horses, on motorcycles, on foot. There were local police, highway patrolmen, and men with no uniforms—only gleaming badges on their suspenders and sticks in their hands. The entire park was surrounded, and I saw something I had not seen since the anti-war rallies in London fifteen years before: hoses attached to fire hydrants.

I hesitated, watching other people who were coming from all directions toward the park. Almost everyone stopped at the sight of the police, as I had done. Many remained standing where they were, watching from outside the ring of police circling the park. Others, like me, began to walk slowly forward again as if impelled by a force they would rather resist. We were passed by briskly marching groups of men and women with determined faces, some with cannery nets waving at the end of a stick, the way Helena had carried hers, some with signs. They looked as surprised as we more timid ones when they saw the scores of policemen, but they reacted quickly and harshly, calling the police "scab herders" and "fascists" (I think that was the first time I heard the word) as they walked through their lines, past their cars and horses, and into the park. One mounted policeman spurred his horse, which kicked backwards, barely missing a man who had shouted "thugs!" at the police.

Within the park there were perhaps a thousand people. Some, like me, moved slowly toward the speakers' stand, our backs to the surrounding police, our shoulders slightly rounded as if ducking a blow which might come from them. Others stood erect, looking all around, at the speaker, at the police, eyes wide with curiosity gradually becoming apprehension. Then there were groups who stayed on the edges within earshot of the police, talking loudly about their hatred of cops and scabs. Scuffles broke out here and there among the men. I saw police step forward swinging their clubs at one or two of the scuffling men, but not at three others, who moved on to another group, provoking another scuffle. I did not at first believe what my eyes showed me—that these three men were working for the police, stirring up excuses for beating and arrest.

The volume of voices talking, calling, shouting, rose and thickened like the burnt air we all breathed. People were not listening to the speakers who climbed up on the platform, and could not have heard if they tried to listen. I could see Helena at the edge of the platform, looking as worried as I felt. The crowd was orderly—except for pocket scuffles provoked by the roving trio—but angry, and becoming more angry as they looked at the police surrounding them. The fainthearted (except for me) had gone home or stood half a block away, out of range. The cautious, the cool-headed, were not here. Those who had entered the park were brave and righteous, but emotional and young and afraid to show their fear. Like the police, they were beginning to mask fear with fury.

I had moved close enough to hear the speaker, standing on the planks stretched across prune boxes, a man who said that the canners' union had voted to be absorbed into a larger union including all agricultural workers. Those near enough to hear him cheered. He shouted, "The AFL doesn't want us, and I quote their leader, 'Only a fanatic would go live in a tent and get his head busted organizing agricultural workers.'" As shouts rose around me, I heard even louder shouts and rumbles from the outer edges of the park. "So we say the hell with the AFL!" He was cheered as he stepped down from the platform, and a few people started to chant, "To hell with the AFL, to hell with the AFL!" Then they stopped, uneasily turning, like me, toward the surrounding lines of police, where scuffles and shouting we could not see or hear clearly were spreading.

The next speaker was a tall, dark man with a stooped back who yet carried himself with stiff, impressive bearing. He wore a wide straw hat which obscured his face. Yet he seemed familiar to me. He spoke Spanish. Someone poked me. "What's he saying?" I translated for a few people around me. "The workers in the fields support our brothers and sisters in the canneries." Mild applause flickered through the park among those who could hear, as the man quickly stepped down. I had recognized his voice. It was Emilio Lopez, Wanda's husband. I tried to get closer to him, but the crowds were pressing inward, driven by the police, who were no longer on the edges of the park, but had begun closing their circle, pushing people inward. There were angry shouts and screams all around the edges now.

Helena raised a woman to the platform, introducing her as a "representative from the needle trades, come down from San Francisco." As the tiny woman shouted her first word, "Workers . . . ." something flew out from the edge of the crowd, hitting her on the head. She fell from the platform. As an enraged shout rose around her, so did smoke, from the place where she fell. A tear gas cannister had hit her, then fallen to the ground, along with others being thrown from the edge of the crowd by policemen.

A crowd of forty or fifty terrified, choking people pushed me before them, slamming me into others. Then it suddenly stopped, moved in another direction, and I stood in a circle of quiet, coughing, my burning eyes catching a blurred glimpse of a man who picked up a cannister and hurled it back at police. A gang of men ran at him, one in uniform, others not, waving clubs, dragging him away by his feet. Then the girl who'd been hit by the cannister was hurried past me, helped by Helena. She saw me and called, "You'd better come with us!"

As I took a step toward her, I was suddenly knocked off my feet. I was rolled, over and over, smashed by a monstrous cold wave. I was drowning, dragged, beaten, crushed by terrible gushing force, pushed across grass and dirt and concrete. And then, just as suddenly, I was still, beached, lying in a puddle in the middle of the street, realizing that I had been hit by water from the hoses plugged into the hydrants.

I was lifted and thrown into darkness, where more gentle hands caught me, lifted me onto a bench, held me with reassurances that I would be all right, nothing seemed to be broken. I realized that I was in the police paddy wagon, that it was quite full, and that the voice of the man holding me, unlike the others, was speaking to me in Spanish. I opened my eyes and looked into his face. "Emilio, don't you remember me?" I asked in Spanish. "It's me, May Lee." Then I passed out again, reviving a minute later as the wagon began to move, driving just around the block to the jail.

This was the first and last use of the van. Other people—about sixty of them—were driven into the street by water hoses, then herded on foot to the jail. The rally was dispersed within minutes. Silence. It might have been any sleepy summer weekend afternoon, except for the smell of tear gas mingling with the charred smell of the gutted old hall of justice, and the steam rising from the wet streets.

Eight of those arrested were women. We were put into a separate cell, with the over fifty men crowded into two larger cells on either side of us. Late that afternoon two boys and a girl were brought in, one holding his wrist, which seemed to be broken. The girl, Harriet, told us they had been part of a group which had tried to rally in front of city hall to protest our imprisonment, but had been gassed and hosed immediately. "I tripped and fell, and Tom and Dick got caught trying to stop the cops from beating me. The others ran away." We were not to worry; there would be lawyers down from San Francisco tomorrow to bail us out. These three were themselves from the City, young "organizers." None had done cannery work or any other work judging from their smooth hands. They were shaken but more cheerful than the rest of us, because because they were Communist Party members, shocked, yet vindicated, even satisfied by what had happened. The violence proved that law enforcement was "only a tool of force used by capitalists against workers."

The rest of the people were simply shocked, with no balancing vindication of ideology. This was their home, most were American citizens, property owners, at least a litttle house, some with even a few acres of orchard. They had never seen the inside of a jail. They were Americans, not some ignorant foreign peapickers. They were too shocked to be aware of their insult to Emilio, until he pointed it out, with me translating. "I have seen the inside of jail before, but not this part of the jail. There is another place, a dirty hole, for Mexicans. They put me here with you this time to insult you. Perhaps they succeeded."

When the guard brought in a local afternoon paper, allowing one of the boys to read it aloud, the shock deepened. A tiny article headlined CANNERIES OPERATING FULL TILT mentioned that police had made "eighteen arrests" of "rioters" in Saint James

Park who had "stormed City Hall" when their efforts to close the canneries failed. Few of those who listened had ever experienced first hand (as I had) the gap between reality and news reported in some newspapers, though all knew this newspaper was owned by the brother of a cannery owner.

In dull silence we heard the guard shouting into a telephone that he was not prepared to feed all these people and had to get rid of some. Whatever was said in reply, he kept interrupting with curses. After he hung up, he carried to the cells the only food available: boxes of half-rotted peaches and apricots. Tom, Dick, and Harriet distributed the fruit among us with careful equality and cheerful assurances that the furious complaints of the guard meant most of us would be released without even being booked. They hoped a few of us would join them in refusing to be released until the lawyers could set in motion a suit that would call attention to the terrible things being done to the workers, who were only exercising their right of free speech.

Tom, Dick, and Harriet. Of course, those are not their real names, just as Emilio and Wanda and Angelina and Helena are not the real names of the people I knew then. But Tom, Dick and Harriet are not real people at all. They are an invented, symbolic trio standing for many young radicals who dropped in and out of our struggle. I have written about them this way because they need greater protection than others I knew. Today, when I glance at an occasional newspaper, I often see their real names and their aged faces in reports of their appearances before some legislative committee accusing them of treason.

No doubt they had political aims beyond what most of the workers knew. No doubt they were blind to injustices among their own ideological comrades. No doubt, as Emilio often said, "They love the poor too much. Save me from such love!" No doubt they encouraged strikes, like this one, that were acts of desperation rather than tools of strategy.

I can only say that when and as I knew them, they were brave and kind young men and women, trying to help people no one else cared about. So I will protect them now by gathering all of them under the names of Tom, Dick, and Harriet.

Sometime after eight o'clock that night, the guard came in followed by a man in a dark suit who kept his hat on and stood well back from the cells, keeping his face in shadow. He looked us over, then mumbled, "All the women." Then he pointed to about thirty men, one by one, who were let out into the hall beside the cells. The chosen ones included men who had been hurt and those who were arrested by mistake, older men (not including Emilio) and one man who had declared himself a diabetic with no supply of insulin on him.

After the man left, several prisoners agreed that they recognized him as the manager of one of the canneries. Forty of us had been selected for release with no record of our having been arrested, before the arrival of any lawyers. But we were not released until the ones left in the cells—party members and militant unionists—had been booked, stripped of shoes and even eyeglasses in a long, humiliating process which the rest of us were forced to witness as a warning of what could be done to us. Compared to this, my arrest in England had been like a coronation. The guard had guessed correctly that those of us who were finally released would be too relieved to complain, let alone sue for false arrest. Harriet tried to cheer us up by saying that we would be met outside by supporters who would give us a "hero's welcome." That was the last thing any of us cared about by then.

It was after midnight when we were herded out into the dark, silent street. No one waited for us; we learned later that police had threatened to arrest anyone on the street after dark. For a moment we all stood in silent confusion. Then, with hardly a word or a look toward one another, we scattered, some to cars parked nearby, others walking.

At least I had somewhere to go. Emilio had thrown me his car keys and told me where his family was.

The ranch where I would find Wanda's tent was only about five miles south of town. I drove in as quietly as possible, but Wanda was standing beside the tent by the time I was within a hundred yards of it, having heard the "squeak in the right rear spring" which always signaled Emilio's arrival. I told her Emilio was unhurt and would be released tomorrow. We embraced and sat down outside the tent, where until dawn we whispered our experiences since last seeing each other.

There were now five children, but Wanda was not pregnant for the first time in years, the contraceptive advice she had received being effective, so far. The next to youngest, Manuel, whom I had nursed during the winter at Dona Ceresita's adobe, was thin, but active and bright, "talks all the time." The gray streaks in Wanda's

258

hair were gone. She was dyeing her hair now. No matter what happened, they were not so poor that she would turn into an old woman. As she lit a candle and placed it on a prune box, I saw that she had arranged a little sitting area outside the tent, with cactus potted in coffee cans and boxes covered by bits of colored material. Arched palm fronds flared from the edge of the tent supported by tree props to make a shady awning. Wanda did not have a house yet, but she was determined to make a home.

The rumor I had heard was correct; they had returned to Mexico, but not by choice. They had been deported as aliens, even though their children had all been born in the United States. How was that possible? Wanda shrugged. How could they leave the children alone here? There were more and more sweeps by local sheriffs, picking up whole settlements of Mexicans, taking them over the border after years of living on this side. It was because of the lack of work. Men came from the cities. Whole families were coming from other states. Emilio and Wanda had made the mistake of going south to pick cotton during the winter and had been caught up in a mass sweep. But they had come right back again in the spring. It wasn't hard to cross the border, if you knew where. "Besides, I think the farmers want us here so in case the Americans ask for more money, they can say they'll give the work back to the Mexicans."

It was not so bad this far north. The thing was to find a regular family or two, small ranchers that you came back to year after year, or, better still, one that would let you stay. If the place was big enough there was work to do all year, and even if they couldn't pay you part of the year, you could grow a few vegetables and get by somehow. The regular family on this farm hadn't come back— probably deported when they went south for the orange crop. She and Emilio were known as good workers; they might be allowed to stay on here, unless his getting arrested became known. Not that she wished he would quit the union work; his drinking decreased when he was in with the union people. No, she had not been tempted to take work at the cannery during the strike. "They just use Mexicans to break the strike and then throw us out again."

Wanda still kept her hope of a job in a cannery and a house in East San Jose. Deported Mexicans were selling little cottages for almost nothing. Further in the future might come the merger of the pickers' union with the canners' union. It was just talk now, but when it happened Wanda might get into a cannery. Meanwhile, she was still adding bit by bit to the savings which had not been completely exhausted by their enforced stay in Mexico.

Emilio did not come home for three days. He spent most of Sunday getting out of jail and talking with lawyers and men from the pickers' union; some of whom accused him of wasting his energy helping the canners. Then he left all of them, drank for a night and a day, slept in a ditch, and returned to his family on Tuesday. His binge was an echo of the complete collapse of the strike. On Sunday the strikers had been denounced in all the churches. On Monday everyone, except blacklisted organizers like Helena, was back at work, so docile and fearful that anyone who even mentioned a union was denounced to the manager. I too was blacklisted as an agitator, a title (perhaps an honor) I had hardly earned, any more than I had ever qualified as much of a cherry pitter or peach cutter. All charges were dropped against those who were arrested, and no move was made to deport Emilio. We were never sure why. Perhaps his good luck was part of the authorities' desire to forget the strike and their role in it.

Wanda announced to her employers (a Norwegian family with slightly more land than Angelina's family) that I was her cousin. I was accepted as part of the family work force, hardly noticed, let alone questioned, for the first fall of prunes was already on the ground. I put on the overalls Guido had sent me, along with one of the straw hats in a pile in the tent, without which no one in the family ever went to work, and then wound wads of burlap around my knees to pad them.

Prune picking was done on hands and knees, each of us assigned to a row of trees, each tree standing in its little purple pool of fallen prunes. Filling a fifty-pound box earned each of us—everyone in the family except the baby—five cents. Men came by with a small truck on which they loaded filled boxes, giving us a tag for each one. At the end of the day I had as many tags as Wanda's seven-year-old, Jesus. Next year he would surpass me. The trouble was my lack of endurance. Yet there was one advantage to picking from the ground on my hands and knees. When I felt faint, my lowered head would often revive more quickly, and if I actually passed out for a moment, no one noticed. And, of course, there was no danger of falling.

It was during this time that the first confusion of my identity arose. It was unusual for women to wear pants in those days, even while

260

doing rough labor. Seeing me in overalls, with a hat on, many people mistook me for a boy. Those who knew me as a woman, like Wanda, called me May. Emilio and the children addressed me as Senora Lee. Many others, hearing them, yet convinced I was a boy, called me Lee. My full name, Mei-li Murrow, appeared on my driver's license and birth certificate (a copy of which I had sent to me from San Francisco after hearing about the mass deportations), but few people remembered my true surname, and sometimes I almost forgot it. On holidays or at Saturday night dances, when I put on my dress, people who had worked near me failed to recognize me. And occasionally, when I wore my pajama suit, I was suddenly transformed into yet another stranger, an oriental. I intended no deception in the beginning, but later, when disguise was an aid and a protection, I made the most of this confusion, switching from one to the other of my three identities frequently.

Apricots were still coming in, and we alternated between picking prunes and cutting apricots, which was done standing up in the drying shed. We cut the soft apricots in half, threw the pits into a barrel (they were washed and sold to oil manufacturers), and placed each half, cut side up to hold the juice, on the long wooden trays that were stacked until the pile was large enough to wheel into the sulphur ovens, and from there out into the sun, where the trays were laid out for drying. Then we switched back to prunes, the second fall to be picked, dipped in lye, then laid out to dry. A third fall would come, carrying the process into October.

As we worked I remembered the long rides down the peninsula when Norman pointed to the huge drying yards where trays lay spread over an acre or two of land. Now I watched them as Emilio did, with one eye on the sky, anxious lest the usual dry fall be broken by early rain. If it rained, everyone would have to scramble to stack the trays again and cover them.

In the prune orchards and prune yards I saw a broader mixture of people than I had seen in the canneries. The children of European families picked alongside Mexicans, Filipinos, a few Japanese. (School would not open until the end of September, after the last prune drop had been picked.) There were older, single men like the one who had appeared on the road to Dona Ceresita's house, and a couple of families from the midwest, with accents so strange, harsh and nasal that Wanda declared them "harder to understand than the

Japanese." They spoke little to us anyway, clearly holding themselves superior to us darker people (and I had become very dark doing this work), their prejudices aggravated by humiliation. They had lost their own farms in the midwest, were suddenly demoted to the migrant status of foreigners, like Mexicans, working for other "foreigners," the farmers of recent immigration from Europe, less "American" than they were.

When October came, the children of the resident farmers got up off their knees and went to school. This exodus of her children's playmates provoked a crisis in Wanda. In the past five years, as the three oldest children had reached school age, she wanted them to go to school. But every penny was needed, and the work of scraping trays and packing dried prunes went on, some of it done by the children. With any luck, the family might even get a week or two picking walnuts, the final crop before the winter layoff. Even if there were no work for them, the children could not go to school without shoes.

Last year in mid-October Juan had gone to school, but after a few days had refused to go back. He had trouble understanding English. Wanda went to the school, where the teacher said he was behind the others ("How could he be behind in the first grade?" Wanda asked) and there was no provision to help students who would only stay a few weeks anyway. The teacher was right about his short stay; in November the family had gone south to pick cotton. But this year they would not leave the Santa Clara Valley, not if they starved, Wanda said. This year Juan, Jesus, and Maria would go to school.

Her resolution required heroic efforts just to get the children ready for school each day. We were always scrubbing clothes in a metal washpan. Bathing the children was easier than on some farms, for, though we had only an outhouse toilet, the enlightened Jenson family had rigged up a shower bath using an old hose, sun-heated as it snaked across the top of the drying shed. Mrs. Jenson supported Wanda's insistence that the children go to school, "even if for only a day, a week," which did not make her popular with her neighbors. She also shared with us a variety of vegetables from her garden and eggs laid by her chickens, presenting them so graciously that it seemed part of neighborly courtesy to accept. She was less adroit in offering some clothes outgrown by her children. A throbbing, inflamed pride was never far below the surface in Wanda, and always right on the surface, like a rash, in Emilio. Clothing, even precious shoes, were refused. For the very poor there were distinctions between those who wear new and those who wear used clothing. Wanda's family had definitely risen to the purchase of new clothing, no matter how inferior to the used clothing offered by Mrs. Jenson. It was a sign of my acceptance into the family that Wanda allowed me to contribute part of my earnings toward buying shoes for the children.

But after three anxious and depressed weeks at school—there was no Miss Harrington to ease them into the classes of Euro-Americans—it was certain that the children would fulfill the teacher's prophecy by leaving. The prune yards were empty, there was no work in walnuts, and the first rain had fallen. Even if the winter proved only normally wet, there might be flooding. The Jenson farm was well irrigated by the Los Gatos Creek, which overflowed during the winter. Life in the tent would bring sickness. The Jensons were sympathetic, but not ready to provide year-round housing. It seemed we might be forced to go south and pick cotton. Wanda cried and prayed, cried and prayed, and her prayers were answered.

Vaino was the foreman in the drying sheds, hired by the Jensons and other prune ranchers to supervise cutting, dipping, smoking, and drying. A Finn with a red, square head and a gruff laugh, he lived south of San Jose in New Almaden, where he was caretaker at the old Quicksilver Mines. Mine Hill was a relic of the gold rush, covered with ruined cabins of miners, shafts still yielding a bit of cinnabar, retorts in occasional, sluggish operation. Vaino was a strict but kindly boss. Everyone, even Emilio, liked Vaino.

On the last day of work on the Jenson ranch, when Emilio and the other men were gathering in the props that had held up fruit-laden branches, storing them with the drying trays, Vaino offered Emilio housing for the winter. The old miners' cabins were empty, and the bosses never visited Mine Hill, never questioned Vaino's judgment unless something went wrong. Vaino felt free to invite sober, respectable families up to the hill for the winter. He even knew how to invite them without touching their irritable pride: they could work at gleaning from the old refining sheds, giving Vaino half of what they found. There must be no drinking; he could not afford to have the law poking around Mine Hill. Children must go to school; he couldn't have them falling down one of the old shafts. Yes, the

Almaden School was right down from the hill. Anyone who was decent and quiet enough not to attract attention could stay until spring.

I still remember how suddenly cold it was on the November day we piled everything on top of the car and drove down the Almaden Road "about a dozen miles," as Vaino told us, to where the road began to cut through hills. The first sign of our destination was the Casa Grande, originally the mine manager's house, a long, porched hacienda now run down and dirty, though occupied. By what? Vaino had been vague about that, but we could see it must be a combined saloon, brothel, and hotel. No need to ask why the people allowed to live in the hill cabins must be sober and quiet beside this flourishing, openly illegal establishment. The hotel made enough money to share with law enforcement.

Behind the Casa Grande were the towers and sheds of old refining and storage buildings, one of which had been turned into a school. On the road beyond it, to our left, was a row of houses where Vaino and other mine employees lived. There was a post office, a grocery store. The last building on the left was a Catholic church. Vaino had told us to drive quietly past all this, to keep our eyes to the right, and to take the third road up Mine Hill. The road was narrow and steep. Vaino had told us to drive to the top and take any cabin we found empty. He did not tell us that the first thing we would see at the top of the road was a cemetery.

We stopped, got out of the car, and walked among the old, sinking gravestones, taking care, as Wanda reminded us, not to walk across graves—as if we could tell where bodies actually lay beneath us. The names chiseled on the stone, sometimes wooden, markers were all Spanish. This had been Mexican Camp; there was even the burnt-out wreck of a tiny old Catholic church beside the graveyard.

Later that winter, during walks when I explored all of Mine Hill, I found Cornish Camp and Irish Camp and the six or seven other clusters of cabins named for the people gathered there to work the mines. I was even told (by Vaino, whose father and grandfather had been supervisors and paymasters) that there had once been a Chinese Camp. The Chinese, he said, had been brought in when the Cornish miners organized and demanded higher pay. What happened then was never fully explained; his grandfather had refused to talk to him about it. The Chinese had disappeared. The rumor was that they had been murdered by the Cornish, their cabins destroyed, their bodies buried in unmarked, mass graves. It was as if they had never been there. But they had. Vaino's father had proof: bowls, a silk cap, a carved ivory bookmark he had found south of Mexican Camp.

Of the eight habitable cabins, three were already taken. We took over two more, Emilio and Wanda with the two babies in one cabin. The older three children and I stayed next door in what must have been a bunk house for single men. There was no heat in the bunkhouse, but a wood stove heated the kitchen of the other cabin, where we gathered at night or early in the morning. Cold water was also piped into the kitchen, and, when a short rain showed only one small leak in the roof, we knew we had chosen the best places available. Before long, even the leaky, half-collapsed cabins were occupied. By Thanksgiving the whole hill was full of homeless people.

Vaino had assigned Mexicans, Filipinos, Japanese and all single men to Mexican Camp. Further north in three other clusters of cabins, he housed Irish and Italian families whose fathers had lost their jobs, then their homes. Some of these had come from as far north as San Francisco. In the old hilltop mine office and store, which had working electricity, he housed a couple of Swedish families who had lost their nearby dairy farms when their bank failed. In the old hill schoolhouse he put two pale, twangy-voiced families just arrived from Nebraska. Although they had as little contact with us as possible, we were constantly aware of their presence because of their religious services: thumping, crying, chanting, singing, which started after dark and went on for hours. The other refugees on Mine Hill (majority Catholic) heard this "holy roller" shouting and stomping with some amusement. But the Okies, as everyone called them, viewed with pure horror our procession down the hill to the Catholic Church early on Sunday morning. The local priest had hastily added a seven o'clock mass for Vaino's hill refugees, warning him to have his people out and gone before the ten o'clock mass attended by weekenders who owned homes in the southern woods.

No one protested the early segregated mass. We did not protest that the Swedes got the electrified housing, nor that the single tramps were housed near Mexican families. We were grateful to be housed at all. For some families, like Wanda's, there were even advantages on Mine Hill that had never been offered so abundantly before.

Like school for the children. Every morning the three oldest children rode down the hill to school with Emilio, who then drove on to seek work for which, when he found it, he was usually paid in goods rather than money, like milk and cheese from the dairy where he cleaned barns every week. This was the most steady supply of milk the children had ever had. After school the children climbed back up the hill, changed to ragged work clothes, and joined their mother and me in gleaning.

We wandered through all the sheds and yards of the reduction works, around shaft entries, through refining and storage buildings both on the hill and down behind the Casa Grande Hotel. Each of us carried a bucket. Wanda also carried a flattened old tin spoon she said helped her to pick through the rocks and dirt as we searched for the rust-red stones dropped during the mining and refining process. Vaino gave us a quarter for every full bucket. Our combined earnings made about a dollar a day, which went to the local grocery store for food.

At night we set a lantern on the kitchen table, where I tried to help the children with their schoolwork—if they were not too tired to keep their eyes focussed on the pages of their books. After they went to bed, I might sit up and write a letter to Stephanie or read one from her which had caught up with me, forwarded to the New Almaden Post Office.

I began to save her letters, carrying them with me even during the years when I was literally on the run, with only the pack on my back. Most did not survive, were lost or reduced to rain-soaked pulp from which I salvaged only scraps. From that winter of 1931 there is only the following fragment, written just after Stephanie had been vacationing in Spain.

> . . . that with no bloodshed at all, a completely new country seems to be emerging from the monarchy, which slipped away almost as peacefully as the old lady you wrote me about. I was in Madrid on the day the vote for women was quite ceremoniously announced in a great leap that makes our bloody fight for it in England only a few years ago seem antediluvian. Every day of my stay there, it seemed that some new pronouncement was splitting wide open some ancient oppression. People strode down the streets with a quite different look, a rather

"American" swing to their shoulders, and with many smiles, especially for us English (who speak up loudly in our own language so as not to be mistaken for Germans).

I was sorry to have to return home where the poverty, though no worse than that in Spain, is unrelieved by their sunny climate, both natural and political. Things are, if anything, worse this year, and it was clear, passing through Paris, that unemployment is beginning there too.

When I got home there was a fuss about trespassers at Chilblains Hall having been treated quite roughly by the constabulary. Since I can't afford staff beyond a caretaker couple, it seems some of the unemployed had sneaked onto the grounds, even managing to get into the west wing, which hasn't been used for years and leaks like a sieve. They did no harm as far as I could see and seemed to be there because they had nowhere else to go. But it was indeed 'cheeky,' as my outraged caretaker-wife said, an act which ten years ago the English poor would not have dreamed of. I call that progress. My caretaker calls it "what you get when the mistress ain't responsible."

I'm trying to resolve the conflict by letting the trespassers stay in exchange for doing a bit of much needed maintenance. That's not so simple or ideal as it sounds, as you and I know quite well from our ill-starred episode among the redwoods. In other words, some of them drink and quarrel and don't want to work at anything, or get sick or . . . anyway, after a dozen trips down there to size up the situation, I've drawn up a list of quite rigid rules, found a firm and fierce man to enforce them (one speedy eviction was enough to establish his authority—he even scares me!), and set a definite time limit for a maximum number of people to use the west wing for the remainder of the crisis, which is sure to end by spring.

The rest of the letter is lost, but this remnant shows how broad was the hope we all held during that winter of 1931–32. We never doubted that with spring would come a pickup of work and wages.

That false hope and Stephanie's letters kept me going during that winter. I wish I could say different. I wish I could say that my certain faith in that thing made me content and grateful to join Wanda's family, or that when I viewed the sunrise from Mine Hill I felt a blessing from that thing. The truth is that I felt nothing but raw, scraped fingers gleaning among the cold rocks. My only conviction was that all efforts for Wanda's children would be in vain. The only revelation I received was that the poor gathered on Mine Hill were no more noble or lovable than the rich, only less lucky. I never felt more alone, more deserted by that thing, than when they were all gathered closely around me during early Sunday mass.

I tried to accept our life. I tried to take every task—gleaning or scrubbing or teaching the children or reading the union literature Emilio brought home—and inject some meaning into it, dedicating it to that thing—which remained real to me, if withdrawn or changed. But I never succeeded in anything but the intent, the thought, the effort, before being overcome by consciousness of cold feet, an aching back, or a furious weariness of the noise of children.

Vaino had given everyone a deadline of April first—the usual end of rain in the valley—to leave the cabins on Mine Hill, but some were already leaving in mid-January for the spinach fields. Wanda insisted on staying as long as possible to keep the children in school, so in February Emilio drove out alone to pick spinach near Half Moon Bay. After three weeks he came back with hardly any money— after paying for gas, a new tire to replace a blow-out, and food sold on the spinach fields at outrageous prices by the Japanese foreman. He had had to contain his rage because the same labor contractor would do the hiring for pea picking in April and May, when there would be higher pay and work for the whole family.

Meanwhile, strawberries were ripening early in fields only two miles away. I volunteered to go with Emilio in the early morning, since Wanda would be busy caring for the babies and getting the older children off to school. With two of us working (and taking our meals at home) we might make a little more money. My optimism came out of my vast ignorance. My sole experience had been in picking prunes. I did not know yet that picking prunes was the easiest field labor, nor that picking strawberries is the hardest, meanest form of "squat labor."

I lasted two days—or more exactly, half-way through my second day and my second fainting spell within an hour. Emilio and Wanda said I would be more useful if I stayed on Mine Hill gleaning cinnebar and caring for the children while they went to pick strawberries. Wanda was a fast picker, especially if she did not have to take the babies with her.

The older children begged to go with her, and it took stern opposition to keep them in school. It was not that they preferred the miserable work to learning to read and write, but that school was a place of increasing anxiety which they could not explain to us or even to themselves. I think they felt the expectation of their teachers that they would give up trying to think in English. Even with my help, they tended to give up on any challenging lesson.

An exception to that attitude was Manuel, whom I had nursed through measles, now three years old, still too young for school. He clutched to him the books his brothers and sister brought home, and by the end of that winter, with a little help from me, he had taught himself to read the first-grade primer. He demonstrated his ability over and over again for everyone in Mexican Camp, giving himself practice that I hoped would stick with him after the books went back to the school and we moved on.

In late March we moved to a camp outside one of the larger pea farms in Half Moon Bay. In the distance I could see the tip of the shoreline hotel where Norman and I had spent weekends in the years when the pea fields were just part of a pleasant landscape. While we waited for the pods to swell, Emilio drove inland to the Jenson orchards to help with thinning the first fruit buds, plowing under the mustard green ground cover and making other preparations for harvest. He had established himself as a steady, versatile worker, and there seemed to be a good chance that the Jensons would keep us through the next winter. Meanwhile, in May, while their fruit was ripening, we would all work in the pea fields, where we could earn seventy-five cents a sack.

That sounded like a great sum to me until I saw the sack, a long canvas bag slung over my shoulder, tied at my waist, and trailing on the ground for five or six feet behind me. The pea bushes were almost as low as strawberries; we stooped, then dragged the increasingly heavy load behind us as we filled the sack.

I moved slowly forward as the younger children did most of the picking, stuffing pods into my sack. I stopped often to catch my breath, while the others did their best to watch out for me. They rarely referred to my "weak heart." They accepted it matter-of-factly as they accepted the terrible toothaches and back pain that afflicted Emilio, the "female troubles" plaguing Wanda after so many unattended childbirths, the earaches, coughs, and sore throats constantly afflicting the children, the mysterious lameness increasing in little Maria. Everyone in camp had an untreated illness, and there was no money for doctors. "If I can keep my health . . . ." meant, if we could keep working despite our poor health.

At the end of our first ten-hour day, when we triumphantly presented tabs for a total of eight sacks, the blow fell; we were to be paid, not seventy-five cents per sack, but only forty. That night in the camp a meeting was called. The dusty clearing with its shacks and tents and three water spigots suddenly became an advantage, a natural gathering point for the workers, including the few Italians and Japanese who lived in their own homes nearby. We all sat on boxes and rolled up sacks in rows of concentric circles, more than three hundred people. I sat in the midst of the Italians, Japanese and Okies, having been asked to translate for them, since the meeting was held in Spanish, the common language of the majority Filipino and Mexican workers.

Language seemed to be the only thing they had in common, for the discussion soon became an argument between Filipino and Mexican men, the Filipinos accusing the Mexicans of being too womanish to strike, the Mexicans threatening to show the Filipinos, right here and now, whether they were men, while Wanda and the other Mexican women defended their men, reminding the Filipinos that they were safe from deportation, which constantly threatened the Mexicans.

In the midst of the argument, Tom, Dick, and Harriet arrived. Someone had made a phone call and brought them down from San Francisco. No, the union was not dead, it was surging up everywhere, not in the canneries but "in the fields where the hardest, bravest workers are." They had come to help us list our grievances, formulate our demands, map our strategy. They spoke in English, and I was pulled up to stand beside them and translate into Spanish and Japanese.

Translation slowed things down, but the crowd reached consensus by midnight: seventy-five cents a sack or strike tomorrow. By midnight Tom, Dick and Harriet were gone, having promised to stay at a safe place nearby. They could not risk being seen, for the sheriff knew them and would lock them up on any pretext. Emilio and one of the Filipino men would carry our demands to the other two camps, where similar meetings were being held. They felt sure of getting a strike vote that would take over a thousand workers out of the fields. We were to go to bed and catch up on our sleep; no one would go to work.

By dawn Emilio was back with the news that everyone had voted to strike. Then he rolled up in a blanket and fell asleep while we waited for an answer from the farmers.

The answer came at noon as highway patrol cars, police motorcycles, and trucks with hastily printed DEPUTY signs on their windshields drove up the road and parked, encircling the camp. Following them was the car of the contractor who had hired us. He said nothing at all, simply walked to the nearest outhouse, nailed a sheet of paper to it, then walked back to his car and drove away. The patrol cars and trucks stayed all day and through the night.

The typewritten notice said that anyone in the camp not working in the field by tomorrow at sunrise would be evicted. It was signed by the owner and by the city and county government officials. Emilio and two of the Filipino men tried to leave to meet with other workers, but the highway patrolmen told them anyone who left camp would not be allowed to return. That was the end of the strike. At dawn the next day we were all back in the fields working for forty cents a sack. The patrol cars stayed, walling us in and others out, for another four days and nights.

Near the end of May, when there remained only a few picking days, we were warned that immigration agents were making a sweep through all three camps, deporting Mexicans who had been involved in the brief strike. That night we rose after midnight, packed in the dark, and drove to the Jenson ranch. When we were discovered there at dawn, we were not welcomed with the friendliness of the previous year, but they let us stay, and no immigration agents followed us there.

The next four months were the usual dawn-to-dusk picking and drying, at wages a few cents lower than last year. We kept hearing of brief, aborted strikes like the one at Half Moon Bay, of Mexicans deported, some even dragged out of their own permanent houses. But we had been promised a full year's work and an old chicken house with a concrete floor and a tight roof, which we could clean out and live in. Wanda and Emilio agreed there was "nothing to do but bow the head" or go back to winter on Mine Hill. But there was no future on Mine Hill, while there might be one in year-round work for the Jensons.

The only hint of resistance came in mid-July, when Emilio learned there would be a meeting in San Jose. It would be too risky for him or Wanda to be seen there, but I might go in their place. (My ineffectual work in the orchards would hardly be missed.) Someone had to keep in touch with the union, if there really still was one. Wanda said, "We must have some hope. Please go."

On a Sunday morning we all drove to Saint Joseph's Church. But instead of attending mass, I changed to my Chinese pajamas and a broad oriental straw hat which shaded and hid my face. Then I walked the three blocks to a large hall where a conference of union organizers was being held. I entered just in time to hear Helena castigating the union for lack of preparation, poor organization, and bad judgment during the cannery strike of the year before.

Tom, Dick, and Harriet unsparingly criticized themselves for their errors. Tom said that too many organizers made speeches of general radical rhetoric instead of sticking to the basic, urgent issues workers could understand. Dick confessed he had rushed workers into spontaneous strikes rather than teaching them how to prepare an effective one. Harriet said that an effective strike could come about only with strong leadership among workers in the fields. "Like Helena in the cannery; we need to respect and develop her counterparts in the fields."

None of them recognized me until I took off my hat and smiled at Helena, who grabbed me and pulled me to Harriet, then left to head a workshop session of canners' organizers. Harriet said they had been trying to find me. They were establishing a union headquarters for the whole valley, trying to develop leadership among the workers. They needed interpreters, translators. "We are mostly white, with no language but English. The workers don't trust us. No wonder! They can't even understand us."

I said I would think about it. Then I went back and reported what I had heard to Emilio and Wanda. They said little except to agree that Tom, Dick, and Harriet certainly had fired up workers to plunge into ill-advised strikes.

One bright spot in that summer and fall was the coming presidential election, on which most of the workers placed great hope. The union organizers devoted all their efforts to registering those eligible to vote for Roosevelt. Even I voted, for the first time. Another bright day was the one on which the children returned to school, including Manuel, who was big for his age and had demonstrated that he could read English.

When Roosevelt won the election, there was a great dance and party in a hall rented by one of the large growers, who was a Roosevelt supporter. Many workers from both canneries and fields came, and even some union organizers showed up. Everyone toasted everyone else with free beer donated by a farmer. Roosevelt had promised to repeal prohibition, so alcohol was already being consumed more openly. It was a loud, gay party at which people made speeches about new harmony and prosperity coming back to the valley. The Jenson family and other small farmers did not attend.

The day after the party the pruners on the land of this same large grower were told that, instead of the pay raise they had been promised, they would take a pay cut. Another strike was called, against this grower and others who followed his paycutting. Pruning had started on the Jenson ranch too, but the Jensons and other small growers did not cut wages, so Emilio did not have to join the strike. In fact, he was told to stay clear of it because of his vulnerable immigrant status. He and Wanda urged me to agree to translate for the union. "We can do nothing this time. You do it for us all."

Every Sunday morning a different person would meet me on a different road and drive me to a meeting where I acted as translator among workers and organizers. Often I was picked up in the middle of the night and taken to a meeting at a restaurant in the northside Chinatown or a bar on the east side, or to a circle of cars on a back road. I alternated the clothes I wore, and many workers did not know that the boy Lee in overalls was the same person as May in a dress, or that May was the same person as Mei-li in pajamas.

The pruners' strike dragged on through the rest of the winter, dying in January with no gains after many meetings in which mistakes in timing and tactics were listed again and again. "The only thing we did right this time was to use translators," admitted Tom, Dick, and Harriet, who—barely old enough to vote—were showing deep lines around sleepless eyes, and even, in some cases, gray hairs.

The letters that reached me from Stephanie that winter were not about our election but about elections in Germany in which Hitler's Nazi party had gained control of the Reichstag. One of the letters which survives described a new tenant who had joined the unemployed at the old country house:

Herr Doktor Rothman is a distant in-law married to a German cousin who died in her second childbirth. Except for exchanging New Year greetings, we never heard from him until I received forms from immigration naming me as his sponsor. Once I remembered who he was, I signed the things. I'd never met him, but had heard he was a quite well-known cardiologist with a large practice. Well, on he came, with his two children and a demand that we instantly get to work on bringing his mother, his aunt, his sister, and countless other relatives. He is convinced that Hitler plans to do something terrible to the Jews, a *pogrom* or something of the sort. He can talk of nothing else.

I asked him what proof he had of this intention and he said, "None." Then why did he leave Germany? It seems that he was looking over his patients one day and suddenly realized they were all Jews. He still had plenty of patients—he's quite famous—but no more gentiles, who used to make up more than half his practice. They had all quietly disappeared. He takes that as a hint of something happening, not just in the rhetoric of that awful man, but deeply in the society to which it is addressed. He promises not to stay long. As soon as he gets all his family out, he plans to leave England, which he predicts Hitler will take over within five years!

I let him and his children occupy my mother's third floor apartment at old Rack and Ruin. It's still in relatively good condition, and he pays rent, keeps a servant, even pays for minor repairs. Aside from being a fearful snob about the unemployed finally moving out of the west wing (he's so frightfully German, insists on being addressed as Herr Doctor and all that), he is an ideal tenant. I hope all his relatives will be as it seems likely I'll soon have the whole tribe there at least for a year or two or however long it takes to rid the German government of Hitler. No one here thinks he can last long, not even dread Uncle Ralph (remember he was a colonel in the War, the one who was always talking about dying for God and country) who says what an effective speaker Hitler is and he could teach our parliament a thing or two. So far I have managed to keep the Herr Doktor and Uncle R. from meeting and starting another war.

In my letters to Stephanie I tried to match her tone, giving an ironic description of the day I spent on the picket line during the interminable pruners' strike. That day I had worn my dress and, deeply sun-tanned by then, looked very much like the Filipino wives who had volunteered to picket with their children. That meant driving to any place pruners were working, getting out of the car, calling to the workers to come out and join the strike. The women took me along, insisting there was no danger because the deputies were unnerved by female pickets. "They break our men's heads, but not ours." They drove around the orchards—fearless, laughing, shouting challenges that might have gotten them shot had they been men. Unlike them, I had been scared all the time, as I admitted to Stephanie. But they were right; we were untouchable. Then. Later, the deputies overcame their reluctance to beat women and children.

It was just about the time that the pruners' strike completed its slow death—in late January—that Hitler was appointed chancellor of Germany. Stephanie made no comment on that in her letters. In fact there were no letters from her during that time, if I remember correctly. It was as if the event struck her dumb temporarily. Except for one mention of Spain—where the government for which she had held such high hopes was already collapsing—she wrote nothing about political events in Europe, confining herself to acid descriptions of the odd assortment of refugees gradually filling her family's disintegrating old country house.

Early in 1933 a federal relief law was passed so that unemployed workers would not starve. Fortunately for Emilio and Wanda, they did not apply even though they were eligible, since during the winter their pay from the Jensons consisted only of the use of the old chicken house. Those Mexicans who did apply were immediately deported. One family known to Wanda and Emilio had their own house (not much better than our chicken house, but their own) and needed to sell quickly. We sat up all night discussing it. Wanda's savings, disclosed to Emilio for the first time, and the money I had, were nearly eight hundred dollars, which the sellers had little choice but to accept. Owning property was next to citizenship, which Wanda and Emilio could not get until they became literate. Leaving the Jenson ranch left them freer to work with the union which might better their condition. Even more important, they wanted to stay out of labor camps, which were increasingly dangerous, often raided by deputies and hired thugs who beat union members.

As for me, Wanda told me bluntly, it was best for me to go on relief, since I was useless in the fields anyway. Then I could concentrate on translating for the union, where I was of some use. I had no trouble getting on relief. A doctor put his stethescope to my chest, rolled his eyes, and wrote a letter certifying me as unfit for physical labor of any kind. With a house of our own, my relief check, and Emilio's earnings, we had hope, which Wanda expressed by pinning a picture of President Roosevelt on the wall next to one of a gently smiling Virgin Mary.

That year, 1933, was the year of strikes, one after another, the year of meetings, one after another. There were large meetings where Tom, Dick, or Harriet listed the increased prices the farmers were now getting for their crops, and smaller meetings where committees were created, and committee meetings where leadership titles were conferred on every worker willing to take one. Strike leaders came from Decoto and Vacaville and from various parts of the Imperial Valley to explain which tactics worked and which ones only gave the sheriff "an excuse for busting heads." The Castroville union secretary came to one large meeting and told how deputies had raided their headquarters, burned their records, and threatened deportation of all Mexicans. But his story did not discourage the people in the packed hall as it might have done two or three years ago. Perhaps they were more desperate—wages had sunk again— yet more hopeful that the new president would back them. Some of them carried pictures of Roosevelt in their cars and tacked them up on the walls of shacks in the labor camps.

In our valley the climax came in June when cherry farmers cut pickers' wages from thirty cents to twenty cents an hour. Since all the workers knew about the increased price the farmers were getting, it took no time at all to call a meeting and agree on a strike if the thirty cent wage was not restored. Emilio was still working on the Jenson farm, which had few acres in cherries and immediately agreed to thirty cents, as did some of the other small farmers, whose children picked and worked along with their hired help. So Emilio was not on strike.

Wanda, with me as translator, was an organizer of mass picketing on one of the larger farms. Nearly three hundred people gathered on the road in carefully disciplined legality, loud but peaceful, at the entrance to the largest of the twenty farms being struck. This time the fact that most of us were women and children did not stop the club-swinging deputies. I managed to get away with a few scuffs and a torn dress, but Wanda was arrested along with about thirty others, including Harriet, whose jaw was broken.

But this time the arrests and beatings did not destroy the strike. That night Emilio and other leaders called meetings all over the valley, and the next day twice as many cherry pickers joined the strike. Within a week nearly all the farmers had agreed to the thirty cent wage. The impossible had happened. The strikers had won. It was the first time they had planned and acted together, and they had won. On the brink of the harvest season, the celebration of our victory was like that June day at the height of summer—long and hot.

Our victory was marred by the fact that when those arrested were released, six Mexicans, including Wanda, were driven south and dumped across the border. Emilio wanted to follow Wanda, leaving me with the children until they could get back, but the Jensons told him that if he left them now, missing the first prune fall, he could not return. I think they almost hoped he would go; having an identified union leader in their employ was making their relations with neighboring farmers more and more difficult. I convinced him that it was best to wait and hope that Wanda would manage to get back. Within three months, she had returned, swearing that if we had done anything but wait and keep her home and her children and her hopes for a good life, she "would have killed you both!" So we celebrated again, and the children, all of them, began the fall term at school.

Our first victory, however, was our last. On the same day that the children started school Tom, Dick, and Harriet went south to organize the cotton strike. Then a few months later they threw themselves into the General Strike in San Francisco and into the industrial organizing that followed it. The next battleground to capture their imagination was far away, in Spain, where no doubt they felt part of a grander struggle than the one in our little valley. None of them ever came back.

Their desertion only slowed our movement. What stopped it was the celebrated National Labor Relations Act, which gave new recognition and power to unions. No sooner was the law passed than the president exempted farm labor from its protections. "Before, our misery was only the custom," said Emilio as he tore Roosevelt's picture from the wall, threw it to the floor, and stamped on it. "Now it is the law."

In December the Jensons told Emilio they had no more work for him, though pruning had begun. He went from one farm to another with no luck—he was too well known. Wanda found occasional work as a servant. Required to live in, she would return after a week with little beyond some food or old clothes given her as payment. During that winter we fed the whole family on the nine dollars a week I received from relief.

On Christmas night we awoke to a crackling sound, loud bangs, three sharp cracks, glass breaking, cars driving away. When we went outside we found a six-foot cross burning in front of the house. I suggested taking the children back to Mine Hill for the winter for safety, but when I drove to Almaden to see Vaino, he told me there was no longer room for people like us. The federal government had taken over the hill to be used as a CCC Camp.

Emilio began to drink again on the nights when Wanda slept away from home. Keeping the children in school became my responsibility, a hard one, since all but Manuel made excuses not to go, often feigning illness, just as often really ill. In school Jesus fought with a boy who had been told by his parents that "Mexicans take work away from real Americans." When Wanda came home, she fought with Emilio and with the children, and the children fought among themselves.

Union meetings were sparsely attended or canceled. So many were being raided routinely, Mexicans deported, others arrested, beaten. The houses of three families nearby stood empty, all of them gone suddenly in a recent sweep. Their homes were being sold for taxes. And where would we get the money for the taxes on this house? Even some of the Filipinos had accepted fare to the islands and had gone back, after the spinach strike in January, when leaders had received death threats. More crosses were burned, more newspaper editorials warned about "communist alien parasites taking relief and jobs from white Americans."

Somehow we held on through the spring, almost the only Mexican family east of the Coyote River without California birth certificates. The children had them, of course, and Wanda often said that when the immigration people came she would leave them with me until she and Emilio could come back again. But when the day actually came, I suppose she was unable to leave them.

It happened in July at the beginning of the fruit harvest, when competition for work at any wage was as feverish as if there had never been a union. The cars from the midwest came in a steady stream now, and the farmers were giving preference to white workers. The union newsletter devoted that issue entirely to the General Strike in San Francisco, with obituaries of the men killed there.

I had been taken to Sacramento, where the agricultural union headquarters had been raided and numerous arrests made, a crisis for which extra translators were needed. I was gone for three days, sleeping fitfully in cars parked on dark roads along with young lawyers who were no more safe than the union members they defended.

When I returned to San Jose, I found the house empty. The few bits of furniture were still there, but clothing and linens—the kinds of things taken in a hasty departure—were gone. Questioning other workers brought me no more information than we had ever gained about families who disappeared with immigration agents. Perhaps they would be back, in a month, in a year. Perhaps never.

I stayed in the house through the rest of the year, putting off the tax collector, keeping the place maintained as well as I could, waiting for Wanda and Emilio and the children, waking at the sound of every car that passed the house during the night, not sure whether to hope or to fear who it might be. I continued to go wherever I was needed, to carry messages, to translate. Since I no longer had Emilio's car, the union gave me an old bike. At the time, I was warned that riding it would probably make my heart stop, but that did not happen. Probably riding the bike helped to keep it going, and kept me safer, less visible for the more risky errands, like taking a message into the labor camps, which now were guarded and surrounded by barbed wire. Even more dangerous, in a way, was taking old, sick Japanese or Filipino men to the relief office and translating their pleas not to be cut off. The danger was that I would be cut off relief too, but I kept my doctor's letter and flashed it whenever I was threatened.

During the long winter nights in the little house, I described these errands in letters to Stephanie, while she answered with descriptions of the refugees pouring into her country house. I have one of her letters from that time, dated 20 December 1934.

> Dearest Mei-li,
>
> It seems after all that the question of what to do with Old Rack and Ruin has been answered for me. The Herr Doktor and his relatives have moved on (emigrated to South America) but have been replaced by others, and the tales they tell are strangely parallel to the ones in your last letter about your Lopez family—I do hope they're back by now—but much more sinister. I am being forced to see that the Herr Doktor was not hysterical or paranoid but quite prescient in guessing there were good reasons to get out.
>
> Don't you ever go to the movies? Your newsreels must be full, as ours have been, of that obscene rally at Nuremburg. All that shouting and prancing and waving of banners and sputtering hatred would be ridiculous if I did not hear endless stories from my unexpected guests and did not know that Hitler's takeover is absolute and secure and welcomed by the mindless mobs who line the streets weeping when he passes. (Again, check newsreels, it's incredible, but there it is.)
>
> One of my Jews presently in residence is a shopkeeper whose store was posted NOT FOR ARYANS. Another's daughter was raped and beaten by thugs on the street while passersby, including police, ignored her screams. Jews have lost jobs in all fields and are now clamouring to get out of Germany. The trouble is that our stupid

government refuses to recognize the emergency and will allow only the usual trickle of entries. The only loophole we have found is one for domestic servants, who may enter the country almost at will, as long as a job is promised to them. All I've been able to do is to "hire" a huge "staff" for old Chilblains Hall, getting people in on domestic servant status and urging them to move on as quickly as possible to make room for more—getting them off to Canada or the U.S. or South America—or whereever a chink in immigration walls will let them through, and finding damned bloody few such chinks. I've learned more about immigration policies throughout the world than I ever wanted to know, and believe me, they are wretched everywhere, not only in California.

Of course, I'm not really doing much of the work, which is handled by a niece of the Herr Doktor, who refused to go on to S.A. with him and has made it her mission to get as many Jews out of Germany, then out of Europe, as possible. I go up to the old house only every couple of weeks, just to discuss money and supplies with her. Then I hop right back to London, to a studio in an old warehouse on the south bank of the Thames (in Bermondsey) where I hole up and paint. I can't paint at Old Rack and Ruin—it's jammed full, like a hospital again, no, like a madhouse with all those stunned, frightened, furious, lost people coming and going.

The truth is I'm too old for all this. You and I will be forty next year, but I feel like two thousand and forty, like a very, very aged Cassandra arguing with old Uncle Ralph (who called the Nuremburg Rally "rather a good show") and the others who say Hitler isn't a bad sort, got the country on its feet again, and so on, until I want to scream.

Instead I paint. I paint the devil who looks like a cross between Hitler and Uncle Ralph.

Do be careful. I loved your description of the sheriff falling into the irrigation ditch, but I wouldn't want him to catch you one dark night.

Love,
Stephanie

In early January, while I huddled under the awning of the relief office in pouring rain with the group waiting for our weekly checks, a child sidled up close to me. She was the daughter of an Okie family that had joined in one of the strikes. She whispered, "My ma said tell you don't sleep at home tonight." Then she ran away before I could ask any questions. There was no point in following her. Her family now lived in a shack on one of the small, outlying farms; the price of this shelter had been breaking contact with the union and anyone still connected with it.

After getting my check, I went home and put my clothes in my pack, loaded whatever food I could carry on the bike, and rode to a deserted cabin about a mile away. That night I could see the red glow of flames from the house I had left, Wanda's first home, and hear the siren of the fire truck, which arrived much too late to save anything.

In a way that fire helped protect me. The rumor spread that I had died in the fire. That is, the Filipino or Japanese boy, Lee, or the half-Russian Chinagirl May Lee, or that white woman in the Chinese pajamas—whatever mixture of identities the tellers of my death perceived. From then on I collected my check very early in the morning and changed living quarters often. A few days with a Japanese family of strawberry pickers, a few weeks in a rented room over a restaurant in Chinatown, winter months in a deserted field shack until flood waters came. Then I would put on my overalls and become one of the Filipino men in a hotel near the canneries. I had been warned that if I left the county, it would be hard to reestablish my relief status anywhere else; moves of recipients were used as an excuse for cutting off payment.

There was always work to do, always someone in need. Very little of the work was for the union anymore. With the depression unchanged after five, six, seven years, most people's needs were at survival level. I went to the relief office to translate for old people. I rounded up children and brought them to the health department for vaccinations. I stayed with the babies of pickers so that their mothers could work.

Sometimes I stole food. I became a delivery boy on my bike, driving through richer streets, making deliveries in reverse—taking boxes of groceries left at the back doors of grand houses, bringing them to a shack where everyone was ill.

My most ambitious burglary was done for the union, almost the last job I did for it during its long death throes. I was lifted through the small window of the local office of the Associated Farmers, from which I stole the file of "dangerous radicals" which had been compiled to be sent to the San Francisco Office, and from there to the FBI. The theft was a symbolic act, since our list was so short and easy to compile again. I was pleased, however, to find myself listed as four different people. One of the listings gave my complete name and other facts which could only have been obtained from the relief office.

My description of that incident makes it sound like a lark, and that was how I described it in my letters to Stephanie. The truth was quite different. The truth was that I remained frightened, tired, and very lonely. The only difference in me was that I no longer suffered such inner struggle. My will had been slightly subdued. Obedience to the demands of the moment had become almost habitual. And once in a while, just for an instant, I felt a clear if faint intimation that I moved in time to the rhythm of that thing.

Only one other letter is left from the ones I received from Stephanie. It was written at the end of 1939, two months after Hitler invaded Poland.

Dearest Mei-li,

I do hope you get this letter. With the submarine activity starting up, perhaps mail will be sunk, so I'm trying one of these new-fangled tissue-paper airletter things, filling every nook and cranny of its meager space and hoping our suddenly appointed censors don't cut great chunks out of what might be the last letter from me for a while—priorities being confused, as usual, and passage even above the Atlantic uncertain.

What is really ghastly about this war is not the lack of preparation for what anyone with half a brain could see was coming. Not the lies, equivocations, compromises, and shameful betrayals, letting that loathsome brute take over one country after another and break treaties and treat one's leaders (!) with contempt. "Low, dishonest decade" indeed, as Mr. Auden says from his safe berth in your country. (Not to judge—probably my staying on here shows only middle-aged inertia.) It's not even the total incompetent confusion of trying to mobilize now that it's almost too late. (If that remark wasn't cut out by the censor, it only proves that even our censors are hopelessly incompetent.) It's not even the way people like Uncle Ralph insisted that Chamberlain was working things out with Hitler, who was really "an interesting and capable chap."

No, what is really ghastly is that now we're at war again, the silly, criminally silly asses have trotted out all the old slogans from the last war, as if they've been in moth balls all this time, ready for use. The old reeking stupidities—how we're going to teach those Germans a lesson this time, how our gallant boys have the spirit to stop even a German tank, how the channel will protect us in any case, how we must all get behind the war effort—and so on and on. It would make you sick to hear the old stuff over again, exactly as before, when what is going to happen, is happening, is destruction of life even worse than before, destruction that should have, could have been stopped a dozen times if these bloody patriots who talk so militantly now could have shown a fraction of that spirit five years ago when that maniac could have been put back in prison where he belongs.

I've no doubt you will be hearing the same blather quite soon because, no matter what your dear president says, the States won't manage to stay out for long, nor will you get off as cheaply as you did last time.

My dear, don't worry about me. I can always go up to old Rack and Ruin with the rest of the refugees and wait this one out. I can't think of what other use I could be. I'm too old for the army—the last war gave us the vote, and this one gives us a chance to join in the killing. Progress?

Actually I'm painting night and day. London street scenes. We're sure to be bombed soon, and things will not look quite the same again. When I tire of that, I'll go to the country and paint my refugees, who are the only people one can talk to these days. The rest all sound like madhouse Napoleons.

If I could believe in that thing of yours I'd say this is a good time for you to shoot up a little prayer to it for us all. But I can't believe in praying to anything that allowed this mess, not to mention how shabbily it's treated you ever since you made its acquaintance.

My dear, I love you and am with you.

Stephanie

By the time of the 1940 strawberry harvest there was plenty of work in the valley, but no cars were driving in, no tents went up. The farmers competed for the experienced pickers but settled for anyone and began to demand that the government "bring back the Mexicans." The people who worked on the harvest that spring talked of leaving to work in war industry, where the wages were said to be "a dollar an hour while they train you, and then more!"

The president continued to say we would never enter the war, but naval bases around the Bay were being built up and new ones created, one of them at Hunters Point. "There are plenty of jobs up there," one of the Okie women told me. "Even for women. Even for niggers. We was up there last week, and I never seen so many niggers. They are moving whole towns of them up from Alabama." Her family left the next day, as did many others in the weeks that followed.

I refused the invitations of families who offered to take me to Hunters Point with them. I could not have passed even the easy physical exam given to people hired to build the ships and bombs. Even were I capable of doing it, such work was not for me. Furthermore, I did not want to participate in the transformation of Hunters Point. I had already seen news photos of the razing of the shrimp sheds, the covering of wooden piers and sandy beaches with concrete and metal drydocks, the covering of the rolling slopes with housing that looked like prison barracks. It was like the sudden invasion of Hunters Point after the earthquake. This new earthquake would transform Hunters Point completely and permanently, and I preferred to remember it as it had been.

Hunters Point in 1880 when Parker S. Murrow moved there with Tatania and their two daughters. *San Francisco Archives, S.F. Public Library*

Parker S. Murrow with Tatania, Erika (foreground) and Sophie. *Effects of Erika Newland.*

Norman Luther Duclar about 1905. *Effects of Erika Newland.*

Karl Goldman in 1912, just before leaving America for Europe. *Family Collection, Joy Goldman Meyerlin.*

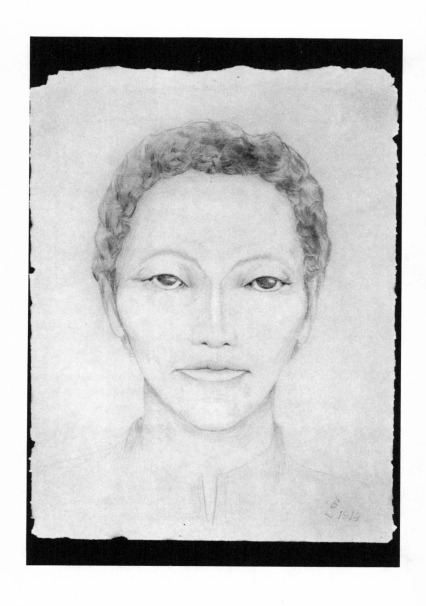

Sketch of Mei-li Murrow by Stephanie, 1914. (Respecting the wishes of Stephanie's heirs, I have withheld the name of her family and of their estate. D.B.)

Redwood grove near Felton, once a trail into "Garden of Eden," now part of Henry Cowell State Park. *California Historical Society, San Francisco.*

Prune orchard near San Jose. *Photo by Gabriel Moulin, 1937. California Historical Society, San Francisco.*

San Jose Canners' strike, 1931. *San Francisco Archives, S.F. Public Library.*

Main entry of Napa State Hospital "castle" as it looked when Mei-li first saw it in 1942. *Napa State Hospital Archives.*

1940–1946

I had spent the winter in a hotel near Saint James Park, and I stayed on through the summer and into fall, seldom leaving my room, sleeping most of the time as if to make up for a decade of unrest. The doctor who had written my letter for the relief office came to see me when the relief office made one of its regular threats to cut me off. He listened to my heart, signed a new authorization for payment, and shrugged. He had not expected me to last this long. Perhaps I would die in this shabby hotel, as an old Japanese picker had died only the day before. The prospect did not alarm me. I only wanted to lie still.

During those long days I had time to think, as I had during the months in Dona Ceresita's adobe, where I had mused on the failures of the Garden of Eden. Now I had a whole decade of failure to consider. Wasn't the pattern the same—years of effort with nothing to show for it? No, not the same, I decided.

The Garden of Eden had been mainly my failure, the result of my folly and pride. But looking over the past decade in the Santa Clara Valley, I regretted nothing I had done. I had listened, had been guided by that thing. I had been on the losing side but had won something. I had subdued my stupid will. I had changed ever so slightly. A victory of sorts.

In the early fall I began to revive enough to go out, to walk the four blocks to Saint James Park, where I sat in the sun, watched the birds and squirrels, and waited. For what? If not for death, then for a new summons, new orders.

They came at the beginning of November 1940. The day had been sunny, and I had sat in the park all afternoon, feeling the town sink into its winter quiet and emptiness. When I got back to the hotel, I was told that a man had been there, had left his card, and would return in an hour. His card seemed familiar. Yes, a letter had caught up with me several months before, from a legal firm asking me to contact them. But the letter had been several months old, and, considering my activities at the time, a letter from lawyers did not make me expect good news. I had thrown it away.

The man came to my room within the hour. He was about my age, in his mid-forties, and he wore the kind of dark wool suit that marked him as a man from San Francisco. Through little round glasses his tired, impatient eyes took in me and my room. "You are Mei-li Murrow, alias May Murrow, alias Lee, alias May Lee, alias Madame Psyche?" As he checked my relief card and my birth certificate, then took a handwriting sample from me, he complained, "This has been very difficult without any photo of you!" I felt like a child being reprimanded for some act of bad behavior I could not remember committing.

"Your sister said we'd find you down here. We traced you through the relief office. Didn't you get our letters? It took weeks to trace you to this place. This is your fifth address in a year," he finished reproachfully. Only then did he introduce himself as a lawyer representing a firm based in New York. "I have some good news for you. Well, first some sad news. An old . . . connection of yours died nearly three years ago. Norman Luther Duclar."

Norman had died of a stroke. His estate amounted to something over three million dollars—a fluctuating figure because of changes in the radio stock where most of it was invested. His wife had predeceased him. There were no children. I was his heir. One brother and two nephews were contesting the will, but they seemed likely to settle for half, which would have been their share if I had not been found within five years of Norman's death, the rest going to several Negro charities. Then there were legal fees and taxes, but I should end up with nearly a million dollars. I might take another few months before I actually had the money, but in the meantime the firm could arrange loans for me so that I could live in the style to which my financial status now entitled me. In fact, judging from my situation— the man looked around my room incredulously—I might as well ride back to San Francisco with him and take a room in a hotel while the process moved toward completion. He put on his hat and opened the door. "I will wait for you downstairs in the lobby."

I sat down, leaned back, and closed my eyes. Norman was dead. I had thought of him often during the past ten years but had never written to him because I believed his last words to me, that he was "not a man to stay alone." But he had after all stayed alone. And he had never forgotten me. The next few minutes were my shortest but not my last period of mourning for Norman. The impatient lawyer was waiting downstairs. I put my few things into my pack and went down to him.

He checked me into the Fairmont Hotel that night and gave me an astonishing roll of cash "to tide you over for a day or two." The next day I found a clean little hotel on Jones Street and paid a week's rent. I spent the next few days shopping for clothes. Having seen a few women actually wearing slacks on downtown streets, I bought three pair with matching blouses, a sweater, a long wool coat, and the first good walking shoes I had owned since wearing out the boots I had bought from George in Felton. There was still plenty of money left for underwear, socks, and meals at a nearby cafeteria.

The following Monday, when I walked to the nearby lawyer's office, he and his partners were furious. I had forgotten to tell them when I left the Fairmont. They thought I had "run away" and that they would have to begin their search again. I could not understand their attitude, which later events made clear to me. At the time, I only shrugged off their sputtering and promised to inform them if I moved again. When would I receive the money? They told me the process could take a year, depending on whether they could make a settlement with the contesting claimants. In the meantime they would advance me an allowance of $1000. I thought they meant $1000 for the year, certainly a good deal more than I had been living on. When I realized they meant $1000 a month, I began to laugh. My explanation, my attempt to make them see the joke of it all, only made them look uneasy. They gave me various documents, including a copy of Norman's will, and we agreed that I would call at their office every two weeks to pick up money and check on their progress.

I caught a heavy cold which kept me in my room through Christmas, readjusting to the damp, chill winds of the City. But with the coming of drier, sunny days in January, I began to explore the city I had barely seen for ten years.

The downtown area was shabby after a decade of depression, but its shabbiness was edged with new, gaudy glitter. There were more bars, more hastily opened jewelry and souvenir shops catering to the young men in dark sailor suits, underfed boys suddenly dressed in good wool, suddenly filled out with meat and milk, suddenly carrying money in their tight pockets. The hotels and apartments a few blocks below me, near Market Street, were jammed with people who had come to build ships and guns. Whole families crowded into a tiny room, paid high rent, rode buses out to the shipyard, leaving their children to play in the street dodging streetcars. The president went on broadcasting his denials that we would ever go to war, but war excitement was all around me.

It had even extended to the other side of Market Street, to the dark doorways like the one in which my father had found my mother more than fifty years before. These rooming houses and hotels were full too, new workers coming in to live among the old tramps and off-season farm workers, who watched the invasion with bewilderment and fear. I recognized one old Filipino man who had not returned to San Jose for the last two seasons. We stopped on the street to talk. He told me that his rent had been raised for the third time, the hotel owner trying to get rid of him and rent his room to half a dozen war workers. I gave him some money and told him I would come to visit him, which I did during the next few months.

When I walked through Chinatown or up and down the streets near my hotel, I glanced at the flower stalls—there were many more of them than before—but did not see either of my sisters. I assumed my father must have died. Perhaps my sisters still owned some flower stalls but employed younger people to work them. What had the lawyer said?—that Erika had told him where to find me. I thought of calling her. I even looked up her number in the phone book, which listed her at the same address out in the Sunset, near the ocean. If she or Sophie needed money, I could give them some. That was one of the things I discussed with the lawyers, who named ways of creating a trust fund for them after I received my inheritance. I decided to wait until I had the money, then pass some of it to them through the lawyers, and let my sisters decide whether or not they wanted to see me again.

At least twice a week I rented a car and drove through other parts of the City. I headed first for the Golden Gate Bridge, which I had never seen although it had stood for three years already. I drove to Sausalito and back, then to Muir Woods and back, making the trip over and over again. The Bay Bridge I had traveled once just after its completion, on the last of trips for the union to Sacramento, but there had been no time then to stop at Treasure Island to see the World's Fair. It had been held over for a second year, but was closing down. I had missed the 1915 Exposition, and had missed nearly all of this one too. Statues and buildings still stood, but everywhere I drove, I saw navy trucks and signs, the ominous takeover beginning even before the exhibitors had left.

I made one trip to Hunters Point. Fences and guards stopped me from going anywhere near the shore or the knoll where I had lived;

that was part of the shipyards now. All around me, people were driving in, the same people I had been seeing for the past ten years in their laden jalopies. Their children were still in tatters, but they were noisy, as if recently fed enough to have more energy. And many of them were indeed black. I had never seen so many Negroes before, shouting to each other from car to car, adding their southern dialects to polyglot Butchertown (which had suddenly lost that name and all the animals which had inspired it).

Once I even drove over Twin Peaks and out to Ocean Beach to the place where I had experienced that thing. I did not expect another revelation or even an echo of the feelings I had years before. I was simply paying my respects to the place and time where meaning had come clothed in ecstasy. I reminded myself that meaning, unlike ecstasy, did not melt away. Then, after only a few minutes of looking at the ocean, I left. It was cold, and I was afraid that, being so near to Erika's house, I might accidentally meet her. I did not think that either of us was ready for that meeting yet.

I wrote letters to Stephanie telling her of the sudden change in my life, of the new look of the City, and of the new people streaming into it. I received one or two short, scissored replies of brittle good cheer, and then, after Hitler went into France in May, no more. I bought a little radio to hear the first live transatlantic broadcasts of war news. I watched the excitement—even gayety—grow all around me, while local radio commentators repeated all the experts' pronouncements that we would never get into this war.

As the months passed my inheritance began to weigh on me. I had learned to deal with my temporary monthly allowance. I used what I needed; then, near the end of the month when the next payment was due, I gave away what was left. Some went to the old Filipino man and his friends down on Howard Street. Some went to a mission that served free meals without a sermon, some to beggars on the street—for there were still many people who were too old or too sick or too drunk to take any of the new jobs. Sometimes I took children off the street and bought them a pair of shoes or a warm coat. Sometimes I bought a book or a hat or a cake from an obviously struggling little merchant, then gave it to someone who might be able to use it or sell it. I never searched for recipients of my surplus; they were still all around, though the glitter of the new prosperity made them less visible.

What weighed upon me was the question of what I would do with the bulk of the money when it came to me. After buying off the contesting relatives, after paying the lawyers, after settling a life income on Sophie and Erika, there would still be something close to a million dollars. A small part of it would be more than enough to support me for many more years than I was likely to live. What would I do with the rest? During my rides and walks, during the hours I spent sitting in my sunny window, looking down on the crowds of people on the streets, I pondered that question.

I had been given this money for some reason. Everything that had ever happened to me, even before that strange illumination on the beach, had happened for a reason. I had often failed to understand the reason, had made many mistakes and miscalculations. But the hard years in the valley had made me a steadier person. I was simpler too, after the humbling failure of almost everything I had tried to do, from the ill-conceived Garden of Eden to my work for the farm laborers. All of my failures had taught me something. Perhaps they had tested me, matured me. For what? For dealing wisely with all this money? Or was the money itself another test I was bound to fail?

It seemed a harder test than the cruel deprivation of the last ten years. I did not want to waste it in idealistic schemes as I had wasted money before. This time I must use my resources wisely, to do the most good. This is what I said to the lawyers during the months when I visited their offices, signing papers, collecting my allowance, receiving reports of their progress through probate. Perhaps they had some suggestions?

They were shocked when I told them the amount which was quite enough for me to live on, but finally they believed in my determination to do something else with the rest of the money. They offered to handle it for me, leaving it in its present investments, paying the income into a foundation on whose board they would serve. They suggested I choose the beneficiaries of my surplus from established charities. The list they handed me did not appeal to me. During the past ten years, the people I had known seldom benefited from the work of these agencies. The administrative costs alone of the plan they suggested were enough to feed hundreds of people year round.

The lawyers were annoyed at my lack of enthusiasm for their plan. "It is your money, madam, or soon will be, and you must decide. Just what do you want to do with it?"

294

I thought for a moment, then shrugged and said that if I could stop this war, I would give every cent of it right now. Did they have a plan or a foundation for that? I was smiling when I asked, but they did not smile back. (I can't remember exactly when they stopped returning my smiles.) We had many more talks throughout the summer and fall, when I proposed various ideas that came to me.

One of my ideas was to buy a row of hotels on Howard Street, clean them up, and provide rooms for the homeless. I had in mind men like the old Filipino to run the hotels, and I insisted that, given a salary and expenses, he would manage a hotel more strictly and efficiently than any charity foundation.

Another idea was choosing a hundred or more older women in Mission-Hunters Point and paying them to open their homes to anyone who wanted to leave children with them during the day. Even if war never came, or if it did and was over quickly, there were always so many children whose parents couldn't care for them all the time, and so many old women with no support.

Or we could take one great lump sum, buy a piece of land near the shipyards, and build housing as different as possible from the barracks going up now. Perhaps Norman would have liked to have his money used to benefit some of the Negro people pouring in. I rejected that idea myself. It would be better to make the downpayment on individual houses chosen by a family. At only, say, $3,000 per family, I could help a great many families to buy the home they wanted, where they wanted it.

Then there were other people to whom I could make outright gifts, people who would never get money from any other source. Girls like Angelina, who should not have had to make the choices she had made in order to earn her education. People who—unlike Tom, Dick, and Harriet, long fled to other causes—would keep trying to help workers like Wanda and Emilio. (I had already instructed the lawyers to arrange for their legal immigration. They never found them, or at least, they told me they could not.) Or perhaps I should give money to lawyers interested in helping the poor. Could they suggest any?

There was always a deep, uncomfortable silence following any of my suggestions. Then the lawyers pointed out the complicated problems involved in implementing my ideas. I had to agree with them. This money was burden which grew more and more heavy.

Would I ever find the right way to dispose of it? Maybe that was the wrong question. Maybe disposing of it, gettinng rid of it, was wrong, irresponsible, full of dangers of evading the task set for me. Maybe my final test was to devote the remaining years of my life to serving the money, making it do its best work. It seemed I had been rescued from destitution only to be captured by riches. Or acquainted with real destitution in order to know what to do with riches. Good enough. I would do my best.

Actually, that last year before the war was a calm, restful, renewing time. I lived in only one clean, warm room for the first time in years, hearing the cheerful and somehow soothingly impersonal noises of city traffic day and night. I frequented a good dentist week after week, who repaired the long neglect of my teeth, no doubt saving them so that, unlike everyone around me now, I still have most of them. I ate plain but good, regular meals in the cafeterias nearby, among convivial, yet courteous, even courtly, old people who gathered to discuss politics and art and old memories of the City. The Salon of Compton's or Foster's, as one old man said, tipping his hat to me if we chanced to see each other on the street. The doctor I visited at the beginning and end of the year said there was no doubt of the general improvement of my health, though nothing could be expected to improve my heart function. This was the first doctor to assert that exercise and minimal diet had probably saved my life. But even he said I could only count on one day at a time.

Near the end of the year the legal work was finally completed, and Norman's estate was mine: three hundred thousand in cash, deposited in various banks; another six hundred thousand in stocks and property now in my name. By this time I had made my decision. I would stay in my cosy little hotel, enjoying downtown city life, making my small gifts to people who had come to depend on me. I would make larger gifts to people who convinced me they would use the money well. No foundations. I would simply have to trust my own judgment to give the money where and when I saw the right person for it. Someone like Helena if I could find her again. Someone like the young writer who worked in the cafeteria, for whom $10,000 would buy years of carefree work on her poems. These and other gifts might not be the ones Norman's lawyers would approve, but Norman would have, and that must be why he had given his money to me. It was the kind of joke he would love, the kind Stephanie would enjoy. (I wrote to her but waited in vain for an answer.) I would trust myself. The only thing I must do quickly was make a will in case my time ran out suddenly. But I decided to find another lawyer for my will, one who might look on my aims more approvingly than the lawyers who had handled Norman's estate.

On the first Saturday in December I met the estate lawyers in their office and signed final papers. From there we went to the bank near my hotel, where various assets had been deposited, to sign more papers. We finally shook hands and said good-bye about 4 p.m.

As I walked down Jones Street I became aware that a car had slowed down and was rolling along near the curb beside me. The car, a tan Ford sedan, pulled slightly ahead of me and stopped. As I passed it I heard my name, "May." I stopped. Before I turned to look, I recognized Erika's voice. She sat behind the wheel after having leaned sideways to swing open the door. I stooped and looked in at her. She smiled. "Hello, May." Her hair was quite white, rolled up in the latest style. Her skin was clear, hardly lined, and so artfully made up that she seemed to glow with natural color. She wore a soft gray dress that showed she had become slimmer since passing middle age, and she was becoming a beautiful old woman. Her glasses gave her beauty a touch of intellectual dignity. "How strange!" she said. "I was just thinking of you. I think of you often, May. I thought you had left the City. When did you come back? How are you, May?" Her voice caught, she swallowed, and then she smiled again, her eyes sparkling and blinking with unshed tears.

As I started to answer, a horn honked behind her, then another. She motioned to me to get into the car. I did, and we moved forward, turning right at Golden Gate. I told her that I had been back for nearly a year, had thought of her often, but had not been sure she would want to see me. I told her about Norman's money and said she would be hearing from the lawyers about provision made for her and Sophie. How was Sophie?

She didn't answer but asked more questions. How was my health? How had I survived the hard times of the past decade? Did I think Hitler would attack us? Had I seen what they were doing to Hunters Point? She chattered and smiled, keeping her eyes on the busy streets as we moved, asking another question before I could finish my answer to her last one. As we crossed Gough Street, she pulled the car to the curb. "There! Now we can talk!" She turned to smile at me, then sighed. "My God, how much you look like your mother. Let's walk. Around Civic Center, just like the old days, when we used to walk to the library."

We got out of the car, and she took my arm, hugging it affectionately, tightly. When we had walked only a few steps, I felt her leading me toward the stairs of a low wooden building attached to one of the court buildings behind City Hall. I stopped. "The library's that way," I said. She did not answer. Her grip on my arm tightened. Her eyes were bright with determination, and her mouth twitched nervously. She pulled at me, edging me closer to the unmarked doorway of the building which, I suddenly saw, had bars on its windows.

I stopped, broke her grip on my arm, and turned away. She grabbed me from behind, throwing her arms around my chest and screaming, "Help, help!" A uniformed man came out of the building, and I heard Erika sob, "Please help me. I've filed a petition, help me get her in . . . I can't . . . my heart . . ." She held me in an iron grip while moaning like a weak old woman on the edge of collapse. The man grabbed me, twisting my arm behind my back in a quick motion that was all too familiar to me from the days in the San Jose orchards.

I knew better than to resist, to fight, or to yell. I tried to make my voice as calm as possible, asking, "Am I under arrest?" He did not answer. He gripped one arm while Erika held the other, and the two of them dragged me up the steps and into a small, dark entry, containing a high bench like a police station. "You can't arrest me," I said, trying to keep my voice from rising. "What crime am I charged with?"

"No crime," the man said as he stepped behind the bench, looking at some papers Erika had handed him.

"Then you can't put me in jail."

"This is no jail."

"What is it?"

"A hospital, just a place to take a little rest for a while."

I turned to look at Erika, whose performance as dignified old lady was only enhanced by the way part of her white hair had come loose in our struggle. "Is it the money? I told you I'd set aside some for you. There's plenty. Erika, stop this right now or I'll . . . I'll tell the lawyers to give you nothing."

298

"Now, now," said the man. "Your sister's trying to do what's best for you. You better be good."

"I haven't seen this woman in fifteen years!" I said.

Erika burst into tears, and the policeman shook his head sadly at her.

"She wants money. A million dollars, to be exact!"

At that he rolled his eyes and smiled at Erika, who gave him a perfect smiling-through-tears expression. The whole performance was so ridiculous that I made the mistake of laughing.

"Now, now, you calm down so I don't have to put you in a strait jacket. Ain't much fun." He took my pack and the change from my pockets. "Just to keep everything safe for you."

He led me through a door, down a short hall, then through another door. The "hospital" consisted of thirteen small cells, each containing a narrow metal cot. The place was dark and cold and smelled worse even than the San Jose jail. There were only bars between the cells, no walls, no privacy at all, even though both men and women were there, the women toward the south end. The cells were so narrow that only by standing in the dead center of mine could I keep out of arm's reach of the person in the next cell. I moved my cot to the center because the woman on my right was reaching through the bars, trying to slap me as she cried and moaned.

The other eight or nine people in the cells were more quiet, three men in a stunned, catatonic state, a woman pacing agitatedly back and forth in her cage, the rest eating from metal trays. A tray was brought to me, slid into my cell on the floor through an opening. I ignored it. After a while the trays were collected and we were taken, one by one, to the toilet. Trying to sound as calm as possible, I said to the woman guard who pushed and prodded me from behind, "I would like to call a lawyer." She laughed as the other policeman had. "Why, honey? You going to commit some crime?" I shook my head. "Then you're all right. Just don't worry."

"What are you going to do to me?"

"Nothing, nothing at all, honey. A couple of doctors will examine you and make sure you're fit."

"And if I'm fit, you'll let me go?"

"Sure thing, honey."

"I still think I should call a lawyer."

"Too late now, time for bed. Call him tomorrow." She kept smiling as she gripped my arm, squeezing it until it hurt. She was a huge woman, and she frightened me more than the policeman had.

It must have been only about seven o'clock, but we were ordered to get into bed. The dim light remained on all night. The woman next to me continued to cry out from time to time. The one in the next cell got up as soon as the guard left, and began pacing again. One of the men coughed and coughed. I had grown used to the quiet of my little hotel room; sleep would have been difficult even if I had not been so afraid. I told myself that this was some new test, some new task. I began to speak to that thing, asking for guidance, for a hint of what I was supposed to do with these new events. I found that speaking aloud was comforting, more real, so I added my chanting prayers to the noises which continued all night long. Off and on I slept until dawn, when we were roused from our cots and taken to the toilet again, fed, then ignored. When I asked the woman guard if the doctors would examine me today, she said, "It's Sunday, honey, no doctors coming today." When I mentioned calling a lawyer, she ignored me.

I sat on my cot wrapped in my coat, which luckily they had not taken from me. Bright sunlight shown through the high window, but the place remained cold, and the only person not shivering was the woman who paced constantly. I no longer found any comfort in my prayers. I tried to speak to the women near me, but made no connection. This was different from the times I had been jailed during strikes. Then we sang songs, cheered each other up. I was kept busy translating stories and jokes and plans for new strategy. Here we were alone, each of us, in an isolation made worse by the sounds of each person's lone suffering and confusion.

So I tried to pass the time with people I loved, who had loved me. I thought of Norman and Stephanie and Wanda and her children and Karl and my baby Joy and my mother and Miss Harrington and Guido. In my imagination I grouped these people in a warm protective circle around me. I even added Sophie to the circle, telling myself that she would come today and get me out of here. She might be dominated by Erika, but there were limits to that domination.

Then I made wider circles around this circle: Helena and the union people; Angelina, who had had to go her own way, but was, I believed, still a kindly person, who might even be teaching children like Manuel near San Jose now; all the workers in the valley; the old men in the hotels on Howard Street and the beggars on Market Street; the kindest members of our commune in the mountains.

And so on and on, building wider and wider circles of advocates, all imaginary, all gone or far away or impotent, not one of them I could call on for help now, except Sophie. Even if I could contact some of the people from San Jose, I might only make trouble for them, without helping myself. I could not think of one without an arrest record or a listing with the FBI. Those who had avoided both were too frightened to acknowledge even knowing me.

Never mind, I told myself. The doctors will come tomorrow, pronounce me sane, and I will be set free. I must relax, remain calm, help those round me whom I could help, ignore the crying, the pacing, and the constantly grating sound of the radio blaring in the outer room where the police and attendants stayed, deaf to screams and calls.

But something strange was happening. As the day wore on, the radio blared with less and less music, more and more talking, portentous announcements just below the volume at which I could comprehend the words. There was less talking among the guards, no laughter, just the radio voice. The guard who brought our lunch was flustered and rushed, ignoring my questions as he ran out again. Now added to the voice on the radio were the voices of more people who had come into the outer office. Even the more distracted prisoners had quieted a little, sensing something ominous in that outer room. At one point in the afternoon the radio fell silent. There was nothing but the sound of the pacing woman, shuffling, exhausted, but still dragging her few steps back and forth. No other sound. I was sure that the guards had left the building.

I heard a faint shout from the street. I pulled my cot to the wall under the window, standing on the cot so that I could see out to the street. I held the bars and peered through the thick, grimy glass just beyond arm's length. I could see a newsboy, waving a paper, shouting "Extra! Extra!" His words came to me through the glass as a dim echo. I shouted, waved my arm, tried to beckon the boy toward the window so that I could see his headlines, but when he saw me he cringed and backed off. He knew this place, as I had not, knew that I was just some old mad woman yelling at him.

When it grew dark, the outer room was occupied again, with the radio on. Trays of food were brought in to us. The woman attendant looked more fierce than ever, so that I was almost afraid to ask, "What's going on? Something has happened. What is it? What's on the radio?"

"The dirty Japs!" She peered at me. "You a Jap?"

Totally confused, I shook my head and waited, but she said no more.

The answer to my questions came about midnight, when they brought in a very old man who was raving, crying, trembling, and praying in my mother's dialect. He fought the two attendants who carried him in, but was so small and weak that they did not bother to use the shackles they threatened him with. When they left him in the cell opposite me, he fell on the cot, huddled into a shivering, moaning lump. He looked like all the old men who lived in the hotels edging Chinatown. I might even have seen him on the street. At first I could not make out what he was saying. Then gradually I understood his repeated, breathy shriek, thin as a whisper, "the white devils . . . kill us, they are coming . . . hide, hide . . . ." He was old enough to have been here during the terrible riots from which my father had rescued my mother, and he seemed to be reliving the terror.

In a quiet moment between his moans, I spoke to him, saying he was safe, trying to soothe him. He answered that I was wrong. "It is starting all over again, over again!" Then he collapsed, sobbing. I tried again. Why had they brought him here? What was happening outside? What had happened to him?

Gradually he quieted enough to be able to tell me. He had been getting onto a bus when three white boys stood up, called him names, threw him off the bus, and chased him. "Dirty Jap, dirty Jap," they had called him, not listening when he said he was Chinese. They chased him, he fell, they kicked him, tore his clothes, took his money, his hat, his shoes. And nobody did anything. Right on Market Street, with people all around, and they only watched or turned away. It was just like 1889, when he had hidden in a dark cellar without food or water for two days, hearing the screaming mobs. No Asian was safe on the street, Chinese or Japanese. "It is starting all over again!" The police dragged him from the doorway where he huddled and brought him here.

That was how I learned Japan had attacked Pearl Harbor. War had come. The fact that I had expected it did not lessen the shock. I lay awake all night, thinking of what Stephanie had said about the inevitability of our entrance into the war. "And you won't get off as cheaply as you did last time."

The next day I tried to tell the guard that the old man was only frightened, and for good reason. He ignored me, saying the doctors decided "who was crazy around here and who wasn't." But he was a younger, kinder man than those who had been on duty during the weekend. When I asked him to leave the door open so that we could hear radio announcements, he agreed, and I was able to hear Roosevelt's address to Congress declaring war. Then someone closed the door again.

Later that day a man came in identifying himself as a doctor. I saw a newspaper sticking out of his pocket and asked him to leave it with me. He shook his head. "Against regulations." I gave him the name of the lawyers for Norman's estate, but he only nodded and did not write anything down. He took my blood pressure and my pulse, gave the usual startled look at placing a stethoscope to my chest, ignoring all my questions, either about the war or about what was to be done with me. When I asked him to bring my sister Sophie to see me, he asked, "Do you often have visits from the dead?" I was so startled that I just looked at him. "Have you seen God?" he asked, looking at his watch. "Would you like to give all your money away?"

"I know who fed you those questions!" I snapped, showing anger, but feeling more fear than anger. To prove my sanity I had to give the right answers, and that might not be so easy as I thought. I looked at this man, wondering what the right answers would be. He only looked at his watch again, offered no more questions. He got up and went to the next cell. He had been with me less than ten minutes. When he reached the cell of the old Chinese man, I offered to translate, tried to tell him what had happened to the man. He ignored me. The old man was, by this time, as silent as the three catatonic men in the adjoining cells.

The second doctor came a few hours later. He looked very much like the first. Both were middle-aged, portly, dressed in somber suits with starched white shirts. Both moved with rigid dignity, and the second one smelled of alcohol. When I asked if he was a psychiatrist, I saw a flicker of annoyance in his eyes. "You speak English?"

"Of course I speak English."

"Why are you so agitated?"

"Aren't you agitated? We're starting the killing all over again!" I was referring to the war, of course. He did not answer me. He asked me who I thought was trying to kill me, but while I was trying to explain, he got up and left. He had been with me about five minutes.

That night, after some confusion and shouting in the streets, our dim lights were extinguished and we were told to lie on the floor under our cots. This I refused to do, since the floor was so filthy. Finally I could make out the shouting in the street. "Lights out, Jap planes sighted!" We were to be bombed, it seemed. But it was a false alarm, and after a couple of hours, our dim light went on again. That night I dreamed that I was in a great hall again, like the one in London, reciting casualty lists.

On Wednesday I persuaded one of the guards to leave his newspaper with me. Aside from the reiteration of the attack on Pearl Harbor, the declaration of war, and the statements of allied countries, there was little information. The extent of the damage and the plans for war were, of course, secret. Instead of information, the papers were full of articles designed to "raise morale." There were interviews with army officers who vowed to "wipe up those little yellow b_____s before spring." There was a photo of pathetically young sailors waving their white caps, supposedly as they boarded ship. It was all as Stephanie had described it, and as I remembered from the last war—slogans and swaggering and regression to utterances of brutal, destructive, delinquent children. There was even a picture of women smashing dishes and bowls stamped MADE IN JAPAN, as most cheap pottery was in those days.

The next day's paper was more ominous. On the front page was an aerial photograph of a large field planted in rows of what might have been artichokes or grapes or cucumbers. The plane was too high to show anything but the familiar lines. A caption stated that this was a field planted by Japanese farmers near Los Angeles, the rows patterned to point toward military installations, to guide Japanese bombers to their targets. When I returned the paper to the guard, I said I could not see how such a ridiculous story could have been printed. He paused, said, "You sure you're not a Jap?" He gave me no more newspapers.

On Friday morning I was taken to a huge courtroom, empty except for a very old judge, a clerk, myself, and Erika, with a man beside her who looked like a lawyer. Erika, all in black, looked more beautiful than ever. Tears trickled steadily down her cheeks as her lawyer explained that she had tried to be a mother to her illegitimate, half-breed half-sister but that, now of advanced age, she found the burden impossible. Her other sister, recently deceased, had also been unstable, and she was still caring for her ninety-year-old father, now suffering from alcoholic senile dementia. She needed the help of the court to make sure that my inherited money would be used for my treatment and care.

That was the first I knew that Sophie had died and that my father was still alive. While I tried to absorb these facts, the judge put down the papers he was reading and looked at me for a long moment before asking if I wanted to say anything. I realized that my slacks and sweater were improper attire for a woman, especially when compared to Erika's respectable black dress. Probably my oriental looks influenced the judge too, not to mention the fact that I had not had a bath and had slept in my clothes for nearly a week. Clearly he was impressed that the elegant, respectable Erika was so concerned about this untidy half breed.

I tried to keep my voice calm as I said that I was perfectly sane and that my sister was lying in order to take my money. The judge gave me a kindly look that froze me. Then he looked down at his papers again. Finally he said he thought I might benefit from further examination at Napa State Hospital. When I tried to protest, a guard stepped forward, clamping her hand on my arm. The judge did not look at me again as I was pulled from the room.

Recently I gained access to the papers that judge was reading— forms filled out with information given by Erika to the two doctors who visited me in the Detention Hospital. I include one as part of this account because it partly explains the attitude of the judge who based his decision on it. It does not excuse his hasty commitment of me, but that was the way such cases were handled at that time. In my case the upheaval caused by our sudden entry into the war only hastened the process slightly.

SOCIAL BACKGROUND INFORMATION

NAME   May Murrow, aka Mei-li Murrow, May Lee, Lee, Madame Psyche, Sy-kee

ADDRESS   Jones Hotel

AGE   46

NATIVITY   San Francisco

SEX   Female

COLOR   Mixed. Yellow and white.

OCCUPATION   None

RELIGIOUS BELIEF   No church affiliation. History of spiritualist worship, claiming occult powers, contact with the dead. Once led a cult based on her "direct contact with God."

EDUCATION   Third grade

CIVIL CONDITION   Unmarried

MAIDEN NAME OF MOTHER   Unknown

NUMBER OF CHILDREN OF MOTHER   Unknown

HAS EITHER PARENT BEEN ADDICTED TO ALCOHOL OR NARCOTICS?   Father alcoholic

HAVE ANY RELATIVES BEEN ECCENTRIC OR PECULIAR IN ANY WAY IN HABITS OR PURSUITS? IF SO HOW?
Mother was a Chinese prostitute brought into home as a servant, impregnated by father of petitioner, who is half-sister of patient. Mother was withdrawn, rarely spoke, possibly paranoid. Died when patient aged eight. No further details available on maternal side, since mother entered USA without papers, family, or family name.

Half-sister Sophie shared patient's delusion of communication with the dead, otherwise functioning normally until death from pneumonia 1940.

WHICH PARENT DOES ALLEGED INSANE PERSON RESEMBLE MENTALLY? PHYSICALLY?   Patient is small of stature, slight. Eyes have epicanthic fold. These are traits of oriental mother. Otherwise resembles father: light skin, straight nose, curly hair (brown and gray), blue eyes. Mental traits resembling mother: withdrawn, secretive, given to panic flights. Resembles father in episodes of megalomaniac speeches which attract a following of similarly unstable people.

306

HAS ALLEGED INSANE PERSON EVER BEEN ADDICTED TO MASTURBATION OR SEXUAL EXCESSES? Long history of sexual irregularities beginning with sexual relation with black man at sixteen. During trip to Europe she ran away with a road show, bearing a child which died. Later became homosexual, encouraging like perversions in cult she led. During the past ten years has repeatedly escaped sister's care to consort with tramps, aliens, communists and other undesirables with whom she has often been arrested.

STATE ALLEGED INSANE PERSON'S HABITS AS TO USE OF LIQUOR, TOBACCO, DRUGS   Alcoholic episodes, for treatment of which petitioner took patient to Europe twenty years ago.

WHAT IS ALLEGED INSANE PERSON'S NATURAL DISPOSITION OR TEMPERAMENT AND MENTAL CAPACITY? Disposition anxious, distracted, restless, imagining herself imprisoned by normal life. Runs away into dangers from which petitioner has repeatedly rescued her. Depression alternates with exaltation, unrealistic plans, trusting unreliable and unconventional people. Mental capacity very high for a woman, possibly causing strain of overactive brain on weak nervous system. Picks up ideas, languages, facts, very quickly, but follows them into erratic actions.

WHAT IS ALLEGED INSANE PERSON'S GENERAL PHYSICAL CONDITION? SPECIFY ANY DISEASE OR INJURY. Extreme heart disrhythmia dating back to near fatal influenza twenty years ago. Pallor, fainting spells. Any exertion or shock could result in cardiac arrest. Otherwise apparently healthy for a woman of her age.

HAS ALLEGED INSANE PERSON EVER HAD CONVULSIONS? IF SO, WHEN DID SHE HAVE THE FIRST ONE? LAST ONE?   First convulsion at age eleven during the great earthquake, recurring once a week during the next twenty years, accompanied by hallucinations of dead people. Convulsions less frequent in recent years.

HAS ALLEGED INSANE PERSON EVER BEEN AN INMATE OF AN INSTITUTION FOR THE INSANE? WHEN AND WHERE? DISCHARGED OR OTHER WISE? In Spain 1919–1920 Sacred Mother Convent for incurably insane and tubercular. Removed by half-sister (petitioner) who hoped to continue non-institutional care in the United States.

307

NUMBER OF PREVIOUS ATTACKS   At least twice a year since the European episode, patient has run away, disappeared, surfacing when in trouble with the law or surrounding community. Largely incapacitated, on relief for the past eight years.
PRESENT ATTACK BEGAN?   Winter 1940–41. Upon notification of impending inheritance patient began giving money to strangers on the street, declined sister's repeated pleas to come home, avail herself of treatment, avoid repetition of previous episode in which life savings were lost in communistic cult. Ignored lawyers' advice, stated intention to give money away.
IS ALLEGED INSANE PERSON NOISY, VIOLENT, DANGEROUS, DESTRUCTIVE, INCENDIARY, EXCITED? Violent resistance when brought to detention hospital. Criminal record in Santa Clara County lists assault, resisting arrest.
HOMICIDAL OR SUICIDAL?   Suicide threats throughout her life, no overt attempts.
HAS CHANGE OF LIFE TAKEN PLACE?   WAS IT GRADUAL OR SUDDEN?   Patient is now in change of life, with possible exacerbation of mental symptoms.
SLEEP   Observed wakeful during the night.
DELUSIONS   Insists she is in prison, examiner not a "real" doctor, sister her "enemy." Fears being murdered. "We're starting the killing all over again."
WHAT IS THE SUPPOSED CAUSE OF INSANITY?
PREDISPOSING CAUSE. EXCITING CAUSE.   Predisposition genetic, both maternal and paternal sides of family. Exciting incident was earthquake of 1906.
OTHER FACTS INDICATING INSANITY   Confusion of identity, possible split personality. Patient has used at least four different names, some oriental, some occidental, some female, some male. Dress and grooming indicate confusion of sexual identity. Wears trousers, short hair, no make up or jewelry. Could be mistaken for a boy.
DIAGNOSIS   Dementia praecox

The second doctor wrote a much shorter report, skipping most of the questions, then giving a diagnosis of "manic-depressive." Both doctors accepted Erika's description of my "insanity," in fact, of my whole life. I was impressed at how closely Erika stuck to the truth, like any good liar, and how well she had prepared for my commitment to the asylum.

She had known about my inheritance before I did, had actually told the lawyers where to find me. She must have kept contact with them during the year of probate, for she had obviously learned of my plans from them. I really don't think they meant to be dishonest. I remember their expressions when I talked of how to use the money. They must have believed that I was insane and that informing my sister of my plans was the best thing they could do for me. If I had called on them for help, I am not sure how well they would have represented me. In any case, my mention of calling a lawyer was always ignored or laughed at by the guards. I have since learned that I did have the right to get a lawyer, but the "alleged insane" at the Detention Hospital were customarily processed through without legal representation.

Later that afternoon two deputy sheriffs drove me north to Napa in an unmarked car with no inside handles on the back doors. The little Chinese man was with me in the back seat. Both of us wore handcuffs attached to a chain which kept us pinned back on the seat, hardly able to see anything through the side windows. "You'll like it up there, nice farm and everything," said the deputy who was driving. "Free room and board, no worries." He kept watching us in his rear view mirror. "Matter of fact, if I was in your shoes, I'd be glad to get out of the City for a while. Not safe there for Japs." I didn't bother to tell him we were not Japanese. What did it matter? Besides, I was beginning to realize that anything I said would, truly, in one way or another, be used against me.

After that comment the two deputies ignored me, speaking only to each other. I listened intently, hoping for some details about the war, but they only talked about whether or not the war would last long enough to make it worth their while to quit civil service for the high wages of the shipyards. Both were beyond draft age. The two-hour drive to the state hospital in Imola was for them a pleasant outing, a break in their usual duties. They planned to drop us off and spend the rest of their day in Napa at a bar run by a man who also worked part-time at the hospital. He would be sure to keep them "in stitches with his bughouse stories."

It was dark when we turned off the highway, though it was probably only about five o'clock. I had a dim sense of being on a broad drive from which we immediately turned off to the left, driving around the back of a long, low building. The deputies took us out of the car but left our handcuffs on until we were inside the building facing a long, high desk. After taking off our handcuffs they handed me my pack, put some papers on the bench, and left. I sat down and looked through my pack. My changes of clothes and my few letters and identification papers were there, but the bank-books and safe deposit key were gone.

A white-uniformed man with a large ring of keys jangling at his belt came through a doorway, saw us, cursed, and opened another door. "Get someone out here from the women's side. The damned deputies just dumped them and took off." He then picked up one set of papers, grabbed the old man by the shoulder, and led him through the door to what I later learned was the men's side. I turned and moved quickly toward the door through which the deputies had left, but not quickly enough. "Where do you think you're going?" A woman in a white uniform had come through another doorway, moving quickly across the hall to grab my arm. She pushed me ahead of her through the doorway she had come from and down a long hallway, her ring of keys clinking at her waist like the warning rattle of a snake about to strike. The walls of the hallway were a dingy dun color which must once have been creamy white. Every few feet was a large metal door with a small window, a few inches square. The odor of Lysol was so strong that my nose burned.

As she led me past these doors, the woman flipped through the papers the deputies had left and called out, "Smith! Smith? I've got another admission here, give me a hand." Another voice called out that Smith was bringing inmates back from dinner. "Then you give me a hand!" But no one came. She opened a door and pushed me into a large room. "Take off your clothes, May," she said, as she took my pack away from me. She stood watching me and, at each hesitation, impatiently urged, "Come on, off, everything," until I stood naked and barefoot. I saw my clothes and pack pushed through a small cupboard door into the next room. Then I was pushed again to the other side of the room and into a shower stall where the water came on sudden and strong, but not very warm.

Still, I would have enjoyed a shower if the woman had not stood there glaring after handing me a sliver of soap. I washed as fast as I could, feeling that her patience would wear out quickly and that I might be yanked out of the shower with my hair still full of soap. I rinsed it out barely in time before the water was abruptly cut off.

When I stepped out of the shower and asked for a towel, she did not answer me, but parted sections of my hair, looking, I suppose, for lice. She walked around me, eyeing the rest of my body and jotting down a couple of notes before handing me a skimpy, gray-ish, damp towel. When I was as dry as it would make me, she handed me a large, shapeless cotton dress made from two flour sacks sewn together, with head and arm holes.

"I have a change of clean clothes in my pack," I said. No answer. She dropped a pair of carpet slippers in front of me. I put them on along with the dress and let myself be pushed out into the hall again, where there were now lines of women waiting to be put into the rooms on the other side of the hall. Two women in white joined my attendant.

"When did she come in?"

"Just now."

"Quiet?"

"So far. I'm going to put her in twenty. Alone. She's homo. Get old Matilda out of there."

"Where shall I put her? The only other solos are pretty mean, and the rest are three to a room."

"Put her bed in the hall. Use restraint so she won't wander. She goes to S Ward tomorrow anyway."

I was led—or rather pushed—down a hallway past women dressed in shapeless cotton sacks and slippers like mine. By the time I reached the end of the hall, it was empty, all the women having been put into rooms. As we turned and started down another long hallway, I was confronted by a huge ruddy face with popping eyes and lips like raw meat, smiling through white cotton fuzz. It was a Santa Claus face, molded from papier mache, brightly painted, tacked to the wall. Yes, Christmas was near, or had it just passed? I was suddenly unsure of the date, and that frightened me more than these large, white-uniformed women bristling and jingling with keys.

I was pushed into a small room, about eight feet square, with one bright light in the high ceiling, a narrow metal cot against the wall, and a large window covered by a heavy metal screen. "We're out of nightgowns, so if you want to keep your dress fresh for tomorrow, better sleep in the raw. Go on, get into bed. Lights out in five minutes." The attendant stood there impatiently as I stepped out of the loose slippers, slid onto the cot, and pulled the thin blankets over me. Then she left, closing the door and locking it. Almost immediately the light went out, switched off from outside the room.

I felt little relief in being alone, having a room to myself, being washed clean. Certainly in the past ten years I had often lacked such comforts, yet now I felt a sick, fearful isolation deeper than any earlier deprivation. My few possessions had been taken from me, and I suddenly realized how much my letters, my own clothes, meant to me. These women in white, with their dozens of jangling keys, talked at me or over me, never to me. When I spoke to them, they seemed not to hear me. One had called me "homo." The other women were to be protected from me. I wondered what else was in those papers that I guessed (correctly) I would not be allowed to see, let alone refute. I had been in jail and knew what it was to be treated by guards as an evil person. This was worse. This was being treated like no person at all.

Suddenly the light flashed on again, blinding me. The jangle of keys preceded the woman who had pushed me in and out of the shower. She was carrying something. "I just remembered you missed dinner. All I could find was this." She smiled and handed me a cup of milk and a slice of bread. I thanked her and smiled back, feeling tears come into my eyes at this sudden, personal kindness. But as I began to eat, she shifted impatiently, told me to hurry up, and, when I handed back part of the bread, glowered fiercely at me. "We don't waste food here!" Her ring of keys gave a silvery hissing rattle. I crammed the dry crust into my mouth, hoping to satisfy her so that she would go and leave me alone again.

I slept well that night in the comparative quiet of my tiny room. I was awakened before dawn, pulled out of my room, and put into a line of women headed for a set of four doorless toilets at the end of the hall. I washed my hands under a trickle from a communal basin, but there was no soap, no towels. Then I was placed in another line that led to the dining room. Given a tray, I stood in line until a dish of cold oatmeal, a slice of bread, black coffee, and an apple were placed on it. I sat down at a crowded table where women ate quickly. Those who hesitated were goaded or threatened

312

by attendants. One or two remained withdrawn, deaf, impassive, but the rest of us were frightened into swallowing everything as quickly as we could. Then we were lined up and marched back to make our beds. I was handed a wet rag and told to "clean everything you can reach."

By this time it was light, and I could see out through my window. I looked onto spacious lawns, tall trees, and a broad drive. I could not see far enough to my left to follow the drive to its end. Directly across the drive were rows of small houses where I guessed, correctly, some members of the hospital staff lived. That pleasant but restricted view of the hospital grounds was all I saw during the weeks I spent on the admissions ward. I was never allowed outside.

For exercise and fresh air we were marched, once in the morning and once in the afternoon, around and around an inner courtyard. As we circled the twenty-foot-square patio like a parody of maypole dancers around the young tree growing in the center, we could hear the men exercising in the courtyard on the east side of the building. We knew of their presence only by an occasional deep cough. Even eating was strictly segregated, no woman inmate entering the dining room until the men had eaten and been marched out.

Between exercise periods came lunch and visitors, then dinner, and then lights out at seven. The rest of the time we sat in rows of chairs in the day room. Of those women who talked, a few talked to invisible companions; others spoke to each other, usually abusing family members who had sent them here. I spoke no more than necessary. It seemed to me that the attendants eyed me sharply whenever I was near any patient, as if expecting me to make a lewd attack on her. I thought it best to remain silent and alone.

Occasionally in the night I heard a scream, then running feet and jangling keys, or during visiting hours I watched an inmate sobbing and begging a relative to "take me home." But generally the days were of a numbing, crowded monotony. The worst ordeal of that month was the Christmas visit of a church volunteer group, preceded by feverish scrubbing, locking up of noisy inmates. During the "festivities," the attendants' fierce smiles warned us to be politely grateful for the handkerchief and piece of candy given us by the church ladies.

When the brief fever of the holidays was over, the routine went on as we all waited, supposedly, for examination and diagnosis by the admissions doctor. Supposedly. The truth was that the hospital was so overcrowded and understaffed that patients stayed for weeks on the admitting ward without being examined. Every day I watched and waited for some sign that I was to be examined, but every day was as empty as the one before.

The only break in the routine was one brief visit from Erika. It was almost impossible for us to talk in the crowded visiting room of the admissions ward, impossible even to find a place to sit. She put her arms around me and whispered in my ear while I stood, frightened and rigid (observed and noted as "withdrawn" by the nearest attendant). Erika whispered that I would be served with papers announcing a guardianship hearing, from which I would be excused, using the doctors' report of my heart condition. If I did not interfere, she would take control of the money, have me released after a few months, make me a small allowance, and leave me alone forever after. "If you make any trouble or call any laywers," she whispered, her clenched-teeth smile touching my ear, "I will sign permission for you to receive a new treatment they are trying out on everyone. It is called electroshock, and it will either stop your heart or fry your brain." She smiled, kissed my trembling cheek, and left.

After a few weeks I got my shoes back and my underwear, put through the laundry and labeled with my name. When I asked about my slacks, an attendant, looking somewhere above my head, proclaimed, "Women wear dresses here." Occasionally I saw newspapers discarded by careless attendants (inmates were discouraged from reading "disturbing" war news) in which I could follow the advance of Japanese forces over the Pacific Islands. It seemed to me that as defeat followed defeat, the new admissions and some of the attendants looked at me with increasing hostility. Perhaps I kept my private bedroom as much for my own protection as to protect other women from me.

I learned not to ask direct questions (almost never answered), but to listen and watch carefully, especially when attendants spoke to each other. Much of what I heard I did not understand until later when I knew the asylum better, but I realized that news of what happened in the most remote areas—wards, out buildings, offices —spread instantly throughout the asylum. By listening to the gossip of this unofficial network, I learned that a new admissions doctor had been found—an old doctor pulled out of retirement—

but had died the second day on the job. Time passed before another came. "Refugee Jew," said one of the women in white, "can't even speak English, and his wife on B Ward. We got a pool on how long he lasts. I took twenty-two days." She laughed and shook her head, accompanied by the jingle of her keys.

One day, after three months on the admissions ward, and without any warning, I was taken out of the afternoon exercise line and brought to an examination room, where I was weighed, measured, tapped for samples of blood and urine, then left in a tiny, locked, windowless room. After half an hour I began to tremble, partly from cold, partly from nerves. This was to be my opportunity to prove myself sane. I must not cry. I must not raise my voice. I must not, probably, tell the true story of why I was here—it was the kind of story screamed by the most disturbed inmates to their imaginary companions. I must do what I was very effectively being conditioned to do: watch, wait, try to guess what the key-janglers wanted, or at least try to avoid saying or doing what they did not want.

I would have recognized the doctor as a European even if I had not heard the attendants talking about him. He was young, probably not much over thirty, but he had that pale, defined, mature look of the European which contrasts so sharply with the expansive, rough, but childlike look of white Americans, especially westerners. The man was exhausted, depressed, disoriented. In fact, if he had been brought in as I had that night in December, he could easily have been mistaken for an admission to the men's ward.

He opened my chart, noted the date of my admission, then shook his head. "Missus Mur-rro," he said, nodding at me. I was not sure whether I was supposed to respond, so I nodded as slowly as he had. He had rolled his r's very broadly, but had not said enough for me to identify his accent. He flipped through my commitment papers. I suspected that he comprehended little of what he read. Then he sighed, put the papers down, and began the physical exam. When he put the stethoscope to my chest, he started, then glanced at my face. I smiled and shrugged as he let out an expression of dismay—in Greek. When he began stumbling through questions in an English so accented I could not understand him, I answered him in only slightly better Greek.

"You speak Greek?" The question preceded a flood of words. As soon as he saw I really understood him and was lucid, he began to talk, continuing his examination of me like a sleepwalker going through familiar motions, pantomiming daytime acts. He tapped and listened and peered, but soon he put down all his tools and only talked.

He and his wife had been put into a concentration camp in Italy after Mussolini's attack on Greece. Their baby had died there. A year later his wife was shipped to a camp in Austria; she had been a well-known singer and was wanted there to provide entertainment for the German staff. The doctor escaped from the Italian camp and made his way along a network of Italian partisans, and then on his own, to where his wife was. With the help of a sympathetic German officer (who asked him to "remember this if we lose the war"), he managed the escape of his wife and himself into Switzerland. From there they used contacts in the international art and music world to get to the United States.

By that time his wife had lost her voice and most of her reason. They had lived in New York, broke, dependent on the help of other musicians who were themselves not well off. After two years his wife was no better, and he was too occupied with her to build up a practice. Then he had heard of the wonderfully curative climate of California. When he heard of an opening at the Napa State Hospital in Imola, California, he took it as providential. Even the name, Imola, was a good omen. It was the name of an old monastery in northern Italy, a town where he and his wife had spent a few days on their honeymoon, almost ten years ago, when life had still seemed bright.

Tears gathered in his eyes. His voice thickened, and I had trouble understanding him. I gathered that he was stuck here for a year to comply with California medical licensing laws, and that his wife, after a suicide attempt, had been put on Ward B. He was beginning to describe the deterioration in his wife's condition that quickly followed her admission, when the nurse opened the door to ask if he was through with me. (This was the first time I had seen a nurse, the only one on the admissions ward.) "I've got seven more patients waiting here, Doctor."

"Yesss...thank you." He switched back to English, wiped his eyes, and picked up another folder. The nurse took me by the arm into the hall and handed me to an attendant, who put me in the line forming for dinner.

316

As I sat numbly spooning cold potatoes to my mouth (all food was overcooked but cold by the time it reached us) an attendant poked me. I began shoveling the food into my mouth quickly—I had seen attendants brutally forcefeeding slow eaters. Was that all? Was that my examination? I had hardly said a word. The poor man had been too overwhelmed by his own problems to listen to mine. The moment I left the room he had forgotten me.

But I was wrong. A few days later I was pulled out of the day room, handed my pack, and told I was being assigned to B Ward. "That's our best ward!" sputtered an attendant, as if outraged that I had won such a privilege. "You better behave yourself there!"

"Who's going to take her? We're shorthanded again and it's bath day."

"Sister Mary can do it."

"Pretty soon Sister Mary will be running this place."

"She might do better than what we've got."

While the two attendants laughed, I tried to read their meaning. At the same time I quickly scanned the visible portion of a newspaper one of them put down on her desk. It carried photos of Japanese-Americans being sent to "relocation" camps. The main photo showed a young white soldier passing a candy bar through a train window to a child. The story under the picture praised the "humane" and "gentle" way these "enemies" were being treated.

Doors were unlocked and relocked as I was walked down the halls, left, then right, to the reception area where I had first entered. Another woman in white waited for me, but this one looked almost like a nun. Almost. Her dress was almost like an attendant's white uniform, yet close examination showed it had been pieced together from parts of a threadbare uniform and flour sacking. Her headdress was almost a classic wimple and veil, but the forehead band was made of stiff paper, the wimple of dingy cheesecloth. Her white stockings were all patches and darns, and her shoes were men's boots whitened with chalk or shoe polish that was flaking off. Instantly I understood the attendants' joke. Sister Mary was an inmate who believed herself to be a nun.

Her plump, ruddy face smiled at me with genuine kindness, and her eyes looked into mine, making contact that attendants and other inmates avoided. "Hello, my dear."

"She goes up to Ward B. You want to walk her?"

"Oh, yes, it's a lovely day. The walk will do her good, won't it, my dear?"

317

"You want to watch her, we haven't tried her outside yet. But she's got a heart murmur so she couldn't get far if she runs off."

Sister Mary smiled at me again. "You're much too sensible for that. But it's brisk out there; she'll need a sweater." We waited while one of the attendants went to the clothes room to get a faded, purple, limp knit blouse with rhinestones sewn into it, one of the items of donated clothing which made us inmates look so strange.

While we waited for the sweater, Sister Mary talked about Ward B. "You'll like it there. It's the best ward. You just behave yourself there, and you'll soon be going home." She went on to give me what I later learned was very sensible advice about Ward B: which attendants were kind, which to "watch out for," how to gain grounds privileges, how to double up socks to keep warm because "the radiators are always on the blink in the castle." I thought her use of the word "castle" signaled some other delusion, but I was wrong. She was lucid except for her unshakable belief that she was a nun whose order had assigned her to work at the state asylum.

Sister Mary helped me put on the grotesque sweater, then took my arm gently with one hand, carrying transfer papers in the other, and led me through the front door to my first full glimpse of the hospital grounds. The broad driveway I had seen from my window was much longer than I had thought, going east across the thick green lawns, shaded by the large trees which lined it. The suddenly open vista took my breath away for a moment. "Beautiful, isn't it," said Sister Mary. "I planted that tree," she said, pointing to a flowering walnut, "nursed it from a seedling that I picked out from the nursery. The greenhouses are back of the castle. You can visit there when you get a grounds pass, but only when the men aren't working. Don't even talk to a man if you ever see one outside the monthly dance. It counts against you more than anything—loose morals."

We walked slowly east while Sister Mary pointed out and identified the buildings we passed. To our left were the medical buildings, the small infirmary for sick patients, then the buildings for student nurses and women attendants who had no homes off the grounds. Behind them was other housing for attendants and maintenance men. On our right across the broad driveway were more cottages for staff people. Further up and to the left were a baseball diamond and a recreation hall. "I know you can't see them yet, but you will as we walk up along there." Beyond the staff cottages stood three large mansions for doctors, "and back beyond that is the new S Ward built by the WPA. It's just the most...."

I didn't hear the rest of Sister Mary's description of the senile ward. I heard nothing because I was now close enough to begin to see clearly our destination—the castle. I shall never forget my first glimpse of it.

The driveway ended in front of a vast, four-story brick fortress like nothing I had seen outside of Europe. In fact, as we approached it, I thought of Stephanie and her wicked jokes about "the drafty corridors of 'Chilblains Hall' lined with the portraits of heirs to its vast, useless spaces." This castle looked even larger than her home, spreading out from its central tower to lesser towers, walls, more towers, walls, reaching back over what at first sight seemed to cover many acres of land. Its dark red brick walls rose like a violation of the softly rolling hills behind it. As we came closer and closer, the rigid brick walls hid hills and morning sun and spread an angular shadow over us.

In front of the main entrance stood a tall, cylindrical fountain—dry. It obviously had not spouted water for many years, although the dry plants around its stone parapet were carefully trimmed. Looking up, I could see an intricate design of white against red bricks decorating the central tower, the windows, the balcony above the main entrance where three marble arches shadowed small doors.

Close up, all resemblance to Stephanie's ancestral mansion disappeared. If her family's castle was pretentious, this one was grotesque. Marble window trim curved downward to form faces, both human and animal, next to naked plumbing pipes added recently. These little carved faces—appearing the way fevered hallucinations might grow out of bumps on shadowy walls—were everywhere, most of them eroded into leprous, menacing expressions by many decades of weather. Other carved faces grinned from columns rising to and from the balcony. Below the balcony, draped human figures stood in arched alcoves. Topping the main entry arch were two bears carrying shields made of—it appeared—bearded human heads, and between the bears a bronze eagle stood on its nest, its outspread wings tarnished green and encrusted with the droppings of real birds. More figures stood, almost lifesize, in alcoves below.

Carved across a strip of stone between the animals above and the human statues below was a scene of tiny human figures, the central ones kneeling to a standing figure, the others standing in a long line stretching out to either side, bodies bent and turned, arms raised in gestures of supplication or worship or . . . I could not tell the meaning of the gestures. Nor could I read the words carved below on the arches of the main entrance. For a moment it seemed to me that they must be Dante's ABANDON ALL HOPE YE WHO ENTER HERE. But when I was close enough to read them, I saw that they said HOPE AND CHARITY DIVINE BE THINE BEYOND COMPARE.

Standing in the shadow of the old building, I suddenly heard music, a thin strand of familiar melody. I turned toward the sound. To my right, across the drive and beyond the fountain, near the superintendent's mansion, was a grassy, wooded area with a white wooden gazebo in the center. Alone in the gazebo sat a man playing the violin. He stood as I turned toward him, faced me, and continued to play a sweet, soothing tune of gently descending notes, like soft steps moving slowly downward toward peace. It was the lovers' duet from Verdi's *Traviata*, one of Karl's favorites.

When the violinist finished, he bowed toward me and said in a soft voice which nevertheless carried across to me, "Welcome to the monastery of the mad."

"That's Paul," said Sister Mary. "He was a fine concert artist, has a collection of posters from his appearances all over the world. I'm glad to see he's out playing again. He was backwarded a few months, but he's better now." Paul, she explained, was a special favorite of the superintendent, who believed in the curative power of music. He spent most of his good days sitting in the gazebo playing, and the breeze often carried the sound back even beyond the castle.

We entered a foyer where there were old chairs and tables covered with lace doilies, flowers in pots, and old-fashioned landscape paintings on the walls. The foyer was empty except for a woman behind a switchboard, which looked like a recent addition to the room. I could tell from her shapeless dress that she too was an inmate. We passed her and went through another room like the foyer, the visitors' room. Sister Mary turned right, stopped at a door, and rang a bell. Then we waited, for of course Sister Mary had no ring of jangling keys. We waited fully twenty minutes; she spent the time saying her beads, which up close seemed to be a string of dried peas. Finally an attendant came to unlock the door and admit us to the places beyond those usually seen by visitors. Sister Mary touched my forehead, spoke a blessing, and left me.

320

The attendant turned me over to another inmate. We stood in the midst of a long, broad, inner hallway where at least fifty old women sat in lined-up chairs. Along the sides of the hall were a few metal cots between open doorways. There was no light in this central hall except for what came through these doorways, which led to small rooms with large windows on either side of the hall, crowded with more cots.

That was when I realized that the castle was not as deep nor as huge as it appeared. Actually, it was only about forty feet wide, shaped like an angular crescent wrapped around inner courtyards where most inmates had their only view of the outdoors, behind walls that hid them from outside view. The circumference of the building and connecting walls was nearly a mile of long, dark halls which were the dayrooms between the inmates' bedrooms. One side of the crescent was for women (the wards named alphabetically), the other for men (their wards numbered), separated by a wing of offices, chapels, and storage rooms that cut the crescent in half. The wards nearest the center of the castle were the "good" wards. The further outward and backward toward either tip of the crescent, the more agitated or withdrawn the inmates were. The very tips of the crescent were quite separate from the rest of the building, reached only through long, narrow halls. Few people had seen these wards, but the threat of them was ever-present. An attendant exasperated by an unruly man would say, "I'll twenty-one you!" or would tell a disobedient woman, "You're asking for N!"

Of course, I learned these details over a period of time. The only thing I was aware of during those minutes I followed the inmate along the central dayroom-hall of A Ward was the smell. It was indescribably foul. It permeated the entire building, though it was much worse, I later learned, on the back wards. It was as much a part of the building as its brick walls and maple floors—indeed it permeated walls and floors, especially floors. It was made up of many things, but its chief components were human waste, dry rot, and floor wax.

My feet slipped more than once on the highly polished yet spongy, rotted floor as we threaded our way among empty beds and full chairs, past doorways to rooms where more empty beds lay side by side, their squared, smoothly made-up corners touching. The old women sat immobile, some almost doubled up, but not allowed to lie in bed during the day. I wondered if many could keep to their feet if they tried to stand or walk. Only one raised her head to look at me as I passed. "Don't go near Marsha," warned the inmate who was guiding me. "She pinches. Other than that, she's okay. These are all okay, senile but clean, just too feeble to go on S, that's the new senile ward, it's lovely, quite well equipped, but too crowded already." She spoke in brisk imitation of the attendants, but her voice was edged by a weak whine and her shoulders slumped.

She led me through an unlocked door and up a stairway. We were in one of the towers, which housed concrete stairs lit only by narrow, barred windows like the slits through which a medieval archer might repel enemy siege. The edges of the circular stairway were sharp at the corners near the walls, but blunted and rounded at the center. The steps were actually hollowed out somewhat, worn by thousands of inmates being marched up and down for their airing in the walled courtyards—twice a day for the past seventy years. The way my feet fitted those grooves in the concrete steps appalled me more than the smell.

A short wait before another locked door, and we were admitted to Ward B. There was a much longer wait after the inmate passed my papers to an attendant seated at a glass-enclosed desk. She was drinking coffee and talking to another attendant. Despite the glass I could hear their discussion as they passed my papers back and forth between them, glanced at me, then passed the papers again and argued about what to do with me. I was careful to avoid eye contact with either of them. I stood as if abstracted, indifferent, withdrawn. I had learned that although attendants talked over me as if I were not there, they were likely to say much more if I gave clear signs of being "not all there." I had, of course, already learned the one inmate joke which was approved by the staff: "We're all here because we're not all there."

From this conversation I learned how much of a problem it had been to place me. I was not old and senile, therefore ineligible for the new S Ward, where the mobile old made up nearly one-third of the total inmate population. I could not be put on the second largest ward, reserved for tubercular inmates. Because of my heart, the doctor had forbidden not only shock treatment (so Erika's threat had been empty) but "industrial therapy," which meant that, unlike the woman who had escorted me, I could not be employed at the many tasks necessary to running the asylum. "I can't even put her on the block," complained one of the attendants, sending a ripple of fear through me as I tried to imagine what instrument of torture this might be. Assignment to the cottages behind the castle was reserved for the elite of the eight hundred working patients. I was not sick enough to be housed in the infirmary nor crazy enough to be backwarded with the disturbed, certainly not with the idiots, where I'd "probably just cause trouble." Since my insanity was of such long standing I probably belonged on "one of the quiet chronics, maybe H," but certainly not on B, the best ward, a "total push" ward whose benefits would be wasted on me. It was all the doing of that new doctor, that Jewish refugee, who said I could talk his wife's language. So the inmate next to her had had to be pushed out to D in order to make room for me.

One of the attendants thought it might be good for the doctor's wife to have someone near who could talk Greek. The other thought such "coddling" would only delay the time when she would "snap out of it." I waited silently while their argument turned into complaints about the double shifts they had worked since two more attendants left. "If this goes on, I'm heading for the shipyards too."

Ward B looked much like Ward A but was not so crowded. Three and sometimes four cots were crowded into each little room. Two alcoves with broad bay windows, which must have been intended as dayrooms, were jammed full of beds. But there were no beds in the hall-dayroom that ran between the rows of bedrooms. Only twenty or so women, most of them younger than I, sat in rocking chairs or on long wooden benches, and some of these wore dresses which were not made of faded cotton sacks. A few even had arranged their hair differently from the asylum style (shingled straight up the back, three inches long on the sides). They had been to the new beauty parlor for curls and waves. I did not realize that there were more than sixty women on Ward B; most of them were working or had taken the trolley to the town of Napa or were on brief, trial visits home.

Another inmate showed me the tiny bedroom I would share with her and the new doctor's wife. There was room for nothing but the three cots, lined up side by side against the huge, heavily screened window. As the newest arrival, I was given the middle cot. I would have to climb over one of the others to get in and out of bed and would face another person, inches away, on both sides. "But there's a box under your bed for your things. We get to keep our things on B, nothing valuable, but our own. And see, our window overlooks the gazebo, and sometimes, especially in the summer when we go to bed in the light, we can hear Paul playing. Even in the middle of the night sometimes he's out there, though it's against all the rules, but the-music-is-so-nice-don't-you-think?''

This girl seemed to be about sixteen. I learned later that she was nearly thirty. She was pale and blonde, very pretty. She smiled as she talked (with sentences that speeded up toward their end, like a car rushing out of control), mostly about going home. "I'm ever so much better than I was when I came. I was very sick, but now I'm almost ready to go home.'' Her eyes darted here and there when she spoke. She never relaxed her little smile or the brightness of her voice. She never relaxed at all, but was always on view, always perfecting her performance of "sanity.'' She had been in the asylum for nearly four years. "The hospital,'' she corrected, when I called it an asylum. She had worked her way up from back wards and hoped to be released soon. Her box was full of pictures of her two children, letters from them, presents she was making for them in occupational therapy—stuffed animals. "The children were just babies when I got sick. They're not too old for these, are they? No, everyone likes a cuddly little animal, don't you think? I make them for the old ladies on A too. You do speak English, don't you?''

She was typical of the women on B, who talked about going home, gauged the chances of the latest one who had left, relayed every word from their visitors, described their trips into town or their walks on the grounds, or the new styles at the beauty shop. They talked most about the ward doctor, whose every word was memorized and analyzed.

These women never relaxed. The tension was like a high pitched sound always shrilling in the background. It rose when the attendants were on the ward, though they seldom were, since the inmates anxiously did everything they could to keep the ward running smoothly without attention from the staff, who, if needed, would conclude and report that the inmates were not capable, not trying, not getting better, not going home. This cheerful anxiety rose to an almost intolerable height on the mornings when, still in their nightclothes, most of the women lined up for shock treatment, which was given on the ward twice a week, in a small room beyond the attendants' office. Talk ceased as the women stood unresisting but rigid, hearing the screams which erupted when the current was applied. There were always inmate volunteers to assist by lying across a shocked patient to prevent broken bones during the violent convulsions. Hours later, when the women gradually emerged from their stunned, ashen catatonia, they asserted that they felt much better. Yes, much better. Yes, ready to go home, really. Although, of course, they were very happy on B Ward, very grateful for treatment, would almost miss the hospital when they went home. *Soon?*

The admitting doctor's wife was the exception to this mood. I think I would have picked her out easily even if the talkative inmate had not brought me to where she sat in a corner, her head drooping like one of the senile women on A. "She doesn't really belong here," whispered the pretty blonde girl. "She's really crazy—suicidal, withdrawn. They had to force feed her. Now she eats, but only enough so they won't do it again. Her husband won't let them give her shock. He's very backward, just a refugee, you know. Doesn't understand the new therapies. She's bad for the rest of the girls. It's very disturbing to have someone like that on the ward, spoils everything. I try not to think about her or I'll start feeling bad myself. I mean, they have to treat her with kid gloves because she's his wife, but that won't help her snap out of it." Like all the other "going home" inmates, the blonde had learned the attendants' language and constantly displayed it like another sign of her cure.

The doctor's wife looked older than I, although she must have been about the same age as the blonde. Her hair was white, her eyelids red and puffy; from her thinness and her pallor it seemed certain that she had eaten poorly for a very long time. I spoke to her in Greek, but she made no response. I sat down beside her, since there seemed nothing else for me to do. Clearly my only reason for being on this ward was to bring her out of the dark place where she had gone. Perhaps if I succeeded, I would win my own release? I would try.

The next day I learned the schedule on Ward B, which was, with few variations, the same throughout the institution and had been for as long as anyone could remember. A few women who worked in the dining room rose at five, the rest of us at five-thirty, dressing and waiting in lines for toilets, then again for wash basins. Then we waited until we were ordered to line up for breakfast, then waited another twenty minutes until we were marched through Ward C to the dining room. Some of the plank tables were set with white patched tablecloths, but there were no longer enough of them to cover many of the crowded tables, where we had to eat very quickly, then hold

325

up our spoons (the only utensils allowed) to be collected and counted by the working patients. Out by seven so that another ward could be fed, we hurried back to B Ward to make our beds according to a rigid, military method, which made all the little cots into square, grey-white slabs. As in the admitting ward, I was given a wet rag and told to clean everything I could reach. When that was done, bedrooms were out of bounds except when we needed to take something from our under-bed boxes.

Then I learned what the "block" was. It was a block of dense, heavy wood about two feet square, almost too heavy to lift. Attached to the top of it by a thick metal pin was a rough pole. Wrapped around the block was a piece of old, tattered blanket. There were a dozen of these blocks in a closet at the end of the ward. After we had made our beds, the blocks were dragged out and pushed across the floor.

In every ward, every morning, troops of patients pushed the blocks back and forth, up and down the long halls, polishing the dark, rotten maple floors which, no matter how permeated with foul-smelling matter dropped over the past seventy years, always shone, slick and slippery. In some wards the block was called the major form of therapy; the first prescription by an attendant for restless, distracted patients was to "put her on the block." In Ward B, the women expressed pride in a freshly buffed floor, running back and forth with the block, then standing in line to wash again, freshen their hair, and perhaps put on some lipstick.

All this activity was the feverish preparation for the arrival, at nine o'clock, of the ward doctor. He spent about fifteen minutes walking around, smiling, saying, "Good morning, good morning," then disappeared into the attendants' office, where he talked for another ten minutes, giving orders based on the attendants' notes from the previous day. Then he was gone. With eight doctors for four thousand inmates, these morning visits could be nothing but ceremonial, but they were the high point of the day, the peak toward which everything built. After the doctor left there was nothing to do.

Working patients left for "industrial therapy," rarely returning before bedtime. At 11 a.m. the rest of us were marched down the tower stairs and outside to the front of the building where the best wards were exercised. We usually walked across the driveway to the gazebo where some of the women joined hands and swayed in time to Paul's violin music. Others played with the cats who came to get scraps someone had saved from breakfast. There were hundreds of cats on the hospital grounds and many more back in the hills where they had gone as wild as the native wildcats. An older attendant said that the cats had always been here, brought originally to keep rats out of the dairy. One of the inmates shook her head and said they were the descendants of pets brought from Napa and abandoned, ". . . just like us." The attendant wrote down a note, and the inmate began to cry. That remark would count against her in her next hearing for possible release. Crying would count against her too. After twenty minutes we were marched back upstairs and put into lines: toilet, handwashing, lunch.

Sometimes after lunch there would be a shout from an attendant, "Mrs. Smith! Visitor!" The woman called would leave the ward to meet her visitor in one of the rooms downstairs near the main switchboard. But most visitors came on weekends. On weekdays, the long afternoon stretched out, with nothing to do but sit like the old ladies on Ward A. Most of the women had passes allowing them to go to town, but many never left the ward. They said it was too cold or Napa was too far to walk or they lacked trolley fare. The real reason was that patients, even if they were able to remove some of the marks of the asylum (faded cotton sackdress, heavy shoes, lopsided haircuts) were conspicuous among the people who lived in town. "I can't stand those people looking at me like I'm crazy."

There were about a dozen old books and a stack of *National Geographics* on a corner shelf, but no one read anything beyond a newspaper that two patients subscribed to, then passed around. The patient library, a large room next to the central chapel, had long been jammed full of beds for overflow patients. Its books, scattered throughout the wards, had been stolen and sold in town by inmates or attendants. Only a few tattered, worthless volumes sat on shelves to be dusted daily as proof of the annual report's assertion that, "A 3,000-volume patient library is kept on the various wards." Few patients seemed to miss the books. Those who could concentrate well enough to read were put to work, and after ten or twelve hours of "industrial therapy" were too tired to read.

In the afternoon the idle women on Ward B sat and talked, discussing war news or hospital gossip. They did not speak to the doctor's wife, who upset them by being so unresponsive, so crazy. Nor did they talk to me. They saw me as a servant attached to her, an oriental at that, possibly Japanese, an enemy.

Once more in the afternoon we were marched out for another walk around the gazebo or into one of the walled inner courtyards where the attendant needn't stay to watch us. There the women from Ward B huddled together to avoid association with the more disturbed patients. "I don't want to be with those women who hear things," said one of them. I could tell from watching her attentive, frightened face that at times she heard things too but had learned to pretend she didn't.

After that airing it was time to line up for dinner, and after another empty hour we prepared for bedtime at seven—ten long hours on narrow cots listening to the sounds of good patients, going-home patients, pretending to sleep, never talking or wandering or giving the night attendant (who expected to have her own sleep uninterrupted) any reason to report misbehavior to the doctor.

During the daytime hours I talked to the doctor's wife, trying to bring her out of her isolation. My rough Greek was rusty, and with no response from her, I had trouble regaining lost words. At first I talked of pleasant places I remembered in Italy, familiar to her as well, but I only made her cry. Dredging up my own memories made me sad too. So I switched to simple, repeated phrases—it is a sunny day, I am your friend, please eat this soup, here is your husband, he loves you. He came every afternoon to sit with her, and I picked up more words from him. Weeks passed before she spoke to me.

Her first words were, "Will they kill us today?" and her second phrase, repeated over and over, in reponse to everything I said to her was, "I've lost my baby, you know." I felt tears come to my eyes, but no words of comfort came to my lips. Her grief only grated at my own; no one ever recovers from the loss of a child.

She spoke to me in whispers, falling dumb as soon as anyone else noticed. "Forbidden, don't speak!" she warned me in a hoarse, hissing whisper. She called the attendants guards and the working patients "capos." When the ward doctor made his 9 a.m. appearance she hid, trembling, under her bed. No one could coax her out until he was gone. To the infuriated attendant this was behavior which could not be tolerated, disobedience, craziness which disrupted her smoothly running ward, the best ward. If the guilty patient had not been a staff doctor's wife, "she would not last on my ward for one hot minute!'' The other patients quickly nodded agreement with the attendant.

I tried to explain. It was clear that she believed herself to be still in a concentration camp. ''A what?'' My answer was cut off with contempt for another delusion. It was only 1942, and the horrors we saw when the camps were opened three years later were only rumors then. I knew more because of Stephanie's letters, but no one would listen to me. The attendants were insulted, furious, and certainly were not to be told their business by an inmate. Only her husband agreed with me when he came to visit. ''Yes, she has come out of the blackness where she hid, but only to the horror that drove her there. And it is true, all true, the horror she sees. No one believes, but it is true.'' He would cry as he spoke. ''The trouble is that this place is very like the camp. It is the wrong environment for her, all wrong, but what can I do? I can't leave her yet and I can't leave her alone, not until she stops trying to join our dead child. She has tried suicide four times.''

She was worst on shock treatment days. To her the line of half-dressed women standing in line must have seemed the line to the gas chamber, and their screams expressed their sudden realization that they were about to die. She would cringe in a corner, weeping, clutching at me and hissing at me to hide, hide. I translated what the attendants told me to say, that the women were only lining up for treatment, as we lined up for showers on bath day, but she gave me a sly look, warned me to agree with anything the ''guards'' said, and stay out of line. ''It is the line to death.''

Her terror infected the other women, who already had enough trouble hiding their fear and loathing of shock. Their agitation expressed itself in little quarrels, in some breaking down in tears, while the attendants raged at this disruption of their carefully organized ward, saying that if only they could ''give her a jolt, she'd behave herself.'' But the ward doctor remained unwilling to ignore his colleague's wishes and would not put her on the shock list.

The climax came one morning when the women stood in the shock line, and she ran to them, hissing warnings, trying to pull them out of line. Two of the patients grabbed and held her while the attendant tried to put a straitjacket on her. She kicked, bit, then desperately gave out her first full-voiced sound, a terrifying scream. The attendant—who happened to be the one Sister Mary had warned me not to cross—grabbed her by the throat and pulled her to the head of the line. We all knew what she was going to do. She would present the doctor's wife for shock treatment. It would be all over in a minute, a mistake, not uncommon. The attendant might be reprimanded, but what else could be done? Attendants were never fired; on the contrary they were placated when they threatened to quit.

The doctor's wife turned toward me, screaming at me to rescue her, to save her. Her screams were a great advance; they proved she wanted to live and even that she recognized another human being as a friend. I was sure that I could take her to our bedroom, close the door, and quiet her. But if she were shocked into the zombie state in which these women spent one or two days of each week, she might retreat into her suicidal shadows again. Besides, though I never dared to say so, I hated this convulsive treatment that had literally broken the backs of some patients.

Full of these thoughts, but without thinking of consequences, I rushed forward to commit the worst infraction an inmate could: interfering with staff. The doctor's wife clung to me as I stepped between her and the attendant and began to speak, to explain why it would be better not to. . . .

The next thing I knew I was lying on the floor against the wall. The side of my head ached. I could not move my arms. I was in a straitjacket. I was being lifted and put into a wheel chair. I was rolling out of B Ward, out of the best ward. I had "assaulted an attendant," and had been "subdued and reassigned to Ward N."

In some ways Ward N was a restful change from Ward B. No one was straining to act "sane." The schedule, though the same as on Ward B, was not so rigid. No one cared about keeping up appearances of the ward or of themselves. As for the ward doctor, they were indifferent to her. Everyone was openly fearful of the attendants, who did not pretend to want anything but our fear and obedience. An exception was one dear lady, a widow with five children on a nearby farm, who took the night shift and brought homebaked cookies every Saturday. It was she who whispered to me, "Just be good and you'll soon be out of here," a hint that everyone knew I was not violent, that I was just being punished. Mrs. Cookiebaker carried scars from assaults by disturbed inmates, but she never inflicted any. She worked on disturbed wards by choice and tried to teach new attendants (those who would listen) how to quiet a patient without hurting her.

Ward N was even more crowded than Ward B or A. There were no pictures on the walls, no tattered and mended curtains, no rocking chairs or books, no boxes under beds with their sad collections of personal property. Nothing but long wooden benches on which, given a blanket, we slept at night. During the day inmates who seemed likely to hurt themselves or others were shackled to a bench. They often protested, when they grew tired of screaming, by urinating on the floor. Others accidentally soiled themselves before they could get released and taken to one of the two toilets for over sixty of us.

The noise was as all-pervasive as the smell. Hallucinating women shouted back at the voices which haunted them as they paced back and forth, often "on the block," which went on buffing the rotting, stinking floor all day long. In the corners depressed women huddled on the floor, folded, curled, as if trying to escape into a silence somewhere inside themselves.

I could no longer hear Paul playing his violin, nor see the gazebo nor the front grounds from a window. Ward N was a back ward on the third floor of the south side of the crescent. The outside windows looked south over the separate low building called Ward P, where an attendant told me I would be sent if I "acted up again." One of the patients said she had been on Ward P once, where there was nothing but concrete floors and concrete pallets. Naked women, walls, and floor were hosed down once a week. Those who did not kill each other often died from overdoses of barbiturates. I have never seen the inside of Ward P, so I cannot say whether this patient's description of it is accurate or another of her hallucinations. I never heard anyone contradict her.

Beyond Ward P were many other buildings, the newest being Ward Q, begun as a new TB ward but taken over and finished by the Navy, which was already moving in hundreds of mental cases from the South Pacific war. A flag was raised and lowered there every day, while a bugler played. From the inner windows of the ward I could see past the walled courtyards to the brick buildings where our meals were prepared. I began to understand why all the food was soggy and cold. Three meals a day for four thousand were cooked then transported underground on rail cars pulled by mules, who, like mules in mines, never saw the light of day. Arriving at the cellar of the castle, the food was raised to each floor by dumbwaiter. Trucks carried food out to the newer, detached wards, the furthest from the castle getting the coldest food.

Beyond the kitchen buildings I caught sideways glimpses of the farm which produced all this food. Unless drowned out by ward sounds, noises from the farm came to us: cocks crowing, hogs grunting, cows lowing, a tractor grinding. Beyond the farmlands rose the hills now turned brown and dry. "All ours," said a patient who believed herself to be one of the doctors (and possibly had been, I was never sure). "All two thousand acres!" I was seldom able to enjoy views from the windows on either side because certain patients claimed windows, stayed at them all day, talking and gesticulating to real or imagined people outside, and furiously defending this territory against anyone who came near. Half the side rooms were closed, locked as seclusion rooms for patients who were dangerous or annoying to others. When one room was occupied, the others usually were as well because the furious, screaming rage or horror of one woman quickly affected everyone else. This spreading wave of panic or rage was almost the only communication among us inmates of Ward N.

Yet it was no harder to get used to this ward than to the "good ward." At least here the women did not stand in dumb, smiling terror in the shock line. They screamed and fought and clung to benches, forcing the attendants to drag them to the electrodes. There was something honest about Ward N.

There was even something funny about it. Attendants and inmates often held comic dialogues, the role of straight man alternating between them, but more often taken reluctantly by the attendant. For these inmates were agitated and delusional, but not stupid, and they had thrown aside all the ladylike inhibitions that usually smother sharp wit. I remember one in particular who, in an occasional peek through her hallucinatory world, would give a brilliantly funny imitation of the nervous ward doctor skittering through on her daily five minute "rounds." Another inmate constantly presided at meetings at which various attendants were considered for "release," which was always denied on evidence of irrational behavior so meticulously described (and so credibly mad) that there was no doubt of a part of this woman's mind being a constant, alert witness to everything in the real world. Sometimes attendants would respond to this teasing by punishing the inmate with shackles, but most of the time they took the jokes and gave back their own rough quips.

What concerned me about this ward was that most of the delusions of the women were religious, and most of the delusions resembled what, from my own experience, I knew to be true. God had appeared to them, God spoke to them, they were God, they had been put here by mistake, but that mistake was also part of God's great plan for them. Their version was a bit overblown, operatic, but too similar to my own to be dismissed. Yet they dismissed each other's revelations, drew apart from each other as they drew apart from me, each of them a lone prophet "crying in the wilderness," as one of them constantly shouted.

Perhaps I was like them after all. Perhaps I belonged here. Perhaps my mind had not opened nearly twenty years ago, I thought, but had merely cracked. No. No, I was sure I had seen reality. But so were they. I would never give up the meaning I had found. But neither would they. Ultimately it was not fear of the attendants which made me "behave." It was my strange connection with these tormented women that kept me silent, subdued.

Most of the work on the ward was done by about a dozen inmates, alcoholics who had come in hallucinating and violent but were, after two or three weeks, quite calm and lucid, if shaky. Among themselves they grumbled about being kept for months as unpaid slaves. They worked hard, cheerfully obeyed the attendants, and never complained to their visitors. They knew the ropes, knew how they would most quickly earn a grounds pass and a date of release.

Usually, immediately after one of them earned a grounds pass, she would come back on the ward singing with good cheer and smelling of alcohol. That was how I learned that the castle cellars contained more than mule-drawn food trains. A still had operated in those shadows for as long as anyone could remember, the quality of its product varying with the inmates in charge, its operation violating hospital rule and state law. It was the wide open secret of the asylum, protected by free distribution to the staff. Patients, however, paid. This policy kept consumption under control, since most patients rarely had money.

Learning about this illicit "industrial therapy" cheered me. It was the first indication that the hospital world was not a solid, rigid monolith of rules and control. It was more like a sponge, full of countless little holes whose space and air also contributed to its shape. Some people had evidently found ways of escaping into those holes.

The still in the cellar started the chain of events that got me out of Ward N sooner than anyone expected for an inmate who had so seriously breached hospital law. One of the worker-inmates returned from running an errand for an attendant. There was a sparkle in her eye and an erect swagger unlike the drooping posture typical of inmates. She smelled strongly of Sen-sen, those licorice flakes that cover the smell of alcohol so well. She was a stout, white-haired woman, probably in her fifties, energetic though often breathless. I noticed that she was gentle when she cleaned patients who had soiled themselves or when she dragged a catatonic to the toilet. But I was surprised when she walked up to me, looked me in the eye, laughed, and began to talk; the alcoholics, like the attendants, were not sociable and chatty with "crazy" inmates.

"You don't remember me, do you, May?"

Startled, I looked at her closely, but had to shake my head. Yet there was something in her voice that seemed familiar.

She rolled her eyes, then closed them and said, "Oh, Madame Psyche, tell me where my ring is!" She opened her eyes and laughed. "I've changed a lot, but you haven't. You look almost the same, must be the oriental blood—they don't wear out as fast as whites." She laughed again, and then I knew her. It was Maisie, one of the girls Erika had paid to enhance my psychic act. "I recognized you right away, but I thought you were crazy. I been watching you. You're all right. How'd you end up here!"

"Norman left me some money, and Erika wanted it."

"Norman's dead? Ah." She shook her head slowly and dreamily. "He was a sweet man. A sweet man." She made no other reference to Erika, accepting my story without surprise. "So many dead. Rebecca died too." At that point the attendant called her, and our talk was over.

Maisie remained friendly but distant. We never had another private conversation. She was too busy working her way out of the hospital. But, although she did not talk to me, she talked about me, and my identity as Madame Psyche spread through the ward and beyond, as any bit of gossip did.

The very next day an inmate from another ward stopped me in the exercise yard, saying that she had listened to me faithfully on the radio and wanted me to contact her dead father. I said I could not, and she began to cry, attracting the attention of an attendant who eyed me sternly. That night Mrs. Cookiebaker told me her mother had always listened to me, and asked for my autograph. One of the Italian patients on N Ward began to make the sign against the evil eye whenever she saw me; this was the only evidence she had given for months that she noticed anything at all. Another patient began to call me Tokyo Rose, the name of a woman who broadcast demoralizing propaganda to American soldiers in the South Pacific. She insisted that I was materializing ghosts of Japanese soldiers who came at night to rape her. To her I embodied two dangers: the oriental enemy and occult powers. But she did not worry me as much as the women who came to ask me to "take away the voices." I knew they were only a step away from accusing me of inflicting the voices upon them.

Denying supernatural powers had no effect. Women seemed always to be following me, watching me, waiting for me to produce a ghost. Rumors came over from the men's wards; a patient insisted that "the witch on N" was poisoning the food. The attendants began to glower at me. I was making trouble without doing anything they could see. I heard one say to another, "Maybe she does have some kinds of powers; I think some of the worst ones do!" They wanted to get rid of me, but were unable to. I certainly had not earned a place back on B Ward, even if there had been room for me there. There wasn't. There was no room anywhere.

Nevertheless they were forced to move me when an inmate decided to execute "Tokyo Rose." It happened, appropriately enough, on July 4, which during that first year of the war was observed with special fervor.

The July 4 celebration was the most festive of the year, with none of the sadness of the Christmas holidays. At the hospital it was a preharvest festival, like the one in the Santa Clara Valley, but more ceremonious, starting with a parade up the main drive to the castle, featuring the male attendants' marching band and floats made by inmates. After the parade, there would be a speech by the mayor of Napa, who stood with other viewing dignitaries on the balcony of the castle. Then came a picnic on the front grounds, followed by entertainment staged on the gazebo, and, as soon as it was dark, fireworks and colored lights at the fountain.

Of course, most of the inmates were not allowed to participate, especially those on back wards like N, which was locked up even more securely than usual so that more attendants could attend the ceremonies. Participation was limited to working patients with ground passes, but these were nearly a thousand men and women. Their visitors, the staff, and their families might add up to a thousand more people. Few inmates saw the fireworks, since regular hours were kept, and all had to be in bed as usual by seven, two hours before dark in summer. In some of the front wards inmates were allowed to get up and crowd near the windows to catch a bit of the glow. But the barbecue, dance, and fireworks that came after five o'clock were for the staff and visiting dignitaries. That year the Navy was to add a marching band and drill team to the parade. The working inmates on Ward N were making jokes about "getting together with a cute sailor boy."

The special holiday schedule assigned attendants to take turns covering two or three wards, relieving each other every hour or two. Theoretically all wards would be covered, but actually during the afternoon hours of the picnic, when nearly all the working patients were out on the grounds, the rest of us were left alone. Knowing this, the attendants put into seclusion rooms or shackled to a bench every inmate who had ever shown signs of unpredictable behavior, including me. My right ankle was chained to the leg of the bench "for only an hour or two" until working inmates would come back with picnic leftovers for us.

Unfortunately, I was shackled to the same bench with the woman who had begun calling me Tokyo Rose. I think that the attendant did this out of a kind of patriotic spite, seeing it as a harmless joke, at worst subjecting me to a harangue by the other inmate. She certainly had no idea that the inmate, who had helped in the dining room before her hallucinations drove her into Ward N, had somehow stolen a fragment of the lid of a can, and had hidden it in a crevice of this very bench, where she habitually sat.

For about an hour the woman simply huddled at one end of the bench (I kept to the other end) viewing me with narrowed eyes and pouring out accusations. Listening to her, I was interested to hear how much of the current war news she had absorbed, perhaps by hearing the radio that one of the attendants kept loud enough to cover inmate noise (which means very loud indeed). She talked of Bataan and Corregidor and the "death march" of our defeated soldiers. Every few minutes she punctuated her recital with a shrill, "Kill the Japs!" or a hoarse imitation of General MacArthur's, "I shall return!"

I had closed my eyes, withdrawing to that thing, or perhaps only willing myself into something like the catatonic doze of withdrawn inmates, when she suddenly leaped at me, slashing at my throat. Fortunately her leg shackle held her back from a full-force strike. She grazed my throat, making nothing but a long scratch which bled profusely but injured nothing vital. As soon as she saw the blood, she began to scream, dropping her weapon and huddling at her end of the bench. In some part of her mind lived a witness who did not share her delusions. That witness was appalled at what she had done. That witness screamed and screamed. Other patients took up the scream, all but the most withdrawn.

After a while an annoyed and breathless attendant came running from one of the front wards, where she had been watching the parade from a window. Her annoyance changed to something near the horror of the screaming woman. "I'm all right," I said. "Lots of blood, but I don't think she really hurt me. See, it's stopping now."

"Oh, God, I hope so. Can you stand?" It was one of the few times an attendant spoke to me instead of at me.

I stood, my shackles were unlocked, and I was led to the attendants' station for first aid, which consisted of cleaning the scratch with alcohol and replacing my bloodstained dress with a clean one.

Hospital rules demand the reporting of all injuries, no matter how small, but few are reported, especially if an attendant—either by neglect or by overt violence—might be held responsible. "You don't talk about this," offered the attendant, "and I'll get you off N." That very night, after dark, while fireworks were lighting up the sky I was moved to Ward K, in the attic.

The attic was just that, a narrow space under the steeply peaked roof of the central front facade of the castle. It had originally been intended for storage but had been finished off in a rough way soon after the asylum was opened, to contain the immediate overflow of inmates. There were no side bedrooms, no dining room, no bath, no toilets, no heat, only long rows of beds end to end, touching each other so that one person turning over sent creaks and shakes along the metal rods in a chain of quivers to inmates sleeping twenty beds away. Trapped under the slanting ceiling, the stale, hot air of July was stifling. In winter the attic was freezing, but still airless.

337

On the other hand there were advantages to being in the attic. There was the view. All inmates had access to windows during the day, instead of being closed into an inner hall-dayroom. Half of the eighty women on Ward K worked, and most had grounds passes, leaving the ward less crowded during the day. Although we had no boxes under our beds, we were allowed to keep what we could carry with us. Most of the women carried sacks or large handbags. After a couple of requests, an attendant found and returned my pack to me, with my few papers intact. I clutched it to me like an old friend. Even the lack of facilities was an advantage. Since we had to go down to the third floor to eat, to bathe, even to use the toilet, we had more freedom of movement. The doors to Ward K were left unlocked.

One thing lacking for the inmates of Ward K was visitors. All of the women had been at the hospital for at least ten years, some much longer. No one on K talked about going home; most had no home. Their ambitions were small: to get "industrial therapy," something to do, with the status and privileges of a working patient. The unquestioned queens of Ward K were two women who worked in the attendants' dining room, where they ate food of a quality never seen by inmates. Their ambition was to earn promotion to an outside job, the laundry or the cannery, whose workers were assigned to Ogden Cottage or Phillips Cottage, low wooden barracks behind the castle among trees and grass.

For the first time I saw cats on a ward. Dozens of cats lived in the four wards of the attic. They belonged to no particular patients but were fed scraps by everyone and slept on the cots with inmates. One of the many hospital rules forbade pets, but the cats were tolerated because the rat infestation in the castle was especially bad in the attic.

All the women on Ward K had spells of depression, delusions, or confusion, but all had learned to mute their symptoms and control their behavior so as not to be sent to Ward N or the other disturbed wards. They knew the rumors about me but were indifferent; some of them claimed occult powers too. They only wanted to be sure that I would conform and maintain the peace and quiet of the attic wards. One of them, as she reviewed the routine of bed-making and cleaning with me, repeated over and over, "You just behave, you'll be all right. You take what comes and make the best of it."

When she was not working, her shoulders and head drooped forward and her arms were clasped around her mid-section as if in protective submission to a blow which might come at any time. On the ward, in the lines waiting to eat or use the toilet, on the exercise yard, everywhere in fact, women stood this way, bent in upon themselves, eyes looking downward, feet shuffling slowly.

No one on Ward K seemed to care about my oriental heritage. No one called me a Jap. In fact they seemed hardly aware of the war or of anything beyond "making the best" of their lives on the ward. The highest excitement I saw during my time there exploded when an attendant gave a favored inmate her own cake of soap. Envy, resentment, threats of a strike (empty threats), ostracism of the favored one (who stood just a bit straighter for a day or two), dominated conversation for a week. By this time I was the one who silently recoiled from the others, from acceptance into this tight world which seemed to be ever shrinking before my eyes.

Another flurry of excitement came when it was the turn of the attic wards to go to the monthly dance in the recreation hall. About fifty of the women signed up to go, and an hour before the Saturday afternoon dance, they were taken to the clothes room on the third floor where "party clothes" (donated garments impractical for daily use) were kept. This clothes room had existed since the founding of the hospital and probably had never been emptied. Year after year, donated finery was added, hung on long racks or stuffed onto shelves from which inmates could borrow items for special occasions.

The women made their choices, then came back up to the attic to dress. It was as if time did not exist, or rather as if all times existed all at once. Having seen little but hospital dresses for years, they knew nothing of style, only of color, texture, rustle. They wore beaded dresses of the twenties with a feathered hat from 1900; a fur neckpiece with a red negligee; a black lace mantilla above a white satin wedding dress slit up the sides. All these remnants of fanciful, funny, gay evenings had been gnawed by moths and rats and smelled of dust and mold. The sight of them reminded me of the earthquake days, when people escaped wearing whatever they could snatch from the ruins. If only the women could have laughed as they draped themselves, could have made fun of it all. But they wanted to look beautiful, not crazy, and they had forgotten what fun was. By the time they were dressed, some were in tears. They lined up as if going to shock treatment (rarely given on attic wards).

It was during that dance, which I did not attend, that everything changed for me.

It was a stuffy, hot fall afternoon. The ward, after the flurry of dressing up and leaving, was quiet. Only about twenty of us sat on benches gazing out the windows. Those of us who had declined going to the dance were confined to the attic, I don't remember why. Perhaps we were seen as unappreciative of the privilege, or perhaps the attendants were busy at the dance. I wandered to the far corner of the ward, stooping under eaves, looking for this ward's share of the "patient library"—five or six tattered books on a low shelf hidden by one of the beds. Down on my hands and knees, I crawled under the bed and pulled the books off the shelf, taking them to a window where I could read the titles. Three were Bibles. One was a copy of Mary Baker Eddy's *Science and Health.* One was a thick book titled *The Evils of Alcohol*, with a publication date of 1890. The fifth book was a sudden vision of my childhood.

It was a picture book of four Greek myths, old, tattered, torn, with half its pages missing. One of the four stories presented in pictures was the myth of Psyche and Eros. It was almost complete, about twenty pictures with the story outlined in captions under each picture. For the rest of the day I turned the brittle, brown-edged pages, examined the pictures, read the captions, trying to fill in the details of the story from memory. I had completely forgotten it. Now, each time I read the words under the figures on the page, more details of the story came back to me. I not only remembered, I rediscovered the story, seeing in it depths of meaning that I had never seen before.

What struck me most at that reading was just one sentence that I had never noticed before, could not remember having ever read. (But it is there, in most versions of the myth I have since found.) It was the advice given to Psyche before she goes to the underworld: to be without pity, deaf to the suffering shades who cry to her for help. The cryptic reference to this in the caption under the picture of Psyche descending toward Hades seemed like a coded message intended specifically for me. Of course, most of the people around me were obsessed by secret messages whose significance only they could grasp, whose hidden meaning was intended only for them. The difference between me and them was that I felt no need to announce my great discovery. I wanted only to think quietly about it and learn why it seemed the answer to some question I had not even begun to formulate.

Two weeks later I was given my first limited privilege. An inmate with a grounds pass was to escort me to the canteen where I could purchase extra things. But I had no money. "Sure, you have. You got more than anybody else in your canteen account!" said the woman. It was another of those bits of gossip that had spread throughout the asylum. I had had no idea that the little store behind the beauty shop was authorized to give me merchandise worth $50 per month, an allowance deposited by Erika.

On that first trip I bought writing paper and envelopes, toilet articles, and as many candy bars as I could stuff into my pack, to distribute on Ward K in celebration. On the way back to the castle I wanted to sit for a moment in the gazebo where Paul was playing as usual, but my escort refused nervously. Escorting me was the first "job" she had been given. She was eager to perform it without trouble so as to earn the privilege of more work and more privileges. It took a couple of weeks before she lengthened our daily walk to include a stop at the gazebo and before she would agree to mail the letters I wrote. Letters were supposed to go out through attendants, but it was common practice for an inmate with full privileges to carry letters to the asylum post office, bypassing official monitoring. I wrote regularly to Stephanie from then on, but received no answer.

After another week I decided to try an experiment. I wrote to a large bookstore in San Francisco, asking them to send me any books they had on the myth of Psyche and Eros, and to bill Erika, whose address I included. Two weeks later the books arrived: *Bullfinch's Mythology*; a newly published *Mythology* by Edith Hamilton; three versions of Apuleius (one in Latin, the other two very florid English translations), a reference book called *Dictionary of World Myths*, and a pornographic French novel titled *Ecstasy in the Garden of Eros*. A note from the clerk mentioned some psychological treatises which touched briefly on Psyche and Eros and named two publishers who specialized in classical civilization and literature. The store would be happy to send me catalogs and to fill all my orders.

While waiting for that first order of books to arrive, I had been reading one of the tattered Bibles, which suggested history and philosophy. By the time my first order of books arrived, I already had another list of books to order. When these arrived, they suggested still others. My sudden absorption in books was like diving into a bottomless pool where I no longer saw or heard the people around me. I felt intensely uncomfortable about escaping in this way. I thought that I should make friends with the women on Ward K, should enter their lives as I had those of my fellow workers in San Jose, should join in their gossip, should allay their fears of orientals, should do my best to ease the conflicts which were bound to develop in our narrow world. But these thoughts would melt away as I unresistingly sank into my pool of reading, diving down and down to a deeper world.

I soon had limited grounds privileges, walking by myself to the canteen, the gazebo, and all front grounds within a short radius of the castle. Yet I felt more and more frustrated by limitations of ward life.

It was growing dark earlier now, and since electricity was used sparingly, we were not allowed lights on the ward. By five o'clock the already dim attic light was gone. I bought a flashlight to carry in my pack, but was not allowed to use it after bedtime, which came at seven o'clock. I did not mind losing most of the morning hours cleaning the ward, but the many half-hours standing in line—for eating, toilets, washing—came to hours every day. I tried to read during these waits, using my flashlight in the dark hallways and in the cold exercise yard, where we were forced to keep moving. I "made the best of it" as did my fellow inmates, but I longed for a quiet place where I could sit in good light and read without interruption.

My longing was satisfied by way of an incident that seemed at first to be a disaster. One disadvantage of being in the attic was my heart, which functioned like a noisy, unreliable jalopy of a migrant pea picker, kept running somehow with ingenuity and luck. My heart kept running too, but climbing three flights of stairs to the attic, all at once, was beyond it. I was quite breathless after a few steps. Everyone knew about the problem, and allowances were made. After coming down in the morning, I was allowed to eat in one of the first floor dining rooms, to sit and read in the visitors' room or out in the gazebo, so that I did not have to climb the stairs again until time for dinner and bed, when I was allowed to straggle, resting every few steps.

But one day there was a new attendant on the ward who did not know about my disability or had forgotten it. After marching us down for morning exercise, she insisted that I climb back up with the other non-workers. When I fell behind, she shouted at me to hurry.

342

She was very nervous, frightened of the inmates as new attendants usually are, anxious about any challenge to her authority over the women who so outnumbered her. She pushed me back into line and ordered me to "march up there just like the others. What do you think you are, a queen?" I knew I could not. So did everyone else. But no one spoke. We all knew the penalty for contradicting an attendant, and if I were made ill or died because others remained silent rather than cross an attendant—well, it would not be the first time they had silently watched an inmate die because of error or indifference or worse.

I was halfway up the third flight when the world went dark and pain filled my chest like a swelling balloon. My first thought was, so, it has finally come, the release promised and delayed so many years. My second thought was, oh, but I haven't read all of Chekhov's stories!

It was a mild attack. I probably would not even have lost consciousness if I had not tripped over one of the cats and hit my head on the concrete steps when I fell.

When I woke the first person I saw was a young man who bent over me adjusting an intravenous bottle. "Hi, Miss Murrow. I'm Buddy," he said in a deep bass voice. He smiled, looking directly into my eyes. I smiled back, but, as much as I appreciated his unusual courtesy, I hadn't the energy to say a word. "You don't want to move this arm if you can help it. The IV has digitalis in it; that will make your heart even out. The doctor says you skipped a few more beats than usual but nothing too bad. This is the infirmary. You know, down near the admissions ward."

I watched him as he straightened my pillow, then moved to the next woman. The room was filled with the usual double row of beds, but with the immense luxury of at least three feet of space between them and, next to my bed, a small cabinet for my personal belongings. On top of that cabinet, in a neat row, were the three books I had been carrying in my pack.

I stared at Buddy because, except for Paul in the gazebo, I rarely saw a man, and never a young man, though there were many on the male disturbed wards and in the Navy's Q Ward. Buddy was twenty-two and looked younger, his skin smooth, cheeks rosy as a child's, his sandy hair thick and shiny and a bit longer than the military cut which came into fashion then. He was tall and gangling.

The attendant's white shirt and pants hung loosely on him but too short to reach his wrists and ankles. I stared at him as I would have stared at a young god who had stepped out of the pages of my picture book of Greek mythology. It had been months since I had seen a young man in good health, a young man obviously well-nurtured since infancy. I looked at him and thought, what a beautiful animal is a human being! At each bed where he checked a bottle or gave an injection, he spoke, smiled, looked into the patient's eyes, called her by name in that voice which was so surprisingly low-pitched for his young, thin frame. Often he received no response but a frightened look. Sometimes a nod or a moan. A few of the women propped themselves up and waved, flirting with him, and one made a gross offer before bursting into laughter. I could see his blush halfway across the ward before he moved beyond my line of sight.

Within a few days the IV was gone and I was sitting up, able to read for an hour or two at a time between naps. Buddy, at my insistence, was calling me Mei-li. He had borrowed and returned one of my books (I think it was Shaw's *Saint Joan*) and made comments which could have opened a long talk, but he never had more than a moment before rushing to the next patient. He came on the ward only briefly to perform medical procedures other attendants could not do. The presence of a man, except for the doctor, on a woman's ward was forbidden, but the shortage of women nurses was critical. Buddy, unlike the other attendants, had had some medical training. When he left he took another of my books, Whitman's poems, promising to return it and bring me his copy of Blake.

Buddy seemed a mysterious figure, out of place. Clearly he was qualified for a better job than he was doing; most of the attendants had no more education than I. Besides, why wasn't he in the Army, a boy in such radiant good health? I began to notice that other attendants were not friendly toward him. One day when I was wheeled outdoors I passed a group of male and female attendants in the hall (the besetting sin of attendants is to gather in gossipy huddles until dispersed by an angry charge attendant). I saw that the huddle did not open to include Buddy as he walked by. They ignored him. Only I raised a hand to greet him. It was obvious that their hostility toward him ran very deep.

The mystery was solved on Thanksgiving night when a suicide attempt was brought in, and, doctors and nurses being even more scarce than usual, a call was put out for Buddy. He stopped the blood (she had cut her throat with a razor she could not have gotten hold of, but somehow did) and started a transfusion of plasma donated by the Navy. Then he sat down at the foot of my bed to watch for an hour, to make sure she was out of danger.

We spoke in whispers and in complete darkness so as not to wake the other patients. Perhaps because it was so dark, because he was far from home on Thanksgiving, because he was so tired, or simply because I asked—he told me about himself.

He had been born and raised in Indiana, where his parents were both college professors. He graduated from college at twenty and began medical school. Then came the war and his refusal to go. "I registered as a conscientious objector and was sent to a camp, 'out of sight, out of mind,' just like all of you here. The peace churches are supposed to run the camps, but they just cushion the orders from the military. I hadn't gone through all this just to be hidden away in some boy scout camp, cutting brush! We had meetings, planned actions, had more meetings. How sick I was of meetings! Have you ever tried to explain democratic action to a Mennonite? Meetings broke into factions, and factions of factions. We had classes, a work strike, protests galore. Anything to make waves, to make it impossible to forget us. Some walked out of camp and got sent to federal prison. When I heard we could serve in mental hospitals, I volunteered. Anything to get out to the people, the community, in the world."

He sighed and was silent for a long time. "In the world," he said, in his normal, deep rumbling voice. Then he was silent again for a while before beginning to whisper again. "Another place to hide people, but this one's no boy scout camp. The two boys they sent with me lasted three months. They had to send them back to camp or they would have had two more patients. I'm not sure how long I'll last or even why I try.

"They keep me on the back wards," he whispered, "with the most withdrawn or violent patients. I got a couple of them tossing a ball last week. Took me all month, but I got them up off the floor, got them washed, into some clothes, and out on the yard. The other attendants say, why bother, they'll just withdraw again. I don't blame the attendants for not caring. The pay is terrible, they get no training, and they've each got seventy or eighty men or more. I'd like to organize them, lead a protest. But I can't, because they won't speak to me." He tried to laugh silently, but I heard the catch in his throat. He was sitting there in the dark, trying not to cry at his isolation, at the terrible things he saw every day. He let me hold his hand for a moment, then stood up, checked his patient once more, and left. I hardly saw him again during the time I was in the infirmary, except when he came to return my book.

The doctor who attended infirmary patients was the admissions doctor, who looked even more pale and worn than when he used to visit his wife on Ward B. I asked him how she was. He shook his head. She had deteriorated further. There was pressure to backward her. "She will never leave here if I let them do it." He stopped more frequently at my bed and talked longer than with other patients. At first I thought he wanted the comfort of speaking Greek, but, when I was ready to be released, I learned that he had been observing me with a definite plan.

He wanted to take his wife off Ward B and move her into the house where he lived on the hospital grounds, "south of the hog farm. I need someone to stay with her day and night, watch her, make sure she eats and does no harm to herself, someone who will get her to talk, to walk, to be in the world. Would you consider it?" Consider it? I jumped at it.

The doctor's house was one of dozens scattered among the rolling meadows behind the hospital buildings. Until the war they had all been occupied by members of the staff. Now half of them were empty and deteriorating rapidly. The doctor and his wife had moved into one of the better ones, a three-bedroom cottage behind a knoll from which the hospital buildings were invisible, except for the towers of the castle, whose topmost spires peeked up over the top of the hill.

The doctor moved his things out of the large bedroom and went to sleep in the smallest room. He kept the third bedroom as a study. The large bedroom had a small alcove where a cot was set up for me so that I could be with his wife all night. The room also held a bookshelf and a small desk. There was a small, stiffly furnished, unused parlor, and a large sunny kitchen, where another inmate did the cooking. Two more inmates came in to clean and keep the garden.

So, after nearly a year on the wards, I entered a life that offered the greatest luxuries: quiet and a little privacy.

My care of Madame Doctor (I addressed her formally with the title and respect she had enjoyed before the war) was simple. At first it consisted of urging her and helping her to get up and dressed and groomed. To eat, to move, to talk. She did not speak for weeks, but I talked constantly, putting in English words where my Greek failed. Sometimes I read aloud. Of course, she understood little English, but I hoped the sound of my voice would be soothing, and would keep calling her to come back, not to sink away from people. She was afraid of darkness, and I could read to myself by the light kept burning all night in our room. Another luxury, the lighting up of evening hours!

I ignored her husband's suggestion that I decorate a Christmas tree for her. I had seen enough of these well-meant observations of holidays on the wards, and was convinced that to a deeply troubled soul they only bring more pain and grief. Instead, I persuaded him to buy a record player. It was Buddy who suggested the music. "Nothing too cheerful or emotional or romantic. Something orderly, symmetrical. I'd suggest Bach, but not the passions."

Buddy had taken over a small cabin nearby where coffins had been stored in the days before the crematory was built, when inmates were buried on the grounds. It was little more than a large box, no heat, no plumbing. But Buddy preferred the coffin house to the angry stares and slurs of the five regular attendants with whom he had been sharing a room above the laundry. The doctor liked him, appreciated his interest in Madame Doctor's health, and invited him to shower and eat at the house whenever he liked. "I will practice my English in conversation with an intelligent young man. Hearing civilized conversation will be good for her too."

Buddy came often. Sometimes he and the doctor argued about pacifism, but Buddy held his own amazingly well for such a young man, tracing back all the inhuman steps which had brought us to the point where the only weapon against Hitler was war. His analysis reminded me of the events recounted in Stephanie's letters during the decade before the war, each exasperating equivocation and disgusting betrayal reviewed clearly by Buddy. "And when these idiots— having ignored every warning, every suggestion by us 'unrealistic pacifists' until trapped with their back against the wall—when they say to me, 'now you must fight to the death, kill them all, there is no alternative'—then I still say, no. We had other choices, other chances. You chose killing. I choose not to kill. No." In fact, Buddy

347

showed himself so much better informed about Hitler and all the history leading to Hitler "than any American I have met; Americans know no history," that the doctor almost forgave his refusal to fight, was happiest when he came home and found Buddy in the kitchen. He did not find him often enough because sometimes double and triple shifts kept him on the wards around the clock.

It rained heavily and steadily that January. Even with heavy boots on, Madame Doctor and I did not go far beyond the garden, neither of us feeling strong enough for long walks through the mud or the thick fog that came between rains. But by the end of the month, I was feeling much better, and she had progressed to getting up, washing, and dressing without much urging. Then the rain stopped, and February came.

Of all the many seasons of the California year, February is the most beautiful. Since June the hills have been brown and dry, and the winter rains have only turned them soggy, still dull in the weak sun of the short days. But in February fresh grass sprouts overnight, a bright, irridescent green suddenly flooding the landscape. Fruit trees bloom, the tule fog disappears, and the sun shines as brightly as in summer, without parching the land. The orchards surrounding the hospital grounds resembled those in the Santa Clara Valley, but in the Napa Valley they were mainly apples instead of prunes, alternating with the little, stumpy grape vines. In that blossoming February of 1943, we began our daily walks.

The doctor had given me a pass allowing us to walk anywhere. We turned away from the buildings on the front grounds, discovering and exploring the world behind the castle. On the first day I took Madame Doctor north through the meadows, following the cows on their wanderings out to the fields to graze, then back to the dairy where they were milked twice a day.

On another day we walked south of the main drive (which kept going straight toward the hills after being interrupted by the castle) around the new hog farm. Beyond the hog farm fence, on the east side, stood a high pile of wood, stretching hundreds of feet into the orchard. All the pieces of wood were the same size, rather flat and broad. All were deeply weathered, etched, and marked. We stopped to turn some of them over and examine them. The marks cut into them were numbers. One that I looked at said 1920. Was it a date? Another, on which I could barely read the number 277, was a cracked, rotted old chunk, nearly disintegrated.

The wood pile remained a mystery until we reached the nursery (as close to the castle walls as either of us cared to go), where an old inmate tended seedlings for a variety of plants and trees. He told us that the hog farm was started on the old cemetery, whose wooden markers were numbered by death count. I had seen the markers of inmates in the order in which they had died, bodies unclaimed and unnamed. "Now they cremate, over there behind the slaughter-house. Can't see it from here. Used to be a big pile of them markers. Mostly used up for firewood."

At that moment the inmate was called away by a frowning attendant whose look showed his strong disapproval of men and women talking together, of women in general. This was definitely male territory. Women worked in the cannery or laundry, but, except for the picking season when all working inmates went to the orchards, outdoor work was reserved for men.

On the days when hogs or chickens were slaughtered or when the crematory smoked, we walked through the northeast orchards. Most inmates with passes went west, down the main drive to the high-way, where they might hitch a ride to town. (Local people usually stopped for the easily identifiable inmates.) So we had the backlands largely to ourselves.

Our favorite walk took us back behind the hog farm, past the crematory, and through the first orchard to Lower Lake. Birds nested in the trees surrounding the lake. Under the trees lay thick logs with hollowed-out seats. Here we might sit for two or three hours while Madame Doctor watched the water and the birds, and I read or talked with Buddy, who sometimes brought a group of inmates with fishing lines, proudly pointing to one or two who were beginning to speak again. Lower Lake was a relatively free place, open to all patients, who often brought visitors there. But in the early morning we were alone there, and Buddy would join us when he came off night shift.

Buddy usually started a conversation with a comment about whatever book I was carrying. Often he had already read whatever it was. He had begun reading at the age of three and had never stopped. By fifteen he was reading philosophers I still cannot under-stand, and historians I find very difficult. He thought nothing of his precosity; all the boys he knew read everything and argued bril-liantly, "then went for a brilliant career and didn't read or argue anymore." They all had commissions in the air force now; he never heard from them anymore. His new friends were the men he had met in C.O. camp. He spent his spare time writing letters to them, and sometimes he read their letters aloud to me. He also had a girl-friend who wanted to come to California and work in the hospital with him. "We'd have to marry. What if she got pregnant? Besides it would be so hard for her. The women are even meaner than the men." I'm sorry to say I could not disagree with him.

His position at the hospital would have been trying even to a more mature man. He was shunned by most of the staff and criticized for being "too easy" with the inmates. He was paid nothing for his work, and though his parents had not repudiated him, they were far away and in poor health, with little money to send him. He was as short of cash as most of the inmates.

Whenever he mentioned a book, I ordered it. I also kept him supplied with writing paper and stamps, insisting that my sister could well afford them. He laughed (knowing a little of my history by then) and accepted gracefully, but he would not let me buy clothes for him. In his off-duty hours he often wore the state-issued gray cotton pants and shirt worn by inmates. This infuriated the other attendants ". . . because the line between us and the inmates is so thin. The only difference is these." He would jangle his huge ring of keys and laugh again, a deep, rich rumble. "I just thought I'd dramatize our true position for my fellow workers."

The clothes looked comfortable. I asked Buddy to look for some small enough for me. He brought me pants, shirt, socks, all in the uniform gray the inmates hated. From the Navy ward he got a P-coat which kept me warm during early morning walks. I was finally free of the terrible flour-sack dresses and could move more freely on the grounds, mistaken for a male inmate with worker's privileges.

Buddy went on dramatizing reality for everyone. He often ate with the inmates instead of in the attendants' dining room, complaining loudly about the difference in the food. He attended every staff meeting with a list of questions. He wrote letters constantly to the state government, complaining of shortages of food, clothing, medicine, staff, space.

His complaints led to the inspection of the hospital by the governor in 1943. His description of the inspection was hilarious. The director of the hospital was willing to show the worst in hopes of getting more money. The attendants did their best to hide what he exposed, expecting the blame to fall on them. The inmates were frozen with fear of joining either side. And the results? Buddy laughed loudest as he repeated the governor's order to "close the attic immediately," increasing the crowding in the rest of the castle, which the governor ordered "condemned." According to older inmates, said Buddy, he was the third governor to condemn the castle.

What gradually won many of the staff over to Buddy was his humor. Whenever I heard him talking to anyone, I heard his sentences separated by low chuckles or deep laughs. He even laughed at the grisly jokes of the attendants. "People have to laugh," he would say. "These guys care, or they wouldn't have to make up jokes like that." He loved fun. He attended all the Saturday dances, choosing as his partners the oldest inmates, the saddest, the most withdrawn. He did not dance as an act of charity but for the fun of it. He really had a good time, especially if he could make someone else laugh.

Of course, there were times when Buddy's energy and humor deserted him. He would join me at Lower Lake or in the doctor's kitchen, pale and red-eyed, looking ten years older, shrunken, as if his tall, thin body had wasted overnight. Then I would hear his account of some horror like the beating of an inmate by the "goon squad" of attendants called to subdue violent men. He would shiver as I held his hand, and his aged look would collapse into one of helpless, stricken boyhood. Then I would remember how young he was— about the age my daughter would have been. In comforting him, I received the most comfort because during those hours we spent together I was temporarily the only friend he had. Just when I thought my few close friends were lost forever, I had been given a new friend.

Madame Doctor and I took longer walks that summer, making interesting discoveries. There were flocks of sheep in the hills watched over by inmates who rarely came down to the main grounds, but lived in shacks they built for themselves. There were caves where discharged inmates lived like Indian fakirs, unspeaking, sitting draped in rags. In the winter they returned to sleep in the castle basement or in some other niche where they could rest unnoticed. It was rumored that one of the caves was occupied by a woman who provided sex for working inmates in exchange for clothing, food, and other comforts which made her life sumptuous. But I never saw any women in the backlands.

Once we came close to the stone village being created by an old Italian man who carried huge stones up from the old quarry where bricks had been made to build the castle. He had made fences, walks, a tiny house. The smaller stones he threw at anyone who came near. We changed direction when stones began to fly our way, so I never saw him, but I heard him whenever the moon was full. He howled like a coyote.

After several explorations we confined ourselves to the area around Lower Lake. There were too many rattlesnakes in the hills, and a long hike was too risky for me.

I made one other interesting exploration on a day when the doctor had taken his wife to San Francisco for the day. It was a quiet, hot Monday in September. I had walked beyond the hog farm and through the broad stretch of farmland where inmates were harvesting tomatoes and rolling in fruit from the orchards, all headed toward the sheds next to the bustling cannery.

Between two orchards, hidden by a grove of camphor and birch trees, was a long, Spanish style stucco building: the crematory. It always looked deserted, even when smoke came from its chimney, and no one ever went there, except the worker (not an inmate) who lived there. Now even he was gone, probably to the shipyards, and an undertaker came in from Napa to operate the oven when an inmate died. The front door, through which bodies were wheeled into a refrigerator, then into the oven, was locked, but a little door in the back of the building had been left unlocked.

It opened into the small room where the former employee must have lived. In one corner was a narrow wooden bunk. In the center of the room, taking up most of the space, stood a small wooden table with two chairs. Under a small window was a small sink and shelves. A worn, sweat-smeared felt hat still hung on the wall. Next to it was the door to the bathroom, and in the bathroom, another door, which I opened.

It led into a large, dark, windowless room. Feeling on the sides of the doorway, I pressed a light switch, turning on a weak bulb that hung from a wire in the center of the room, which was even larger than I had thought, at least thirty feet long. All four walls were lined with shelves, from floor to ceiling. Filling the shelves were rows of fruit jars, three deep. I walked closer to the shelves and saw that the jars were labeled, each with a name and a date. The contents of the jars were gritty gray. Each contained the ashes of a dead inmate.

There were egg crates on the floor which contained the overflow of jars from the shelves. Most of the crates were full. On the wall next to the door to the bathroom, the crates were stacked to the ceiling. Other full crates were already being stacked against full walls of shelves.

Of all the strange but invariably true rumors which spread through the hospital, I had never heard about this room. Inmates never worked here; some sense of the humane, the decent, kept the attendants from employing them in disposing of their fellows. Perhaps the attendants did not even speak among themselves of this room. Sad as it was, it was an advance over the numbered markers on the old graveyard-hog farm. These remains were at least named and dated, kept for family or friends to claim. That so few were ever claimed was not the fault of the asylum.

Buddy's situation improved a little in 1944 when he was assigned to the new children's ward, whose all-woman staff was having trouble handling the teenagers brought in off the city streets, out of control though not necessarily out of their minds. Buddy worked the late shift with the boys. He took them on long afternoon hikes, stayed up late talking with them, and slept on the ward. In his off hours he wrote letters or attended meetings where he continued to push his growing list of reforms, now more often supported by other staff members. Somehow he found time to meet me at Lower Lake almost every day to talk about a book I was reading. "Hey, I *make* time. Without you, I'd go crazy here!" He showed me letters from other resisters working in asylums, saying he planned to collect enough for a book that would expose the universally terrible conditions.

When it rained or when the numbing winter fog settled over us, he came to the doctor's house, where we listened to music on the radio or to the war news. Together we had followed the allies' progress from the invasion of Italy through victory after victory. By early 1945 there was no doubt that Hitler would lose. The only question was how long he would prolong the slaughter. At the asylum the war was felt in deeper shortages and the increase of new admissions. Some were soldiers or nurses. Most were old or weakminded or misfit people who had scraped by outside with a little help from relatives or neighbors until they were abandoned in the excitement of the war effort. How fragile a thread had connected them to "normal" life!

353

The war in Europe ended just as the Napa days were turning hot. Buddy managed to get a week's leave to go to San Francisco for the conference establishing the United Nations. He came back with many more addresses to write to and with rumors that a huge force was being prepared to leave San Francisco to strike Japan. Now, even on hot days, we sat near a radio, hardly speaking, listening for hints of the coming battle. What we heard instead were the horrors found as the concentration camps were opened. Even Buddy had not believed in anything so terrible.

It is strange, but I cannot remember actually sitting and listening with Buddy when the news came of our sudden victory won by dropping atom bombs on Japan. I know we heard the news together, but I think my mind must have refused to hold onto this new horror we shared.

There were fireworks that night at the dry hospital fountain for the first time since the beginning of the war. Patients on the front wards or workers' cottages were openly drunk on liquor freely distributed from the castle basement. On the back wards there were three suicide attempts and a dozen attacks on inmates or attendants. They were an echo, our institutional version of the rapacious riots with which San Francisco celebrated the coming of peace.

It was the only time I ever saw Buddy lose heart. He stopped writing letters, stopped reading the newspapers, stopped reading anything at all. During his off hours he sat with me at Lower Lake, hardly speaking, or at the Doctor's house where I tuned the radio to classical music. To make matters worse, he learned that he was not to be released now that the war was over. A few resisters had been released, but complaints were made that they were "getting all the good jobs before our fighting men can get home." The sad rumor was passed to Buddy in letters—resisters might be held for another year, to be discharged last.

I was of little help to him, being preoccupied with more sad news. Word from England had finally confirmed what I feared. Stephanie had died early in the war in one of the bombing raids on London, all her belongings, all her work destroyed with her. My letters, stamped UNDELIVERABLE THIS ADDRESS, began drifting back to me, almost weekly reminders that I had nothing left of her but a few letters and the portrait she had drawn of me. The pain of those days is, mercifully, blurred in my memory. When I think of them, I remember sitting with Buddy at Lower Lake in long, numb silences.

354

Madame Doctor improved steadily. She was eating well, putting on weight, taking interest in her appearance. An inmate who had been a seamstress made her some new clothes, and her husband took her to town to buy shoes. She came home smiling, with three pair of brightly colored, high-heeled, totally impractical shoes.

Shortly afterward, her husband told Buddy and me that he was leaving to set up a practice in San Francisco. It was now quite safe to leave his wife alone during the day, and he was convinced she would recover faster in the City. She had even found a voice coach and planned to begin singing again, perhaps taking a few students of her own.

A few days later Buddy (who was at work on his letters again) asked me what I was going to do. We were sitting beside Lower Lake at dawn of an already hot, dry fall morning. "I'm sure the doctor will recommend for your release if you ask him. And this time you know what to say at your hearing."

This was a reference to the hearing I had had just before fainting on the castle steps. The committee of doctors and nurses had asked me if I felt the hospital had helped me, and I had answered with the truth. Five minutes later I was on my way back to the ward. The last thing I heard a doctor say as I left was, "Too bad we can't shock her and stop this slide into paranoia." He was quite sincere, a passionate believer that he had found a cure, quick and permanent, for all of us. I told Buddy there was a little imp in my throat who might just cough up the same unacceptable truth as last time.

"Then skip the hearing and just walk away. People do it every day."

"Yes, and come right back again. Where could I go? What would I do? Jobs might be plentiful now, but I can't work anymore unless I can sit most of the time. And I don't even know how to type."

"Get your money back from your sister."

"How?"

"You know how. Get a lawyer. I can name three who'd gladly take the case and probably advance you money to live on until you win. In fact, if you start something, Erika's lawyer might advise her to make a settlement, and you won't even have to go to court. You could be out of here in a week. I know how to do the writ of habeus corpus that would start the process."

I made some weak objection, and Buddy lost his temper, a spectacle which was awesome to witness. "You don't want to leave here!

You're getting to be like Sister Mary and all the others who regress as soon as there's a chance they'll get out. You've been here nearly five years, and you could have gotten out in one. That's why you told the truth at your first hearing—you knew they'd punish you for that, knew they'd keep you. You're becoming institutionalized. You'll soon be sent back to a chronic ward, then further back until you never see anything but the walls of the exercise yard and the church ladies who come at Christmas time, and by that time even they won't get on your nerves, you won't care anymore, you'll be "settled down nicely," as they say, a good patient, a woman who has found a home, a woman weak in the head but lucid enough to be trained to change diapers on the idiots!''

There were tears in his eyes as he shouted, and tears in mine as well because I saw how much he cared, even if what he wanted was not right for me. His anger reminded me of those last scenes with Stephanie before the end of the Garden of Eden. Why did I have to infuriate the people I loved best? I waited until he stopped scolding. Then I tried to tell him, and myself, what it was I really wanted. "There is some reason why I was brought here, something I'm supposed to do.''

"And what is that?''

"I don't know. I need time to find out. Time and peace and quiet.''

"Peace and quiet is the last thing you'll find back on the wards, even if they put you on B.''

He was right, of course. I couldn't live on a ward again.

"You can't live a normal life, anywhere on this place.''

I laughed. "I've never lived a normal life, and I wouldn't want to try to start living one now. Listen . . . .'' I asked Buddy to think of Paul, the violinist in the gazebo, and his greeting to each new patient. "Welcome to the monastery of the mad. I like that—a monastery, a place removed from 'normal' life, a place distinctly abnormal, like this one, where nothing is touched up or disguised or smoothed over, where all the jagged wounds of the soul are exposed, unashamed, an honest place in its way. You know, if it weren't so awful, it would be wonderful!''

"Yes,'' Buddy said patiently, "but it *is* awful.''

Then I told Buddy about my image of the asylum as a sponge, a place full of holes where some people had found a place to hide and live a life apart, within its shelter yet not crushed by it.

Buddy looked at me silently for a long time. "All right, then we must find a hole for you."

Finding a hole for me was not easy. True, inmates lived in odd corners all over hospital property, some in abandoned houses, some in sheds scattered beyond the orchards that surrounded the main grounds, some even on the edge of town. But they were men with outdoor jobs and freedoms never given to women. Women worked as servants and sitters in all the staff houses, but they slept on the wards; my live-in job had been a rare exception. The caves or shacks back in the hills were beyond me; I knew I was not strong enough for such austere conditions. I could probably find an empty house or room on the grounds, but staff houses were filling up again. It was likely that if I picked my "hole" among these buildings, I would very quickly be discovered, remembered, removed, and reassigned permanently and strictly to a ward. I had to find a place where I could be forgotten.

Then I thought of the crematory. I described it to Buddy, who, like most people, was barely aware of it. "No one lives there anymore, and weeks go by—between deaths—without anyone going near it. They can't suddenly decide to use it for something else, because it's full of those jars that I'm sure they don't know what to do with and probably would rather not talk about or even think about. The place is almost completely hidden by trees. I could come and go when few people are around. I have my grounds pass. As long as no one sees me going in and out of the place, they'll think I sleep and eat on the wards."

Buddy smiled. "Hide in plain sight, eh?" I could see that the idea appealed to his sense of fun. "But speaking of eating, how will you manage that?"

"There are plenty of fruits and vegetables I can eat raw along with some milk I can pick up at the dairy."

"And carry back in one of those fruit jars?"

I nodded and Buddy guffawed. This would be the best joke of all. He immediately began to plot my move, going to the crematory after dark to inspect and prepare it for me. The first thing he did was to stack crates of full jars against the door from the storeroom to the bathroom, covering the doorway completely so that no one would accidentally enter my hiding place. The very existence of the room in the back might be forgotten.

Next he ordered (and charged to Erika) white paint from a local hardware store. "No institutional green for you." He also ordered a small electric heater, a shower curtain, a mattress and blankets for the bunk, a small radio, a reading lamp, blackout curtains for the window (to hide my presence at night) and a paring knife. "What else?"

"Bookshelves." Even while he was pounding the shelves into the walls, no one interrupted him or questioned him. I was right, everyone had a superstitious fear of the crematory and kept as far away as possibly. A patient died during Buddy's remodeling work, and Buddy withdrew until the undertaker had come and gone. A new jar was added to the others, but no notice had been taken of our presence in the building. It seemed that I had found the right "hole."

Getting from the doctor's house to the crematory could have been a problem. It was not easy for a patient to be "lost." But the doctor solved that problem without my asking him or saying anything that would compromise him. On the night before he and his wife left, I saw my transfer papers sitting on his desk, all alone, the last piece of business for him, left, "forgotten." Nothing but my name had been filled in—no reassignment, no signature. I did what I think the doctor meant me to do. I took the papers with me when, at midnight, I picked up my pack (Buddy had already moved my books) and quietly left. The doctor had known, of course, that I planned to "escape," but even he did not guess the nature of that escape. In my pack I found some money and a San Francisco address, where I hoped the kind doctor and his wife finally found some happiness.

It took only a few minutes for me to walk from the doctor's house, around the back of the castle, past the nursery, the hog farm, and the chicken houses. Only the cats took any notice of me, a half dozen forming a silent escort, then scattering as we reached the trees surrounding the crematory.

Just before he left three months later, Buddy did me one last favor, misfiling my medical records with the "congenitally disfunctional" so that my case would not come up in routine reviews for discharge. There has never been, to my knowledge, any thought of moving me from here. I have become familiar yet forgotten, like the old man of the stone village, who still howls when the moon is full.

358

FROM THE LETTERS
TO BUDDY

1947–1959

Mei-li Murrow's autobiography ends abruptly with her move to the crematory. For information about her life from 1946 to 1959, we are dependent on her 108 letters written to Doctor Garin "Buddy" Buddell during those years.

The original plan—to publish all the letters—presented problems. Much of what she wrote is confusing or meaningless without Buddell's side of the correspondence, which, except for three fragments of letters, is lost. Many of her letters recount experiences which are more fully detailed in her autobiography.

Therefore, it seemed appropriate to excerpt only those portions of the letters which can stand alone and which describe Mei-li's life and state of mind during her last years.

January 5, 1947

My best wishes to you both. After your long separation I see why you ran off to New York with the money Nancy's parents might have spent on a big wedding. You'll need every bit of that money for medical school since you'll have no benefits as a war veteran. You and I know, nevertheless, how well you served your country and at what cost.

Nancy's interest in the occult is a good thing in a psychologist—shows an open mind. But I am the wrong person to ask. Although I amused you with some stories of my early career, I am not interested in the occult, never have been, least of all when I was in the business of staging fake seances. She asks if some occult experiences are genuine. Who knows? Some must be. But they seem no more miraculous to me than electric power or the motion of a dancer. I agree with the eastern guru who, when his disciple bragged that after twenty years of austerities he could walk on water, replied, "You could have paid a coin to the ferryman and saved your energies for something better."

November 4, 1947

Congratulations! And thank you for the book. Yes, it is a thin book to come out of all the letters you collected. Yet those hundred short scenes of asylum life—chosen from how many?—tell more than volumes of history, statistics, and argument. I have ordered two more copies as gifts to the staff library. I intend to write your real name next to "Editor, Ernest Bedlam" (a good joke, but I hope you won't sign your next book with that name).

Was it really necessary? And necessary to omit the names of the witnesses of these scenes? I suppose your publisher knows his business. If continuing hostility toward conscientious objectors would hurt sales, then he was wise to conceal the way the book was compiled. Yet I am sad to think that the work of three thousand young men should be erased from memory, lost like a piece of life burnt out of a patient's mind by electroshock. Our written history is like a mind after a million shock treatments, a series of thin bridges over dark gaps.

February 16, 1948

I have just come from viewing the exhibit of valentines in the recreation hall. It was the idea of a volunteer art therapist that patients create cards and posters to be pinned on the walls for the "Cupid Capers" dance on Valentines Day.

There were, of course, dozens of fat baby cupids, grinning and drooling, and shooting arrows. Then there were some in which Cupid-Eros is the handsome young Greek, with wings. And then—the wild, frightful ones. The hearts dripping blood, the arrows of fire, the winged Eros diving through the air like a deadly rocket, the wild explosions of the heavens, dismembered lovers like millions of meteors falling.

I thought of what I have read on early images of Eros, born of Night and Wind, a golden-winged, four-headed, double-sexed force that created earth, sky, and moon, then set the universe in motion. How did that Eros ever become the fat little Roman Cupid? That old Eros seemed to be bursting through the valentines of these patients—that Eros and how many other visions of Eros!

November 8, 1948

I am reading a book by Christopher Isherwood about Ramakrishna, the Hindu saint who often taught in parables. Here is one of his stories. A serpent had threatened a whole village until converted by a holy man. When the holy man returned months later he found the snake half dead. "What on earth has happened?" he asked. The snake answered, "Since I became your disciple the boys from the village torment me. I'm wounded and starving, afraid even to leave my hole under this rock."

"Fool!" said the holy man. "I told you not to bite. I never told you not to hiss!"

I laughed aloud and thought of you and of how I miss you and your benign hissing and your quoting Emerson, "Your goodness must have an edge to it."

I tell you this story also to remind you that it does not matter if twenty-three journals have rejected your article attacking lobotomy. Go back to the top of your list and start submitting it all over again. Keep hissing for those who are too weak even to hiss.

September 9, 1949

No, my days are not dull or lonely though they might seem so if I describe them. I am usually up before dawn walking in the backlands. Returning, I pick up some milk at the dairy, bread and fruit from the kitchen. After eating I read, then take a nap. If the weather is mild, I go to sit by Lower Lake with a book. Later I eat again, then read before going to sleep. Between eating, sleeping, walking, reading, there are long silences. These silences are the heart of my life here. In them lie, I think, the reasons for my staying. About these silences I have nothing to say, not even to you.

So, am I a total recluse, contributing nothing to the asylum except the money Erika pays for my care? No, I have a job now, my own exclusive "industrial therapy." Unofficial, of course.

You remember the rule that dying patients must never be left alone? It may be the only rule of the asylum that everyone respects, and the hardest to keep. Sitting with the dying is a steady job here. Sister Mary used to do it when staff could not, but she is getting old, is often ill. And this is not a task casually assigned to other patients. Mrs. Cookiebaker often comes to me to ask if I will take the after midnight hours of sitting with a dying patient. "It's hard on the young nurses, but it doesn't scare you."

Yes, it does. Dying is so hard, seldom as dignified as it is in the movies or in opera. It takes everything else away before it finally gives up and lets life go. The mystery of that agony stuns me. Yet it deepens the silence I am seeking here. So I am the right person for the job.

By the way, the crematory is no longer used. The dead are sent to an undertaker in Napa, and I don't know what he does with the ashes. So no one comes to this building anymore, and it seems unlikely to be taken over for any other use. What would they do with all those jars? They prefer to forget them, and as long as the crematory remains a "forgotten" building, I have a safe and very private home.

It may still be here long after the castle is gone. The most recent condemnation of the castle is to be enforced. Patients were moved out last month, temporarily crowded into Q Ward now that the Navy is gone. A new building is slowly rising in front of the castle, a low modern "facility" as these things are called now. Upon completion, the builders say, they will tear down the castle. No one believes them.

363

February 2, 1950

Back in the thirties, when I spent some time on my knees under prune trees, I was usually exhausted to the point of fainting, always conscious of the hardship of the people working near me, and even more frightened than they were of the forces that kept us on our knees. Yet sometimes as I touched the fruit, the dusty lavender skin suddenly cracked, releasing a shining burst of gold, pouring sticky sweetness over my fingers. And—still with aching head, back, knees—my consciousness of our suffering was lit by joyous color. Through my exhaustion would ripple an irresistible thrill, a shiver of delight.

That same delight echoes in my mind when I think of those days. I remember, not our hardships, but the sights and smells and sounds of the seasons of our work.

I remember the thump of irrigation pumps starting up, like a deep pulse in the earth, in regular rotation, one thump answered by another miles away, and another and another, like the arteries of a huge heart vibrating deep beneath the orchards. I remember the smell of fresh mustard greens and earth after the plowing under of ground cover; the sweet smell of rotting prunes fermenting, creating air like wine; the dry hot smell of hay; the smoky dawn during pruning when the piles of branches burned; the thicker sulphur smell of the smoking ovens; the almond smell of apricot pits piled high in barrels.

I remember the naked trees in winter, row upon row of wispy skeletons reflected in the flood waters when the two rivers rose, and the trees reached like thousands of drowning hands grasping the air above the waters as the rain splashed all around them. The fresh smell of that clean, drenched air, like a blessing after the hot, dry fall. As the waters fell, the smell of muddy orchards, of thick, rotting black clay, sticky and stubborn and impenetrable by shovel or tractor blade, like glue, like excrement, like the living body of the earth.

Then the brief flowering, the white and pink clouds of blossoms covering the trees and the ground under the buzz of a million bees, and the growl of the tractors like beasts calling to each other across the orchards, calling a warning that the fruit was coming, and the workers, and the frantic gathering before everything drowsed off into the hot, dry fall again.

June 2, 1950

The castle is no more.

During the past few months it was stripped of statues and marble ornaments which are supposed to be kept on display in offices in the new building, but are already being smuggled out to antique dealers. I have a souvenir, HOPE in stone, a fragment from the motto over the entry. It makes a good door stop.

The wrecking ball, the trucks, the dust and noise have been part of life for months. But until today the central tower stood against all pounding. Finally this morning they laid a charge of dynamite that shattered every window in the new building. The tower lurched and swayed. Then slowly, still intact, it fell with a crash as loud as the dynamite explosion.

Hundreds stood on the grounds watching. Some cheered. Others cried. Others laughed at the ones who cried.

I heard an old man arguing with some young volunteers who had laughed and cheered. "You don't understand, you people will never understand." He remembered when the castle was built, had attended the dedication ceremonies at the age of five. His grandparents and parents had worked at the asylum, as had his wife and himself. His daughter still oversees the cannery, and two grandsons manage the dairy and maintain machinery.

"It's what was meant," he kept saying. "It's what the castle was meant to be that you will never understand. It stood big and grand like the Statue of Liberty—give me your tired, your poor. That is what the word asylum means, a safe place, solid, big, built with respect, a city for the poor crazy people. Now they're stealing this place from the crazy people. It was a grand idea, even if it didn't work right, and now even the idea is going."

As he raved he pointed west to the new junior college across the highway, where most of the young volunteers are enrolled. I suspect the people hearing him missed his point, have already forgotten that only a couple of years ago that campus was an orchard belonging to the asylum. There is talk of closing the hog farm and the shoe factory. Everyone seems to know that in a few years very little will be left of the world I entered here ten years ago. "Good riddance," is the reaction of the young people, "nothing could be worse." But I side with the old man. When this place goes, what will take its place? (The most innocent, foolish, most often disproved words in the world are "nothing could be worse.")

July 8, 1950

War again. And so few years since the last horror. Who, even among the most pessimistic, did not give us at least a decade of cold war before real killing began again? Who would have picked Korea as the place where we would light the fuse to explode the world? I have seen two other wars start with singing and waving of banners. This time I see only fear and the certainty of doom. We can never go into war in cheerful, patriotic ignorance again, and yet we still can go, it seems.

Yes, I share your feelings, but I do not understand your question. It implies that I have, and that I owe you, some explanation, if not a solution. No, I have no "answer to the question of nuclear holocaust." I'm not even sure what you are asking. I'm only sure that you are suffering. As I am. I think of inmates who name the date of the end of the world, then revise and recalculate each time doomsday comes and goes without their prophecies being fulfilled. Now that we have invented the means to fulfill their expectations, we may have to concede that their grip on reality has always been firmer than our own.

Do I have faith that something will intercede before we destroy the world? No. Do I think that we will prove faithful enough to our own self-interest to stop short of nuclear bombing? No. Our history, especially during my lifetime, tells me we usually do our worst.

Is that a statement of despair? No, I do not despair, if only because I know I live in darkness and ignorance. There are so many truths which my thinking cannot include, which I have not the least capabilities to know or to understand. Am I saying that these unknown truths will keep us from destroying the world? No, only that our world is part of something beyond its own existence and our capability to know.

Does that sound as if I await the explosion complacently? Oh, Buddy, if only you could see me shivering with dread as I write about this.

366

January 7, 1951

What I like about the Psyche and Eros myth is its way of going on and on and on with elements of one myth after another linked together. Where another tale would end, this one absorbs an ending and moves on.

Psyche's beauty places her in competition with Aphrodite, who sets out to humble her. Another myth would end there, with the girl turned into a spider or a tree.

Aphrodite's plan backfires and, instead of shooting Psyche with a disastrous love arrow, Eros falls in love with her himself. In the tradition of disastrous tales of a mortal woman loved by a god, the story should end when Eros deserts the disobedient Psyche, leaving her in a loveless world, like Eve being cast out of the Garden of Eden.

But the story goes on, with Demeter sending her back to Aphrodite for more punishment. And suddenly we're in a tale of tests and challenges. Such adventures typically let the young hero win his love after three tasks, and the story ends.

But not Psyche. After three incredible successes, she is sent to Hades, from which hardly anyone ever returns. Yet she does return, bringing back the prize, divine beauty in a box. End of story? No.

Curiosity and disobedience undo her again. She opens the box and collapses. Surely this time she is, like Pandora, finished. She has had her last chance. No. Eros revives her and carries her to the gods, to immortality, to divine marriage and divine motherhood. The End, finally.

All the earlier endings were new beginnings. All Psyche's mistakes were doors opening. All her punishments were tests that transformed her and the gods as well. "All goes onward and outward, nothing collapses/ And to die is different from what anyone supposed, and luckier." That's from part of a poem Erika recited at my mother's funeral.

November 20, 1951

Emily May. A lovely name. How can I tell you what it means to me to know your little girl will bear my name next to your mother's?

I embrace you—all three—on the beginning of new life, your baby's and yours. Nothing will ever be the same again, believe me. Write me about everything she does—the pitch of her cry, her first stare of recognition, her first smile, her way of falling asleep and of waking, her sounds of pleasure, her first rolling over and her look of astonishment at this accomplishment, the tight grip of her tiny fist on your finger as you feed her—everything. No, I will not be bored by this "parents' prattle" as you call it. I will revel in every word. There is nothing like a baby, a new life, a fresh beginning.

Coincidentally, a baby was born in the infirmary last week. The institution made its usual response, canceling grounds passes for women, "suggesting" a sermon on morals at all religious services, berating attendants on the ward of the mother, interrogating suspect attendants, workers, and inmates. The mother can tell them nothing. Being hardly aware of her own existence, she does not recognize or believe in her child. She has no family and little hope of recovery.

Why am I telling you this sad story? Because somehow in the midst of the accusations and head-shaking, there is an irresistible surge of joy. Mrs. Cookiebaker brought the baby to show me before it was taken away. "Poor little thing," she said as she rocked it, her eyes radiant. Then she crooned and smiled and made all the foolish noises we make at a baby. It will be adopted by the childless cousin of an attendant. None of our "poor little things" arrives without three or four families competing to keep it, even with the risk of its inheriting the mother's ills.

Does anyone here look about and say, but all of these lost souls were once babies like that, see what it all comes to? Never. At the sight of a new life, all the hard truths melt, as I believe they are meant to. We are given this irrational moment of wonder and hope with each tiny new life, to teach us how we should continue to look at each other, and to give us comfort when we cannot.

October 3, 1953

I have come to Steinbeck's "Grapes of Wrath" very late, but in 1939, when it was published, I was not doing much reading. This book takes me back to my years in the fields only slightly north of Steinbeck country. Only one thing is wrong with it. All the characters are white, all migrants from the midwest dustbowl, all "real" Americans. The cast of characters is incomplete, bleached of color, missing the people I knew best and think of often, especially last week when I happened to see a San Jose newspaper.

I read that among the teachers hired for an eastside grammar school was a Manuel Lopez. If Manuel, who could read at the age of three, did not lose that ability, and if his family re-entered the country as *braceros*, and if—so many "if's," follow them with me —if Wanda was one of the Mexicans hired by the canneries during the war—if Manuel stayed in school—if Wanda kept working and pushing him through to San Jose State College—he would be just about old enough to be hired as a teacher on the Mexican side of town.

Of course, Lopez is a common name.

July 20, 1954

You will be pleased to hear that compulsory attendance at religious services, either on the wards or in the chapels, has been officially abolished. This is mainly the accomplishment of a young minister who came to lead Protestant services two years ago and has now been hired as our first chaplain. I do not attend services, but I see the young Reverend sometimes at Lower Lake. He is about to marry and plans to make a life here, splitting his time between a congregation in Napa and whoever needs him here, wants him, comes voluntarily for worship or counseling.

He mentioned, and I ordered, an interesting book by one of his teachers, a psychologist named Boisson, who has spent much time in asylums, both as a patient and a minister. Boisson writes of the similarity between the mystic and the lunatic, recognized by the folk saying that a lunatic is "teched," that is, touched by God. The revelation, the opening, the crack in the walls of the mind is the same, he thinks. The difference between the mystic and the lunatic is pride. The lunatic refuses to "walk humbly with thy God." The lunatic says, "I am God." The mystic says, "We are God."

January 3, 1955

I have been trying to write, in chronological order, some of the things I told you about myself, some of the things I have written about in my letters to you, and some things which I have never told you.

The trouble is that I write a page or two in the evening, then go to sleep. When I awake in the morning I am full of memories aroused by what I wrote the night before, events left out, and then I feel that I must start all over again. I think I could spend the rest of my life writing successive versions of the same incident over and over and over. I can't imagine how writers manage to finish books!

Yet I feel so strongly impelled, now that I have started, that I must agree you were right to suggest it.

July 12, 1955

I love praise as much as anyone, but I must say you are mistaken about my "gifts." I have only one gift, and it has made some difference in the way I look at things. That gift is the damage done to my heart by influenza. This damage has never seriously inconvenienced me. What it has done is to remind me constantly of the certainty of death, an imminent possibility. Every day death "knocks at my door," with sudden inner pounding for a moment or two, reminding me that this may be the last day, the last hour, the last moment. This gift of awareness is what most people call a morbid preoccupation, but it does not feel morbid to me at all.

Remember the Huxley book I sent you? Somewhere in it he describes the absolutely centered, concentrated bomber crew under attack, the mobilizing force of crisis. (Is that why men love war? Does it return to them the banished awareness of death, the great reality which crowds out a million petty cares?)

My shaky heart has provided a steady reminder of this reality, of the shortness of this form of my living, of the vanity of all kinds of worries and distractions. In other words, this crippling defect has given me freedom.

March 1, 1956

Of all the inmates who believe themselves to be Jesus Christ (did your count reach 183 during your first year here?) the only one I see regularly is a new one, a young man who often comes to Lower Lake in the early morning on his way to work at the dairy. Unlike some other inmates whose delusions are religious, he does not rant or strike attitudes. He is "gentle, meek and mild," well read, and, I have been told, the holder of many academic degrees. He is open to all ideas and opinions except on that one point, his quiet conviction that he is Jesus.

The other inmates are strident and aggressive with him, for inmates are brutal toward each other's delusions. Often I overhear an inmate bringing to bear all logic and evidence to attack the identity of this Jesus. The logic is formidable, prepared carefully, refined from earlier arguments. His response is a sweetly reasoned refutation of their logic with his own. He always ends with a promise to intercede with his father on behalf of those who attack his identity as the son of God.

One of his most determined challengers is a man about his age (thirty) who is quite rational, except for the suicidal depressions which engulf him regularly as clockwork for three days every three weeks. This man, also well educated, has identified himself closely with the young, progressive staff. He wants to cure people and get them out "into the real world" (though he keeps postponing his own departure), and he is determined to cure his fellow inmates first of all of their delusions.

One day last week while "Jesus" and I were sitting alone on opposite banks of the lake, watching the sunrise cross the water, I saw this man coming toward us, his arm around another man he was pulling along. He stopped in front of Jesus, presenting the other man to him, then left the two men alone and walked around to sit beside me. "This guy thinks he's Jesus too. This is his first time off the ward. I've been wanting to get the two of them together. Maybe I can cure both of them at once!" He sat beside me watching intently as they two men talked. "Boy, I wish I could hear what they're saying!" The two men began to walk around the lake together, each of them nodding politely as the other spoke. At about the time they were approaching us and could almost be heard, an attendant arrived to take the second Jesus and his escort back to the ward. The two Jesuses shook hands, smiled, and waved goodbye. As soon as the attendant and inmates were out of earshot, Jesus shook his head and softly said to me, "Poor man, he thinks he's me."

Later I learned that his counterpart was saying the same thing to the challenger who had brought them together. Each of them respected and treated tenderly the desperate need of the other to cling to something that perhaps maintained a fragile balance.

The next day Jesus was back at the lake still giving quiet answers to his relentlessly curing friend. "How can you believe that I performed so many miracles, including my own resurrection, and yet deny that I could be here with you now, in this place where there is such desperate need of me?"

Perhaps for this time and place that sweet young man is our Jesus, our Buddha, our Krishna, our tenuous intermediary between us and reality. We make do with what we have.

May 16, 1956

You may be right—your victory over lobotomy may be only its replacement by the latest "cure," the so-called tranquilizing drugs. (They may stun a violent patient with less damage than an attendant's fist, but that remains to be seen.)

In my fifteen years here I have seen one "cure" after another introduced—electro-shock, insulin shock, lobotomy, drugs, each with advocates who pronounced it, at long last, the genuine cure. (And convinced others—remember that Nobel Prize for lobotomy!)

I have seen some patients get better and leave, and some leave without getting better. But I have never seen one cured by any of these miraculous cures. And those who leave are quickly replaced by more of the sick of soul.

December 3, 1956

Last month I saw a news article which quoted one of Angelina's brothers, fighting to save the family orchard from annexation to become a freeway and housing development. "They are destroying a good way of life. Hard but good."

Last week I read letters dictated to a volunteer by an Indian patient who died at age ninety-six. The old man described the oaks that once covered the Santa Clara Valley. To him, the orchards that replaced them were "rows of stunted sticks, lined up like the white man's army." The oaks had fed his people "without the slavery of men on their knees under the orchard army." He concluded, "They destroyed a good way of life. Hard but good."

By the way, the volunteer who showed me the letters is Mrs. Cookiebaker, who has now retired but still comes almost every day. She keeps the letters in the patients' library that she has established in an old hydrotherapy room (another "cure" gone out of fashion). I have begun to give her my books, which threaten to crowd me out of my room. The new director is sympathetic and promises her that the new building will contain space for a real patient library.

January 7, 1957

That little group of young attendants (they are now called psych-techs) has won. The site of the old hog farm will not be used for any other purpose, though their request to place a stone memorializing it as the old graveyard was denied. The land has, within only a couple of seasons, reverted to a grassy, tree-lined meadow. I think it must look much as it did before the asylum was built.

Last week, as I was walking to Lower Lake, I passed an old woman, a visitor, who stood on the edge of the road looking across the meadow as if searching for someone. She turned to me and said, "I think my mother must be buried here." Then she told me about the beloved mother who "died" when she was a child. Only recently, in old family letters, she discovered that her mother actually had been sent to the asylum and never spoken of again.

Now this woman, near the end of her own life, wants to put up a small stone for her mother, "for all those buried here." She has been told that law and rules forbid it. I smiled and shrugged to give her a hint of how easily she might find allies to help her bend the rules, then said, "Talk to Ellen," one of the young psych-techs. She thanked me and nodded in a quite determined way. So I would not be surprised to find, on one of my future walks past the old grave-yard, an illicit marker dedicating this land to the forgotten.

That same night I had a dream. I saw my daughter Joy wandering through the grounds looking for me. She was not a baby, as she al-ways is, of course, when I dream of her, but a middle-aged woman. Yet I knew it was Joy. And although I was invisible to her, I watched, patient, content, certain that before long she would see me.

Such dreams must be wish-fulfillment, and how deeply and tena-ciously my wishes hold on. I like to think of myself as wishing for nothing now, having learned at last to accept whatever is given. But there, you see, at base I am just like my poor sister Sophie, like all my clients of the old days who longed to believe that their lost children were growing up in the "spirit world."

Every time I begin to believe I have made some progress in my work here, something happens to show me that I am only at the beginning. Each day I start again.

April 12, 1958

Mrs. Cookiebaker has achieved a subscription to *Life Magazine* for her patient library. I took our first issue outside into the first bright sunshine after a long rain. I went to sit in the gazebo, the only structure left from the old castle days. Paul, the violinist, died eight years ago. For a while an accordianist took his place, but he was re-leased last year. Now Obadiah, a Negro jazz saxophonist, plays almost every afternoon.

I opened the magazine and saw a scene that took my breath away —a golden afternoon on long green lawns stretching outward from a grand English country house. It was Stephanie's family home, not crumbled into ruin as she expected and hoped, but restored by her niece and the industrialist she married. It is supported largely by the visits of tourists awed by the pretensions Stephanie despised. Yet it is beautiful and full of treasures to whose maintenance Steph-anie's niece, has, it seems, dedicated her whole life.

As I turned the pages I imagined the comments Stephanie would make about the elegant facade, the shining galleries, the rows of ancestral portraits, the view of the park from the trophy room, and so on and on. The article briefly noted that the "great house suffered neglect and hard use as a hospital in the years between the two world wars." I can almost hear Stephanie's guffaw, her caustic, "Suffered? Those were old Rack and Ruin's days of glory!" But she would have liked the photo of village children playing in the fountains.

June 8, 1959

I attended a funeral today, a mass funeral. The group of psych-techs who preserved the old graveyard took as their next project the respectful burial of all the jars of ashes stored in the crematory. The jars were carefully transported by three large trucks to a nearby cemetery, where many staff members and patients gathered for the memorial service conducted jointly by our Catholic, Protestant, and Jewish chaplains. The burial was in a common grave where eventually a slab will be placed. Their hope is to etch on the slab the names from the labels on the jars.

It was a proper and a very moving ceremony, but it means that this crumbling old building is no longer inviolate. I have moved all my books to the patient library where they sit in boxes awaiting the move to a larger room in the new building, a real library for patients. I think it is best to keep them there, for the eventual use of everyone, in case I should be suddenly evicted from here.

I needn't fear being put back on a ward. The new "cure," as you know, is to be "community care," which means inmates who are not helpless or violent will be handed a bottle of pills and put out on the street. It is only a matter of time before I will be one of them.

The possibility does not concern me, one way or the other. I am ready to go at any time. Yes, I'll call on you if I need help negotiating with Erika. She is in poor health and wrote me a strange letter saying she must come to talk to me when she is better. Since she has nothing to gain by seeing me, I can only assume that illness and old age have softened her a little.

August 1, 1959

A woman comes to sit by Lower Lake every day at exactly three o'clock. She carries an old-fashioned windup record player and one record, Edith Piaf singing *Non, je ne regrette rien.* No, I regret nothing. She plays this record again and again as she sits looking into the water. Yesterday she gave me a faint look of recognition, almost a smile, and she hummed a little. One of her good days.

I regret nothing. It is a brave, wise song, which I can now sing by heart and which I try to think of whenever I remember any part of my life as an injury or a deprivation. I regret nothing. Especially not the injuries, errors, and accidents which drove me to despair.

If I had not been pushed to the end of my rope, I don't know that I would have fallen, ever, into the reality that has given my life form and meaning. Some—perhaps a George Fox or a William Blake—can break through their walls (mixing metaphors? can't help it) without being driven to the opening. But I was a very hard case, rather like my sister Erika, without her strength to go on as she is. It was the combination of losses and my own weakness which saved me. If I had been rescued from even a little bit of that suffering, I might have been able to go on without changing, like a sleep-walker in a nightmare, wandering blindly, flailing in all directions with yearning and pain and fear. I was saved from that life, but at a price. The price was everything and worth everything.

No, I regret nothing.

Napa State Hospital records list Mei-li Morrow's date of death from "heart failure" as August 24, 1959, three weeks after she wrote this letter.